TEMPTATION
OF A HAUNTED
HEART

by

Sophia-Rose Johnson

A Tell-Tale Heart Retelling

Published: S.R. Johnson L.L.C.

Editor: Susan Stradiotto, Bronzewood Books

Cover Design: J.A. Armitage, Enchanted Quill Press

Interior Design: Sara Sines

For those who cannot trust their minds

Content note:

Before you begin reading, please be aware that parts of this gothic horror romance novel may be triggering for some readers.

The Temptation of a Haunted Heart depicts several difficult topics through either mentions or depictions: blood and gore; death of parent, partner, friend; consensual as well as dubious and non-consensual sex; mental health; and violence.

While the whole book does not pertain to such topics, please remember to use self judgement before reading. A comprehensive can be found on my website: sjohnsonbooks.com.

Take care of yourself.

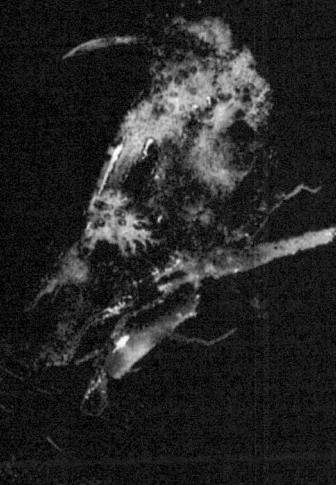

One

I froze in the doorway, swallowed by the sitting room's floral wallpaper—my dress disappearing into the pattern like it had been cut from the same cursed bolt of fabric. So much for my good impression. I wasn't often invited to the Cox residence, so I thrust myself into the party, shoving past the butler at the door, with the invitation in hand for January 6, 1843. The matriarch of society, Mrs. Cox, gave me a wide berth off.

Raising my chin, I forced a placid smile. The sleeves of my dress puffed up enough to brush my chin when I turned my head, and the waistline hugged the underside of my breasts. The Godforsaken corset pulled my midsection in until the smallest movement threatened to break my ribs.

Mrs. Cox returned to her bustling flock of followers.

They don't know the details of my past, or so I repeated to myself like a mantra to keep the whispers at bay.

These were my peers. I had lost my place with them, the same way I had lost Ethel.

I glanced to my side as if she would materialize, stepping from the shadows. She had acted more like a child who played hide and seek than an adult in high society. Then again, she hadn't been a woman of high society; rather, she had dragged me into the shadows.

Now, I was elevating myself. If I could climb to grace without the elite knocking me to the ground again.

The dagger-like societal whispers ripped me open, leaving my blood and organs on the floor for the vultures. It all started with how I was unchaperoned this evening. The gossiping old biddies commented on everything from the sizes of my kidneys to the redness of my blood, calling me *different*. Abnormal.

As Mrs. Cox left the sitting room, a trail of women on her heels, I had half a mind to follow her and insert myself into their conversation. Of course in doing so, I would only prove myself a fool and gain more enemies, so I let the women depart.

There were ways to return to their good graces, no matter how large their memories were, but they were not the reason I came to this gathering. I needed a husband.

Specifically, I needed someone who could hoist me from social ruin.

While the women had tracked my movements over the last few months, the men seemed less interested. Holding a glass of bitter wine, I swept the outer perimeter of each room at the Cox residence. While men and women—at least the siblings and the married couples—arrived together, they split quickly. Men went to smoke or gamble, and the women went into the parlor to gossip. Their voices filtered through the house like small shrill birds.

As I passed a hoard of men, they glanced over their shoulders at me. Women weren't banned from the men's unholy places of worship. Men prayed to God to make them money, attending to Him here more than any church.

"Miss Jones," said a man, and I schooled my features from viper to doe. "It's good to see you. Please let me offer my condolences on your parents' passing. I know how hard it can be to lose them."

I blinked at the man, feeling the sear of his words and trying to parse through my memory to recall who he was. He looked familiar. It was clear he knew me, but everyone did. Did they have my portrait in their pockets like criminals did on posters, meaning to collect bounties?

"Miss Jones?" prompted the man.

I cleared my throat. "Yes, thank you. You are too kind, sir."

He frowned, like he was expecting something further, but I thought myself smooth for not calling him by a name. He was perhaps ten years my senior and had a good face. I should turn my attention to him and scoop him up in conversation, but did he have a shield against the blows that polite society threw?

"Mr. White," Mr. Cox called to the man addressing me.

Like a dog beckoned by its master, Mr. White ducked his head and returned to the gambling table.

As the son of my neighbor, Mr. White would've done fine enough. I cursed myself for my idiocy. I needed to keep my hold on society, but days, weeks, months had passed since I was last with these people. Their faces muddled. Those I could remember were like water slipping through my grasp.

When the dinner bell rang, I followed the herd of men. I needed to catch the eye of stragglers, but men chased food as if starved. None, however, had ventured into the kitchen to lift a helping hand.

There—Mr. Martin met my gaze from across the room, bodies blurring between us like a rushing stream. I waded into the torrent of bodies. Men liked to play heroes, didn't they? If I was run over by a hungry pack, wouldn't a man have to play my hero?

"Mr. Martin." I clasped his tense arm in an unladylike gesture, and his eyes grew wide, panicked as if I could infect him.

He wasn't my first choice either—a man double my age with two adult children and a dead wife. I was closer to his son's age, but he wouldn't be on the marriage market for another few years. The last time I heard, he was somewhere in Europe.

"Miss Jones." Mr. Martin twitched his gaze to where we were connected.

"Are you enjoying the party?" I asked.

"Very much," he said shortly.

"Likewise. Did you see the new wallpaper in the front sitting room? I like it."

"I have not seen."

"Let me show you," I said, willing to drag him.

We were about the same size. As I stood in my skirts, corset, and every heavy layer meant for the winter chill, we were also practically the same weight. One of us, however, had the added strength of desperation.

He looked like he would almost take me up on that offer—like he finally realized there was no gentlemanly way of removing himself—when Mrs. Cox called out to him.

"Mr. Martin!" She sauntered over, other ladies acting as her wings. "And Miss Jones."

Her voice sounded less than enthused, and I let go of him. The years of etiquette lessons manipulated my muscles.

"Might I steal Mr. Martin, Miss Jones?" Mrs. Cox slipped her arm through the crook of his elbow.

Could the man not speak for himself? Not defend himself? He used these clucking hens as protection.

When they melded into the crowd, I flexed my hands. The night was young. Mrs. Cox threw exorbitant parties—the type that had stunned me speechless when I was young—so she had a variety of events planned. I only needed to wait.

Mrs. Cox—for all her posturing about being a Godly woman—invited a mystic, the Marvelous Auguste, to her residence. She paid him to tell us fortunes and talk to the dead, tipping him for every morsel.

Interlocking my fingers, I held myself back from the group cluttering the mystic. They told him everything about their lives, but these people had money; their lives seeped into newspapers and gossip pamphlets. The Marvelous Auguste had no magic, just the ability to read. Mrs. Cox should've known he had no mysticism when she had referred to Ethel as a witch.

The past fought to the forefront of my mind, the memories of Ethel swirling.

A flash of a woman slipped past the corner of my eye, but when I turned toward her, it wasn't Ethel. However, the woman moved to reveal a scowling man on side of the parlor. I thought I knew most—if not all—people at the party. Except him.

I must've been looking at him for too long or he felt my gaze like I often felt Ethel's, because his eyes flickered to me. My breath caught in my throat at his handsomeness.

Raising his glass of brandy, the man smirked at me. Heat graced the back of my neck.

No, Ginny.

I wouldn't be so enthralled. This was only business.

What about love, Ginny?

Love wouldn't protect me from the vultures I used to call friends.

Rolling back my shoulders, I slunk across the parlor, and he straightened from the door frame. He gave me a once over but dragged his eyes back to the mystic. I stood beside him, not needing to fill the void, and watched the crowd.

The mystic played his part well—a flare of hands, mumbled Latin, jacket shimmering in candlelight—and the partygoers hung on his every word, dangling their mouths open as if to catch flies. I would've been like them if it hadn't been for Ethel.

Don't think of her now, Ginny.

"Do you not find the mystic entertaining?" whispered the man.

"I have been distracted," I said.

I peeked from the corner of my eye, and his handsomeness overwhelmed me again. Heat brushed my cheeks.

I focused forward. "Do you find the mystic interesting, sir?"

"Perhaps entertaining," he said, grimacing, "if this was a carnival."

"Do you not believe in the mystic?"

"Do you?"

What would he want to hear? I tried to clear my mind of him and my wants. A husband or a lover?

Mr. Martin was in front of the mystic, sitting with Mrs. Cox, and he would've been a husband.

Society overlooked the man beside me, perhaps a few years older, with chiseled features and kind eyes. He clearly wasn't one of us. As a man without a name, he wouldn't be able to offer me protection. I needed to look elsewhere, yet I rooted myself beside him.

"No," I answered, breaking from the mold I was trying to fit into for Mr. Martin. "I don't believe the mystic or whatever he says magic is."

"You don't believe in magic?" asked the man.

"No." The word slipped from my mouth before I thought about what he wanted to hear. I pressed forward regardless: "I'm not a child and do not believe in fairy tales."

The man dropped his smile but faced me fully, and I braced myself for what was to come. How had I angered him? How had I misstepped?

Why couldn't you keep your mouth shut, Ginny?

He stared at me for a few long seconds, but then the sparkle returned to his eyes. It was like he was opening a new universe, and I was the sun he revolved around. I would happily swoon to have his hands upon my body. He could cradle me against his chest, and I could meet his gleaming eyes.

"Do you?" I asked, finding my voice. "Believe in magic, I mean?"

"No." The man glanced at the mystic. "It's a farce. No truth. But we are humans, fighting with and against society and our ancestors. We need to work with nature."

"You speak like a scientist."

"I am."

That would be why I hadn't seen him at these parties before. He truly wasn't one of the elites. Mr. and Mrs. Cox selected their fellows to attend such gatherings. Perhaps this man would be the next on the stage to perform. If he proved to be one of the Coxes' scientific scholars, then he was worth the name and my lackluster patience because the Coxes had to hold him in high regard to not only invite him to this soiree but fund his research at the university.

I smiled up at him, and he looked down. A rope tied us together. I meant to make it strong, knotting it repeatedly.

"Does that please you, miss?" he asked.

"You may call me by my name," I said, extending my hand. "Virginia Jones."

"Arthur Hunt."

He raised my hand to his lips and planted a kiss upon my gloved knuckles, yet I could feel his hot breath through the thin fabric. It set me alight. His grasp remained gentle, allowing me to pull away, but I wouldn't. I didn't believe he would either.

"Miss Jones," he said, lowering my hand again, "tell me more about yourself."

"I would rather hear about you," I murmured, fluttering my eyelashes. I would collect the information and tuck it into my mind, rereading it later so that it would enter my dreams.

"Where would you like to start?" he asked.

"With the mystic," I said.

Others were looking toward us now. Perhaps we were disturbing them, or Mrs. Cox would drag another man away from me. I didn't latch onto him. If he really was outside the societal pull, he wouldn't know the black cloud that followed me.

"I came to this party because of the Marvelous Auguste," answered Mr. Hunt. "Or the likes of him, nonetheless."

"Did you?" I asked, drawing my eyebrows together.

I hoped it showed interest, not confusion.

"Yes. Mrs. Cox has been inviting me and my colleagues to her parties for some time, something about combining culture and science." He sounded quite sour. "I had a break from my research, so I thought I might join this evening."

"Yet you don't believe in magic?" I asked, keeping a teasing tone in my voice.

Men grew defensive when you challenged their thoughts, shoving their own words into their faces. They were delicate creatures like that.

Mr. Hunt cracked a smile. "I don't believe, no, but it is not a bad idea—I think—to take a pulse on what others believe. Magic and superstition and all. I, as a scientist and researcher, must formulate my own opinions."

"What are your opinions?"

"That he is boring, and you are lovely, Miss Jones."

Red rose from his high collar. His throat looked unable to bob with such a tight shirt and jacket. It was poorly tailored, perhaps not originally his.

"You speak too kindly, Mr. Hunt," I said, purposefully playing coy. "You've only just met me."

"I already know I wish to speak to you," he said,

A spattering of applause echoed in the parlor. Voices murmured and people pointed at the mystic. Others slunk toward the food and drinks, but I was caught in Mr. Hunt's lofty gaze. Mrs. Cox strode toward us, her cane cracking against the floor, and I took a pace back. She narrowed her eyes on the scientist, but I couldn't let him slip from my grasp.

"Will you share a drink with me, Mr. Hunt?" I asked, perhaps being too forward. "Let us speak more. The night is still young."

"Yes, it is, Miss Jones," he said, leading me toward the wine.

With my back exposed, the pointed gazes hooked into my dress and dragged down my skin. I shook them off as I accepted the glass Arthur held. The wine matched the winter dresses, a deep burgundy. Mr. Hunt sipped his wine, so I mirrored him, letting the liquid grace my lips but never pass them. The taste still leaked onto my tongue.

"Do you prefer brandy?" I asked after he lowered his glass.

"I cannot say that I have a preferred taste," he said. "Or one so refined."

I paused, trying to measure my response and possible lie, but I could only study him for so long, letting the silence yawn. I needed to have him closer before he found better entertainment. At least, I didn't have to contend with the mystic, but other women eyed Mr. Hunt. They fluttered like hummingbirds, a near constant buzzing thumping against the back of my head.

"No preference," I lied.

"Do you attend these parties often?" he asked.

"It varies," I said. "We are just coming off the holidays, so I have been away from these gatherings. There are positives for these events, though I cannot say I always agree with the entertainment. As for the people..." I tried not to grimace. "It is important to find those who are likeminded. Mrs. Cox has invited you, so she must feel that you fit well here."

"That is a very kind way to think of it." He took a sip from his glass. "I can say that you have made this night worthwhile."

I didn't push further, balancing between polite society and science. "You thought it was for naught?"

"I believe Mrs. Cox has invited my colleagues to further educate the masses, but I cannot say that I am the most helpful. I leave that to John McCarthy, who talks up a storm. I would rather be in a lab."

"Is it where you feel most comfortable?"

"Yes."

"Tell me more of your work. The funding must be difficult."

"We get by at the university," he said. "We are not New York or London, but Boston is making large strides. In a few years, we shall rival them."

"My father often donated to the university. He believed in the further improvement of humanity." The words flowed freely, and tears threatened to do the same. "The university does just that through science and art, welcoming us into a new age."

Mr. Hunt raised his glass.

"I could not agree more, Miss Jones," he said before taking a sip like it was a salute. "Enough about work. Tell me more about yourself."

My cheeks warmed. "I am no one of interest."

"I doubt that very much."

"You shall be sorely disappointed." The words slipped from my mouth before I thought better of them, and I lifted my hand as if to snatch them back.

"Let me decide." With a kind smile, he offered his arm to me again, and I clung to it, holding him at my side. "You prove to be interesting, more than just the way you think but how you speak. I would be very interested in what you have to say."

"As long as it's not about the mystic," I jested, following his lead around the room. I forced lightness in my tone, something so ladylike that I didn't recognize myself.

"Let us not speak of him again," agreed Mr. Hunt. "Let's speak of everything else."

With Arthur occupying my mind, I left my house door open for a moment, breathing in the chilly night as if I could hold him a little longer. The carriage that brought me home pulled away, the wheels and the horse hooves clattering over the cobblestones. The wind whistled down the street and fluttered the curtains, dispelling Arthur by the second, so I shut the front door.

Closing my eyes, I sucked in a deep breath. Arthur's cologne filled my nostrils; it lingered on my dress. I wouldn't wash the fabric or myself if it meant another moment of him.

Pushing off the door, I strolled up the stairs. I had sent all the servants away after my parents died, so I undid my cloak and let it drop to the floor. There was little use for servants when I lived in this quaint house alone. I was a modern woman, able to cook my meals and clean my house and mend my clothing. However, tonight I wished I had a maid to tell everything to.

I had to let something out, so I hummed. The music carried me through changing into my nightgown and brushing out my hair.

Something white fluttered in my peripheral vision. I spun from the vanity, holding the brush as my weapon.

There was no one in the doorway of my bedroom.

"Ethel?" I asked aloud.

No one answered, especially not Ethel.

The flickering candlelight and the lit hearth and the flapping curtains and the howling wind clogged my mind. The white was a trick of the light. I had been distracted.

Setting the brush on the vanity, I flexed my hands. My knuckles cracked. I forced myself to hum again, thinking back to Arthur, though Ethel hovered in the corners of the mind, her one blue eye and one green eye staring from the shadows. I didn't look at her eyes, instead sliding into the cold bed in my childhood bedroom, alone.

I dragged my hand down the side of the bed that had lost Ethel's indent. Her hair used to fall across the pillows, and she would wrap herself in the blankets like they were luxurious. These blankets were scratchy and old, knitted and bought when I was a girl.

Ethel's scent wafted off the bed, and I turned away. My hair fell around my face. It smelled of Arthur, a mixture of cologne and something sterile that had to be from his research. As I closed my eyes, I remembered his smile. His kind eyes. His cutting features, a strong jaw and thick brow bone. His fingers had been gentle as if I was glass that he was scared to break. Little did he know how close to shattering I was.

Two

October 31, 1842

With my head ducked, I peeked out from my cloak hood. Broken windows let out the cries of babies and screams of women. Everyone moved hurriedly on the street except the whores. They stood in the mouths of alleyways, waiting.

Watching.

Calling out.

The clamor rattled my already pounding head. I pulled the hood to cover my face like a shield against the noise and the rancid smell leaking from the clogged buildings and the too-bright day. I hurried on.

Skidding to a halt outside a shop with wooden boards covering the windows, I glanced at the soggy paper in my hand. The numbers matched, same with the street and this district of Boston that I never should've come to. Desperation—a mixture of fear, sadness, anger, and whatever else threatening to topple me—clouded my head, turning my blood sluggish.

I stood in an old dress, strings hanging off and chunks of fabric missing. If someone were to pull on a loose string, I would come undone. Every part that made me a living human would be suspended. I didn't want to die, but it was like I had forgotten how to live.

Before my maid left the house—a recommendation and extra wages in her hand as well as the promise that she would say nothing of her time in the Jones household—I had asked for guidance to...heal. I needed someone outside of polite society. The physicians servicing the wealthy proved unhelpful, offering the asylum as the hallowed answer.

I checked the sidewalk and the street before pushing myself inside the shop. I might as well have been dead if Boston's finest learned of my existence here.

"Hello?" I asked the empty apothecary.

I had expected someone would greet me, telling me to try this new relaxation tea and my problems would be solved promptly.

When no one answered, I tiptoed further into the clutter, sidestepping wooden crates and strewn tables. Parchment, books, and jars covered the counters. I placed my hand on the coin purse tucked into my skirts, feeling the weight. Perhaps it was too much for a place like this, or perhaps the money was what they wanted to see. Only then would they deem me important.

The door squeaked behind me, and I spun on my heel. A woman stood in the way, shoulders hunched. Water dripped onto the already molding floor, the aged wood sloped. The woman peeled back her hood. She had one blue eye, one green, but she was...stunning.

Heat washed over me, and I looked away, unsure why I was acting as such. I had seen many beautiful women in society, admiring them from afar and not daring to speak to them out of turn. I wasn't sure I would be able to speak to this woman either. My tongue intermingled with my building saliva.

She dragged her mismatched gaze across me, though my hood still covered my face.

I cleared my throat. "I'm looking for—"

"I don't work here," said the woman with a huff.

Bypassing me in the main aisle, she peered into jars and pushed books aside, peeking through the contents. She seemed to know where everything was placed and hated where it was located.

I peered toward the back of the apothecary and then ventured toward the heavy-looking curtains that cut the shop off. The woman stepped in front of me. Our skirts brushed against one another.

"What are you doing?" she demanded.

"I need help," I murmured.

"And you thought to come here?"

"My maid suggested this would be the best place for me."

"Your maid is a fool."

"Or vengeful."

She cocked an eyebrow at me. "Why would she be vengeful? What did you do to her?"

I gasped, but I had done something to the maid. My choices had been limited, and there was no reason to keep her on. She hadn't been happy either.

"I had to terminate her," I said. "Not just her—all the servants."

The woman crept her gaze down me again, taking me in, but I doubted I was different. I felt like an eggshell as always. A hard knock would leave me broken and my yoke oozing across the cobblestones.

"Have you lost all your money?" asked the woman.

"No. I can pay." I touched my coin purse under my cloak.

"Don't touch yourself like that around here," she said, yanking my hand from my person. Her skin was like ice, burning me, but as soon as she pulled away, I wanted her to hold me again. "People will know to pickpocket you. Or worse, they'll just attack you."

I blanched. "But you will not...do either?"

For a long moment, we stared at one another. Her one blue and one green eye dredged up my soul. She could've sucked my soul from my veins and drank my bone marrow. I, on the other hand, had my thoughts of what she would taste like.

"No," said the woman, her voice wavering. "I won't attack you. I help people."

"So you can help me?" I asked meekly.

"It depends." The woman pursed her lips. "What ails you enough to bring you to this part of Boston?"

The words knotted in my throat, because they'd been prepared for my explanation to a physician or even an apothecarist. While I somehow trusted that this woman knew herbs and what would heal me, I couldn't tell her. I was exposed while standing fully clothed.

"I'm Ethel," said the woman.

"Virginia," I replied.

She harrumphed.

I balked. "Did I do something wrong?"

"You should not speak your real name here," said Ethel in a hushed tone.

"There are many Virginias."

"Not in the ruling class. It would be easy to find you."

"What if that is my intent?" I asked, emboldened.

"Is that your intent?" she questioned.

"No." I hesitated. "Is Ethel your real name?"

"Yes. Ethel Brown."

"You don't hide it?"

"I make money on my name. The more people know it, the more they will ask after me."

"What do they ask for?"

"*My* help."

"I came for the apothecarist."

"Yet he isn't here."

"He left his shop unattended, door unlocked?"

"It must be your first time at this apothecary."

I straightened, feeling like a child. This woman was less than ten years my senior, though our lives were vastly different, aging our features too. It gave her a harder, more defined face that exalted her knowledge. I thought I looked innocent, child-like with my rounded face that easily pinked. My old governess once said it was how she knew I lied.

"Yes, it is my first time here," I admitted, choosing the truth over a lie.

Ethel huffed. "Of course it is. Otherwise, you would know he is not in his right mind. He wanders off."

When I needed him the most... Tension coiled in my sour stomach. My head threatened to swim, and then perhaps I could sleep. I needed help; Ethel could give it. She said she could.

"I have the money to pay," I said.

"I know," she replied. "You told me."

"Will you help me?"

"I need to know what ails you." She repeated the words slowly like I was daft.

Perhaps I was, which explained much of my life. I never claimed to be intelligent, nor could anyone say so in my life. I couldn't speak multiple languages or play an instrument; I had only done well with lessons because my father took his time to walk me through the teachings.

My heart broke thinking of him. When I hadn't been able to learn like everyone else, I would cry, and my mother would hold me, rocking me in her arms like I was a baby again, soothing me with her notes. I missed them. They had died too soon, and it was shameful that I wasn't taken with them.

Pressing my hand to my chest, I stumbled from Ethel before the memories overwhelmed me. She caught my hand, her grip strong.

"Is it your heart?" asked Ethel, tone like the physician's that serviced polite society.

"Yes." I swallowed. "No. Not physical pain."

"It appears physical."

"It is." I dropped my hand from my chest.

She didn't let go of me yet, brushing her thumb across my knuckles.

I said, "I fear what has happened to me…is not my heart."

"What has happened to you?" she asked.

I nibbled on my bottom lip, scared of the words. I had said them many times, in person and writing. That mattered little. Each time I spoke them, it was another stab that left me hunched, wheezing. I knew what had happened—woke every morning without my family and went to sleep in a silent house—but it didn't lessen the pain.

"My family is dead." I flinched at the callous words. "They died from the fever, but a lot of people died. I'm no different, and I'm fortunate because of my wealth, and I should be—"

"You don't have to be anything," said Ethel fiercely.

It sizzled my skin where her gaze lingered.

When she spoke next, her tone was softer. "What has happened since?"

"I cannot sleep," I admitted. "I cannot think. I cannot eat. I'm ill and tired, the thoughts so powerful. My maid suggested opium."

"No!" Ethel shook her head. "Not that."

"I've seen others use it," I pushed. "And if it will help…."

"You shall need something else." She let my arm go.

With her gone, I missed her. I rubbed where she had touched me, the fabric warm.

Ethel was looking through the jars and then the plates, pushing things away. Her nostrils flared like a hound's. Hunching her shoulders, she followed her nose through the apothecary.

I took a deep breath, but the swirling scents mingled with one another. It was disgusting, musky and smelling of skunk. Nothing smelled floral, but that was the only scent I knew, walking through flower shows in spring and summer. Just like my mother's perfume.

Suddenly, Ethel held a jar of greenery like it was a prize. "Here it is."

I ventured forward a tentative step. "What is it?"

"Hashish."

"I don't know what that is."

"I would imagine not."

I narrowed my gaze. "What does that mean?"

"I don't mean to be rude," said Ethel, holding out her hands like I was a cornered animal. "Not many in the ruling class know this herb."

Ethel started looking through the jars again, turning her back to me. She moved faster now, set to the task, but I hadn't agreed to it. Nor did I have any idea what it was.

"What will it do to me?" I asked, forcing my voice to be stronger.

Though, a strong wind would've blown me over, my limbs like the branches of a willow tree and my stringy hair like leaves. No wonder Ethel wouldn't look at me with more than a scowl: I was ugly and ragged, no better than a whore on the street.

When Ethel turned toward me, she extended a wrapped bundle. "The herb will help you relax."

"Relax?" I nearly scoffed. "I need to sleep. I cannot think or eat, I'm just so tired. Everything hurts, and I think of dyi—"

"It'll help you."

Help, like it was so easy.

Tears splattered my cloak and dress. I would drown. I had heard that was a nice way to die; perhaps I should go to Boston Harbor.

"Don't cry. Please." Ethel held out her arms like she was about to touch me but paused, perhaps thinking better of it.

Yet her hands hovered there.

I couldn't remember the last time someone held me. Or slapped me and told me to keep myself together. I was succumbing to the sadness that would turn me feral.

"How?" I asked her.

All air expelled from my lungs with the singular word.

It took me a moment to regain my strength. I asked, "How do you know this will help?"

"I'm a healer," she said in a simple, kind tone.

"What kind? You come to another's apothecary."

"I travel to heal, coming down from Salem."

While I shouldn't have been struck by such a town, the history of Salem, Boston's twin, was dark. And then to be an apothecarist from such a place.

"Are you...?" I studied her through my bleary gaze.

Ethel smirked, like this was a challenge. "Say it. Don't be scared."

I gulped. I wasn't scared of her or anyone else. Except for the fever that kept me up late at night as the house groaned like my parents had on their deathbeds.

"Are you a witch?" I asked.

A smile bloomed on her ruddy, angular face, her pink lips pulling back like petals of a flower. I should've feared a woman who didn't say she wasn't a witch but wanted to be closer to her. Her grin was beautiful, peeling back a hard layer of age and life. I inched toward her.

"No," said Ethel finally. "Though others would say so."

"Why?" I asked.

"Because I'm a woman. A healer. Because of who I help—those who need it the most. Including the whores you passed on the street, the beggars in the alleys, and those coming off the ships from far-off places."

Leaving the bundle of herbs on the counter, she returned to searching the stacks. When she tilted her head, her hood fell, and her loose curls cascaded down her back. I wanted to coil them around my pointer finger and give a gentle tug.

"What kind of help do they need?" I asked.

"Probably the most." Ethel plucked something off the shelf and inspected it. "I help my patients how they most need it. Like I know you need to relax."

"I'm not your patient."

"I'm trying to help you, so don't act proud." She placed a vial on the counter, still searching the stacks. "It will help you relax, which then you can sleep and eat and be better."

"Will I be happy?"

The truth hung between us, glaring, and neither of us could ignore it. I had tried.

She faced me, the light having left her eyes. "Based on what you've told me, Virginia, I'm not sure you'll ever be happy again."

A sob slipped from my trembling lips, and I slapped a hand across my face. The truth was the most painful, especially when exposed by another.

"Then what is the point of living?" I asked in an anguished yell. Salty tears rushed into my mouth, drowning me as I stood on land.

She glided across the room, not hesitating as she wrapped her arms around me. I fell into her, my head resting in the crook of her neck. I hadn't fit into another person besides my mother, but my body had come from hers.

With Ethel, we were pieces taken from different vases and brought together, fitting so well. It was only natural.

I held her tight, so close that her breasts pressed into my chest. For the first time since my parents died, I felt something. It stirred in my lower belly. It moved up my veins and into my heart until I was only beating for her. At the same time, it slid down my body, into my core; I pressed my thighs together.

Ethel pet my hair. "I know, Virginia, but it will make you better. For at least a little while. Smoke it tonight."

She held me for another moment. Perhaps it was because I clung to her, breathing in each of her exhales. She took a deep breath too, quaking us both. Our bodies vibrated. She slid her fingers through my hair, careful of the tangles. I locked myself around her further, our cheeks melding together in slickness.

Then she pulled away from me, and I nearly collapsed, my knees weak. I grabbed the counter as my leverage to keep myself upright.

"Go home now," said Ethel as her hands fisted her skirts. "You need rest, Virginia."

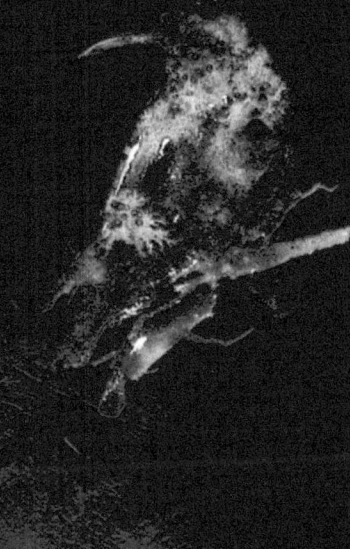

Three

fter a solitary breakfast, I dressed in my work clothes and aired out the rooms. Once the house had been opened up, I closed my eyes and recalled everything about the night before. And Arthur.

The music replayed in my ears, and I spun across the sitting room, pretending that Arthur and I were dancing, not only standing and talking, not daring to touch one another. I smacked into the table, and a vase fell. I didn't slow as I swept around the room in a joyous waltz.

Knock.

Knock.

Knock knock knock.

I halted, the skirts of my dress swishing around my ankles. My heartbeat resounded in my ears, quickened by my haggard breathing. I set the broom aside and moved toward the door, smoothing my dress. My house was in no state to entertain; neither was I. I had eaten alone this morning, accompanied only by the memories from last night.

Glancing over my shoulder, I considered hiding, just as Ethel did in the sitting room.

Another knock rattled the door, repeating the same quick bangs, and I called out, "Coming!"

At the door, I checked over my shoulder and down the hallway and then peeked at myself in the mirror. I was…horrid. Ethel said there was nothing wrong with hard work, but my back was hunched and my hands red, muck under my fingernails to turn them black.

A third pattern of knocks rattled the front door, and I whipped it open. Thankfully, it wasn't Mrs. Cox or the ladies of elite society, or I would officially be excluded from any upcoming gathering. The so-called queen of Boston and commander of my destiny would post servants at the doors like castle guards.

A boy stood outside, a messenger satchel swung across his bony shoulder. "I have a letter for…"

He withdrew paper from his satchel and then stared at the scrawled handwriting, but we both knew he couldn't read.

From his memory, he said, "Virginia Jones."

"That's me," I said.

"A servant?" he asked.

I snatched up the note, and he held out his hand, expecting a penny. I wouldn't give it to him after his insolence, but then I opened the letter and read.

The boy could have all my money. Arthur had written to me.

Placing a hand to my sputtering heart, I read the short letter three times before I could comprehend his hesitant words.

Dear Virginia,

I had a wonderful time last night speaking with you. You are a unique creature, one refined and knowledgeable and worldly. As a woman in such polite society, you must already be busy. However, if you are not—and would have interest in, of course—I am hoping you would accompany me for a river walk stroll at midday. It is understandable if you are not available at such is a hastened date, but you weigh heavily on my mind.

Ever your friend,

Arthur Hunt

"Ma'am?" asked the boy.

Now he knew how to talk to me.

"Will you run a response back?" I asked.

"Are you paying?" he questioned.

"Of course. Stay here."

Inside the house, I wrote to Arthur and then threw that letter into the growling hearth. Sweat dribbled down my wrist, smearing the ink. Cracking my knuckles, I drew back. Immense anticipation of meeting him quaked my knees, the same thrill running the length of my body. Once I swallowed my feelings, I wrote out my agreement to Arthur.

The boy was still waiting outside when I returned with my coin purse. He had trampled through the flowerbed, but I didn't yell.

I handed over the letter and a few coins. "Take this back to Mr. Hunt."

Snatching both, the boy sprinted off.

Running late, I tripped on the hem of my dress, but as a woman, I was supposed to be late. It would be too forward of me to be waiting by the harbor. I fastened my gloves tighter around my wrists, but a cool winter breeze slipped in. The small hairs on my arms stood.

Arthur lingered next to the harbor walk under a streetlamp. I could easily pick him from the crowd. He stuck out compared to the bustling maids and butlers and the strolling ladies with parasols. I had left mine at home but now wished I hadn't. It would give my fingers something to do besides twitch.

"Mr. Hunt," I finally said when I was within a few strides of him.

He snapped his head up, pink coloring his cheeks as though I'd caught him in the middle of something indecent. "Miss Jones. Hello."

I wished he would use my given name but kept that to myself. There were too many prying eyes.

"I hope I didn't keep you waiting," I said, trying not to sound breathless after practically running to meet him.

Getting ready took longer than I expected; none of my wardrobe looked fashionable. I wanted to impress him but feared I had done up my corset too tight. Then again, a woman didn't need to breathe if her corpse was beautiful.

Standing beside him, I realized it wasn't the corset that was the issue but his features. His handsomeness held my heart in its grasp, tightening its grip until I wheezed. I clamped my teeth shut and forced a smile that perhaps came off as a grimace.

"It's a beautiful winter day. Unseasonably warm," I commented, lacking anything else to say.

"You have only made it prettier," he said, extending his arm to me.

I slid my hand through the crook of his elbow, and we started our walk down the river. The public was our chaperone, but perhaps I should've hired one for tonight. I didn't have the time and knew even fewer women who could attend to me. On this boardwalk, I could pretend it was just us, and my own imagination rose to do just that.

Boston notoriously smelled of fish and the sea, but in this section, near the port and river, steamboats huffed off-color clouds. The stenches fell away as I inhaled his cologne—smokey like brandy, with a tinge of sweetness. I held it in my lungs as if it could imprint into my chest.

Though our arms were linked, we kept a formidable distance. He faced forward, jaw set. I didn't like how he focused on something other than me.

"Have you made this walk before?" I asked, pushing a light tone into my voice. Unfortunately, I sounded more like a squawking seagull.

"I have not," he admitted. "One of my colleagues suggested it."

"You don't sound pleased."

"I'm distracted."

"Not by me."

He spun toward me, eyes wide. "Oh, Miss Jones. I should be."

"Then who distracts you?" I asked.

Who had time to burrow into Arthur's mind after he had written to me? I glanced up and down the boardwalk, but he could've found many of the women here more beautiful.

"It is not who," he said. "My work."

His work, Ginny?

"Is it because you skipped out early today?" I asked, knitting my eyebrows together.

"I have another meeting tonight. My work is important to me, but I know my worth. As does my mentor. It is just... I shouldn't have listened to my colleague when he suggested this location. While very romantic"— his gaze flickered— "I fear I am distracted by the birds and the sea. The birds are skimming as the tide comes in."

I led him to the edge of the raised boardwalk. The wind would have to be hefty to blow us both into the water. Once we were looking at a boat shimmying in the flow, he relaxed.

"Are you a sailor, Mr. Hunt?" I asked.

He barked a laugh. "I never found my legs for it."

"But you've been on a ship?"

"A few times. Yourself, Miss Jones?"

"Yes."

"It would be hard to look out at the sea rather than looking at you."

"Yet you've done it."

"I'm a fool," he said, glancing down at his shoes.

"You are not," I disagreed.

"You are too kind."

"You are a man of science."

"Lacking in the skills a man should possess when courting women."

"That is not a bad thing." In fact, I preferred it.

He ducked his head. "I have been a horrible person to speak with."

"Our time together has just begun," I said.

He gave me another dazzling—albeit hesitant—smile. He really was a man who had no interest in other women, so it was hard for me to understand why he wished to spend time with me. What did he see in me? What did he want with me? Was it possibly love?

Not now, Ginny.

In my search for a husband, I had set my sights on old and decrepit men. If a man around my age, accomplished in his own right had interest in me, I didn't need or want to question it when I had blooming affection toward him.

"Shall we continue?" Arthur backed away from the edge, towing me along the water.

The crowd enjoying the fine day parted for us, though I didn't miss how the high-society ladies looked pointedly at Arthur and off their noses at me. Their thin pink lips turned down in disgust as if I were an imposter. I had the same right as any of them to stroll here on the arm of a man.

When a lady of polite company came too close, I steered Arthur away like my father had once taught me to guide a horse. I acted as though I had seen something on the water, and Arthur joined me at the railing. A mix of steam-, coal-, and wind-powered ships speckled the harbor, the older ones with white sails puffing like billowing clouds.

"Are you Boston born and raised?" asked Arthur.

"Yes." I faced him. "I live in the house I grew up in."

"How wonderful."

"Yourself?"

"Not a Bostonian." He cracked a wavering smile.

"Where are you from?"

"Nowhere of note. I came here for university and fell in love with the city."

"Would you ever move home?"

"Absolutely not." He chuckled. "I must sound mad to move closer to my family and to not."

"Your studies are here," I reassured him. "Do you still write home?"

"Yes," he said. "To my parents and my brothers. Some childhood friends."

"Your parents must be very proud of you."

"Yes and no."

"You're a scientist. How could they not be?"

"They wished me to be a physician and come home to be the local doctor. Especially my mother." He shook his head. "I do not do well with blood. In fact, I'm a coward with it."

"I shall keep that in mind," I replied.

Waves rolled up the harbor wall, pushed in and out by the tide. When the waves calmed, the flashes of people reflected on the water, even Arthur and me. Our shoulders brushed. A wooden fence kept us parted from the sea, though it was safer than falling in the water after a possible swoon. Arthur had his hand clapped over my own, so there was no possibility of me tumbling in.

"What do you like most about Boston?" I asked.

He smirked, his eyes glinting mysteriously. "Shall I say you?"

My cheeks heated. "Only if it is true."

"It is true." He brushed the skin exposed between my glove and jacket sleeve with his fingers, offering me his warmth. "You have made Boston lovelier since I met you."

"We only met last night."

"What a night it was. Far better than the time I spend in research." Red tinged his cheeks. "I should not be so forward."

"Please be forward." I could not be with the constraints of womanhood.

He raised his head, peeking at me from under his dark eyelashes. "I am very fond of you, Miss Jones."

My breath hitched. "I am as well, Mr. Hunt. Of you, I mean."

Red blossomed on his neck, looking more like a rash than a flush. "I am very pleased to hear that, Miss Jones."

I had a hard time finding the words when my body felt feather light, as if I would rise with the next hefty gust and fly away. All thoughts left my head, and I would take blissful stupidity if it meant holding this moment close to my heart. It already beat for him.

There was a flash from the corner of my eye, probably a dreadful seagull. As much as I wished to ignore it, something white landed on the ebb, its mismatched eyes burrowing in me. I hated to look away from Arthur and only meant to shoo it away, but it wasn't a bird.

It was Ethel, her reflection on the water. Her blue eye was the same color of the waves, outlined in black. It had a wicked glint.

I gasped, and Arthur asked, "What is it?"

I tore my gaze away from him, looking at where Ethel should've been standing behind us, but she wasn't there.

Some people hustled down the street, while others walked leisurely. I searched between the bodies, but she had disappeared. I would've recognized her anywhere but couldn't find her in the crowd. The passersby looked at me now too, eyes large, mouths downturned in scowls.

I spun back to the harbor, finding Ethel's reflection as clear as day. Her eyes burrowed into me, catching my soul and crumbling it in her icy grasp. Like the witch she was proclaimed to be.

I stumbled back, tumbling over the hem of my dress, but before I fell, Arthur caught me in his bony arms. My face landed against his chest, and his heart beat strong, thudding against my already racing mind.

He pulled me to my feet. "Let us sit."

I only nodded, unable to find the words I needed for an apology.

Arthur led me to a nearby bench. His head was bent toward mine; his breathing returned to normal. I imagined this was how he looked at his research subjects, eyebrows knitted and concern etched into his face like a plaque hanging on a building. No physical harm had come to me, so relief melted his features. The same couldn't be said for mine.

Why had Ethel followed me?

I didn't want to turn away from Arthur, but I craned my neck to find Ethel. She had most likely fallen into the background like she so commonly did, leaving me to the aftermath.

"Thank you for helping me," I murmured, heat sparking my cheeks. "How embarrassing."

He must've thought I was weak minded. Weak willed. Women didn't just fall over.

"No reason to be embarrassed," he said. "I'm just happy you're all right."

"I am. Thank you. This has never happened to me before. I have always been in good health." The lies slipped from my mouth.

My thoughts forced me back in time to when I first met Ethel at the apothecarist shop. Through the haze, I had barely been able to understand the situation. Since then—with Ethel at my side—I had been fine.

"That is good to hear," said Arthur.

While concern imprinted his face, terror filled his eyes as if I were a siren rising from the sea with my song to suck out his soul. We had been so close and then Ethel had to ruin it.

Why couldn't she allow me to love again? In the brief time I had known Arthur Hunt, a tether had wound its way around my heart, connecting me to him. This was his time to sever it and leave me in tatters.

"Can I walk you home, Miss Jones?" asked Arthur. "Perhaps you should rest."

"Yes, rest is exactly what I need," I agreed.

And him, Ginny.

I took his hand, and he helped me to my feet. The skirts of my dress fell, and my corset no longer cut into my skin like a blade. As my arm slipped through the crook of his elbow yet again, I studied our surroundings as if Ethel would appear with a satisfied smirk. Many cast glances our way, but none were Ethel.

Arthur strolled slower now, as though I were a newly born doe finding footing. I ground my shoe heels into the road, purposefully standing taller than I had before. I wanted to show Arthur—and anyone who might be watching—just who I was. Not a weak or sick fool. Not a person who had fallen under the spell of a witch.

As we turned the street to my house, I stiffened. We hadn't spoken on the way home. However, the silence didn't feel wrong either. I had snuggled against him, and he had held me close. I no longer felt weak, though embarrassment still made me warm.

"My house is just ahead," I said.

"Perhaps I should speak with the staff about your state," he said.

"That won't be necessary."

"Miss Jones—"

"There is no one there to tell," I said, cutting him off in an unladylike fashion. "I sent them away."

"Why?"

I swallowed over the growing lump in my throat. "It is only me now living in the house, and not enough work for them. Someday, I'll bring them back. When I am a married woman, and hopefully with a child on the way."

"Why is it only you?" asked Arthur in a kind tone. "It is abnormal, isn't it?"

Questions like those gave away that he wasn't a man of the elite. No, he was a man of science and would fall into high society—playing our silly little games—to keep the money pumping into his projects. My father had often given money for further exploration, and as the remaining member of this family, I had followed suit. There were no male relatives to wrestle it from my hands or pluck every coin off my body for gambling.

Suddenly, Arthur halted. "That was an inappropriate question to ask. My apologies. It is none of my business."

"I think it is, if we are courting. Though, it is hard for me to speak about." I faced him, puzzling out what our relationship exactly was.

He didn't disagree about us courting, only pink bloomed on his cheeks like flowers in spring. It was adorable. So innocent. I trusted him more because I could read him like a book.

"May I officially court you, Miss Jones?" he asked.

"You may," I said, the weight removed from my shoulders.

He let out a soft breathless chuckle as if he couldn't believe it. I giggled too as though I were a young girl coming into my first crush. I had had many crushes in my day. Excruciating pain usually followed.

"I do not know if you would have interest, Miss Jones," began Arthur.

"I can assure you I have much interest," I said.

"You don't even know what I am about to suggest."

"If you have interest, then so do I."

"It might be terribly boring."

"I doubt it."

He laughed again—a loud burst of sound upon the quiet street that left people glancing our direction. It was one of those laughs that people in society didn't allow to happen because it drew the wrong type of attention. I placed a hand over my mouth, covering the shrill chortles.

"Then," he finally said after collecting his breath, "I would like to invite you to a science symposium."

I managed to get a tight hold of myself as well. "Like with exhibits and panels?"

Arthur winced. "I did warn you; I am quite boring."

"It will not be boring," I assured him. "I will admit that I won't be the most knowledgeable guest."

"It is open to people from all knowledge bases."

I stepped closer to him, the laughing having distanced us. "Will there be people to teach us about such science?"

"Of course. And there will be plaques."

Bless the man who still didn't understand what I was asking, so I chose to be less coy: "I was hoping I might have special attention. Would you be able to provide me with such help, or should I be looking elsewhere?"

"No," he squeaked and hastily cleared his throat. "I shall be your mentor, Miss Jones."

"I promise to be a very good student."

"I have no doubt."

His words sent a shiver down my spine. I had played student before, not only to proper teachers or tutors, but to Ethel as she used my kitchen to make her tinctures.

"Oh, goodness, look at the time." Arthur snapped his pocket watch shut. "I do apologize, Miss Jones. I do not wish to depart so quickly—or at all—but I must hasten to a meeting with the faculty before the symposium."

Breath left my lungs at once. I tried not to wince, instead painting a demure smile on my face that perhaps showed too many teeth. It wasn't that I thought myself more important than science, but rather I wished to be more important to him than his science. But given his passion, his pursuit of knowledge might always be the wedge between us.

Calm, Ginny. You're looking for a husband. Just be happy he is not a man on his deathbed.

"Of course"—Arthur paused—"I look forward to seeing you at the symposium. I will think about you until we meet again."

He took my hand in his, raised it to his lips, and kissed me on the knuckles. In the blink of an eye, all my fears dissipated until they were part of the normal Boston fog.

"I shall do the same, Arthur," I said, venturing to use his first name.

While it may have been improper, what I dreamed of him was also improper.

"Thank you...*Virginia*. Until then." He gave a curt nod and walked away.

I waited until he was down the street before I ran into the house and slammed the door shut. I wanted to call out to the servants to pull out every dress I had and ensure they were dusted off, bring out my mother's old jewelry, and then—while they were at it—to refurbish the house. We needed to make it a home for Mr. Arthur Hunt.

Alone, I stood in the front entryway, the words caught in my throat. Who would I talk to?

"Me, Ginny," peeped a voice.

I refused to look at Ethel in the front sitting room. Shadows loomed over her pale form.

"I must go out," I said, even though I had just entered my home. "I'm in need of a new dress."

Something that preferably didn't look like wallpaper.

I slammed the door before she could follow, but she would climb through the windows or crawl through the cracks in the stone to haunt my every step. I wouldn't let her ruin this for me. I wouldn't lose Arthur after I had lost so much because of her.

Four

Feeling like I was being watched, I stepped onto the street to call a cab. Despite all the levity I should feel with Arthur, the weight that was in my belly pulled me toward the cobblestones, turning my feet to iron. As a curtain fluttered, I whirled to face my house.

Ethel had been watching, even if she pretended to hide.

Unfortunately, hers wasn't the only gaze on me: Mrs. White also watched from across the street.

Arthur's offer for courtship blinked into my mind. With my past, if he were to do so unchaperoned, it would ruin him. We needed to play by societal rules and show others how well we were suited. Though she hadn't attended elite events as long as me, Mrs. White had become a confidant to Mrs. Cox, having her ear to the tea-table chatter. Hopefully, she would have the mouth too.

I started to cross the street only to feel the back of my neck prickle. I spun toward my house as the curtain in my front window waved like a hand.

"Damn it, Ethel," I muttered and then met Mrs. White's gaze.

From her perch in the house's front window, she had seen it all, including how idiotic I must look. How forlorn and useless. I should let myself slip back into the vastness, remaining forgotten and lost, but I needed Arthur. Being courted by him might be my last hope.

I stalked to the White house, my fist raised to knock. But the door flung open, and I met a servant directly. She must've been waiting for me, watching through the peephole as I had stopped and started. Undoubtedly, this was one of my woes that would be passed from house to house by the gossiping servants.

"I would like to speak to Mrs. White," I said without greeting. I attempted not to cringe at my tone; Ethel would've scolded me for using it.

The servant blinked her big brown cow eyes at me. "What?"

"I would like to speak with Mrs. White," I said, pointing at the old woman.

She hadn't risen from her perch in the window to greet me. Apparently, the servant learned her manners from the woman.

I continued, "It is urgent. If I could..."

"You cannot," said the servant.

I locked my jaw, astounded by the insolence, and then craned my head toward Mrs. White. Her wrinkled skin bunched around her neck.

"Miss Jones?" asked the servant, bringing a whiff of onions. "Are you all right?"

"Fine," I snapped, backing away from the White residence.

Mrs. White and the others would get nothing from me when they needed my parents' money for another art or science exhibition. They would have to grovel at my doorstep for the new railroad money or reach into the coffers they'd already depleted from their time in European nobility.

I stepped into the street, ignoring Mrs. White as well as Ethel. They were like two sides of a coin, but I would show them who I could be. I headed straight to the seamstress shop, only pausing when I touched the first fine fabric.

Until my fingers traced across the lace and bows, I hadn't realized how much I missed these dresses. I wanted to see the latest fashions from New York. I would strut up the street and into the parties, fashionable and adored.

I tore my hands away when gazes chipped at my bones. Three ladies of society—worse, their maids too—stared at me like I was a spider they could crush under their heel. I looked down at my hands as though I had left a string of web, but they were clean. Thankfully.

"Good day," I said to them, because we couldn't pretend like we didn't know each other.

They turned their backs on me, acting no better than children.

I tried to focus on the kaleidoscope of colors, how lush they were, so vibrant. The murmurs and vitriol they spouted behind me made it clear that the women expected me to brandish my claws and rip the fine fabric to shreds. It rocked me to my core, and I gripped the table to keep myself upright. This time, Arthur wasn't here to catch me.

Brushing my thumb across green fabric that reminded me of moss, I wondered if Arthur would like this color. It would bring out his eyes.

Unfortunately, the voices in the seamstress shop popped like fireworks. "Did you see her with a man last night at the Cox Residence?" and "Any man, woman, or child should steer away from her."

Her?

Yes, me, Ginny.

If they did not speak my name, I could pretend it was some other girl. How terrible for her. I could've added my voice to the chorus of gossip to agree that no man should waste his time on her; it would ruin his standing, his prospects. What would he have without those, especially when he came from no money or family that could trace their lineage back to revolutionaries?

"Her and that witch," seethed a woman.

I pinched my eyes shut.

This isn't about me, Ginny.

"Ethel was the witch's name."

Not a witch, Ginny.

The words stabbed me in the back, cutting through my dress and corset and dragging the blade down my rib cage. A piece of the blade lodged between my ribs, pumping with the flow of blood into my body. It sliced through my fat and into my organs before the tip of the blade lodged into my heart, and I pressed my hand to the ache.

"Can I help you, Miss Jones?" asked a voice.

I forced my eyes open and pasted on a placid smile, dropping my hand. The seamstress stood before me, done up in bows and layers of rich fabric.

A lump had formed in the base of my throat, and I gulped. It landed like a boulder in my stomach, threatening to weigh me down, but I stayed upright.

I proclaimed loudly, "I need a new dress. I'm attending an event with Mr. Hunt. Do you have something in this green?"

I withdrew my weighted coin purse from my pocket and placed it on the counter with a loud *thump*.

Wearing a dress bought from the seamstress, I sat on a hardback chair at the rear of the crowd, facing Arthur, who read aloud from a sheet of paper. Sweat wetted his temples, and he licked his upper lip like a thirsty dog.

When he had invited me to the science symposium, I didn't know he would be speaking publicly. I wasn't sure if he was nervous because he was speaking to his colleagues, the amassing crowd, or me—as I liked to hope. While his nerves made him stutter and hunch his shoulders, his work sounded remarkable. More than a few of his colleagues, all wearing fashionably tailored jackets and speaking jovially, nodded along. Others in the crowd—those like me without higher education—were glassy-eyed, tilting their heads to the side as if trying to decipher a harsh accent.

"Thank you," finished Arthur with a wavering breath.

As others stood to leave, I clapped and promptly received annoyed looks, likely for being boisterous. While embarrassment on his behalf warmed my cheeks, I couldn't help how my breast swelled with pride for Arthur and his wonderful science. I was standing in a room of the future.

A deep red flush crept across Arthur's face when he spotted me, and I dropped my hands, wondering if I was too out of turn. I smoothed my new dress, my fingers catching on the intricate lace.

Arthur walked to my side, giving me a small bow. "Miss Jones, I'm happy you made it."

"I wouldn't miss it," I gushed. "Though, I didn't realize you would be speaking."

"I didn't wish for you to see my poor performance. I'm not much of a speaker. I've never done well on a stage. Speaking to colleagues, yes, but to everyone else…" He grimaced. "The masses terrify me."

I understood better now. "You did marvelous."

"You humor me," he said.

"I do not," I lied, hoping to replicate my mother's honeyed tone. "It probably didn't help that I arrived early."

"I'm happy that you did," he said.

"You are?"

"You grounded me. When I became nervous, I looked at you. I felt better."

His speaking skills must be truly abysmal if he thought he did better because of me.

I gave him my best reassuring smile because Arthur had many wonderful attributes. I shouldn't judge when I often had to stop myself from talking, the words gushing like a waterfall. It would be nice if he did speak well publicly to be my protection against the gentry and any lingering rumors, but alas, that would be a battle I would wage alone.

"That is too kind," I said. "I'm happy I could help."

"I'm happy you ignored my time to meet," he said, extending his arm to me. "Would you allow me to take you through the rest of the symposium?"

I slipped my arm into the crook of his elbow. "Yes please. I wish to learn more. Your presentation was so interesting."

He chuckled as he walked me through the cramped halls. Other stages had been set up with experiments and samples, pieces of paper placed beside them with black cursive ink to explain what they were. I had bypassed them previously when I saw Arthur Hunt's name as a presenter. He was on a fairly long list that seemed like a cast on a playbill.

Candles had been lit in bunches, the high chandeliers radiating above us, and hot wax pooled at the bottom of each holder. Smaller holders were set beside the parchment.

People bent down, noses practically touching the ink. They squinted as if the action would help them better understand. However, the exhibits included breakthroughs in medicine and astronomy and math, so most of us couldn't understand a lick of it. How boring I must be to Arthur.

I needed to showcase some comprehension—or pretend to—and as I was about to, a man clapped Arthur on the shoulder.

"A very good lesson indeed," said the man.

"Thank you," said Arthur, returning to his normal nature that first attracted me to him. "Many people have come tonight."

"Mr. and Mrs. Cox have been telling everyone," said the man.

He faced Arthur like I didn't exist.

Perhaps I was a ghost, unable to be seen or heard, but that was also the life of a woman—to be looked at or looked through.

"We'll hopefully be seeing more interest and funding in our projects," continued Arthur's friend.

Arthur cleared his throat. "Mr. John McCarthy, please meet Miss Virginia Jones."

He looked at me off the tip of his nose, though we weren't far apart in height, and then took my hand. His scruffy beard dragged against my knuckles as he gave me a kiss; I wished I had worn gloves. I had been so interested in touching Arthur that I hadn't thought about all the people tonight, let alone his colleagues. It was a failure not to see past my own wants.

"Pleasure to meet you, Miss Jones," said Mr. McCarthy, releasing my hand, and I politely—albeit quickly—tucked it back into my dress skirts.

"It is my honor to meet one of Mr. Hunt's colleagues," I said, taking the gamble that the two of them worked together.

Neither of them corrected me.

I didn't celebrate, rather cautious about how the man still looked at me—puzzling me out like I was a specimen in a jar. I recognized the look that sent a shiver down my spine. He knew the rumors surrounding me like a plague of locusts.

"You're too kind," said Mr. McCarthy, wrinkling his brow. "I must borrow Mr. Hunt. There is an investor here who wishes to speak with us. Come along."

He turned on his heel and started walking through the crowd, whistling for Athur like a mutt.

Bowing his head, Arthur turned to me. He opened his mouth to speak.

But I spoke first, "Go ahead."

It was what every wife should say to their husband, allowing them to work as we took care of the household and children.

Arthur furrowed his brow. "I don't wish to. I've never liked this part of science."

I whispered, "It's a necessary evil for the greater good in research."

He laughed heartily. "You are right. Please stay at the symposium. I wish to speak with you further."

"Do not worry about me," I said. "I shall be content."

He raised my hand to his lips and kissed my knuckles so tenderly I might've swooned. The small touch, mixed with heat and devotion, lit a fire in me that made me want to kiss him on the lips and scramble out of my clothes. I kept myself at bay, nodding to the simple touch and ignoring the fire raging inside of me.

"Excuse me," he apologized and then followed Mr. McCarthy through the crowd, chasing down an investor.

Sliding to the outskirts of the hall, I bent beside one of the science exhibitions: the stars mapped out on canvas and notes about comets circling the Earth. In Boston, streetlamps were lit nightly, so I rarely saw the stars. Although, I often huddled inside my house at night as well, hidden under the blankets and fending off sadness.

I tried not to think of that now, instead focusing on what I could learn and impress Arthur with.

The symposium dragged into the night as I heaved myself through the exhibit, looking over my shoulder and hoping I would catch a passing glimpse of Arthur. He proved to be allusive, burrowed between men and hidden in talks.

When I had done a full tour, I stopped beside the front windows to collect my breath. I didn't know when I had begun trembling, terrified I had lost Arthur to his colleagues. I would need to start over, going back to my old plan of finding a decrepit man who might take pity on me if it meant he could fuck a warm cunt. I would be no better than the whores on the street, lurking in the shadows to find a lonely and wealthy man.

Nose pressed to the glass and fogging my reflection, I faced the tension in my chest, chains wrapped around my heart. The pain wasn't quick to subside once I started recalling memories of Ethel.

When I squeezed my eyes shut, I recognized the spark of the love I once had for Ethel now in Arthur. But the ache was monstrous, roaring in my ears. I blinked away burning tears before the agony of loss overwhelmed me. The bricks I'd carefully laid in creating a new life would be knocked over by my hysterics.

The emotions would drown me—not just my tears—and I would be a pool on the floor, dripping through the floorboards, seeping into the soil and breathing my last breath.

The fog cleared from the window, and I gasped, staring straight into one blue eye. It was attached to no body, hovering like a spider on a web. I stumbled back, clutching my chest.

Why was the evil eye following me now?

Why hadn't it left with Ethel?

Catching myself before I fell, I turned my back to the window, refusing to descend into the evil spirits but also wanting someone else to see.

Quiet people wore open disdain, and I pointed at the window. They had to see, didn't they? The evil eye had been there, pointed not only at me but at them. It would consume us. I was only the beginning.

"Virginia," said a voice, cutting through the rising panic.

Arthur had suddenly appeared, holding my forearm in his firm grasp.

Stop, Ginny.

"Are you all right, Virginia?" asked Arthur. His gaze was tender. "You're pale."

"I'm quite well," I lied, compelling my words to be calm.

I took a deep breath, or as much as my corset would allow me. I couldn't have another fainting spell with him around. No more fainting spells at all. I was well and healed.

"Apologies for being pulled away like that," said Arthur, seemingly reassured by my lie. "I don't enjoy the talk of business, but it often happens at these events."

"Think nothing more of it," I forced myself to say because it was what every woman should say as men did important work. "I hope it was a good conversation."

"It went as well as expected. How have you been through the symposium? Found anything of interest?"

"I have found much."

"Is there anything you would like me to translate? Though, I suspect you know more than you let on."

Warmth spread through me, and I sucked in a deep breath to stifle the flames. He was already making me feel better. This must be love.

"Was the discussion profitable?" I asked, walking through the displays with Arthur at my side.

"Originally, yes," said Arthur. "We spoke to the benefactors, but then I was pulled into a discussion about my findings. It did become heated."

I blinked at him. "Heated?"

"As much as scientists can be. We are not men of fists. Rather, I was questioned on my findings and my research. This man wanted every detail." He huffed. "Enough about work."

"No, please," I whined. "Continue. I like when you speak passionately of your work."

"I rather not speak passionately about these details. As for my other passions, those you will make you wish me to close my mouth."

I smiled. "Never."

"I was hoping you would say that. As well, I hope I am not too forward in making a dinner reservation for us after the symposium."

I halted between the cases showcasing animal skeletons with extra limbs. The stitching was bad on the bones, and the little drill marks were covered in plaster. The scientists needed to hire better help. As did I without a chaperone, not that he was thinking of that regardless.

"Or not," Arthur added hastily. "I will not hold it against you if you say no. If you have no interest or are too tired. Or—as I know—it is improper. We should—"

"That is not what I was going to say," I peeped. "I would very much like to supper with you. When shall we leave?"

Five

Arthur held the chair out for me at the restaurant, and I sunk onto the worn cushion. I tried not to squirm, Arthur sitting across from me at the circular table with a white cloth. I wanted to be solely focused on him but couldn't help the nagging feeling that had followed me from the science symposium.

Others dined around us. Forks and knives scraping plates broke any silence. Huddled around their small tables, people murmured. Any proof of their talking came from the way the candlelight danced. Arthur and I were seated in the middle of the room, in full sight of everyone to cast their judgement like lightning bolts.

"I hope this is all right," said Arthur, sipping from his glass of wine.

"This is wonderful," I said, returning my attention to him.

"Truly?" His head was bent, and he looked up at me with glistening eyes that reminded me of a child filled with fearful hope.

"Yes."

He released a shaky chuckle. "Good."

"Were you scared?"

"Yes."

"Why?"

He shook his head. "It is foolish."

"Tell me anyway. Please."

"Well." He cleared his throat, raising his shoulders to sit taller. "A man might say he wishes to take his woman—that is a woman he is courting—to a new place to impress her, but rather, I've never been here before. I would dare say you have."

"Yes, I have."

"I assume you like it. Or should I take you somewhere else?"

"This place is lovely. I'm happy to be in your company."

He let out another nervous chuckle, making him appear younger than he actually was. "Thank you, Virginia, but it is me who should be happy in your company."

"Can we both not be?" I asked.

"Yes, we can. Of course. However, I should say that I enjoy you...the mere thought of you as...in my—"

He picked up his glass of wine and took a long gulp. A tendril slipped from the corner of his lips. When he put the glass down, he wiped his napkin across his face instead of dabbing, which when he realized his mistake made his cheeks redden.

"I'm very pleased to be here tonight, Virginia," he stammered. "Thank you for joining me."

Though his actions were unconventional, my stomach fluttered all the same.

"Thank you for having me," I said.

Something about him being so nervous took the pressure off my shoulders, allowing me to enjoy the company of the man before me. There was no need to hide behind pretenses when we were so boldly in public together. Our night would make it back to every drawing-room conversation.

We ordered supper—tonight's special—and having had it before, I could say it was the only thing edible on the short menu. Once the waiter scurried away, Arthur reached across the table, acting as if he were reaching for his nearby empty wine glass, but his fingers brushed the back of my hand. The smallest skin-to-skin contact stoked the ember burning in my stomach.

As quick as he touched me, he pulled his hand away like it was indecent and twisted his head at a painful angle as two women strolled toward us. I froze in my seat.

I hadn't noticed Mrs. Clark and her daughter Miss Clark when we arrived, though they had found us. But now that I considered the uneasy sensation I'd been feeling since we'd been seated, I concluded it had most likely been their eyes that I had felt in my back like pricks of a needle. I prepared myself for the initial stab of judgement, undoubtedly starting with where my chaperone was.

"Mr. Hunt, lovely to see you this evening," said Mrs. Clark.

"Um, yes." He stood and reached for their hands. "My apologies. I cannot remember your name—"

"Oh, no bother," said Mrs. Clark. "We are admirers of your work. We've only met once at a party held by Mrs. Cox."

"Mrs. Cox?" echoed Arthur, his voice squeaking as though he were a young boy.

The sound forced me to my feet. Then others were looking at us too, and I halted. The audience was growing.

"Yes," said Mrs. Clark, looking past me. "There was a wonderful mystic there that night. Very entertaining. Don't you think so, Agatha? Agatha—my daughter—had such a wonderful time at the Cox residence. Didn't you have such a wonderful time, Mr. Hunt? And the mystic... so insightful. Oh, apologies, Miss Jones. I didn't see you."

I bit my tongue, tasting metallic blood pooling between my teeth, as to not ask how Mrs. Clark couldn't have seen me if she could see Mr. Hunt so clearly. The last time Mrs. Clark and Agatha Clark saw me, I had been wearing a dress that blended into the wallpaper, quashing my hope of returning to polite society.

Mrs. Clark had surely not forgotten. Neither had Agatha by how she glared at me from the corner of her eye.

"Miss Jones and I are having supper," said Arthur as if there were nothing amiss.

Men rarely saw through what was in front of them, forgoing the quiet remarks women spoke to one another.

I could never recall my mother speaking to another person this way, but as I had entered Boston's finest, I had been met with remarks meant to shake me to the core and leave me crying in cloak closets.

"Yes, and we apologize for interrupting," said Mrs. Clark, oozing patience. "Though, I do wonder, Mr. Hunt, how much you know about Miss Jones?"

No, Ginny.

Not him, Ginny.

I couldn't breathe. My mind had gone blank like a fresh piece of paper, the creamy film washing across my mind. I couldn't find anything to say. Nor could I hear over my pounding heartbeat. I swore my heart would rip from my chest, thunking on the table, coloring our dresses crimson.

"Miss Jones and I are learning each other," said Mr. Hunt. "We met at the Cox residence during the mystic's show, if I recall correctly."

That lilt in his voice demanded that he was correct, but I wouldn't disagree.

He continued, "Miss Jones and I were speaking then, and I found her—and continue to find her—quite appealing. Ever so wonderful. Very knowledgeable. Suitable."

The last word calmed my heart for the briefest of moments, but the look on Mrs. Clark's face leeched away the calmness. She rolled her shoulders back and clucked her tongue, letting her mouth dangle open to suck the air from the room and then bellow out whatever she had to say.

"No, Mr. Hunt," said Mrs. Clark. "You do not know Miss Jones well. I ask you to take my heed. Miss Jones has an unsavory past—"

"I—" I tried to cut in, but the words died on my tongue if I ever had them at all.

Arthur trained his gaze on Mrs. Clark and Miss Clark as if they were a puzzle to solve. He nibbled on the inside of his cheek, the skin drawn in to create a dimple. I imagined that this was how he looked when he was working, and then I realized this would be the last time I would see him as Mrs. Clark revealed my past.

"These things have colored her," continued Mrs. Clark. "It will color you too, so you must understand, Mr. Hunt, that Miss Jones is not the woman you think she is. So many people already know who she is. It is why she is past her prime to become a married woman. Other men pass her by because of her history and her family situation. You would do better with a nice girl, like my daughter."

"Enough," snapped Arthur, holding up his hand to physically repel the words. Perhaps he couldn't take them anymore.

I released myself from the floor, taking one small step back and then another. I glanced over my shoulder, wondering how many steps it would take until I reached the door because once outside, I could run. I would lock myself in my house and never leave.

"Mr. Hunt," said Mrs. Clark, "I know this must be difficult."

"I wish to hear no more of it," he said.

Mrs. Clark flashed a satisfied smirk at the damage she had done. "Allow me to acquaint you with my daughter, Agatha—"

"No," said Arthur, opening his eyes. The ink-black pupils narrowed into pinpricks at Mrs. Clark. "I will not hear this idle gossip, for I draw my own conclusions. I will not be acquainted with your daughter, nor will I listen to your outlandish claims, nor will I allow you to speak about Miss Jones so falsely in public—or private. How dare you, Mrs. Clark? Have you no shame?"

Her jaw dropped, but this time, she released a small huff, exhaling into the room. I took in the long opium-heavy drag of her air. It made my head woozy, and I grabbed the chair for support.

"You are supposed to be a woman of God, yes?" asked Arthur, continuing in a whispered tone. "How dare you treat another person this way, especially one of your own society who has had a difficult time since her parents passed, like so many did in the latest fever. And these rumors—"

He spat out a deep breath like he didn't want the tainted gossip on his tongue, then continued, "Are preposterous. Sickening. I am shocked that a respectable woman like yourself speaks so. You are excused from my table and my sight, Mrs. Clark, Miss Clark. I am having a private meal and conversation with Virginia."

He returned to his seat, placing the napkin on his lap.

Mrs. Clark gasped as tears swelled in Agatha's eyes. The younger woman looked between her mother and Arthur at a pace that had to hurt her neck, a crack ringing out. Finally—and with her head bowed—Mrs. Clark scurried away with Agatha on the tail of her dress.

"Please sit, Virginia," said Arthur in a kind voice, though a vein rose from his neck.

The throbbing matched the pulsating in my heart.

"Virginia, sit," ordered Arthur.

I lowered into the seat opposite him, still trembling. It felt better to sit than stand, and I felt scared of falling and having to wait for him to catch me. I wouldn't blame him for letting me fall.

Only now were others turning away from our table, having caught a free show with their supper, but their peeled gazes watched Arthur like I did. I, too, couldn't predict his next move or what he would say.

He drank from his glass until the wine was gone and then set the glass down with a thud. I wished to offer him my untouched glass of wine, but the words were lost. I was unsure if I would apologize or dismiss Mrs. Clark's accusations.

"I'm sorry that happened," he said.

"What?" I blinked. "I mean, pardon?"

"That shouldn't have happened," muttered Arthur. "Not to you. Or anyone because it was—simply put—*wrong*. However, you… I hope you do not think me out of place, but I do like you, Virginia. Very much. I don't like people who drag another through the muck. It does not raise them."

"But the…accusations?"

"I don't want to hear of them."

My erratic heartbeat didn't calm.

I began, "I am grateful for your assistance, Arthur, with Mrs. Clark and others because I am sure there have been others—"

"Do not think of it," he said.

I grimaced. "Then you already know of the rumors surrounding me."

"John mentioned them at the symposium. He was laughing. It could've been a jest. He likes to stir trouble."

Tears collected in my eyes. I turned my head away, the burn worse than possible.

"I don't believe what they say, Virginia." Arthur reached across the table and took my hand. "Nor do I want to hear them. People are cruel, and what I've seen in high society is not something I like. I do not wish to be part of that."

"Then you don't wish to see me?" I asked meekly.

"No, Virginia. I didn't say that." His voice was kind. "I don't see you as one who looks down on others. I have felt drawn to you since we met at the Cox residence. These rumors have given me resolve."

I raised my head to look at him, his appearance hazy through my tears. "They do?"

"You are friends with someone not in the same class as you?"

"Not anymore," I said, unable to speak her name.

"You were, though?" he asked, ducking his head.

"Yes."

"That's good to hear," he said, "because what people fail to realize— or perhaps cannot see past their own bias—is that I am not a man of the ruling class. I was not raised in Boston society nor raised with much wealth. I have created my own. We both have rumors surrounding us, Virginia. People are cruel for no reason. I hope you do not take it in the wrong way—for I mean it not to sound as such but cannot pick my words carefully now—is that I don't trust many of the people in the old families. The women are vicious."

I murmured, "You have no idea."

"They talk of witchcraft," he said, shaking his head. "They speak of witches like they mean to start the next trial. They treat each other as competitors, meaning to burn them at the stake. If I had a sister or a daughter someday—"

The words warmed my chest.

"—I would love for her to have friends," he continued. "Life is hard enough as it is. She does not need to look over her shoulder for the watchmen, taken before the court of our peers."

I straightened my fork.

"As if witchcraft is real." He scoffed. "Thankfully, you and I have the same opinion on the occult, Virginia."

Our supper finally arrived. We both ate a concoction of sausage, buttered vegetables, and pumpkin with bread rolls. Seasoning was shipped to Boston, but I couldn't stomach anything more than salt. Arthur, on the other hand, had blends of orange and red spices, turning his sausage from gray and brown to a sunrise of colors. I watched him take a bite, consider it, swallow, and then take another, finding it palatable.

"You enjoy it, then?" I asked, motioning to his plate.

I had cut into my sausage, the innards sliding out from the wrapping, and steam clouded my nose.

"Yes, very much so. You?" he asked politely.

"Yes," I said, though I hadn't taken a bite. "Thank you for asking."

I was used to making stew for myself, so anything not wet and needing a spoon would be tasty.

"You do not need to thank me," he said. "I care for you, Virginia. I wish to know what you like and do not like."

"In food habits?"

"In *all* habits. I wish to know you."

I tried not to blanch, and when I thought myself unsuccessful, I dabbed my lips with the napkin. "I would say you know more than most. Truthfully, I am not interesting. I would like to hear more about your work."

He chuckled. "I shall go on for days."

"Then please start," I said.

"Virginia, I will never stop talking about my work. I will have to be dead to never utter another word of it," he said. "While our night started as business with the science symposium, I do wish to court you in the fullest, which means that I should know you. In turn, I will speak on your behalf."

I swallowed and shifted in my seat. "Very well, where should we begin?"

He laughed nervously under his breath as if he had something to hide. "To start, I know that you are an only child. I have three older brothers, and I would like to have a family. Would you?"

"Yes." The word was immediate—a grunted response that was expected of a woman—but I did mean it.

A smile pulled on his lips like I had already told him he was to be a father. I could see our future play out. He would be a good father, loving and kind. Mindful. So helpful that I would have to shoo him from our child's room when he wanted to watch them sleep.

"The gender of the children doesn't matter," said Arthur. "I will love them all, but I would adore a daughter. I would dote on her."

"My father did the same to me," I said. "While I have no siblings and my father had no son, I don't think that it caused a rift."

"I will do the same," said Arthur. "Knowledge is not meant for only a few. It's why funding for university projects is so important. I know my research could revolutionize the world, but it needs to be in the hands of the masses."

"I couldn't agree more," I replied, thinking back to his speech.

"Apologies." He gulped. "I said no work. Do not let me curtail the conversation."

I nodded. "How many children would you like?"

"At least four. Having grown up with three brothers, I'm used to all the sound. It is odd to be somewhere so quiet. It was nice to have playmates. While we could be rough as boys, it was nice to have others around my age."

"I, too, wish to have a house full of children." The house was too quiet as it was, and I wanted to have sound rushing through the halls again. "I was a lonely child. My parents tried their best to be around, but they had other duties to attend to."

"It is understandable," he said.

"Yes. Are you interested in teaching?"

"At some point, I might be, but I am far more interested in the science now. However, universities have some of the best resources. Being a professor would have more possibilities. We could expand the house when the time comes."

We.

Butterflies quickened in my stomach, and I knew I wouldn't be able to eat. He was thinking of our future. Courtship and companionship were one thing, but this could develop into love. The crinkles around his eyes said that he, too, was growing accustomed to the idea.

When I re-entered polite society, I hadn't thought I would be so lucky for love in a marriage, so I had thrown myself at whatever man would have me if it meant that I would have a comfortable home and a shield of protection. It was my duty to carry on the family and fortune. Arthur was more than I had ever dared to dream of.

Six

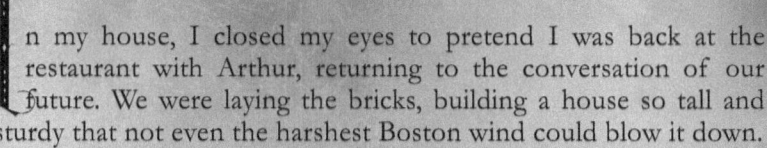

In my house, I closed my eyes to pretend I was back at the restaurant with Arthur, returning to the conversation of our future. We were laying the bricks, building a house so tall and sturdy that not even the harshest Boston wind could blow it down.

Of course, we would live in this house. Arthur would move in once we were married, and we would sleep in what was once my parents' bedroom.

"Don't," I said without opening my eyes, but I knew she was here.

Her presence was a chill, seeping across the floor and sliding up my legs. Her phantom fingers pressed into my skin, like she used to touch me.

I forced my eyes open to meet her gaze.

Ethel leered at me from my bedroom doorway. This used to be our shared bedroom before our life collapsed. Her reflection in the mirror blurred white, and the hearth shed light onto half of her.

I ran a brush through my hair, catching knots and yanking. The strands fell around my feet, and I kicked at the ticklish hair. They were like spiders crawling up my legs. I slapped them away until I hit myself, pain sizzling. I bit back a hiss, instead turning my attention to the looming Ethel.

"What do you want?" I asked, tightening my grip on my hairbrush.

My knuckles ached, protruding from my pale, taut skin.

Darkness clouded her eyes—the same way it had when we had spoken of love huddled in the blankets of my bed, our limbs intertwined, and she had a devilish thought—but then she lowered her head.

"Why are you here?" I demanded.

She still said nothing.

Anger bubbled in me like fire. Whirling from the mirror, I threw my hairbrush at the now empty doorway but missed wide. It thumped against the wall and clattered to the floor. I lingered like she did, counting each raging heartbeat that threatened to explode from my body.

Returning to the doorway, Ethel said, "You're lonely, Ginny."

The words flowed past my ears and wrapped me in a warm embrace; I was falling into them like I had fallen into her arms so many times. I shook my head to free myself.

"I'm with Arthur," I said. "I have Arthur now."

"He's not here," said Ethel. "I am."

"He'll be here soon."

"Tonight?"

"You know not tonight."

"Then we have tonight."

"No!" I turned away from her, gripping the vanity to anchor myself here instead of crawling into her arms and feeling how our bodies pushed and pulled against one another.

We had created Heaven in this house—in these blankets and in these haunted halls, filling them again with laughter and music. We'd made love and were in love—but then we burned it down, leaving us in constant Hell.

"You don't need Arthur," said Ethel. "You have me."

I know bubbled in me, but I clamped my teeth shut.

I wouldn't!

I couldn't.

"I'll always be with you," continued Ethel in the doorway. "We'll never be parted."

I pressed a hand to my chest, the words striking me like a searing brand; *Ethel* would be written across my breast. Her mouth would move to my nipple, and I would hold her head in my hands. Then she would sink her teeth into me, sucking out my blood and soul, and I would give myself over.

My mind.

My sanity.

It was all for her to claim.

"No," I repeated.

Ethel raised her head again.

"We are done," I shouted. "We are over. What we had is buried in the past. You need to leave!"

"Do you think it is that easy, Ginny?" asked Ethel.

"It should be," I said.

"It is not."

"I know."

"Then how can you ask such a thing of me?" She raised her voice until it was a howl.

Pinching my eyes shut, I tried to ignore the pull toward her—the warmth rising in me at the thought of us together in the cold that had overtaken the house. A chill ran down my spine, my body reacting before my mind could. It wanted me to run, but Ethel would follow me like a hound. She knew my blood as well as my scent. She knew where I would hide, not that I had anywhere else to go.

But I did now, didn't I?

"Tell me about Arthur, Ginny," said Ethel. "How was the date tonight? I know how you like that restaurant, though it was Arthur's first time. Who would've thought he liked the taste of something more exotic than salt?"

"You were there. You were spying on me," I accused.

Ethel said nothing. She wanted to provoke me, and she would use it against me to anyone who listened.

I had played into her hands before.

"I have the right to be happy, Ethel. I have the right to move on and find love. *Be* in love," I pleaded, hoping she would understand.

I would want the same for her if our positions were reversed.

Ethel laughed, a high-pitched bark. I flinched.

Burning tears blinded me, but I blinked them away before Ethel could see me cry; I was just being a spoiled child, crying over my own mess. I had neither servants to do my bidding nor Ethel to take my orders. Although, I never asked her to.

Pushing off the vanity seat, I flew across the room and slammed my door, shutting Ethel out, but her laughter echoed underneath. It haunted the halls, reverberating until it rattled the windowpanes, threatening to crack and let Ethel out. Her laughter turned into the cackle of a witch.

With the sound rattling around my skull, I jumped into bed and threw the blankets over my body and the pillow over my head. Ethel's smell lingered on the bed, no matter how many times I washed the linens. It was as though she were lying beside me. This bed was one place we didn't have to hide. In fact, we truly came alive with who we were.

Seven

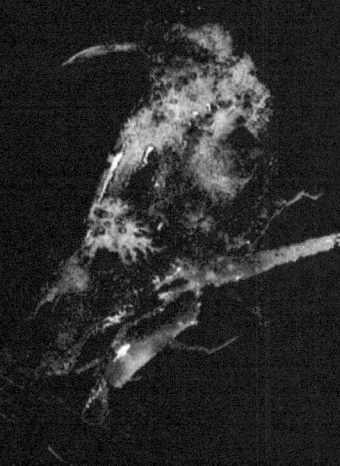

November 15, 1842

After months of neglect—even from the servants—the house needed to be cleansed. I scrubbed, washed, and dusted. My knees and shoulders ached, and I walked hunched like a hag instead of a young woman. It made my corset more important. I tightened the laces until my body was shaped foreign to me, such a narrow waist and pressed breasts that nearly toppled out.

I made tea and bought sweets. I didn't know what my guest would like, so I bought two of my favorites and one of everything else. I even bought a meat pie for a proper supper. Licking my lips, I walked past a newly dusted mirror, my hair pinned up fashionably. I wondered if that was what Ethel liked.

A knock rattled the front door, and I tried not to flinch. It was the time I had asked Ethel to come, delivering the next batch of herbs to help me relax. Her last remedy had worked wonders. I had returned to the apothecary, meeting the apothecarist but not her. He gave me her address, and I sent her a letter. Had it been rude of me to call upon her?

No, Ginny. This is business.

And if I wanted more than that? A companionship that transcended the word, my heart swelling under my breast and my stomach in knots. I couldn't remember ever feeling like this.

I walked toward the door as I had seen servants do: without rush. We were a house of Boston's finest; we didn't rush for attention that may not be deserved. At the same time, I wanted to run to the door, so when I whipped it open, I glowered at the empty space.

"What?" I gasped, stepping into the day, and spotted Ethel walking away from my house.

With her head bent, she had the same shawl over her shoulders like she did days ago, though it wasn't water-logged. Today could've been a nice day if it wasn't for the biting wind coming off the harbor. Autumn bled into winter.

"Come back!" I called to Ethel.

And then—like an improper lady, my shoes reminding me of how bad of a decision it was—I chased her.

To feel the wind through my hair and my arms pumping back and forth, I felt like a child again. My parents would take me to the beach, where no one cared that I sprinted through the sand and surf or flew like a seagull, extending my sleeves as wings.

Ethel waited back on her heels as I neared her, reminding me of a spooked deer. I slowed foolishly but that was exactly what I had been—a fool. Mrs. White would no doubt spread the word. I should've hidden inside the house and let Ethel leave. However, I had chased her, knowing in my heart that it was the correct decision.

"You're leaving?" I squeaked.

Ethel faced me. "Do you have the funds? I have your…medicine."

I wanted to thank her for speaking in such a vague manner. Already, the people on the street were watching us. I needed to get us out of public; too many prying eyes were skinning me alive. It didn't look like it bothered her.

"Yes, in my home." I stood out of the way, sweeping my hand. "Come along."

We made it to the door before she stopped on the threshold, gazing up at the front of the house, the two columns twisted and carved in stone. In comparison to the other houses on the street, it was plain, but it was my home, including the chipping paint and dusty curtains. While the other houses had primed gardens and hordes of servants, I could clean this house caught between colonial mansions.

I held the door open for Ethel. "Please come inside."

"Inside?" she breathed, astounded.

I didn't think I could catch her unprepared. She was worldly, if not otherworldly.

"Yes," I said. "Please."

Please, I wanted to repeat until she stepped into my house. I wanted her inside to trap her, make her speak to me.

Did that sound odd?

To any woman in polite society, it would, but I didn't wish to have the same dull conversations about marriage, birth, and children, all culminating in our deaths when we were gray, wrinkled, sagging with old age, and addicted to imported gin.

When I spoke to Ethel, it was like I fed off her. I had been thinking much—perhaps too much—about our previous conversation, the words creeping into my mind long after we had parted.

With her gaze lingering on me, Ethel stepped inside the house, and I closed the door behind her. The sound outside hushed, like a candle snuffed out. The world was gone, and we were together, huddled close in the large front entryway. Ethel's skirt brushed my own, and I tucked my hands behind my back so I wouldn't grab ahold of her skirts and drag her further into my house or closer to me.

She faced me. "The money—"

"Have supper with me," I blurted.

Red graced her cheeks. "I cannot."

"Why?"

"Don't be imprudent."

"I'm not."

"You are."

"You have not told me why you shall not supper with me."

"You have not told me why you wish to have supper with me," she said, shooting the words back into my face with a huff.

Her hot breath licked my skin.

"You have not asked," I said.

"I am now."

"You did not previously. I did."

"Must you bring that back?"

"Why should I not?"

"Will you just pay me?" asked Ethel, hand in her pocket. That must've been where the hashish was kept from me until she decided to administer it.

"Will you have supper with me?" I asked.

"No," she said.

"Then a glass of wine?"

Ethel worked her jaw as though I had angered her, but she was no longer arguing with me. I had three more replies to whatever she said, but I didn't often think before I spoke to her. The words flew from my mouth. It made me question if this was like to be free—no, not free, because was I not free as a woman with means and no position? Ethel had calloused hands, and nature had bitten her cheeks. Still, she was gorgeous. Determination illuminated her eyes, and her pink lips pinched to look like a budding flower.

"I don't understand why you want to share a drink with me," said Ethel.

"I like your company," I said.

That was too simple of a statement, though it was filled with every hope that thrummed in me of all the things I could not admit. Nor could I explain why I wanted her to stay for supper or why I felt so connected to her. I had never felt this way toward any other person, certainly no woman. I had never been close to them. Perhaps it was why Mrs. Cox thought me so peculiar—a sentiment that had only worsened since my parents died.

Ethel studied me for a long moment, punctuated by my quick heartbeat. "Will a glass allow me to be paid?"

"Will it not make you want to stay longer?" I asked, the question slipping from my mouth before I thought better of it.

I bit my tongue as though I could take back the words.

She harrumphed. "Lead on."

In the dining room connected to the kitchen, I opened a bottle of wine, the bitter kind my parents used to drink, and poured a serving for Ethel and myself. When she took the glass, her fingers brushed mine, and a shiver sizzled my skin. It warmed more than just my chest. She withdrew her hand, now with the glass of wine, and rested it on the table. I put the bottle down and then sat opposite her.

"Won't you sit at the head?" asked Ethel, inclining her chin to the width of the table.

After my parents died and I still had servants, I sat there. I'd been running the household and family line, but the endearment from others about me being a modern woman had quickly parted. I only sat there when I still wanted to smell my father's cigar smoke or feel the indent of his body, but no, I was not made for the head of the table.

"I would be far from you," I said, meaning the words.

Ethel laughed so heartily it sounded almost like a man, but it was natural. She didn't hide it behind her hand or shift the octave higher to sound more girlish.

She wheezed like it was the funniest thing she had ever heard. I didn't much appreciate being laughed at, but it didn't feel filled with malice, only disbelief. I could concur just how in disbelief I, too, was at my own actions.

"You don't think I smell too much?" asked Ethel when she recovered.

"No." I sniffed but then shook my head. "What would you smell like?"

"I spend much time with herbs and in the kitchen. I would imagine onions and potatoes. Perhaps sweat."

For some reason—not that I wanted to admit to myself—*sweat* made me clammy. Perspiration collected on the back of my neck and behind my knees, dripping down my calves. I took a sip of the bitter wine that brought me back to the days I had supper with my parents.

"I don't think you smell." I could only smell the meat pie coming from the kitchen.

My stomach grumbled.

She laughed again. "That would be a first. I would think many in the ruling class would think of me as a terrible choice to sit at their table—or be in their house—because I would stink it up. Or cast a hex."

"You are not a witch," I said, reminding her of the words she once said to me.

"Others think I am," she said, leaning toward me.

"Because you hail from Salem?"

"As well as my ancestors, who were hanged during the trials."

I blanched, and Ethel smirked at me, though her eyes shimmered. The hard shell of the woman seemed to have cracked. I was trying to piece together what I knew and thought I knew about the woman.

"But you are not a witch," I said again.

Ethel sipped her wine, puckered her lips, and then decided it was good enough to take another drink. "What do you think?"

"There is no such thing as witches," I said. "They were fairy tales concocted to scare children."

Ethel raised her eyebrows like she was impressed. "Is that all?"

"What do you mean?"

She hesitated, watching me like I would break, but I kept my gaze even with hers. This wouldn't be allowed in polite society, but Ethel had made it clear that she wasn't interested. I felt like something else was in her gaze: a burning.

A yearning.

"Well, I must say I like a woman who uses her own mind," she said.

"I try, but do not inflict flattery when you mean something else," I responded.

She flattened her gaze. "Do you think those fairy tales were only meant to scare children? Or do you think they were meant to scare adults too?"

We were deep in gray territory now, darkening by each spoken word of things I had never said.

"I have never given it much thought," I admitted. When the thought struck me, I quickly blew out that flame. I didn't need my imagination to catch fire.

"Will you think about it now?" asked Ethel.

"I assume I have no choice," I said.

"I never had a choice. My mother taught me everything I know about healing others, including the plants and tinctures that can be created from this very land. Don't think that imported plants and medicines will always help you. Generations have thrived off this land before others razed it." She sipped her wine. "Before my mother, it was my grandmother and so forth. Back in the old days of Salem, before it was a booming port. People had to survive on what was there, including anything native. These herbal remedies have been passed down."

"Do you write them? For others, I mean."

"If they so wish, yes, but most people do not. They don't want to learn, only to have their problem fixed."

I scratched my heavy head, thinking about the dreamless sleep I had had since Ethel waltzed into my life. "Will you write down the remedy for me?"

"Yes, though yours is simple. Yours is nature itself. No mashing, cutting, and boiling required."

"What about these practices for future use? Your own descendants."

Ethel shook her head. "I do not see any future descendants of my own."

I blanched. "You don't wish for children?"

"No. Do you?"

Yes, to grow and birth a child who looked like me like I did my mother, to watch the child grow into an adult and have other siblings running around, to have a house filled with laughter and joy. That was what life was meant to be.

However, her question fractured me.

"Doesn't everyone?" I asked meekly.

"I do not." She ran her thumb around the rim of the wine glass, no longer meeting my gaze. "All I ever wanted was to help people, like my mother and grandmother did before. I want to help those who cannot help themselves. I was never meant for a frock, nor am I holy enough to be a nun. I've never had the money or training to become an apothecarist, and I like to think of myself as an herbalist, but it matters little what I think."

She looked at me, like she expected me to say something—*anything, Ginny!*—but when she spoke so eloquently of her own wants, I didn't know what to say. I would rather let her speak, hanging onto every word like it was breath itself.

"You're here. Let me serve you dinner." I was off the chair and in the kitchen, the door swinging shut behind me, before she found her next argument as for why she couldn't dine with me.

As much as I loved when she spoke—her sultry voice was like bonfire smoke, her accent added a lilt to her voice, her quick words left me breathless like I had just run a race—I didn't want to hear another argument about supper. I served it quickly, dreading that she would be gone when I re-entered the dining room. She hadn't moved. I placed the warm meat pie on the table and began to cut. The juices rolled out, meat and vegetables—not perceptively different looking—falling out in chunks as the flaky crust crumbled.

I placed a piece in front of Ethel and then returned to my seat with my own slice, fighting my rumbling stomach. The sound only increased as I took a deep whiff and prepared to eat this meat pie like it was my last meal in this world. When I took a bite, I tried to swallow my moan with the food, but the flavor lasted on my tongue and the chunk of meat pie filled my stomach.

Ethel hadn't taken a bite, but the steam rolled up to cloud her face. The food bits were like discolored organs on the white plate, mixed with congealed brown gravy. She took a drink from her wine, setting down her goblet, empty, and I rose to grab the bottle and refill.

"Don't," she said, placing her palm flat over the rim.

If I did pour, I would splatter her red, the wine rolling from her hand like an open wound.

She had said one drink—no supper—but I would've pumped the wine and food into her until she was bloated, stuck in the chair, and unable to move from my home, let alone my sight.

With her other hand, Ethel motioned for me to sit, and I sunk into the seat, holding the neck of the wine bottle. By some chance—perhaps my lacking strength as a woman—the bottle didn't shatter.

"What about you, Virginia?" asked Ethel.

"What about me?" I squeaked.

"What do you want?"

You.

I took a sip of wine to clear my thoughts and the word, but then I was swaying—damn the wine—so I took a bite of the meat pie. A chunk lodged in the back of my throat, so I had to drink more wine while the old grandfather clock ticked, letting me know just how long I had let pass.

"I don't know what you mean," I said.

"What did you expect your life to be?" asked Ethel, still watching me. "Do you want to be married and have children?"

"Yes."

"Why? Don't say it's what women do."

I frowned. "Then I'm not sure what to say. You already expected my next words."

"What if you had a choice to do anything else?" she asked.

"I do not."

"If you did—"

"You're growing close to the territory of fairy tales," I said, "and we've already spoken about you not being a witch."

She smirked. "Then, without a choice, what are you, Virginia?"

I could come undone with her speaking my name, half whispered and half taunted. I took a bite of the pie because, while delicious, it offered a moment of clarity.

"I've always known what I would become," I said, "what my parents expected of me."

"You are not what your parents expected of you," she accused.

"You didn't know them," I snapped, tightening my grip on the fork and knife.

Ethel grimaced. "That is not what I meant."

"You were speaking of my parents like you knew them. You've never met them. You never knew how good of people they were. You never knew what they wanted from me—"

"You just said you wanted to do what they expected, and you want to be married, and you are not," said Ethel in one breath. "You are going against your own class in your home, no servants and sharing food and wine with a woman like me. What will others think?"

I looked down at my lap, hanging my head. My shoulders rolled forward, body only held up by the corset. While I should've felt foolish—Ethel's words were like stab wounds to my heart—I knew what she was asking: she, too, knew how dangerous this was for me.

"I've never been the best at what society thinks I shall do," I admitted in a small voice. "It didn't matter very much when my parents were alive because I only had to deal with society when outside, but since they have died…it is like society has entered my house, lays in bed with me at night, whispering about what a woman like me should do."

Ethel drew her eyebrows together. "Are you not what a woman in the elites should be?"

"A woman like me should already be wed, having children and running a household."

I let out a soft, mournful laugh, because I had lost that part of myself when my parents died. I had fallen into a hole, and until I met Ethel, I thought I would never crawl from it.

"A woman like me," I continued, "would have charities or hobbies, but I am no great painter or musician, nothing so accomplished like many women looking for husbands. In fact, I'm boring."

"You're not," said Ethel.

"Do not lie," I growled.

"I do not."

"Then you treat me like a child."

"I do not."

"Then do not—"

"You are not boring, Virginia," said Ethel earnestly, reaching across the table. She stopped before touching me, her fingers hovering. "I recognized that from the moment we first met."

I rolled my eyes. "So I amuse you."

"I did not say that."

"You must've thought me daft."

"Only naive. It would be hard to blame a person for that."

"Yet you did."

She plucked the wine bottle from my hand and poured herself another glass. When her goblet was full, she set the bottle on the table with a thud, a reminder that she wasn't taught how to be as quiet as a mouse.

"The reason for my attitude in the apothecary and even today is that I envy you." She sipped her wine.

"Envy?" I asked, astounded. "Because of the money and the dresses?"

"No." She laughed, though not with malice. "Because you are amazed by everything. Because you have so much to learn. Because you are open and curious. You are proactive—no, don't try to hide it, Virginia. It is what brought you all the way into the slums of Boston, where you were most likely told to never go, and why you wished to survive when the world wished to only swallow you into the murky depths. You are strong, Virginia."

I couldn't help but laugh, like this was all some jest, because this was far from the truth. Perhaps I was a much better actress than I thought, but my memory was too terrible to remember lines from a play.

"I'm only a watcher," I said, shaking my head. "While you may see me as daring, I am a wallflower. I am passed over."

"I don't believe that," whispered Ethel and then straightened in her chair and took a drink from her wine as if it could give her courage or luck, perhaps both. "If you think you are, then we will need to change that."

She cut into her meat pie.

I wasn't sure how I would change that when it was expected of me, but the moment of rest allowed me to think further about how to draw myself from this conversation. I was a mad woman to society, and with women already having weak constitutions, I would be hard pressed to find a man who was willing to put up with my mind, emotions, and body.

"Not to push the topic further but I wonder," began Ethel after swallowing a bite of pie, "how did your parents die?"

"The fever," I said, trying to use the same cold voice the physician used when he told me there was nothing left to do.

Ethel nodded. "That was a hard bout. Many died."

The newspapers reported such numbers, but I didn't spend my time reading sadness.

"I've been alone since," I murmured.

"I know the feeling," said Ethel. "My father was a dock worker, died when I was a babe in an accident, and my mother died when I in my youth."

"Then you are a proper orphan."

Ethel shrugged. "Everyone—well, most—become orphans one day, losing their parents. For parents to lose a child…that may be heartbreaking."

"You have no siblings either?"

"I do not, but I cannot say I've ever been alone. I've had my work and friends. How about you?"

My cheeks burned. At the beginning, I had others in society sending well wishes, but those petered out as if I were no longer allowed to mourn and was unable to cope. I should've written back, but I let the letters collect dust and finally threw them into a lit hearth in a bout of sleepless late-night rage. It was a terrible thing to do—abandoning the people who only showed kindness. I cast myself out of society.

"You said you had servants once," said Ethel. "Shall you bring them back now?"

I shrugged and then cringed, how unladylike. I had taken the motion from Ethel, and I needed to leave it with her. If Mrs. Cox or Mrs. White saw, they would spread the word that I had fallen out of ladylikeness.

"I don't mind being alone in the house," I admitted. "I didn't realize how quiet the house would become. It is small enough for me to do the upkeep. Cleaning is one of the few things that keeps my mind busy."

"What happens when you aren't busy?" asked Ethel.

My head ached at the thought, the rush of everything rising like a wave coming to sweep me out into the harbor.

"Your medicine has helped," I said.

She released a small smile. "I'm not sure it can be called medicine."

I didn't want to think about what it was—only that it worked—so I said, "I don't know if I want the servants to return. Not yet. The house isn't ready for them."

"What do you mean?"

I bit my tongue until I drew blood because I couldn't say it—couldn't even think it—and not seem like a madwoman. If there was anyone who might understand, it would be Ethel because she was a descendant of the Salem witches.

With her head still drawn toward me, her eyes calculating and her ears pointed at me like a listening hound, I said, "I think the house is haunted."

A smirk pulled across her lips.

I winced like I had been slapped; I should've known better than to say that aloud. How foolish I had been. I didn't know this woman.

I tried to pull my hands to my lap, but Ethel grabbed one. Under her touch, the small hairs rose across my body. She wrapped her fingers in mine, hanging onto me, and as much as my mind wished to pull away, my body wouldn't move.

"I don't mean to torment you, Virginia," said Ethel, voice soft. "It is that I do not believe in ghosts."

I gasped mockingly. "Yet people call you a witch and you do not believe in ghosts?"

She laughed, understanding my jest.

Thankfully, I had hidden the throbbing pain. I had seen mystics claiming to speak to the other world, and I had attempted to bring one into my house to speak to my parents, in hopes it would urge them to the afterlife and give me peace. When he arrived, I couldn't open the door, and I huddled in my parents' bed, breathing in their lasting scents.

"My mother and grandmother believed in ghosts," said Ethel. "Even tried to speak to them. I remember them practicing with mystics when I was a girl, but I didn't believe it. I refuse to believe in ghosts or otherworldly creatures. It is so easy to be caught up in so-called magic and miss what is in front of us."

Was I doing just that? Perhaps I was hiding from society and myself behind these ghosts, and I should've re-entered with the flourish of a woman who was not desperate. I wasn't *that* good of an actress.

"Would you like a tour of the house?" I asked.

Ethel placed her fork down. "Is that what you would like to do?"

"I would like to show you where it is the most haunted. Where I think it is most haunted."

Where I could hear the ghosts and where it would grow cold even at the height of summer, leaving me shivering. I could show her where I saw them from the corner of my eye, but they disappeared when I tried to face them.

I thought she might laugh at me again, but she said, "Yes, show me. I can put your mind at ease."

We started on the main floor, passing through the dining room and sitting room as well as the library and study that hadn't been aired out since my father died. For a long moment, we stood in the wonderful eastern light that shone into the sitting room.

I waited for her to hear the ghosts, but she didn't blink an eye. They were silent, and I could only assume it was her that kept them away.

We walked up the grand staircase, the floorboards creaking under our weight. Before my father passed, he had been planning to replace the steps, but now, I refused, needing the familiar sounds to break up the breathing of the house that seemed to have a soul of its own. The bones had long since settled, and the heart lay somewhere, deep in a place I had yet to find. I was sure it was here somewhere, but I had been searching since I was a child to no avail.

On the landing, Ethel smiled so genuinely it made me stumble over an uneven floorboard. She thankfully didn't notice. Her eyes were trained on something else, and I wondered if she saw a ghost.

"I can imagine you running down these halls as a young girl," said Ethel.

"I was admonished by the servants for running," I admitted.

"Did you listen?"

"No."

"Did your parents scold you as well?"

A smile pulled on my lips as I thought back to them. "They never did."

"How long have you seen ghosts?" asked Ethel.

I ducked my head, wondering if she was making fun of me or perhaps testing me, and peeked from the corner of my eye to study her. She was watching me expectantly, eyebrows raised.

"Since I was a child," I explained. "I cannot tell you who they are, cannot make out their faces or what they say, but I know they are here."

"I believe you," she said.

"But you don't believe in ghosts?"

"I *believe* you." Ethel held my hand, locking our fingers together. "Also, I thought you might want me somewhere more private."

I couldn't tell if she was joking with me, worming into my soul like the gossip did. The house was already private, but I was taking Ethel somewhere that no one else was meant to go, not even the ghosts, which was why I shouldn't have taken Ethel upstairs to where I slept. Some part of me wanted to take her somewhere that others didn't see.

I hesitated at the door to my parents' bedroom, wondering if I was willing to air it out and lose their trace by bringing Ethel inside to reveal my secrets but draw her closer. Her scent lingered, brought closer by how she continued to hold my hand. By now, I knew the herbal scents on her cloak. They were probably interwoven in her hair too. I bit my bottom lip, pretending it was a clump of her hair caught in my teeth as I tugged her until her lips met mine.

I already loved when she smiled, the light dancing in her eyes and red tinging her cheeks, creeping down her neck to hide under the high collar of her dress. But her pink lips were set in a consistent frown. If I kissed her now, I hoped I would make her smile. I would be graced by God's light, warmed and blinded and never ending, but Ethel was glancing away as if she couldn't look at me any longer. I was losing her.

"Are there ghosts in there?" asked Ethel, inclining her head toward the closed door.

"Yes," I whispered.

I dropped my hand from the brass doorknob, and she dropped her hand from mine, tucking it into her cloak. I wanted to reach out and wrap her fingers in mine, keeping her hidden in the house, our skirts wrapping around our ankles and our bodies close together.

"I can let you in the room," I said, hoping she would stay.

Gaze wavering, she had already stepped back.

I returned my hand to the door, about to push it open and reveal what was inside to Ethel. If she would stay, I would show her the whole house, my whole life! But she was backing toward the staircase.

"Why are you leaving?" I asked.

"Why would you like me to stay?" asked Ethel.

"Why must you ask these questions of me?"

"The why questions?"

"Yes."

"I want you to think."

"I do."

She frowned.

Though she didn't speak it, I felt the spank of pain that I never experienced with my servants telling me to be on my best behavior.

"I need to return to Salem before it's too late. Walk me out?" she asked.

"You may stay here," I said. "I have more than enough rooms."

"Will people not think it improper?"

No died on my lips, leaving me puckered and leaning toward her. I only needed to gather her up and kiss her like I had seen my father kiss my mother. We were protected in these hallowed halls, not even the prying eyes from outside or the ghosts could see us.

At the same time, I wanted to tell her I hadn't seen or heard a ghost since she entered my home. They had never hidden from a guest before, so it was Ethel herself who was my protector.

Ethel continued, "Nevertheless, I have business in Salem this very night."

I nodded before walking down the hallway, her a step behind me. I wanted her to walk as my equal as she had done when we first came up the stairs, speaking about ghosts in hushed whispers like two friends, but I was now a woman in polite society, while she fell into the servant's role, the original herbalist she'd been when she walked into my house, called by me.

In the front entryway, with my medicinal herbs and her with money, I held the door open as if I were the servant and she the lady. As she stepped outside, giving me a curt nod, it was apparent that she was not. Others on the street took notice, the same way they had when Ethel had arrived. The curtains were peeled back, and old Mrs. White watched everything.

"Good evening," I said to Ethel, but she had already turned her back to me.

I gripped the door frame like I wished to grip her, digging my nails into the fabric of her cloak, keeping myself upright by being anchored to her. I returned inside the house and closed the door, slumping against it when I could stand no longer.

 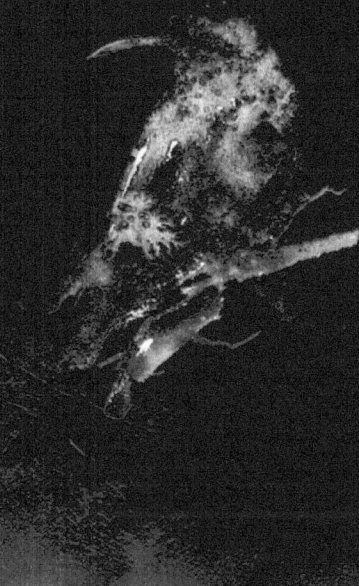

Eight

A knock rattled the front door in the morning, so I stopped my daily chores, letting my hummingbird-light feet carry me. It wasn't until I had my hand on the cold brass doorknob that I stopped, realizing the state of myself. Not needing a repeat of what happened with the messenger boy, I waited for the person's shadow to disappear.

I peeked through the peephole and checked the surroundings before grabbing what was left on the front step. Then, I closed the door, locking myself inside the house again.

Flowers waited in my hands, and I took a deep whiff. Perhaps the mayflowers would grow into my lungs, clinging to my bones and using my blood as water, growing up my throat. I would be such a beautiful garden.

The flowers crinkled, a leaf falling to the floor along with a splat of something harder. Peeking around the white bouquet, I kicked a note, the cream-colored paper folded in half. I dropped the flowers to pick up the note, petals and leaves fluttering like in autumn. When I unfolded the letter, I recognized Arthur's handwriting as if it were my own.

Dear Virginia,

I had a wonderful time last night. The conversation was riveting. You continue to prove yourself knowledge and graceful. If you would be so kind, I would like to see you at the upcoming ball.

Yours truly,

Arthur

The words swirled. I forced myself to read the note thrice to collect every detail. With my knees quaking and my mind in a haze, I hugged the letter to my chest as if the words would write across my skin.

I loved him. I knew it in my heart and in my bones—every part of me that mattered—and I wanted to marry him. I wanted a future for us.

What if he doesn't want you as you, Ginny? He will play you a fool, and he will discard you for your faults. A man cannot be blind to them.

I ground my teeth until I felt they would break.

No, Arthur loved me.

"Do not give me that look," I snapped at Ethel, who lingered at the edge of the sitting room. "Don't ruin this for me. And do not follow me!"

I stomped upstairs, slamming the door to keep her out... If only it were that easy.

She swept into the room as if she was still welcome, trailing after me like a lost cat wanting cream, but I had no more to give. I turned my back to her, shifting through my dresses in the wardrobe to find something fitting for an upcoming party.

The Cox servants took my bonnet and cloak as I arrived. Stepping into the house, Arthur handed over his hat before he held out his hand, and I slid my arm into the crook of his elbow, returning to his side. We stood a wall against the imposing elites. Their noses pointed in our direction like hounds smelling blood.

"This way, I think," said Arthur, towing me from the front entryway.

Murmurs clawed at my back, and my thick dress acted as armor.

The side room offered some ease and a glass of wine, but I kept my lips pinched together and my fingers on the stem. The world was already spinning. The side room had a few other couples relaxing, not that they paid much attention to us, for we had purposefully escaped the bustle.

Arthur took a sip of his wine. "Do you like these parties?"

"Yes," I lied because I should like them.

He drew his eyebrows together.

I asked, "What is it?"

"I didn't think you would," he said.

"Why do you say that?"

"You act like you would rather have your teeth pulled."

I snickered, and he chuckled. I tightened my hold on him just to feel how his body vibrated.

"Am I that transparent?" I asked after my fit of giggles.

"Perhaps. I can understand why you may not enjoy these parties." His eyes were pointed at Mrs. Clark and Agatha as they stepped into the house, surveying the room, and Arthur spun my back to them. "I do apologize."

"You have no reason," I replied. "It is I who should apologize to you."

"I don't wish to hear it."

"What do you wish to hear?"

"Have you ever enjoyed these parties?"

"I used to."

"Not anymore?"

"Things have changed."

"Such as your parents' deaths?" he asked.

I grimaced.

"I'm sorry, Virginia. I didn't mean to—"

"You're correct," I said hastily. "Their deaths stunted me. It didn't help that I became such a recluse. For society, I mourned them far too long."

Arthur shook his head. "There is no one way to mourn those you love."

"Thank you." The words were a balm to my pain. "The parties where I used to dance were my favorite."

"I imagine your dance card was filled most often."

"At times."

"Do you think there shall be dancing tonight?" he asked, eyeing the door.

Guests trickled into the house, hosted by the Coxes and other wealthy families in Boston. Soft music played in the distance, probably a quartet, and the laughter was like a clap of thunder, only matched by the clank of glasses.

"One can hope," I said.

"Then I should fill your dance card early," he said.

"I will admit that I didn't take one." I rotated my empty wrist.

"Then I will get you one now."

He stepped away, but I locked my hand on his elbow. My grip startled me, an impossible strength. My arms still ached from the cleaning and movement over the past few days.

"Dear Virginia, I don't think you wish to dance," said Arthur in mock conspiracy.

"I wish to dance tonight," I said, "but only with you."

He raised his eyebrows. "What if another man asks?"

Since Ethel, I had been on the outskirts of the elite as well as the dance floor. Besides Arthur, no man had stepped toward me or even met my gaze. Arthur was braver than them all.

"Then I shall say no," I said to Arthur, unblinking. "You are the only man I wish to dance with. Though, I should ask if you wish to dance with other women—"

"I do not," he cut me off. "Though, I feel I should admit that I am not much of a dancer."

"I do not believe it."

"I do not have the training."

"Then we shall not jig."

"I do enjoy a good barn dance."

I laughed. "Those are not the same things."

He saluted me with his half-full wine glass. "I look forward to many waltzes with you. As well as much time spent."

Warmth sliding across my skin like melted wax, I clamped my lips together to give a demure smile. My cheeks quaked from the pressure of hiding the full grin that wanted to erupt. I felt like a child again, in the time of innocence and love in fairy tales.

"What is it?" he asked, candlelight glinting in his eyes.

"I've missed you," I admitted. "I have been waiting to meet you again, and I'm scared to let you go. That is how much I've missed you."

I regretted the words as soon as I said them, no matter how true they were. With a huff, I turned away. Arthur caught my chin in his forefinger and thumb.

"I'm sorry," I gurgled. "It was foolish—"

"It wasn't," he whispered, his voice as smoky as the hearth. "I feel the same way, Virginia."

He leaned in, and I puckered my lips for a kiss, no matter how inappropriate. I wanted it! It was society that kept us apart. The damn rules. He kissed me on the cheek, lingering his face close to mine for a few pregnant seconds, his hot breath scorching. This winter dress was too thick, too confining. Too many layers parted us.

When he pulled back, Arthur's smile left my heart fluttering and my knees weak, a throbbing opening inside of me that was hungry for a taste of him. I hid the heat sliding up my body, ignited by only his smile. A craving wiggled from my lower belly. Someday, I would have his child growing there and would feel the movement—until then, it was primal desire.

"Shall we dance now?" he asked as the music swelled.

"It's a little early," I said.

"There is music."

"There is."

"Then it is the perfect time."

He led me from the sitting room into the ballroom filled with the pounding voices that hushed as we entered. The eyes burrowed into my body, wishing to see every part of me I didn't want to exposed. He didn't allow me to turn away. I was forced to look up at him, rolling back my shoulders and drawing up my head, fighting the crushing weight.

"Shall we dance now?" asked Arthur.

"No one else is dancing," I said, tilting my head to the floor. "The appointed dances haven't started."

"Then we should start them."

I giggled. "You're being ridiculous."

"I am?" he asked in mock surprise.

"Yes, and you know it."

"I do know it very much."

He touched his fingers to my chin, and more heat slid down my body. I bit my bottom lip, or I would nip at his thumb, taking his nail between my teeth and indenting his skin. Perhaps I would get a speck of blood.

"I wish for no one to make you feel unwanted, or as if you do not belong," continued Arthur in a soft voice. "You are meant for this life, Virginia. Far more than me."

"I wouldn't be here without you," I said.

He chuckled. "Don't blame this party on me."

I laughed, unable to hide the small wheeze escaping my mouth. He just made me feel so alive, safe, and sound.

"What is so humorous?" asked Agatha, having joined us in a blink of an eye.

Her perfect curls framed her long face, and her tight corset made her longer.

"It's Miss Jones, isn't it?" she asked, facing Arthur. "Yes, she is quite laughable. I often find myself and my friends—the connections to the well-bred, Mr. Hunt—turning away from her. My mother has mentioned her past—"

"Enough of this," interrupted Arthur.

I tried not to grimace at him or her.

Glancing over her shoulder at Mrs. Clark, Agatha nodded with new-found determination and then returned to Arthur and me. "Miss Jones hasn't been truthful with you, Mr. Hunt. If she was, then you would turn away from her. Miss Jones is a harlot—"

"Stop," hissed Arthur, placing his body between Agatha and me.

I wished he wouldn't. It would only hurt him more.

Others were looking toward us, sipping their wine like it could hide their faces. Arthur stepped up to Agatha, hovering over her like a beast instead of the kind man I knew.

I drew him back, hand latched on his elbow. "Don't."

"But, Virginia," he said.

"Please, *Virginia*, do let this continue," goaded Agatha, an evil glint in her blue eyes. "Everyone already knows it, so you might as well let him in on the secret too."

It was no secret, for Agatha and her friends had made it clear, spreading rumors that I was a *harlot* across society until the servants whispered it too. The gossip started when Ethel and I had stepped from the house together. How the men had jeered, and the women had said my parents would be ashamed. Not even Ethel could comfort me that night, though she tried and pleaded and broke down in tears, but I had screamed.

Arthur shook his head, the tremble moving through his limbs and jerking me back to reality. I exhaled, grateful to be distracted from the past rising in my vision, the shadows and the burning hearth and how Ethel had cried out, mixing with the disapproving faces.

This was all too much. I never should've come to the party. I never should've survived when my parents did not.

I tried to back away, but Arthur clamped his hand on mine.

"Miss Clark," said Arthur, "I do not know what is wrong with you, but I will not allow you to speak to Miss Jones that way. Nor will I let you speak to me at all. Good evening."

He swept me onto the dance floor, though it was hardly the time to dance. We fell into the waltz, ignoring that it wasn't the dance required of the song, but with eyes already on us, it hardly mattered the dance or timing. It didn't sedate the burn in my eyes or the way my cheeks flamed like I had been slapped.

"You shouldn't have done that," I said.

Arthur raised his chin. "I would do it again."

"Your reputation—"

"I barely have one."

"Don't you want it?"

"Not with these people if that is how they act." He snorted in disgust.

As much as I knew others watched, I forced myself to meet his gaze and push out the world that would knock me back into the rock-bottom reality. Instead, I flew in his arms with the waltz, soaring like a bird did over water, rushing toward the endless starry night.

Others joined the floor in their colorful dresses and suits, and we became one of many couples, slowly being swallowed with every pass of a dress. A flutter from my eye tore my gaze from Arthur.

"It has grown crowded," said Arthur, tugging on my hand. "Come, let us retire to somewhere private."

He did not ask for a chaperone, and at this point, I wouldn't either. I trusted none of these women.

We wove through the bodies, leaving everyone behind. We weren't just together but alone. The rumors of me being a harlot would only grow, but as Arthur took me into the frozen garden in the back of the house, I didn't care what they said or what would haunt me tomorrow.

Lifting his head, Arthur craned his neck like he was searching for something specific, so I tried to look too, spying only darkness.

Voices tumbled from the house, mingled with the playing orchestra, and light filtered from the windows. Silver moonlight shimmied across the brown grass, speckled with frost, that crunched under my boot.

"You're not too cold, are you?" he asked in a rush of white breath. "We should've retrieved your cloak."

"I'm quite all right," I said. "I'm a Bostonian. I can handle the chill."

"I apologize nonetheless."

"It's not necessary. I'm warm from dancing."

He chuckled. "I as well. It clouded my thoughts."

"Does the coolness make your head clearer?"

"Yes, but I will say that I've had a clear mind, except when dancing with you, I was…" He grimaced. "I'm making a mess of this."

I drew my eyebrows together, confused, because we had been having such a lovely time, aside from Agatha's and her wretched mother's interference. Arthur had been my shield against any blow.

"I don't think so," I said.

"I am," he reiterated. "I have always preferred science, having never been good at words."

"I think you do well at speaking."

"You appease me."

How close he stood to me…each of his warm, haggard breaths sizzled on my face. I blinked to see Arthur clearly, but he appeared like a stone statue with his mouth set in a thin line. He was thinking hard.

Not liking that look, I tried to brace myself. I thought we had an enjoyable time dancing but could've been wrong if my past finally didn't reach his standards. He would brush me aside. It was honorable that he was at least telling me, even if I would be left in a pool of tears.

"I had a lovely time dancing with you tonight," Arthur said, "and I wish I could dance my night away with you. As well as my life."

I felt the break of his sentences in my bones. It weighed me to the ground. I couldn't flee even if I wished to.

"There is something I must do," he said breathlessly. "Something I have been considering since the night I first spoke with you. I didn't want you to think me rash, and perhaps I am yet. I cannot wait any longer."

A fracture ran the length of my pounding heart, the ventricles coming undone from the other organs like tentacles releasing from a ship.

I only saw darkness. It hurtled toward me. I blinked feverishly.

Arthur lowered himself to one knee, ensuring that I stood over him, and still clasping my hands, he asked, "Will you marry me, Virginia?"

I sucked in a deep breath because I was sure my body had faltered, playing tricks on my mind.

Arthur was waiting, so I nodded, unable to find my voice.

Pushing to his feet, he pulled me into his arms, swinging me like I was a small child. I squealed, having forgotten what it was like to fly. My father had been the only one to ever do this to me.

"You are making me the happiest man in the world, Virginia!" he spoke into my ear.

"I am already happy," I said, pressing my cheek to the warm skin of his neck.

A little further and I could've kissed his vein.

"I will make you happier," he said.

I murmured, "I don't know how that's possible."

"I promise I will."

"I believe you."

He set me on the ground, and I found my feet, my knees quaking, the same buzz sliding up my bones. Without a second of thought—and ignoring how inappropriate it was—I kissed him on the lips.

He startled, and I winced at my own mistake. Then he returned the kiss, wrapping his hand around the nape of my neck. My body brushed against his.

Pulling back from the kiss, I said, "Apologies. I was so swept up."

He released his hold on me as red bloomed on his already pink-tinged cheeks. "It is I who should apologize."

"Please do not."

"Only if you do not."

I tasted Arthur on my lips. "I shall try."

"I want you to know that I would've asked your father or another family member but seeing that..." He winced.

I understood, glancing away before emotions overtook me.

Arthur continued, "I didn't want you to think that I would do this improperly, and you are very independent, Virginia, so it is I who should've asked you directly."

"I'm very excited to marry you," I said. "I'm in love with you."

I stood taller with him now that I could breathe. I would be getting married to a man I loved, re-entering Boston's finest. Someday, I could leave behind those rumors and grow from my past.

"I don't want a large wedding. Only you. I want to marry you as soon as possible," I said, not mincing my words.

I was clinging to Arthur as the sun that he was, willing to give me life as much as burn me.

"Come," he said. "We will let everyone know."

He pulled me inside the house before I could tell him no, but why would I want to keep this quiet? Why shouldn't I scream it from the roof to let Boston know our joyous news? Thus, I galloped with him into the ballroom, where women swirled in their floor-length gowns, whipping each other like horses. I didn't stop him as Arthur rushed to the raised platform where the small orchestra played.

When the song abruptly ended, Arthur clanked a full wine glass with a silver knife to gather everyone's attention and quickly announced, "Miss Virginia Jones has agreed to become my wife!"

There was only a smattering of awkward applause. Someone coughed.

My smile died like a candle near the end of the wick, same with the happiness; it was worse than when others glared at me. Now, I was overlooked and ignored, much like Ethel had been throughout her life. Agatha and her ferocious mother shared an all-knowing gaze, as if they were God themselves!

"We could not be more excited," said Arthur, though his voice wavered and his shoulders slumped. "I am proud that Miss Jones is allowing me into her family. And to continue my research."

Taking my hand, he kissed my knuckles, letting everyone see how he touched me so openly. I wished he would kiss me on the lips, show how he would take my body as his own.

"What wonderful news," said Mrs. Cox, hobbling from the back of the crowd. "Congratulations!"

Then she started to clap, leading others to do the same. They mirrored Mrs. Cox's smile. Warmth illuminated her eyes, and her bottom lip wobbled when pulled so tight.

"Pull out the champagne and pour glasses," ordered Mrs. Cox, "and the music must start up again. We are here to celebrate."

Giggles bubbled from my lips, shaking my body. The orchestra played a joyous jig. Before I could step away, Mrs. Cox lumbered toward us, the smile revealing her browning teeth.

"Congratulations to you," said Mrs. Cox.

"Thank you," I said, wishing to throw my arms around the older woman for her kindness.

I was not a young girl and she not my granny, but with her blessing, the others would have to accept us.

"Thank you," said Arthur with a small bow of his head.

Mrs. Cox only nodded like she was a queen and had bestowed this gift on us, and then she turned to me, her smile tightening. "I never thought I would see the day, Virginia. Your parents would be proud of you."

A lump formed in my throat, and I tried to talk over it. "They love Arthur."

"Yes, they would've loved Mr. Hunt," agreed Mrs. Cox, but her gaze didn't waver from me. "You take good care of yourself and Mr. Hunt, Virginia. We'll surely be keeping an eye on you."

Then she reached in, gave me a quick peck on the cheek and stepped back.

"I shall move on," she said. "Others are lining up for their time. I dare say you two will be popular tonight. Finally, some weight off my shoulders."

She laughed as she walked off, and like she had said, others rushed forward to give their well wishes.

"Congratulations," said a woman, but I looked past her, raising to my tiptoes to see the elite's matriarch Mrs. Cox glide from the room. Someday, I could be like her.

Someone shoved a glass of champagne into my hand, bubbles fizzing on the surface. I didn't get a taste of the expensive wine as more people arrived, offering their congratulations and kisses on my already flaming cheeks. Warmth spread across my body, and I wished to be in the garden again with Arthur, alone with ourselves and the night chill.

"Congratulations," said another voice as the orchestra played. There wouldn't be additional waltzes tonight, only lively dances to celebrate love.

"Thank you, Agatha," I said and then turned to Mrs. Clark at her daughter's side.

"Yes, congratulations," added Mrs. Clark as she leaned in.

Her hot breath sunk across my exposed throat like a cord wrapping around my neck.

"You'll ruin him," whispered Mrs. Clark. "You will destroy his life like you have destroyed your own."

I panted, losing air like I was in the harbor drowning, reaching for help but unable to get my arm from the water. I was slipping beneath the surface.

"I never liked your parents," continued Mrs. Clark in my ear. "With you and Agatha born at the same time, you two were bound to fight one another, but I never had to destroy you when you did it yourself. I knew you would do it when I met you as a child, your parents too."

I tried to rock away, but she clamped her hand on my elbow, holding me against her chest like a babe meant to suckle.

"That whore," Mrs. Clark hissed, and I knew immediately who she spoke of. "No matter who you marry, we know you. You will never be welcome in *our* society."

She put her sloppy lips to my cheek, giving me a small kiss, and then stepped back, fixing a cold smile to her face.

"Come, Agatha," she said. "We've taken enough of Mr. Hunt's time."

Mrs. Clark and Agatha stalked off, replaced by others in the extensive line. The voices were high like sopranos and bounced off the rafters. I forced a smile until my cheeks ached. I was swimming and then sinking, only returning to the surface when Arthur kissed my temple.

"People are too kind," said Arthur.

I nodded, missing my words. I tried to collect them, but we only had a flash of a moment before more people congratulated us.

Nine

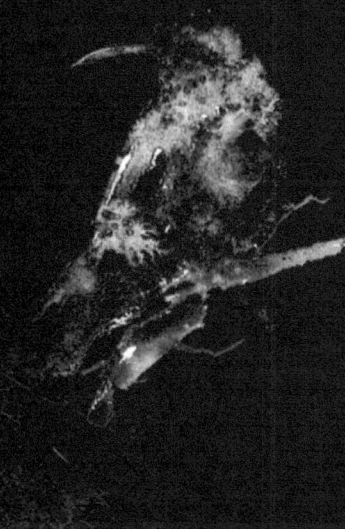

Arthur hopped out of the carriage at my house, offering his hand to me while calling to the driver, "Wait a moment please."

The horses neighed, shaking their heads and trembling the carriage. My body buzzed from being so near Arthur inside the carriage and perhaps the champagne. I didn't trust my own legs, much like my own mind. When I took his outstretched hand, I stumbled from the carriage.

Arthur caught me. "Are you all right? Should I send a physician to check on you?"

"I'm fine," I said.

Arthur drew his eyebrows together, a crease wrinkling his forehead. He hesitated, and I wished he didn't. We had a wonderful time tonight, or so I continued to tell myself, ignoring how Mrs. Clark had acted. Mrs. Cox had welcomed us.

"Please do not worry," I said, touching his arm. "I had too much liquor."

"Let me walk you to your door," he said.

I slid my arm into the crook of his elbow, and we strolled across the sidewalk and up the few stairs. The curtains fluttered, and I grimaced; Ethel had been watching. I would have to tell her that Arthur and I would be getting married, and she would need to leave. I had told her before, but she had no choice now. I couldn't have her here!

Arthur looked down at me, worry aging him, and I cupped his cheek. My fingers had to be like icicles, yet he leaned in, closing his eyes. I could imagine us in the future, him sleeping upon my chest and me brushing the hair from his face.

"I'm very happy you accepted my proposal," said Arthur in a rush of breath. "More than happy or excited. I am not a man of words. I do not know this one. You're too good to me."

"Never." I brushed my fingers across his cheekbone. "It is you who is too good to me."

He kissed my palm. "There is nothing too good for you. You deserve the world, and I will only be able to give you a sliver."

"You are my world," I told him. "You have become every part of me. You are my dreams, alive and awake, and I cannot wait to spend the rest of my life with you, devoting my body and soul to you. To wake up with you and fall asleep with you."

A grin covered his face, cheeks turning crimson. "Virginia, you take my breath away. It is a shame I cannot say these things to you, but I will practice."

"No need. You are perfect to me."

"One should always improve. I will do my best to only get better for you," he promised.

My heart skipped a beat.

The driver snapped the reins, and the horses stomped.

Arthur glanced at the cab driver. "I should go. Are you sure you are all right?"

"Yes," I said. "I am quite fine."

"Then I bid you good night."

He kissed my knuckles and then went down the steps. I placed my back to the door, hoping he would ignore how the curtains moved again, waving like a ghostly hand.

Ethel was still watching, her eyes burning the back of my head, the evil eye tracking Arthur as if he were prey. As he stepped into the carriage, I didn't leave the front stoop, though Ethel murmured inside, hums slipping under the door like a siren call. When he was gone, I opened and then slammed the door shut behind me. Her singing stopped.

I couldn't face her when I was floating in the clouds with love, my chest rising toward the sky like a hot air balloon soaring toward the stars. I brushed past the front sitting room, where the curtains continued to dance as if she were looking at the departing carriage, and headed upstairs, pulling off the heavy clothes sticking to my sweaty skin.

Sitting at my vanity, I brushed out my hair. I refused to look at her lingering in the doorway, though my body ignored what my mind wanted: her dressed in a white nightgown. I remembered how heavy and rough the old nightgown was, unlike the comforts I wore to sleep, and when I had tried to offer her one of mine, she chose the one that she always had. The days—and nights, truly—of offering what was mine to her were long past.

Ethel waited behind me. For all her eavesdropping, she already knew what I didn't tell her now. How long had she watched Arthur and me on the stoop? How long had she been at the front window, waiting for me to come home? What if the neighbors saw the woman in my house when I was trying to return my life to how it had once been, and how was I to explain that she wouldn't leave?

How much longer could I beg?

No, Ginny.

I shouldn't have hidden from my future but needed Ethel to leave the past behind us.

"I am getting married to Arthur," I said, looking at her reflection in the mirror. "He will be moving into the house. You cannot stay here any longer. I've tried to be kind, and I know how we ended things wasn't…"

The words caught in my throat, and I hunched over, about to be sick. Clamping my lips shut, I breathed deeply through my nose, but I could only smell blood.

When I could finally clear it away, I said, "I need you to leave, Ethel. You have to leave."

"I cannot, Ginny," hissed Ethel.

"Stop!" I threw the hairbrush on the vanity and stood, but I ducked my head to the side, unable to look at her without my heart breaking. "I don't want to hear it. You have a choice. You could go."

"I am bound to you."

"Arthur will be bound to me," I said. "Same as I will be bound to him."

"Not in the same way."

"Don't, Ethel."

"You won't even look at me, Ginny."

"It's what you want."

"Of course, it is! You cannot pretend I'm not here."

"Why not? You don't need to be here."

"You think I can just leave?" Ethel barked a laugh.

I winced like she had slapped me, not that she had ever raised her hand to me.

Ethel demanded, "Look at me!"

I couldn't—*wouldn't*. It might've broken me to face her when we had spent so much time together and I had loved her deeply.

She had been my reason to breathe, pulling me back from the brink of death. She had been my sun on a cloudy day. If I looked at her again, meeting her gaze and tracing her body... I couldn't trust myself.

Ethel screamed like a banshee, shaking the mirror and me as though I were a reed to be snapped in a half. I clung to the vanity, digging in my nails until I pulled away strips of wood.

"Stop!" I finally looked at her or where she had been in the doorway to my bedroom.

Even when I looked at her, she ran, playing this childish game.

I continued to the space she had once been, "You need to be quiet. Or the neighbors might hear! I don't need the watchmen called."

Ethel laughed, the sound hitting the walls and bouncing off the windows, but it was disembodied. Where had it come from?

"Ethel?" I asked, spinning around in my bedroom.

I swore she had just been here, so perhaps she had run into the hallway, giggling for me to chase her like I had before taking her in my arms and kissing her. After our games, I took her into my bedroom and laid her down, trailing kisses lower until she was coming on my mouth and I was drinking her juices.

Her laughter had been closer, not vibrating in the hallway, so she had to be in my room. Perhaps she had stashed herself in my wardrobe or hidden under my bed, much like I had done as a child playing hide and seek alone. Arthur and I would have many children, so none of them would ever have to play alone.

"Where have you gone, Ethel?" I asked, balling my hands into fists and trying to understand why she hid from me now. "I won't chase you."

"Come play, Ginny," called Ethel in a singsong voice.

"This is not a game," I snapped. "I am marrying Arthur, and you shall leave."

Ethel didn't answer.

The house was silent for the moment, and then she was humming like she used to do when working on one of her remedies. I recalled her shoulders hunched over a boiling pot, steam turning her hair unruly. Perhaps she had gone into my kitchen, where she often made her potions.

"Ethel!" I stomped from my bedroom. "Ethel, are you listening to me?"

Her humming increased, strengthening into a song that sounded more like a wail than a musical note, but she had always said she wasn't a good singer. I hadn't believed her until I first heard her sing. With a voice like hers, people would think she was being murdered.

I marched down the steps, bypassing the kitchen toward the sitting room, where she would curl into a ball and read one of my father's old books after blowing off the dust and cracking the yellowing pages. Instead of lounging in a chair by the lit hearth like she so often did, she knelt on the floor.

I stepped into the doorway. "You told me to look at you and you told me to come downstairs, and now you won't even look at me. What is this, Ethel? Look at me!"

Slowly, she rose to her feet, her body tilting sideways as though she were about to fall. Her head slanted forward. Her hair had darkened, tinted maroon.

I had the queerest feeling that I was dreaming, lost in a nightmare, because now I understood why Ethel's hair color had changed: it was blood. The crimson ink was splattered across her white nightgown, spilling from her skull much like brains did.

"What—?" I gasped.

Finding reality before me—a Hell I would never escape—and gasping, I stumbled back and gripped the doorframe. I needed to be prepared to run, but instead, I grabbed my stomach—my nightgown unmarred, my skin taut—and heaved up tonight's supper and champagne.

Ten

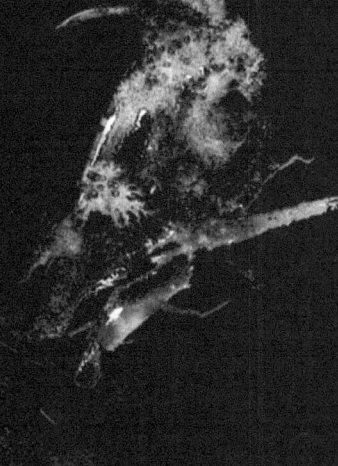

November 30, 1842

Ethel hadn't written back to me, no matter how many letters I sent. My hand had cramped by how I sliced the words into the page like I'd been breaking into skin and using my blood as ink. Through my silent tears, I swore words appeared that I hadn't written—as if Ethel were writing on the same piece of paper as me—but when I blinked, the words were gone. I looked over my shoulder like she would appear.

I couldn't stay in this house, tossing in bed and howling at the moon. Without having meant to—or so I assumed—Ethel had cracked open my chest and taken my heart. How was it that I lived while my parents, in the prime of health, had fallen ill and died?

After another day—though I couldn't say how many had passed— and no response from Ethel, I decided to go to her. With the old cloak around my shoulders, I tried to leave the house, but my feet were like iron. I was burned by the brass doorknob.

Go, Ginny.

I whipped open the door.

My heart tugged me forward like I was a dog on a leash. I crossed Boston, the sun beating down on me like a hammer, and headed straight to the apothecarist shop where I first met Ethel. Prying eyes bored into me, but I pressed onward, trying not to run into carriages and walls. If I could just be smaller, maybe the nosey onlookers would turn their gazes elsewhere.

"Come here, girly!" called a whore on a streetcorner. "No reason to hide! Let's see your pretty face!"

"I'm sorry. I must go," I mumbled, spinning from her grasp.

"You got a penny for me, poppet," called out a beggar, shaking a tin can at me with something already rattling inside.

It could've been a tooth for all I knew, one of the many missing yellow teeth hanging from his white gums.

Voices were rising from the depths, brought from the ocean, unloaded with each ship. The apartments were brimming with the sailors or other people poking their heads from the open windows as if they could catch a whiff of air that wasn't fishy.

"She don't belong here!" called the whore, pointing her spindly finger toward me.

I dropped back a step.

"She must have something good!" said the beggar, hobbling closer.

He smelled rancid, like he had uprooted his clothes from graveyards.

"Excuse me," I said, holding my purse close against my chest like it was a shield.

I hadn't brought much since Ethel hadn't been interested in anything I offered except for payment for the medicine, but these people would pluck each coin from my dead body. They would hold it up to the light and pretend it was gold.

Running from them, I found the apothecary again and stumbled inside. "Ethel! Are you here? I need you."

I slammed the door shut, the bells jangling above, but Ethel wasn't here to greet me. Nor was the apothecarist.

Go, Ginny!

I forced myself out the door, only to be slapped by voices: the whores on the corners and children playing with a ball in the streets and chasing each other with sticks. So many eyes burrowed into me, peeling off my skin and laying it down for others to walk across.

"Out of the way!" yelled a man.

I barely had time to jump from the street as a carriage sped past me. The hooves clattered, and the horse neighed in an angry burst.

"Off the road, mad bitch!" called the man, whipping the reins.

The carriage shuddered the ground like cannon fire, and I scurried out of the way, running face first into the whore. She pushed her chest up toward me, her plump cream-colored breasts surging forward.

"Have a touch," she said, "for a pretty penny. Come on, girly, give me nipple a twist."

Putting my head down, I sprinted into a tight alleyway between two buildings. The windows were open, people yelling out and a baby screaming. The loudest pelted me, and I tripped over the ground—no, a foot hanging out from a lump of a man lying in the alleyway.

He startled as much as I did, jumping to his feet and hollering, "Who are you? What do you want?"

Swinging a broken glass bottle, he darted into the shadows, terror shining in his eyes like I was a ghost haunting these streets. Perhaps I was. Death had claimed me and now I haunted the unsuspecting.

My wobbly legs and tiredness after many sleepless nights weighed on me until I slid down the wall. Fat, hot tears sprung from my eyes, coating my cheeks like a heated summer rain, turning the ground to mud under my shoes. I was soon drenched, sucked into the muck. I would turn into one of the buildings, and someday, the people of Boston would inhabit me.

"Virginia?"

Raising my head, I tried to look through the tears hazing my vision. It took me too long to realize the person who spoke was Ethel. She was reaching for me but dropped her hand before I could take it. I needed to hold her—touch her. I cried harder at the missing touch.

"Virginia, what are you doing here?" demanded Ethel, a hard tenderness coursing through the words. "You shouldn't be here. What if someone sees you?"

"I had to come," I said through my sobs. "You weren't answering my letters."

"I'm not at your beck and call."

"I wasn't asking you to be."

"So you came here anyway. That's foolish."

"I don't care if someone sees me."

"Good, many have." She huffed. "You need to go home. Now."

"I won't." I grabbed her skirts, hooking my fingers in—she couldn't leave me. "Please, Ethel. You have given me peace like I've never known. What you have done for me—"

"It's the hashish," she hissed, turning her head away.

"It isn't."

"Don't be foolish," she snapped.

More tears welled in my eyes. "I'm not."

How could she think me a fool when I meant to bare my soul to her? How I was here to hand myself over to her if she would take me, including my body and money and home? Everything I had—and was—was hers.

For a long moment, Ethel looked down at me off the tip of her nose. I was caught in her gaze, ensnared—her creature to do with what she wished. Her mismatched eyes were flashes of fireworks, a kaleidoscope of colors that shone her emotions. I saw in her eyes and how she held herself that she couldn't walk away—I knew! She just had to give in. To give herself to me too.

"Go home, and I will come to you," said Ethel in a small voice.

I didn't release her skirt. "Do you mean it?"

"Yes. I have business to attend to, but once I have finished here, I will come to your home." She placed her hands on my forearms and lifted me from the ground, her strength unmatched. "Please go home, Virginia. I can't bear to see you this way."

Unable to find my words—as if I were swimming in depths too close to death—I nodded.

Twiddling my thumbs, I paced the length of the house, crisscrossing through the front entry room and the kitchen, the sitting rooms and the dining room, going as far as placing my foot on the first step of the grand staircase, listening to the groan of the wood, and then stepping back. I needed to be close to the door when Ethel arrived.

What if she doesn't come, Ginny?

Cold crept across my skin, leaving a wake of goose bumps. I curled my arms over my chest as if I could hold back the chill, but it grabbed at my bones, gnawing on my marrow and sucking me dry. I swayed sideways, barely catching myself on the wall. My knees trembled.

Stop, Ginny!

I shoved myself from the house. The unseasonable Boston warmth that had the stench of a dog's breath hit me. The sun had dipped behind buildings, the golden tendrils snaking through the alleyways and down the street to catch me in their embrace. Unlike before—when I had flinched away because of my pounding heart—I stepped into the sunlight like a madwoman. I let the whole street see me clearly, feasting upon the crumbs I had become.

"Miss Jones?"

I gasped, spinning around, supposing I had been caught doing something untoward by polite society. I didn't need Mrs. Cox's judging eyes, but alas, it was thankfully not her.

"Ethel," I greeted, marching toward her with my hands outstretched to take her into me, but she kept her hands to her stomach, fingers interwoven.

"Are you feeling better?" she asked in a distant, hardened tone.

"Now that you're here," I admitted on an exhale, the weight slipping off my body.

"Not before?"

I drew my eyebrows together. "Why do you ask?"

"You're outside."

"Would you prefer me inside?"

"I thought that's where you would be."

"Come inside," I said, walking toward the door.

"I don't think that would be a good idea," she replied, remaining outside the front gates.

How I wished to tear them from the ground.

People out for their evening strolls glanced toward us, and Mrs. White across the street had pulled back her front curtain, her pale face illuminated in the windowpane. She frowned.

Anger burned my face like I had been slapped. I tried to remain calm, holding my hands at my sides until I lost feeling in my fingers. It would've been easier to live my life if I had lost all emotions, leaving me pointed in the direction of the future instead of adrift in this life.

With my knees quaking, I marched toward Ethel. My stomach was in knots, pulled tighter when she said no. I could've begged—I was halfway to my knees already—and held on to her dress like I had done before, threatening to tear the flimsy fabric.

"Why not?" I asked, spitting the words through my building tears.

Ethel wouldn't meet my gaze, so busy staring at her boots. The ground wasn't so interesting!

"Please, just tell me," I begged. "I can't go on like this. Please."

She slowly raised her gaze to meet mine, tears pooling in the corners. I wanted to kiss them away. I couldn't have her in the same pain as me. I didn't mean to do this to her.

"I've been staying away," admitted Ethel.

I silently begged for her to say more because I didn't understand.

A small dog yipped, charging at us from his leashed state. Two people walked behind him, watching us openly.

Ethel lowered her voice. "Let's go inside to speak about this."

I motioned her into the house first, not trusting that I wouldn't turn my back and have her run. That would break me like a vase, the shards lying upon the ground for others to grind their boots down into dust, washed away in the next Boston storm.

Ethel walked into the house, and I closed the door behind us. We didn't make it three steps inside before she spun to me. Her speed ruffled my hair.

"The way I like you... It is more than one should in our lives," she said, voice wavering. "It is romantic. I have always felt a pull toward women that I had never have toward a man. You are not the first woman I have been attracted to. You are the first in the ruling class, which is why I've stayed away. You have the ability to destroy me—"

"I won't," I promised.

"I have loved women openly before," said Ethel like she didn't hear me. "I haven't needed to hide from anyone...unless you count the judges or holy men. This is my warning to you, Miss Jones, to stay away from me, and I shall stay away from you."

She tried to walk around me, but I stepped between her and the door, locking her in my house.

"No! You cannot leave," I said.

Tears ran down her pinking cheeks, her eyes swollen. "Please, Virginia, move."

"Not until you listen to me," I begged. "I feel the same way about you, Ethel."

"Perhaps you shouldn't."

"Because we are women? Because you are supposedly less than me?"

"Because it will ruin you."

"I am already ruined, and that had nothing to do with you. You are the one healing me."

"Then you do not have romantic notions for me." She blinked her tears away as she found her superiority over me again. "Rather, you are confused by me being your physician."

"Don't tell me how to feel," I scolded.

"Tell me, Virginia. Have you ever felt this way toward another woman?"

My mouth dangled open as my mind knew the truth. "I've never given it much thought."

She raised her chin like a victor did. "Then you have not."

"That is not what I said."

"But you've never loved another woman?"

"I've never had the opportunity. I have not been allowed to love a man or woman or anyone else, but I've always known that my destiny in life was to marry a man and produce an heir."

"You cannot do that with me," said Ethel.

She tried to brush past me, and this time, I let her slip through my grasp like water. She took a piece of me with her stream. I would be with her forever.

"Please stay," I whispered.

"You only want me to stay because of the ghosts." Ethel tried to jest, but the words fell flat, lying between us, like she had ripped up the floorboards of the house to create the expansive space.

Spinning around, I grabbed Ethel's head between my hands, interweaving my fingers with her hair. I planted my lips to hers as if I could give her a seed and we could grow a flower between us and watch it bloom each spring. We would water it desperately in summer and fall so it would stay alive that much longer; I wouldn't let us die in winter, keeping the vine to my chest to feed off my blood.

In a moment of miracles, Ethel returned the kiss. She twisted her tongue with mine until we warred for space. Our lips touched, and then our bodies ground against one another. My limbs moved before I could control them, urging me to cup Ethel's face and then run my hands down her body until I knew every part of her.

The fabric of her dress held us back. My corset squeezed me so tightly I couldn't breathe, reflecting my desperation for another mouthful of Ethel. Every chunk I took from her, she took a larger piece.

I dragged her deeper into my house, showing her what was mine and what I could offer her.

Eleven

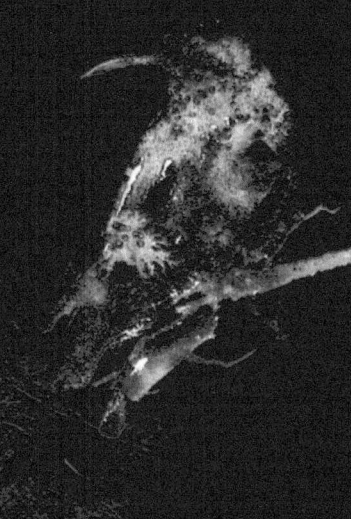

Arthur had truly become my knight in shining armor. I, his princess. With his arms looped around me, he carried me across the threshold of my—*our* house as a married couple only a day after we became engaged. There was no reason to wait when this love was meant to last.

Our wedding had been intimate—though others would've called it small and hidden—meant for our love, the priest, and a few guests, such as Mr. Hunt's colleagues, their wives, and Mrs. Cox. The whole time, her servants plucked at her like chickens with crumbs. So when we returned home alone with night creeping across the sky, I welcomed a quiet and clean house, bringing my husband into what we would create together.

"Put me down!" I tapped Arthur's chest. "You'll hurt yourself."

"You're as light as a feather," he replied before easing me to the floor.

"You are a liar," I said, though I felt like I was a cloud.

"Or high on the day." He kissed my lips, pulling me close, and I fell into him.

The layers of the wedding dress left me puffy and out of style, but it had been my mother's. I didn't have time for alterations, nonetheless I liked how close my parents had been. It was as if they had stood beside me on the dais, listening from the afterlife.

When Arthur pulled back from the kiss, I said, "We should see if your things were delivered from the university housing."

"Please, Virginia." He took my arm, sliding his thumb across my elbow. "Let's not worry about it now."

"We're going on our bridal tour tomorrow. We don't know how long we will be gone," I said. "We must worry about it now."

"Perhaps I'd rather be in the nude on our tour."

My cheeks warmed. "We cannot travel with you in the nude."

What would his family think of you, Ginny? A harlot turning their son into a whore.

With a cheeky grin, he acknowledged, "That is very true."

I strengthened my smile. "Let me see if your things are here."

"They aren't much."

"You know I have never cared for extravagances."

I only needed to peer into the small room off the way to see that indeed his few trunks had been delivered. His whole life was stored in those trunks, including what he had brought from his home; it showcased how he had lived in Boston until he met me. His small apartment didn't fit much, but he was not a man of materiality.

"Well?" he prompted, standing off to the side.

"I believe it's all here," I said. "Perhaps you should check."

"I shall believe you." He took me in his arms again and planted a kiss on my lips, tilting back my head to meet my gaze fully. "Today, you've made me the happiest man in the world."

"It shall be my goal to make you the happiest man in the world every day," I replied.

"I hope I can make you a happy woman."

"You already have."

"You must tell me when you are unhappy."

"I don't think that is possible."

"But you must, Virginia. Promise me you will say so."

"You are too kind. Other husbands would never care, but you are…"

The words escaped me, though I wasn't sure there was a word to explain how it made me feel or who he was.

"I will," I said finally.

In our bedroom that used to be filled with my parents' old things, Arthur poured me a glass of brandy, setting it on the vanity beside me. Wearing just his pants and shirt, he drank from his glass and perched at the edge of the bed, elbows on his knees. He looked at me in the reflection of the mirror. At least, it was his face and no other.

I had been scared to bring Arthur into the house with Ethel lingering, but she had made herself scarce tonight. I hoped she would continue to stir no trouble.

Brushing my hair, I dragged my gaze down his body. He had to be waiting as much as me. Ethel had been much different: we had been trapped in the lustful woes that swept us into each other's arms.

Arthur met my gaze in the mirror. Setting down the brush, I took a sip of the brandy, hating the burn, and faced him.

"We should consummate the marriage." I pushed off the vanity and sauntered toward him. "I wish to have you. All of you."

I sunk onto his lap but did not feel the prick of his cock.

"Do you wish the same?" I asked.

Arthur murmured, "I do."

He wrapped an arm around my waist, and I leaned onto him farther, liking how he began to ball my nightgown into his fists. His chilled fingertips grazed my skin, and I stifled a shudder. I wanted to bury my face into the crook of his neck, suck on his vein, and leave a mark upon his skin.

We were man and wife. I would ensure he knew how close we were meant to be.

I took a sip from his brandy glass and then handed it back to him, which he chugged too, blowing out a hot breath. It danced across my chest. I was illuminated, burning, encompassed, especially as he snaked his arm across my waist, tightening his grip on me. I listened to how our hearts matched in their hammering, filled with anticipation and lust.

"What do you wish this night to be?" I asked.

"It is your wedding night," he said, his voice wavering with nervousness.

Perhaps he had never touched a woman like this before. I would be the one to teach him.

He kissed me, though he kept his hands down by my waist and on my thigh, brushing his fingers across my skin but not daring to go further into my warmth.

When he gasped, sounding like a heaving fish on land, I pulled back to study him. Not just the chiseled features I had known since the moment I set eyes on him but the man with his quirks.

"How soon do you want children?" I asked. "You said you wanted many."

He gulped. "I do."

"I would like a child soon."

A relieved grin crossed his face. "I would like that as well."

I shifted on his thighs, burrowing my hips closer to his center and swinging my leg over his lap. He let out a breathless chuckle, his hands still limp, so I took them in my own, showing him how I liked to be touched, one on my hip without any fabric in the way and the other on the small of my back, pressing us closer. This was how I had been touched by Ethel.

I grimaced at the rushing memories. I couldn't shake them away, though it had been a different room and a different bed. We had claimed many rooms as our own, conquering them like queens. This was the one room we hadn't touched, but tonight this bedroom would be mine. And Arthur's, of course.

Feeling how he reacted to me, I rocked on my knees and then ground my body against him. His trousers were growing tight across the groin.

Arthur wanted me, though I hadn't had doubts after he cut off the priest by saying "I do."

I pressed my lips back to Arthur's and then parted his lips with my tongue. I dug my knees into the bed, holding him down, and dragged his hands closer. When his fingers began to move of their own accord, I allowed myself to travel over his body. His clothes kept me back, even when I slipped my fingers under his shirt, and he hissed. Too hard. I retracted my nails.

I pawed at him, wiggling under his shirt until he took it off, letting the fabric pool on the floor. Tomorrow, I would be a good wife and hang the clothes so they didn't wrinkle, but I was a new wife tonight. I would make love to my husband, letting him come inside of me and hope a seed would take root, blooming a child we would give all our hopes and dreams to. I could practically hear them running up the hallway now, and through the kisses, I glanced over my shoulder. It wasn't a child watching us... but Ethel.

"Virginia," whispered Arthur, slowing his kisses, "is something wrong?"

"No," I declared, ignoring Ethel.

I wouldn't let her take this from me. I deserved happiness!

As I kissed Arthur, pleasure mounted in my body. I grabbed for his trousers, undid the buttons, and let his cock burst free. The head was purple as a bead of cream blossomed on the tip.

I swallowed, not used to how the slit stared me in the eye. The cock seemed too large, heavy, and thick for my body. I, of course, knew how a woman became pregnant, but when holding a cock meant to be inside me, pleasure started slinking away. This wouldn't be like how it was with Ethel.

"Lay on the bed," said Arthur, tapping my thigh.

I didn't want to move my weight grounding him. When I didn't move, he took my lips back in his, pressing our bodies closer.

Then he repeated in a husky voice that melted my bones, "Lay on the bed."

I rolled off him, lying on my back with my legs dangling off the edge.

Arthur loomed over me. Unable to touch him and wishing he were upon me, I squirmed, my night dress rolling up. It caught on my hips, making Arthur halt from his war on clothes.

"You're beautiful," he purred, pink rising to his cheeks.

I giggled.

"You don't think so?"

"I don't think you've seen all of me," I said.

He licked his lips, dragging his gaze up my legs and then up to my covered breasts. The hearth warmed the cold night, and I was already sweltering in the thin, white nightgown. I didn't know how I would survive the night if I made love to Arthur as I did to Ethel, our bodies sparring yet working in tandem.

"Virginia, I do not want to pressure you," began Arthur.

"Say it," I begged, loving his kindness but hating how he crept toward what he wanted when I was laid out for him, ready to be eaten.

"Remove—" He cleared his throat, his jaw jutted. "Remove your nightgown. I want to see all of you."

I tore off the fabric and then caught myself on my elbows, my breasts looking plumper. My perked nipples pointed toward Arthur, and as he licked his lips again, I imagined how it would feel with his mouth on me.

"You too," I said, jerking my head toward the trousers hanging loosely on his hips.

Dark hair trailed down his lower belly. It was a shade darker than what was on his head.

Arthur kicked off his trousers and then walked toward the edge of the bed, pressing his knees into the mattress. He dragged his fingers up my leg.

"Arthur, please," I begged.

He gave a curt nod like he was about to start a business project and then placed his hands on my thighs and peeled them apart. I wondered if he knew how this would go because he was a man, whereas I was like a naive doe, wide-eyed with a cock. He slid his fingers down my folds. I let out a soft whimper, anticipation riling me. He didn't drive his fingers inside, only taking a hold of his cock and then pressing the tip to my entrance. He eased inside of me.

A whine built in my throat, tears collecting in my eyes. This was more than I thought it would be. I wasn't sure how much I could take. Or stretch. It burned!

"Breathe, Virginia," said Arthur with his knees pushed into the bed and his cock halfway into me, his hands on my thighs to keep me open.

I sucked air through my nose, scared another whimper would escape, but I couldn't hide the pain and certainly not the tears that twisted my face.

"Virginia, it hurts too much." He placed his hand on my waist as if he meant to pull out.

I grabbed his hand, lacing my fingers with his own, and pulled him close to me. I wanted him closer—not just inside of me but enveloping me until our skin melted together and molded us into a new being.

"Please," I said, my hips aching from the strain. "I need you."

He drew his eyebrows together, questioning, but then slid himself into me carefully.

The pressure was overwhelming. I breathed like I was birthing a child instead of taking a cock. I wanted the pleasure that was supposed to come with this, but perhaps those were lies I had heard from the servants. Or maybe I had misunderstood the whisperings of married women. I wasn't sure how any woman could like this.

Arthur slid his free hand from my hip and up my pulsating belly. Each of my breaths pulled my skin taut, but his hand crept higher. I stilled. He crawled his fingers between my breasts and flicked his thumb across my nipple. It was only a small wave of pleasure.

He took the pain away by cupping my breast, and I let out a soft moan. He drew his thumb around my areola, beckoning me to jump into pleasure. I could not name my hesitation, though my want was reaching toward him and clenching his cock.

"I like it," I said. "I want more."

He moved his hips, and I rocked to meet his thrust, our bodies colliding in a slap of skin. He moved me, the groaning bed, and seemingly the whole room that twisted around me with an increased force that left me breathless. I yearned for air as much as I craved him.

Around Arthur's lithe body, I spotted Ethel's reflection in the mirror. She drew nearer, and I wrenched my face away, pinching my eyes shut. Unfortunately, she was in my mind too, haunting my dreams and waking hours.

"Virginia?" asked Arthur, slowing his pace. "Did I hurt you?"

His voice was loving, but his fingers left my breasts. I slapped my hand on top of his, holding it close to my tender flesh.

"Don't stop," I begged.

His eyebrows were drawn, but he quickened his pace. When he thrust inside of me, he released soft grunts that boarded mutterings. I couldn't admire him when Ethel was caught in the reflections of the windows, her eyes narrowed exactly on where Arthur and I were joined.

"What is it, Virginia?" asked Arthur.

Ethel pinched her lips into a snarl, and I silently begged her to leave, because she didn't need to see how I loved Arthur. I blinked, and Ethel dissipated into the nothingness.

Arthur pulled out of me, and I reached for him but missed, falling. My body was weakened from pleasure, though my mind hadn't been terribly involved. I wanted him back inside me.

"Please, Arthur," I whined.

Tears built in my eyes for how foolish I'd been and how I ruined our wedding night with such distractions.

Without the pleasure, the pain grew. My nether lips ached. I was sure I was bleeding but was scared to look. The damage had already been done, but what else could his cock do to me?

"When we wed, I took the vows very seriously, Virginia." He came to the edge of the bed, not touching me. "In sickness and in health—"

"I'm not ill," I said.

He sunk beside me on the bed. "I only mean that you are my everything, Virginia. I will do all that I can to help you. Sickness and in health, for richer and for poorer—no matter what. I do not want to see that look of terror on your face again. Perhaps you should rest. We'll be traveling tomorrow, so it will be a long day."

"No!" I gripped his hand, nearly digging my nails into his flesh if it meant he would stay. "Please, Arthur, I need you. With me. Beside me. Inside me."

He dragged his knuckles down my cheek, brushing his thumb over my lips. "Are you sure?"

I kissed his thumb. "Yes. Please."

I pulled open my thighs. The chill slipped between my slick folds. He stared deeply into my garden for seconds that seemed way too long, quickened by my thundering heartbeat. I felt caught in the middle of the storm until he guided his cock back inside.

I couldn't lose him, so I would need to focus on him. Every part of me loved him and cared for him. He was putting in the effort with me. I would do the same for him.

Thus, I met his thrusts halfway, and he raised his eyebrows, impressed or confused. Both of us needed to work together. I placed his hand back on my breast and then my hand between my thighs above where he entered me, rubbing my peeping nub. I moaned, pleasure building in my veins and across my bones. His eyes grew large. He studied our connected bodies like he meant to fathom how a woman might enjoy the act.

Arthur quickened his pace, red blotching his features and his breathing ragged like he had run hard and fast. With my hand circling my nub, joined with his efforts, I tipped over the edge into oblivion.

Black dots exploded before my eyes, whipping me into the convergence of pleasure and wonderment, only to pull me back to reality as Arthur howled. His seed spurted into me, crawling up my insides until it bloated my stomach as if I were already pregnant.

When we both came out of our haze, I patted the bed beside me. "Lay with me."

Arthur crawled into bed and then placed my head against his chest. With the heat compounding between us, my breathing evened out, and I found my eyelids drooping toward slumber. I glanced at Arthur like he would do the same.

"I love you," I murmured, not wanting to break the steady silence between us.

He kissed my forehead. "Will we sleep now?"

"As opposed to...?" I asked, giving him a smirk that I knew was devilish.

He chuckled, pink flushing his cheeks.

Warmth spread across my chest. Even though he made love to me, he still blushed when I spoke in such a straightforward manner.

"Yes, sleep is the best option," I agreed, laying my head on his chest again.

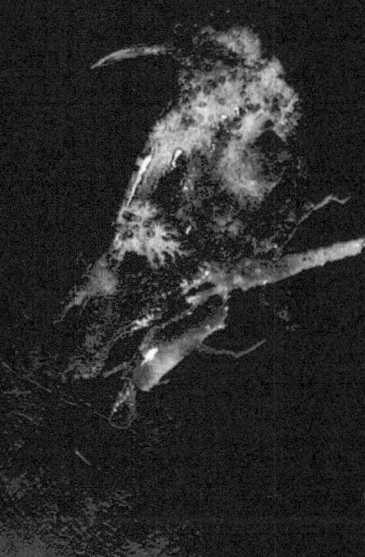

Twelve

When Arthur said he planned our bridal tour, I hadn't batted an eye. Our bridal tour wasn't extravagant—no month-long trip to Europe or the countryside. Instead, we were visiting his family in a nowhere village in our home state of Massachusetts. I clung to Arthur's arm as he brought us through the train station.

Aboard the shuddering metal beast, I stared out the window from our personal cabin—a splurge on his part to give us time alone—and watched Boston fall into the distance, the sea rising on the horizon. I pressed my nose to the window like an excited child.

"Remind me where your home is?" I questioned, trying to keep my voice light.

He'd never told me the name of the town. Perhaps I should've pushed harder, but at the time, any pushing would've turned him from me. I locked my hand on his thigh, anchoring myself to him.

Arthur looked up from the newspaper, quirking a smile. "I told you it's nowhere interesting. We'll take the train and then a cab. I don't miss the journey."

A lump strangled my breathing. "We're heading north."

He glanced out the window like he was checking. "We are."

"Are we staying close to the coast?" My voice squeaked.

I cleared my throat, eyeing the divide of trees and knowing the road ahead.

Salem.

Ethel had many stories to tell about Salem and her childhood and the witch trials that no one spoke about, a dark cloud hanging over humanity. She knew which roads to take to get to Boston, and she used to tell me that she would spend the whole ride staring at the trees, never bothering with putting her head in a newspaper or a womanly craft like embroidery.

"We'll pass through it," he said in a simple—albeit bored—tone. "We'll stay there for the night. They have such a booming port. It rivals Boston. Something about deeper water."

He barely glanced over the top of his newspaper that reported runaway slaves and arriving immigrants.

Tension curled around my neck. As if Ethel had her hands on my skin, sucking my air into her lungs. I wheezed. The sound echoed in the roomette.

Arthur dropped his newspaper finally. "Are you all right, Virginia?"

"Yes." I forced a smile. "I just wasn't aware we would be in Salem for the night."

Though the light didn't reach his eyes, he chuckled. "Don't tell me you believe in the old ghost stories of Salem, the witches and such."

"No, of course not," I said, spitting the words out because they were true. "Thank you for planning this and taking me to see your family. It is wonderful. So thoughtful. Very kind."

He returned to his newspaper. "I only wish to give you the best, Virginia."

I pulled myself away from the window to lean against him in the carriage, letting him read the newspaper and ignoring the large black headlines. I protected the crystalized bubble around Arthur and me, one filled with love and swelling with potential. We would have more privacy if we pulled the curtains over the roomette door, but Arthur said he wanted the light to read and for when food was brought. I indulged him and rested my head on his shoulder.

We arrived in Salem at dusk. The Salem smell wasn't better, though the fishiness of Boston had been replaced with historical grime. The sea clogged the space between cobblestones, turning them slick. The waves roared in the distance, bringing in the chill that left our breath white.

"Blasted," muttered Arthur under his breath after standing outside the train station for a moment.

People hustled away while others stood in line for horse-pulled carriages, and Arthur stepped off the curb, looking up and down the street to no avail.

"We'll never get a cab this way," he commented. "Not with all these people. We'll have to walk."

It was better than standing here. I glanced over my shoulder, waiting for Ethel to appear. We needed to move before she found us.

Sliding my arm into the crook of Arthur's elbow, I said, "It's a lovely night for a walk. Not too cold for winter."

Arthur blinked at me as though I were speaking a foreign language. Had I spoken out of turn or not understood what he was thinking? Men could be very confusing creatures, and I wasn't well-versed in interacting with them.

"You are marvelous," said Arthur.

A blazing smile overtook his features, and I was warmed as if sitting by a lit hearth.

"Don't give me that look," he said. "You have found a way to be positive about this."

I squeezed his hand, his fingers as chilled as mine. "I am happy to be with you."

Tears collected in Arthur's eyes, and though he tried to turn his head away, I saw them illuminated by the lit lamps. I wouldn't let anyone ruin our time together. Silently, I promised Arthur and myself I would make the best of the short stay in Salem, which included eating at a restaurant and then walking toward our inn.

After we dined and by the time we reached the room he'd let for the evening, I regretted the suggestion to walk. My shoes pinched my ankles, and my toes felt ready to fall off, the hem of my dress heavy with snow and muck. I practically fell into the lit hearth in our room to warm myself.

Brushing my hair in front of the small mirror, I glanced at Arthur over my shoulder. Shoulders slumped, he sat on the edge of the bed, gazing at me under his gorgeous long eyelashes.

I put down the brush and then faced him. "What is it?"

"You're stunning," he murmured dreamily.

My cheeks warmed. "You're tired. It's been a long day."

In one fluid movement, he crossed the room, standing over me, and slid his hand under my chin. I was falling inside the vastness of him, his eyes brilliant like stars. He ran his thumb across my lip, leaving fire on my skin, illuminating me from the outside, and eating toward my soul. Damn the hearth when he heated me so.

"You are, Virginia," he said. "You're beautiful. Marvelous. Wonderful."

"You're too kind," I said.

"You just do not see yourself clearly." He placed his hands on my shoulders and pointed me toward the small mirror, smudges on the sides and a crack in the corner. "Please look at yourself, Virginia."

I wasn't sure I wanted to, so used to Ethel hovering over my shoulder, but I raised my head like Arthur asked me to. Unfortunately. My hair was stringy, the color faded, sticking to the sides of my face. Sullen cheeks aged me ten years, my bones poking from the grayish skin. It must've been him who needed to see clearly when a haggard monster glared at me, my lips drooping in a curved frown.

Bending beside me, Arthur pressed his cheek to mine. "You are lovely, Virginia."

I giggled, looking at him because it was easier than looking at myself: his youthful glow, the light glinting in his endless gaze, a smile so natural that it ached.

"You see it too, then?" he asked.

I saw him and answered his question with a kiss.

Wrapping my arms around his neck, I pulled him close, our chests rubbing against one another through our thin cotton clothes that now felt like sand.

"Arthur," I pled through the kisses, "have me."

He pulled me from the vanity chair with more strength than I thought possible for him and then laid me on the bed. He kissed me deeply, contorting his body to continue the touch, and I clung to him, expelling the last part of my strength. He pulled off my nightgown and pushed my thighs apart.

"I want you inside of me," I moaned.

Pleasure seeped across my skin. It started in my throbbing nether lips and worked down my limbs. I would offer myself to a pyre if it meant that Arthur would come inside me, swelling me with his child and finally giving purpose to my spinning life. Arthur had already given me love, and I couldn't imagine what he would do if we had a child, injecting his love into them as well, sharing it between us.

He removed his trousers. His freed cock reached toward the ceiling, but I didn't shy away from it as I had done the previous night. He lined up to my entrance and then eased himself in, holding down my squirming hips.

"Does it hurt?" he asked in a panic. "Do you want me to stop?"

"No," I practically screamed.

My body opened for him like a blooming flower, and his stinger found my center. I locked my legs around his hips, pulling him deeper into me. I didn't think he could potentially get any deeper. His hands fell to either side of my head, bracing his face above mine.

"You are beautiful at every angle." He built my pleasure brick by brick. "You are wonderful, Virginia."

His words could melt my frozen heart, but Arthur already had. From the moment I met him, he had been thawing me. At one time, all I wanted was a husband for protection and an heir; Arthur had offered me more than I thought possible. I was the luckiest woman alive.

He ground himself into me, and I stretched to take him all in. I slipped a hand down and rubbed my nub, the pleasure increasing. With his tongue between his teeth, he glanced down like he wanted to touch my nub too, but his hands were braced on either side of me. He hung over me, jerking with every pound.

His hot breath licked my face, burning my already buzzing lips, bringing tears to my eyes. The heat enlarged as he moved faster, harder against my body, deeper in me.

On the edge of ecstasy, I looked away, wanting to stare at him but my body aching. I should've looked at him longer—never taken my eyes off him—because I wouldn't have seen the crystalline blue eye with the blown black pupil and narrowed white glaring at me.

Ethel had finally arrived.

"Arthur!" I slammed my hands into his chest.

He drew back. "What is it? Did I hurt you?"

"Look!" I pointed at the window.

He whipped his head around.

It was when I blinked and he looked that she was gone, melting into the Salem night.

"I don't see anything," he mumbled.

"We were being watched!"

"Watched?" He slid out of me and stalked straight to stand in front of the barely parted curtains. "I don't see anyone—"

"I know what I saw," I interrupted.

He tried to look down only to fog up the glass. "I don't know how anyone would be able to see in. We're on the second floor."

She had been there, watching Arthur fuck me!

"They couldn't scale the building," he continued, rubbing his jaw.

He worked through the situation like a scientist as I curled my knees to my chest.

"There is nothing to climb." He twisted his head up. "No ivy or vines. The inn is mostly brick. Possibly setting in the grooves and then using rope. Though, I don't see where they would hang the rope, nor do I see any rope. Could they have started on the roof and rappelled down?"

He grabbed the bottom of the window and started to pry it open.

Only a crack would've let in the cold air and…the evil eye. Not Ethel but her evil. It would've been upon me like spiders, crawling across my skin and flooding my mouth, nose, and ears, climbing into my cunt and laying its eggs in my womb.

"Arthur, don't!" I ordered.

He jumped. The windowpanes rattled in the sill, cracks threatening to spiral up.

"Fuck!" He pulled his hands to his chest before looking down at the precious digits.

I hadn't meant for him to get hurt. I only wanted to protect him, save him before he let in evil. It would devour us just as Ethel had said it would. Evil was in my body, and someday, it would come to claim my soul—

No, Ginny, she didn't say that.

That was too much witchcraft; Ethel wasn't a witch.

"She is," I snapped. I knew what I saw!

"What, Virginia?" asked Arthur, eyeing me from across the inn room.

It was practically barren, only made up of a bed, a wardrobe, and vanity.

"I know what I saw," I said through my tears, each ragged breath salty and leaving me drowning, my lungs yearning for air.

He should open the window to let in the air and let my past consume me. It would save both Arthur and me the trouble. Ethel too.

Why wouldn't she leave us alone?

Why couldn't she let me be happy?

This was supposed to be our time, filled with love that would leave us floating in the life we were about to create.

After closing the curtains, cutting off the moonlight, Arthur padded to the edge of the bed, reaching toward me. I drew back.

"I know what I saw," I repeated.

"Virginia." He touched my knee, and I flinched. "Virginia, I believe you. There had to be a vagrant out there."

He was humoring me—I knew it. How would he react if he knew about the evil eye? About Ethel?

No, it hadn't been her. She hadn't followed me. It was a vagrant, like he said. Just some criminal. Ethel wasn't a witch, and she couldn't scale a building.

I pushed, "You just said—"

"I didn't see anyone, but it doesn't mean someone wasn't there. Oh, Virginia—" his voice cracked— "I hate seeing you like this. I'm sorry."

"You didn't do anything," I replied, trying to collect my tears.

"I was unable to protect you." He crawled beside me, his nude body rubbing against mine.

His cock was still elongated.

I was his wife. I needed to make him feel good; I needed to bear his children. It was the duty of a wife. Therefore, I gripped his cock and started to rub like I had seen whores do in the streets. He placed his hand on top of mine. Would he show me what he liked?

"Don't, Virginia," he said. "You don't have to."

I began, "But it will—"

"I only wish to hold you now, to provide you comfort when you need it the most. I only wish to provide for you—to give you everything you need, Virginia. At least what your money cannot. Today has been long, tonight no better. We will rest."

So he tucked us into bed, wrapping his arm around my shoulders and bringing my head to his chest, his breathing steady and his heartbeat steadier. He laid a blanket over us.

While he dozed, I couldn't sleep. I stared at the window, where the evil eye had been, now sure that Arthur was right. How foolish I had been to think it was only eyes. Or that it was Ethel. Of course, it wasn't her.

The fear didn't leave me. I no longer shook, warmed by Arthur and the hearth enough to sweat through the blankets.

Tiredness weighed my lids, but before closing them, I saw another glimpse. The gaze in the window tapped on the glass to be let in. My eyes flew open. The vagrant could've come back—we weren't safe!

I sat up.

Stirring, Arthur blinked his bleary eyes. "Is it morning?"

"No," I said, wincing at how I had woken him; one of us should sleep.

"It's still dark." His words slurred like molasses. "Have you slept?"

"I can't."

He bolted upright. "Has the man returned? Has someone else looked through the windows?"

"No."

The curtains were still shut, occasionally waving like there was a draft. Someone might've peeked inside. They would see us still naked, touching. I curled my knees to my chest.

He brushed his knuckles across my arm. "Then you are just scared."

I snapped, "Don't say it like I'm simple."

"I'm not implying that, Virginia." He tightened his grip on me. "I understand why you're scared, and it is unfortunate that we have nowhere else to go. I don't like this place."

I peeked at him from the corner of my eye. "What do you mean?"

"Something about this inn…." He downturned his lips. "Something about Salem just doesn't feel right. I don't like it here, and it makes me want to go home. Back to Boston. We can't see my family in such a state. We shouldn't even travel in such a state."

Tears started to build in my eyes again, the love we were supposed to have tearing apart. "You don't wish to continue our time together?"

"Oh, Virginia." He laid his forehead against mine, his skin cool. "I don't wish to continue here. We need to plan something better for us. Away from the harsh world. I have failed."

"You haven't," I swore.

"We should go back to Boston tomorrow, yes? Will that make you feel better?"

I wanted to travel on to see his family and where he grew up, learn a piece of him that I didn't know, but then I glanced at the covered window. Memories swirled. I would never be able to love Arthur properly here, and he was correct: I wasn't in a state to meet his family, unable to showcase my real self. I would only bring shame upon him, and how terrible I would seem as a wife.

"But your family," I pushed, cringing when I said it.

The emotion was false.

"My mother will understand," he said. "Though, she is very excited to meet you. Or I know she will be once she replies to my letters. This will also give my brothers a chance to make themselves presentable. They need time—years if possible."

He pulled me back into a lying position. His coolness was almost like a phantom across my body. After wrapping us in blankets, he settled back, his breathing even. His eyelids drooped.

"Rest," he ordered.

I stayed awake all night.

Thirteen

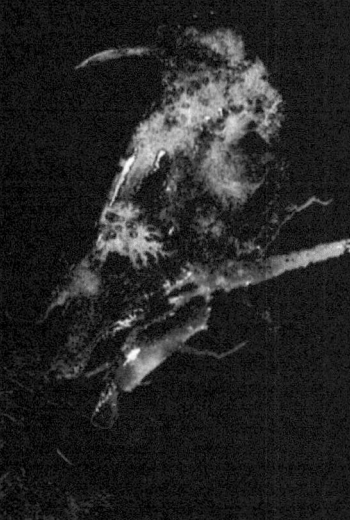

When the carriage rolled to a stop outside our house in Boston, I was a shell of who I had been when I left. As a husk, I pressed a hand to my lower stomach, praying a child was taking shape.

"Give me a moment before we enter," said Arthur, stepping out of the carriage after me. He took my coin purse. "I need to pay the driver."

I hadn't shifted my gaze from the house. Not having thought we would be back so soon, I had boarded it up for just that case, hopefully keeping Ethel trapped.

Mrs. White had her curtain parted, staring out at us like she was a hawk and we her prey. Others moved down the street, taking afternoon strolls in the warmest part of the winter day. When they saw we had returned early, failure pricked my skin. I bared my teeth, refusing to recoil, because unlike these bastards, we were in love. We would never be broken apart.

"Virginia," said Arthur, taking the crook of my elbow.

I transformed my face into a demure, sad smile.

"Arthur." I looked down at his hand on my elbow, liking how he held me even if his fingers pressed painfully into my skin, his nails digging through my clothes and threatening to draw blood. "I want to apologize again for—"

"Do not apologize," he said. "I only want to ensure you are all right."

He had been saying that since we boarded the train from Salem. We had sat with the other passengers, and I'd pressed my forehead to the icy glass. Our conversation had been stunted at best, repeating the same things:

"I'm sorry," I would say.

He would answer, "I'm happy you're all right."

And I would say, "I'm all right with you."

And he would say, "We'll be home soon."

There was no more talk of last night. Perhaps we could leave it in Salem.

"I'm only tired," I said.

With his eyebrows knitted, he continued to give me a weary look as if trying to see through my admittedly weak lie. My frame was no more than a reed, my dress like the leaves about to fall and scatter across the ground.

He crinkled his nose. "I think I need a bath. I smell like a barn."

My cheeks burned. "I imagine I don't smell much different than you."

"You smell like a flower."

"It's only my perfume," I said.

"Then I am indeed lucky and you, unfortunate. You should've spritzed me on the train."

"It wasn't necessary."

He grimaced.

He was ever so polite, though I wished he weren't.

"You should rest too," I said, hoping he might come to bed with me.

Now that I was feeling better, I knew how to atone, growing us back together by intertwining each other in our limbs and mangled hair.

I ventured, "Perhaps you would like to join me—"

"I should bathe," he said. "I'm offending myself. Shall we head inside, Virginia?"

So we did. His hand was still on the crook of my elbow, keeping me steady. He moved me from the sight of others, and I was thankful to leave their judgement behind. I already felt better with him, but I did balance on my shoe heels to keep myself from falling sideways.

As Arthur returned outside for the traveling cases, I took a deep breath of familiar homey scents. The same spiced trace fluttered from the curtains and my mother's perfume embedded in the walls. I coughed.

Something was…off.

The smells rubbed against the back of my throat, itching and burning in my nostrils and making my stomach twist. I was going to be sick, but I couldn't name the reason until I heard it.

Thump.

Thump.

Thump thump thump.

I stumbled back, grabbing my chest.

In my house, Ginny!

The realization dawned on me like a punch in the stomach: someone was in my house.

Arthur lugged in the two cases, depositing them just inside the door, and then he began to close it, but I called out.

"Wait!" I grabbed his hand.

His eyes widened to moons, his mouth dropping to an O like I had burned him with a hot poker. I pressed my pointer finger to my lips.

"What?" he asked.

"Can't you hear it?" I whispered, but the pounding had stilled.

They heard us.

"Someone is in my house," I hissed.

Arthur locked his hands on my waist, backing me out the front door.

"Wait here," he said, depositing me on the sidewalk, and then turned to the house.

"No, Arthur!" I said, holding his hand. "I don't want you to leave. Be here with me."

"Someone needs to investigate."

I eyed the looming house, so like the others with spiral columns and brown brick and the painted shutters. This was my home.

"Do you wish for me to call the watchmen?" asked Arthur.

"No!" I winced at how the sound traveled down the street, so I repeated in a smaller voice, "No. I don't think it will be necessary."

I didn't want them in the house, looking around.

"You may go." I peeled my hands away from him. "If you promise to be careful."

"I will." He shuffled back inside.

He left the door open as he turned toward the sitting room, disappearing into the shadows. The drawn curtains fluttered.

Arthur's name built in my throat. I wanted to call him back but thinned my lips together because I couldn't give away where he was. Nor could I distract him. If there was someone inside... I narrowed my gaze on the curtains, waiting for Ethel's nose to be pressed against the glass like a child's.

"Oh, Virginia," said a high-pitched voice behind me. "Returned from your bridal tour already?"

I froze. If I didn't move, Arthur returning to my side safely, then they wouldn't see me. I would be like one of the statues popping up all over Boston of deceased men from the Puritan or Revolutionary days. Birds shat on statues. Like those birds, these women wouldn't stop plucking at me until they had taken out my eyes and tasted my organs.

Pasting on a smile, teeth aching from how hard I ground them, I faced Mrs. Clark and Agatha Clark, who—though they didn't live on this street—were strolling by.

"Yes, we are. I see you're enjoying Boston's winter weather," I said.

Agatha, while she tried her hardest to be regal, looked about to snap in her tight corset and layers of clothing, her mother dressing her as a brood mare. Mrs. Clark thought prowling the streets might scrounge up a match for Agatha, but it would only give them frostbite and flaky skin.

The things women suffered in the name of finding a husband, of course, weren't things said aloud in the gentry. The same could be said about Mrs. Clark's ever-so-silent barb, what it meant for me to be home from my bridal tour early—that Arthur was not happy to have taken me as his wife. Though not true, the news would burn through society.

"Come along, darling," said Mrs. Clark, pulling on her daughter.

The older woman had an evil glint in her eye and set her face in a firm line that only meant trouble.

With their heads bent together, Mrs. Clark and Agatha clucked like hens as they departed.

I sucked in a deep breath. I wanted to scream about what had happened. Mrs. Clark and Agatha were women and should understand the terror I felt over being watched by a *vagrant*. That was what Arthur had called our onlooker after all, and they would believe him.

"Virginia!" Arthur stalked from the house, running his hand across his unshaved jaw.

"Arthur, are you all right?" I asked.

"Yes."

"My house?"

"Empty."

I drew my eyebrows together. "Are you sure?"

"Yes." He stepped off to the side, waving me forward. "Come inside."

Raising to my tiptoes, I glanced around him at the open door, darkness like a mouth ready to swallow us whole. He said no one was in the house, but I knew there was.

"Virginia?" He took my trembling hand.

"Thank you for checking," I said past my clenched teeth, fear pulsating my chest, but I wouldn't be forced from my home.

When I stepped inside, an immediate chill hit me, colder than outside. Shadows crawled across the walls. I tried not to step on the tendrils slithering across the floor. While no one was in my house, according to Arthur, the walls or floor vibrated with each bang.

Thump.

Thump.

Thump thump thump.

Who was in the house? How were they moving?

"You've checked the house?" I asked.

"Yes," he said, standing beside me. "No one is here. Besides us."

Us. The word fluttered my heart.

"I've looked everywhere," he continued.

"Everywhere?" I echoed.

How much was everywhere? There were so many places to hide, behind the curtains and under the beds, but it was more than that. What about the sitting room? Had he gone down into the bowels of the house, under the floorboards?

"Yes," answered Arthur, exasperated. "Everywhere."

In the front entryway, I waited for him to continue.

He drew his eyebrows together until they were one hairy caterpillar, a deep crease slipping up his forehead like a crack. Perhaps his skin would rip open and his skull would shatter, his brains oozing out like egg yolk.

My stomach growled, which seemingly broke the trance between us.

"Come," he said. "I will make you something to eat along with your tea."

"It is I who should be making food for you," I said, the words numb on my lips.

"I am a grown man, Virginia. I can, in fact, make food for myself. I've had to do it before." He took me into the kitchen, where the kettle was already blowing steam on the stove.

As we made love that night, I focused on Arthur—never tearing my gaze from my husband.

Yes, Ginny.

This—*him*—was what I wanted.

His skin slapped my own like thunder, leaving me sizzling. We sucked in each other's breaths, his burrowing into my lungs. If his cream wouldn't reach my womb, then perhaps his breath would grow a child in my lungs. I dropped open my jaw.

I drew my knees around his hips, keeping him deep inside me. He thrust faster until he hollered and then slumped forward. His arm was slung over me, our collected sweat dripping onto the sheets. When he regained his breath, he slid out.

He rolled over. "Are you all right?"

His face was seemingly caught in this perpetual concerned look, his pupils narrowed to catch every one of my ticks.

"Yes. That felt very good," I lied.

I was coiled tight for pleasure that would never come. Arthur had been reserved tonight, not even touching me between my thighs except to guide himself in. This was what other married women must've felt, existing in the world for a man's pleasure. I didn't pretend with Ethel like I did with Arthur now.

As I lay in his arms, Arthur brushed my hair down like how a man petted a dog. I fell asleep and stayed asleep until a boom shook the house.

Gasping, I sat up in the darkened bedroom, the hearth only burping embers now. Dimly lit night surrounded us.

Arthur faced away from me, his breaths rising and falling in soft motions like waves lapping a beach. I couldn't relax like he did. Sleep inched away, and I meant to chase it, especially when the thumping banged in my mind like a drum. I flinched.

Someone was in the house, even if Arthur couldn't find them. I would have to.

I stomped out of the bedroom without Arthur stirring. The thumping was on the walls, running from me. I tried to catch the phantom hurtling away from me only for my hand to fall through the air. I chased.

The balls of my feet slapped the floor. My toes dug into the rug and then wood. I followed the thumping through the house, skidding to a stop in the sitting room. The banging also ceased.

"Hello?" I asked.

Silky hums ran the length of the room like musical notes before falling to the floor, lying in heaps until the bang started again. It was only one thump on the floorboards, but I jumped, nonetheless.

I stood nude in my sitting room, how irresponsible of me. I should've gone upstairs and tucked myself into bed beside Arthur or, at the very least, wore a robe. I tried to turn away from the knocking on the floorboards beside the sofa, but there was another thump. Surely, Arthur would wake from this if he hadn't done so already. He needed his rest, much like I did, so I tiptoed across the room.

While the banging paused, something shifted under the floorboards, scratching at the wood.

Like I was a small girl, I pressed my eye between the cracks in the floorboards. Darkness stretched out, like there was everything there and nothing at all. I pressed my ear to the floor and listened. I waited until my lower back was sore and my knees ached.

Not one more sound.

No more movement.

I sat up, and my head spun, all the blood rushing back until my ears scorched. I sprawled on the floor, yet the world twisted like a ship thrown into storm waves. I flexed and scrunched my toes to get feeling back into them; my skin buzzed like an army of bees.

When my breathing returned to normal, I studied the bleary sitting room: the sofa perfectly positioned for absorbing the eastern sun, a mahogany desk in the center, ornate objects on the polished imported tables—all free from dust after I had cleaned a few days ago.

Everything had a place. I was just being foolish.

I pushed up from the floor, my body still aching, and didn't stop moving until I was standing at the edge of our bed.

The banging hadn't awoken my sweet husband. I ran my hand over the blankets, yet he didn't stir. I crawled into bed with him, though I couldn't say I was tired. When I closed my eyes, sleep was as far from me as ever.

It wouldn't come easily, much like a skittish animal, so I watched Arthur instead.

Fourteen

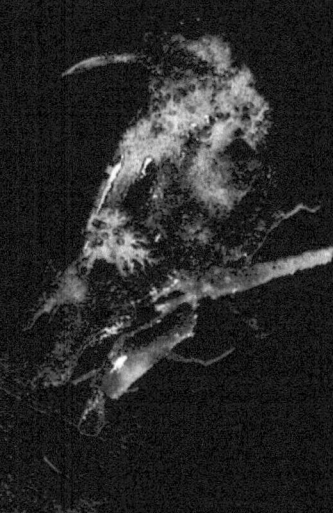

December 07, 1842

Leaning on my bed, hands braced on either side of my sitting body, I craned my neck toward Ethel, who straddled my center. My muscles stretched like wool, and I dropped my jaw. She caught my tongue between her teeth and chuckled, the heartiness shaking us both where we balanced on the edge of the mattress and of oblivion.

Ethel's chest rubbed mine. We had shimmied down to our underclothes, yet it was too warm, and too much fabric still separated us. I needed to break free.

I slipped my tongue from her teeth. She released that hold on me, though her hands locked on my cheeks, her narrowed eyes peering into the depths of my soul. Each breath we shared, our stomachs grinding against one another, until I was swimming in the mattress from the loss of oxygen.

"You're gorgeous," I mumbled.

Ethel laughed again. "Is that all you have to say?"

"You're powerful." I gripped her thick thighs beneath her underdress, pressing my fingertips into her flesh.

"You're intelligent." I slid a hand up her body, touching each part of her bare skin I could reach.

"You're lovely." I stripped her dress over her head and twisted my fingers in her hair at the base of her neck, holding her so close we might become one.

I kissed her deeply, roughly enough that our teeth cracked against one another, our lips turning to heated wax and slipping down our bodies.

Ethel returned to me when she could, and when she was here, I was alight with possibilities rather than darkness. This wasn't the first time I had brought her into my bedroom, where my childish dolls sat on top of my wardrobe and my old tea set collected dust in the corner, but this would be the first time we made love.

"Tell me now," I said.

I danced my fingers up her bare skin, goose bumps rising in my wake. I was a child begging for attention.

"What am I?" I demanded, though my voice wavered.

Tightening her grip on my hair, she lowered to my eye level. "What do you wish me to say?"

I shook my head. "Don't play these games with me, Ethel. My heart cannot take it."

She slipped one hand from the back of my head, down my neck and my chest, finally resting it against my raging heart. "You should see an herbalist about that."

"Ethel," I whined, withdrawing my hands.

"No," she said, locking her hand on the back of my neck and shoving her forehead to mine. "What can I say, Virginia? You have become everything to me. You make me rise in the morning and run here. I have become nothing without you."

I giggled like a young girl.

Ethel bit her bottom lip. "Was it not as you expected?"

"I expected compliments. Not imprisonment," I jested.

"I gladly give myself to you."

"It took you long enough."

"I was blind to not see what we could be."

"I only see you," I murmured. "It shall only be you, Ethel, for we are bound. I am both your captive and captor."

"With these chains"—she glided her hand down my torso and then under my nightgown, creeping her fingers up my thighs, and then she found my center—"I declare you mine, and I forever yours."

She kissed me again, pulling me closer to her and sliding her palm against my apex.

"Please," I begged through our breath-stealing kisses, "let me see all of you."

"I want to touch you," she said, rocking herself against me like we were on a ship at sea.

"I shall never stop touching you. I shall be on you. I shall be in you—in every place that aches for me."

"Do you promise?"

"With my life. With my health. With my soul."

She laughed. "You must really want to fuck me."

I knew she kidded, wondering if she could truly let me in, for she had built her castle walls so high that they seemed impossible to penetrate, but I worked hard to climb.

"More than that," I said to Ethel. "I want you. Every piece of you."

I kissed across her jaw line, stretching my neck to see how far I could reach, but the clothes and the binds of our mortal bodies only allowed me so far.

"Please," I beseeched, willing myself to lose all pride, because ego didn't have a place in love. "Let me see all of you."

"If you plead so, then I will let it be." She climbed off me, taking her weight and kisses.

I suddenly felt cold and empty. A desperate hunger opened its wide mouth for another taste of her.

Ethel peeled the fabric off her skin like a snake shedding an extra layer. By that time, I lost my ability to breathe, and my lungs ached to be full. I could've been high on opium for how I lost time and meaning of life as I stared at her.

She put her hands on her hips, bunching the skin. Her thighs were dimpled, and I could see where my hands had bitten into her flesh. If only I had canvas and paint...but I was a lousy painter and would never do her justice. Not even the finest artist could capture the starkness of her collar bones or the swell of her breasts heaving with every deep breath. No paint could recreate the shade of her pink-brown nipples.

"Is it everything you expected?" asked Ethel.

I nodded, still trying to find the words. There would be none to give, for they were too simple and my mind too empty. Not even a dictionary and a smart man could describe Ethel in her true glory.

"Your turn," she prompted.

I didn't leave the bed, my fingers twisted in the blankets like tree roots. I was sliding further into the mattress, like the fabric would rip open and the feathers would grab ahold of me.

"Come along, Virginia," said Ethel. "It is only fair that I also see you naked."

"I agree," I found myself saying.

She waved her hand at me. "Then undress."

"I'm not sure I can."

"Why not?"

"I do not trust my own legs to stand," I admitted, feeling like a newborn calf.

Surely, I would fall.

She giggled.

I said in a small voice with my cheeks heating from embarrassment, "Please don't laugh at me."

"I'm not laughing at you," said Ethel.

"You are."

"Fine, but not in the way you think." She pressed her chilly fingers to my face. "Rather, I laugh because no one has ever spoken this way to me—acted like this toward me—before."

I placed my palm against her cool hand, startled. "You've had other lovers."

"They are not the same as you."

I grimaced because that meant that I could not make love to her as well as they had, but we hadn't truly started yet. I still had a chance.

"That is not a bad thing, Virginia," continued Ethel in a soft voice. "You have opened something in me that I didn't think I had. My chest aches, like my heart is too big for my rib cage. It scares me, Virginia, if I must admit, and you on this bed—telling me you cannot stand because you look at me—it is more than I can take."

Suddenly, I stood, surprised by my own power. If she was startled, she didn't show it.

"I'm sorry you've never felt that way," I said, holding her close.

She put her hand to my chest. "Have you ever felt that?"

"No."

"Do I make you feel that way?"

"Yes."

"Show me."

The nightgown was a massive cobweb, and I pulled only for it to cling to me. Ethel gathered the fabric. We shredded it together, leaving the tendrils of cotton at my feet. I braced myself for the comparison of our bodies—they were different in cut and color—but Ethel admired me regardless, walking around me and dragging her fingers over my skin.

I grabbed her body, drawing her to my chest—between my ribs—as if I could absorb her like cloth did water. Her hard nipples scratched across my paper-like skin. I ignored how deep she cut me.

We fell into each other and into bed.

She slunk her hand down my body—through the small crevasse between my breasts and down my stomach, reaching my secret folds like she had before—and then wrapped her fingers in my lower curls. My hips bucked against her hand, and she giggled like a madwoman. I opened my mouth, swallowing the sound into my burning lungs. I only released, gasping, when she pressed a finger into me.

"Do you not like this?" she asked.

I tried not to wince as she slid her middle finger a little deeper, swirling it. Her palm pressed to my nub between my lower lips. The feelings combined with each thrust of her hand.

"I've never felt this before," I admitted, trying to kiss her, but she pulled her head back.

"Do you want me to stop?" she asked.

"No."

"Does it feel good?"

She worked her hand faster, peeling open my lower lips and driving her finger inside, rubbing her palm against my throbbing nub. A tingling sensation washed over my body, and then I was hurtled into the deep sea.

"Don't stop," I moaned.

Ethel pushed so deep inside me that I didn't know if I could stretch any further—I didn't know I was so deep—and the pressure and the pleasure built until I was teetering on the edge of insanity. Never ceasing her movements, Ethel pushed me over the ledge.

Light burst in my eyes, cascading down like falling stars, and then dancing dark dots covered my vision, blotting out Ethel. I feverishly blinked them away as the world spun. I gripped the bed. A high wind had picked me up, and I became a blowing leaf. I quaked like a leaf too.

Through the blood pulsating past my ears, I heard my own voice: "Don't stop! It feels so good! Ethel!"

She pulled back her hand as I fought to catch my breath and whirling thoughts, but did I want them? It was easier to belong to this bed, living in this house like it was a fortress, meant to keep others out and us hidden.

"Did you like that?" asked Ethel.

I released a shaky laugh. "You know I did."

"I want to hear you say it."

"I loved it. I loved what you did to me. I want you to do it again. I want—"

The words died on my buzzing lips as Ethel raised her fingers—the fingers that had been inside of me, the hand that had been on my nub—to her mouth and began to lick. She cleaned herself like a cat, moaning in pleasure as she ate me from her fingers. I couldn't let her have all of me when I hadn't had her.

"On the bed," I ordered, my voice near a growl.

Ethel drew her eyebrows together. "What do you want?"

"I want you to lie down," I said, rolling to my shaky knees.

"Why would I do that?" she asked, smirking like this was a game.

Willing to play, I grabbed her by the shoulders and threw her down onto the bed. Flipping her hair from her face—the curls wrapping around her neck like a pair of hands—she swung around, baring her teeth.

"That is why people think you are a witch," I said, shoving her hips into the mattress.

"This is why women don't like you," she said, wiggling under my grasp but never breaking free. "You order people around. You look down on others."

"Do I?" I asked, knowing it was my station.

With her ass cheeks at the edge of the bed, I shouldered her thighs apart, licking my lips at the sopping sight in front of me. Juices slicked her puffy nether lips, the pink folds blooming like a flower. The inside petals were a darkened abyss, red and leaking. Their owner shook as I breathed her in.

Ethel grabbed my hand and wove her fingers in with mine.

I said, "I have you now."

"You do," she agreed.

"You shall never be free from me."

"I never want to, Virginia."

Then, like I was a vampire in the night, I started to suck. Her pink folds enveloped my face, pulling me in further, and I gladly pushed into her, using my tongue and teeth to take one bite and then another, drinking her juices like they would give me life itself. I felt reawakened, reimagined, and recreated. My organs had already been rearranged when she fucked me. I was now rebuilding her piece by piece with my tongue.

My teeth were on her, fighting to have more of her.

Her cream was on my tongue, down my throat, and settling into my stomach, coating me like I was her.

"Virginia! I'm going to—"

Ethel tried to slam her thighs together, so I released her hand to brace her thighs apart unless she wanted me crawling inside, my head in her garden for the rest of our days. I could always fuck her from the inside. However, I stayed outside, keeping my shoulders broad like a trained soldier fighting off her bodily attacks. I fucked her mercilessly with my tongue, taking every last drop, but there was always more.

"I'm—" Ethel moaned, sounding like a ghost in the halls.

Instead, she was casting out the spirits with how she came on my mouth, rocking us on the bed. I was sure as I drank from her that I heard her scream my name, and I expected there to be applause like I was a performer.

She tugged on my hair, and I released my hold to crawl up to her side. Our limbs, sweat, and nectar intertwined. I placed my hand on her chest, listening to her rattling heart, and sighed in contentment because I was tired, spent, and overall happy. I couldn't remember the last time I had been the latter.

With Ethel, the weight lifted from my body, so I could breathe again. The tension freed from my shoulders, allowing me to stand straight. My bones were like melting ice that might shatter from impact. She laid my head on her chest, her chin brushing the back of my scalp.

"Is this when we speak?" I asked like an innocent doe, but I had never handed myself over to someone.

"Or we could sleep," she offered.

"Is that what you want?" I asked.

"What do you want?"

"I asked you first."

"You asked if I wanted to speak. You surely have something to say, Virginia."

"I was offering it as either of us could speak," I said.

"So you do not have something to say?" she asked.

"No." Yet not another word came to my lips.

"I would be scared if you had nothing to say. You always have something to say, Virginia."

I rolled my eyes.

"I could feel that," she said.

"I would only be concerned if you could see me roll my eyes," I said, tilting my chin down so she could only see the top of my head.

"Then I really would be a witch."

I giggled. "Witches cannot do see without their eyes."

"How would you know?" asked Ethel.

"I would ask you the same thing."

"Because I am a witch," she said, and I rolled my eyes again. "Yes, I felt that one too."

"You are not a witch."

"Others think so."

Unable to take this back and forth about witchcraft, I pulled my head up to meet her gaze, my neck straining. "That is because they don't know you."

"You make it sound simple," she said in an easy tone, yet I caught a shimmer in her eyes.

"Isn't it?" I asked. "You are an herbalist. You help people."

"But I don't wish to know others. Nor do I wish for people to know that much about me."

I frowned. "Here I was thinking I could take you to the Cox residence and—"

"No." Her tone had lost all playfulness, coldness sharpening her single word to a blade.

I blinked away my pathetic tears. "You didn't hear what I had to say. If I take you to the Cox residence, we can perhaps get an apprenticeship. We can introduce you to society. The rumors would all but dry up."

"It will not make a difference," she said, brushing my tears away. "Please don't cry."

"I mean to help you, Ethel."

"I know, but it will not help."

"But—"

"Your heart is in a good place, Virginia, but it is rather your…"

I propelled away from her and to my knees. "My what?"

"Your mind," she said, exasperated. "Your naivety about the world."

"Don't," I spat with a huff.

She pushed into a seated position. "I do not wish to have this conversation again."

Both of us were naked and covered in sweat, begging for each other to understand. This was when we were at our most dangerous stalemates.

"It is not just the Cox residence," pleaded Ethel, flexing her hands. "You cannot take me anywhere. We cannot be seen together. I have already turned my back on what others want from me, but you have not, Virginia."

"You cannot expect me to turn my back on all I have ever known," I said, wrapping my arms over my bare chest.

I was exposed and hated it.

"Nor would I want you to, but your life will be harder because of this. Because of me."

"I love you."

Though I had been thinking the words—the feeling expanding in my chest and warming my body, making me kiss Ethel even after only hours apart—for some time, this was the first time I verbalized them. Now that they were in the world, I wasn't scared. Nothing felt more right than the words, because what we had was meant to be embraced, not huddled in the dank shadows of the cellar.

Ethel ducked her head, and pain ached in my chest more than I thought possible, worse than when my parents had died and I couldn't sleep or eat. Perhaps this was what death felt like, but I should know it wouldn't be so immediate. I would have to wade through the pain, slipping further into the water until I drowned.

"I love you too, Virginia," said Ethel in a small voice that left me straining to hear her, but I waited on it.

And her.

She loved me, and my heart swelled tenfold, rubbing against my rib cage.

I was shattered again when she continued, "But think of everything you want—a family, living in society. I cannot give you that. Our love will not save us."

I didn't tell her otherwise. I didn't argue with her.

I lay in bed with her, our tangled bodies heavy from lovemaking, swearing to her silently that my love would save her.

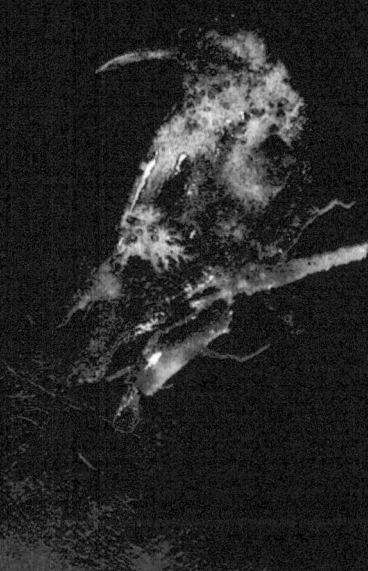

Fifteen

With winter-tinged sunlight streaming through the curtains, I blinked dust from my eyes, unsure if I had been asleep or dead. It felt like death. Heaving myself from the brink, I hooked my claws into life and pulled myself into a seated position.

"Oh," said Arthur from the far end of the room, pulling on his boots. "I didn't mean to wake you. You need the sleep."

"As do you." I yawned, stretching toward the ceiling. "Come back to bed."

"I cannot." Finished tying his boots, he stood, wearing his workwear. "I have a busy day."

I swallowed another yawn, as close to alert as I possibly could be. "Where are you going?"

"To work," he said. "I have ongoing projects at the university, which are now funded thanks to you. I was going to leave you to sleep."

"But it is our bridal tour."

"We're back in Boston."

"But—" I didn't have an argument.

Yes, he should go back to work; there was no point in us lounging around all day. He was a hardworking man.

"Yes," I agreed, my tongue sour. "I understand."

Arthur walked to the bed and kissed me on the top of the head, though I chased his lips. He stood out of my reach as if I meant to pull him into my secret garden, and perhaps that was my plan after all.

"I will see you tonight, Virginia," he said before strolling out of the bedroom.

I rocked to my knees, palms flat on the bed, and listened to his footfalls on the floor, quieting the further he walked away. The old wood creaked, especially on the stairs. However, there wasn't the sound of the knocking like there had been yesterday, not even as the front door squeaked open and then shut.

I waited for the banging to restart, but it did not. Perhaps Arthur was still lingering, so I whipped off the blankets, flew down the stairs, and pressed my nose to the glass. His form was retreating into the busy streets of Boston, most people beginning their day.

I turned away from the front window, the curtains falling into place. "Ethel?"

The house didn't stir, not even a hum from her somewhere down the hallways.

"Ethel, come here," I said.

Since Arthur had moved into my house, she stayed in the shadows, keeping her distance like I had asked. I should thank her, but I had the right to be ungrateful. I couldn't live in this house if that banging continued, but the house was now silent, so eerie the outside slipped under the door to fill it with voices. I wouldn't allow ghosts to return to my home!

I stomped through the house as loud as I could, slamming doors. I banged on the walls like Ethel had, sprinting into the sitting room and landing on the floor with bruising knees and palms.

I would do anything for Arthur. The same way he would do anything for me, dedicating his life to me with our holy vows of marriage.

Arthur wouldn't be safe if Ethel stayed in the house. At some point, she would grow bored of playing solely with me. Perhaps she would be so angry that I didn't love her anymore she would attack Arthur! I needed to protect him.

When Arthur returned home, I had supper ready and an open bottle of wine. I was a good wife, taking his jacket. When I had servants again, I would teach them to anticipate Arthur's whims, but he was such an easy man to please.

He was kind, especially when he returned home and said, "Oh, Virginia, the food smells amazing, but you look like you have been on your feet all day."

I tried not to wince. I had washed, brushing out all the knots from my hair. To ensure that I had missed nothing, I had cleaned the sitting room, and much to my approval, Ethel hadn't made a sound.

"No, not all day," I lied, smoothing my dress. "Sit, please."

I held the chair out for him, and he lowered himself down and took a sip of the dark wine, smacking his lips like he enjoyed the taste. I was sure he would like the dark wine over the sweet wine because he preferred brandy. Much like my father.

"Let me serve dinner," I said.

"Let me. I insist." He took the fork and knife from my hands to cut into the meat.

I sunk into the seat beside him and then sipped on my own glass of wine, trying not to grimace at the taste. My father had so many bottles in the cellar. I had plucked a bottle from the collection, wiping away the gray dust that seemed to take over the house like snow. Every day, no matter how much I scrubbed, there was more. It wasn't just in the corners or untraveled areas but on the floor and doorknobs.

"You said you rested today. Good. You needed it after…" He cut into his slice of meat, took a bite, chewed, and swallowed. "I felt you in and out of bed last night."

I tasted dry chicken. I needed to hire a cook and then servants to run the house.

"I also heard the floorboards creaking," he continued. "The stairs as you moved up and down. Almost like a banging."

I dropped my fork and knife. A piece of half-chewed chicken stuck to the topside of my mouth, sliding backward like a maggot with each tug of its body.

"I think we should renovate the house," he said without additional preamble.

The word stuck to the top of my mouth too, and I curled my tongue to say something.

As he waited for me to respond, he took a long gulp of wine, his throat bobbing and the liquid splashing in his glass like foam blooming on the sea. Finally, half the wine gone, he set the glass on the table and wiped his mouth with the formerly white napkin. Grease now stained the cloth in the outline of his mouth and jaw.

"I'm confused," I said.

"The state of which the house is in," he said like he was choosing his words, plucking them from the depths of his expansive mind. "Virginia, I don't mean to be rude, but the house is… Well, while it's livable for us and likable for who we are, it is in need of upkeep."

"I…" I glanced around the dining room, looking for the wear and tear that Arthur had noticed but not myself.

Was it how the floors creaked when they were walked upon? The stairs were the worst offenders, and my parents—before they passed—had spoken about having them replaced. Or perhaps the wallpaper was out of fashion. The paint was chipping in a few places, specifically the corners and where the ceiling met the walls, but I hadn't thought it was noticeable. Perhaps it was the discolored drapes. Or was it the missing rug in the sitting room and the scratched floorboards?

"Do not worry about it," Arthur added hastily. "I'm not sure anyone would notice."

"But you have," I reminded him.

"Yes, well…" He took another sip of his wine. "I'm a scientist. I am trained to look for the minutest detail."

As if elite women wouldn't see how terrible this place was, torn and worn and decrepit, whispering amongst themselves that this place—including me—was meant to stay on the outskirts.

"We should hire someone to renovate it," offered Arthur.

No, Ginny. They cannot. You know what they will find.

I rubbed my temples to ward off an oncoming headache.

There were a hundred ways for this to go wrong, but only one worker needed to take initiative for something that wasn't asked of them.

I tried not to flinch as he scrutinized me, the cogs in his head working to catch the wheels. I wished I could burrow into his skull and see inside, catching the thoughts before he said them. His word would be final as the man of the house, though it had been once my house and my money. He was now the usurper.

Arthur had long since fallen asleep, but resting was impossible for me when the house was breathing.

Thump.

Thump.

Thump thump thump.

Pinching my eyes shut, I nestled my head into the blankets and pillows, but the sound only grew. It slid into my ears and down my throat, pooling in my chest. When the pillow and blankets offered no protection, I pressed my face into Arthur's back; he was now turned away from me, still snoring. I had been so close to falling asleep, but then the knocking returned like Ethel's knuckles were on my heels.

Snapping to a seated position, I kicked off the blankets and stared into the darkness at the end of the bed. The soft hearth embers allowed orange light to creep across the floor, revealing it to be empty. Ethel wasn't here.

I twisted away, reaching for Arthur to draw back his hair from his peaceful face, but then *thump, thump, thump thump thump*. While I loved Arthur's ability to sleep, I wanted him to hear this. Ethel wouldn't leave me alone.

With my finger lingering above his shoulder, about to prod him awake, the thumping ceased. I released a deep breath, a heave that rattled my ribs like they were wind chimes. If only the sound would stay away…

I tiptoed down the hallway to surprise Ethel, hopefully catching her in the act. I could scare her like she scared me! Upon entering the sitting room, I paused.

Ethel knew the house as much as I did. I had shown her every part of it as I had shown her every part of me, opening every room and displaying the cobwebs in the servants' hallways.

"Ethel? I know you're here." I padded around the empty sitting room, pressing my ear to the wall.

A moment passed, and then there! The wall wheezed, and I followed, trailing my fingers along the peeling wallpaper. I slammed my fist against the wall, and the wood underneath groaned.

Silence.

Then something scratched against the wall, one long nail that dug up the wood, and then the person was moving again. I followed, tripping on the leg of the table and falling to my knees.

Pain jolted through my bones, but I had drawn no blood. Hopefully, I would not bruise, or Arthur would have questions. No, I couldn't have him ask because I didn't know how many more lies I could tell him. Our marriage and the rest of our lives couldn't be built on lies.

Rising to my feet before the window, I peeled back the pale curtain and stared into the dark night. Silvery moonlight slanted across the cobblestones. I dragged my eyes to the ground, only raising my face when I saw that I was being watched.

Mrs. White was sipping her steaming tea, staring at me from under her bushy gray eyebrows.

Her face transformed into a reflection of Ethel in the window. I spun around, reaching for her. She slipped through my fingers like a splash of cold water. Ethel was gone, and I stood alone in the sitting room.

"Ethel," I demanded, stomping my foot on the floor. "Don't hide from me."

She knocked on the floor. The small vibration brushed my toes.

I dropped to my knees and pressed my ear to the floorboards. Her nails scratched the wood, dragging across the floorboards like she meant to claw her way out, but she already knew how to get out.

She had been out and around the house, hiding in the shadows, watching Arthur and me.

I reached into the cracks between the floorboards and yanked up, my muscles groaning in protest. Dirt sprayed my skin. It was in my hair. Across my vision. I blinked quickly, hating what I saw. My stomach clenched.

Maggots scurried into the dark soil and across the ruined red rug. My mother had once loved that rug, having imported it from somewhere exotic. The color had once been wonderful, dulling after the years and then transformed, wrapped so tight like a butterfly in a cocoon. It was where Ethel hid, pretending to sleep. I should pull her out and shake her until she was yelling. Her head would wobble back and forth on her thin neck, and her hair would bounce like it always did.

She didn't fool me. Neither did the rancid scent. I raised my hand to cover my nose, seeing the skin on my arm squirm, and I bucked, terrified a maggot was on me. I nearly fell into the hole, succumbing to Ethel's game. When I looked at my arm again, it was bare of any insect.

This was exactly how Ethel wanted me. Distraught like her. But the end of our relationship hadn't been easy for me either.

The rug was lumpy but not like a person rolled up, snuggled into a blanket, but rather, she had stuffed it when she escaped. I had known girls in society to stuff their beds with pillows to sneak out with boys.

I grabbed the edge of the rug, rust-colored flakes caking my nails and fluttering across my nightgown, and began to pull, exposing the truth.

The scratching echoed behind me, and I spun around. Ethel stirred in the shadows.

"Ethel, enough of this," I growled, but the thunder of feet was moving away.

She was tunneling deeper into the house.

With a huff, I threw the floorboard back into place, hiding my mother's ruined rug. She would've been disappointed. Pushing to my feet, feeling Ethel move with me, I sprinted out of the sitting room and up the stairs.

She was climbing higher now. She aimed toward our bedroom.

Was she after Arthur?

My heart jumped to the base of my throat, shortening my breaths. My lungs burned as I raced faster, skidding to a stop in my bedroom. Arthur snored softly.

He was fine.

Safe.

Sleeping.

He was so peaceful. I wished I could crawl into his arms and have him hold me. I wished to have him inside of me, his tongue and his cock, eating me and impaling me. When I was in his arms, him inside of me, I belonged to him, and I fell more in love with him every time.

Ethel knocked on the door, and I cringed. Of course, I had brought her up to the bedroom, throwing Arthur into the game I didn't want to play. I spun to the open door, *no* on my lips, but Ethel was already running away like we were children playing hide and seek. She wanted me to chase her like I had done before.

I lingered over him for a moment to calm my galloping heart and rickety mind and then backed out of the room. I closed the bedroom door. The hair on my arms stood, and I slapped myself only to find nothing there. My skin sizzled, a welt raising that would become a bruise.

My feet were dirty, and I was covered in grime. Arthur would have questions when he awoke and didn't find me in bed. I couldn't return to him like this, dragging muck into our marriage bed, staining him with my filth. I needed to move quickly, but when I took a step, I pitched forward.

My mind swam, my breathing ragged. The floor was moving… Or it was just me? I tiptoed down the hallway, aiming toward the water basin and a fresh nightgown, but darkness slunk across my vision.

Sixteen

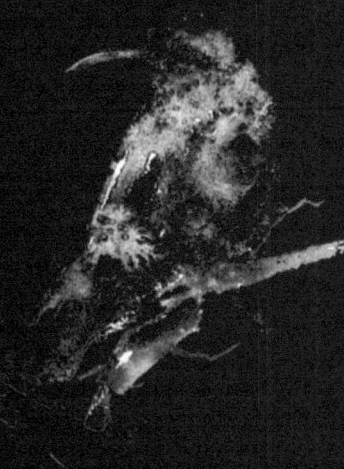

A haze clouded me, brought on by tiredness grasping my bones. I snapped my eyes open, focusing on Arthur hovering above me. Dark creases etched his pursed lips. A breeze fluttered my eyelashes, partially from his heavy breathing and the way he carried me from where I had fallen.

Had it been in the hallway? I couldn't remember the details. They slid into the dark reaches of my mind, the outlines blurry.

He grunted as he hefted me onto the bed. I landed with a thud. My neck jolted back.

Arthur was now covered in dust too. Smudges tinted his chin as red blossomed on his cheeks, but that was all the color in him. He seemed to have gone ghostly pale.

"I will call for a doctor," mumbled Arthur, slipping his hands from me.

"No," I said.

The word snapping from my mouth was a surprise to me as much to him. He startled, like an animal caught unaware, frozen where he stood, unsure if he should run or attack.

"Please, don't," I added, forcing myself to make amends for the harm I was most likely causing.

I let my words turn to syrup, the sweetness lingering on my tongue, and I snuggled into bed like I meant to rest.

"That's not necessary. No doctor." I couldn't have another person in the house—not while I was unclean and unwell.

A doctor was bound to investigate, stating he was doing it for the good of the patient. In the end, the doctor would say that I needed more exercise and the sun but also needed more rest, and then he would prescribe something that wouldn't work, which ultimately would make me travel to the parts of Boston I wasn't meant to be in. That was, after all, how I'd met Ethel.

"Please," I said again, my voice measly because I was sure that I had lost this battle.

He was the man of the house, and I was only a woman.

Kneeling beside the bed, Arthur pressed his lips against my fingers. His warm breath lifted the hair on my arms. His eyelids fluttered shut, and I didn't know how many seconds passed in the state of his praying. Where there was once love, patience, and kindness, there was fear, though I had no reason to be terrified of Arthur. He only wanted the best for me.

He opened his eyes, watching me for another long moment that made me forget how to breathe. "Virginia, why were you out of bed again? Why are you so dirty?"

Tears collected in his eyes, and I reached across my body to brush them away. The heat was sloppy on my fingertips, splattering the bed. He leaned into my touch.

"I couldn't sleep," I began.

Arthur blinked slowly like he couldn't comprehend my words; for him, I was probably not speaking English at all.

"Like the previous night?" he asked.

"I'm anxious to be back in the house," I said.

"Because of what happened on our bridal tour?"

"No," I said, though I wasn't sure if it was the truth.

He drew his eyebrows together, much like he did when he was thinking hard, and dragged his eyes across my body. My skin crawled. How could he see me so clearly?

"I must ask…" He crinkled his nose. "Where did all the grime come from? It smells like an animal died in the house."

I balled my soiled hand into a fist, tucking it under my nightgown. My nose twitched at the newly recognized scent.

"I'll clean it up," I said in a rush. "It's most likely just the cooking from last night."

"You don't need to," he said. "You need rest, Virginia. You had such a fright in Salem."

I winced at his decisive tone, picking through his kindness because that's all it was. He cared for me, wanted to help me, and I was the one who dragged him into this. I couldn't have the blood on my hands stain him too.

I would need to deal with it—specifically Ethel—before renovators arrived to tear apart the house and create something anew. Then, officially, the house wouldn't be my own. I wouldn't be able to see Arthur's children running down these hallways with me chasing them and yelling for them not to run, silently giggling at their exuberance.

With a huff, he said, "Don't do it now. You need to rest."

"I'm fine," I said, pushing into a seated position and ignoring how the room spun. With my free hand, I twisted my fingers in the sheets to root myself.

"I want to believe that." He glanced toward the hallway. "It will now be seared into my mind finding you there. In that state. I thought you were… I shall stay with you today—"

"No! You've told me how important your work is. Your work has funding now."

Your funding, Ginny.

"You're important to me, Virginia," he said.

My cheeks warmed. Those words were the perfect reminder of how lucky I was to have married Arthur.

"Please," I said, smiling so hard that my teeth began to ache. "I shall rest while you're gone, but you must go to work. You need to be out in the world. I'll handle things here. It is a woman's duty to take care of the household."

He dropped his jaw open like he would argue, the stillness stretching between us like a canyon, but then he nodded promptly and rose to his feet.

I waited until Arthur was gone. He shuffled through the house like an old man and then finally closed the front door. By that time, I had thrown off the too-hot blankets. I jumped to my feet and then ran through the house, pressing my nose to the front window and watching Arthur wander into the distance.

Away from the window, I peeled off my dirty nightgown and left it in the heap. It was one of the many things I would need to clean today, but that would have to wait until later, when I had cleansed the house of the decaying scent leaking into the wood and any and all fabric.

Ignoring the dirt under my fingernails and how it clumped in my hair, I threw on a maid's uniform and the cloak I had first worn when I met Ethel. I needed to be hidden, though Mrs. White was watching me. Always. I scampered down the street and then took a left, heading deep into the bowels of Boston.

When I still had servants, the cook and the maid would use salt on meat to keep it longer. They would put it somewhere dark and cold. When I had my first bleeding, I was given salt for my old blood-stained clothes, before they were too worn and needed to be burned. Perhaps that was what I needed to do with the rancid scent.

While I didn't need to travel far for salt, I was scared Mrs. Cox's servants might see me. I was a woman who did my own shopping, and I wasn't ashamed of it. However, I did buy the largest bags of salt I could carry, balancing them in each arm and feeling how my muscles burned. I tried not to trip over the hem of my dress, my cloak wrapping around my ankles. I dashed home, dropping the bags of salt in the front entryway. Only then did I pause.

Thump.

Thump.

Thump thump thump.

"Arthur?" I asked the house breathlessly.

How long had I been gone? His work was too far to meander home and check on me. Nor did anyone answer my call. Arthur would've answered, not waiting for me to venture further into the house only for him to jump out at me.

"Arthur?" I repeated louder this time.

The knocking stopped. As did my breathing.

The house was silent, not a groan on the floorboards or the scurry of rats in the walls. I was alone.

I hefted a large bag of salt and then shouldered my way into the sitting room. The horrid scent hit me, and I rocked back on my heels. Now that Arthur had pointed out the smell, I couldn't escape it. It wrapped its taloned hand around my neck. I couldn't suck in another breath without the stench in my nostrils. I backed out of the sitting room.

You have to do it, Ginny.

I plunged into the sitting room once more. The curtains were drawn, murky gray light shifting in at an unnatural angle. I should open a window to air out the room, but what if the neighbors smelled the stench? What if the neighborhood rodents slipped into my house? I couldn't have that, but my stomach was knotting further, squeezing so tightly that my insides were liquefying.

I backed out of the room, this time on a mission to grab coffee from the kitchen. I remembered one of the newer servants had burned coffee and how much worse it had smelled. The servants had to open the windows in the middle of winter, and I, as a young girl, bundled in dresses, a jacket, and a cloak and sat by the fire.

With the canister of coffee pressed under my nose, I returned to the sitting room and built a roaring fire in the hearth. I ground up the coffee and set a pan to boil, intent on leaving it to scald. I knew it wouldn't be enough to hide the scent of death, but it kept the bile at bay.

Like a hound, I tracked the scent to the middle of the room. It rose from the cracks between the floorboards.

Of course, Ginny.

I ripped up a floorboard more efficiently than I had done the previous night. Splinters cut into my hands; my fingernails chipped away. I laid the floorboard aside, already huffing from the exertion.

The scent hit me. Bitterness clawed at my throat at the same time excuses populated my mind. I swallowed.

Maroon splotches covered the tattered rug as if it had been stained by spilled red wine. The lumpiness was more human-like in the daylight.

A maggot crawled from the top, the slimy tiny body inching toward the light. I wanted to flick it off, offering Ethel any remaining dignity. She deserved it…if she was actually in the rug.

Peeling back the corner, I gasped and almost dropped the salt, which would scatter across the floor, and I would have more of a mess to clean. As if I hadn't done enough damage.

Not looking like herself, Ethel was covered in dirt, discolored inflated eyes staring into the distance. The once vivid color was fading. The rest of her was puffy as well, her skin now grayish.

Apologies bubbled on my tongue. If I opened my mouth, more than a sorry would fall out.

It's not her, Ginny.

Like a witch meant for the gallows, she must've changed herself out for another, or she purposefully painted herself grotesque, hiding a dead animal under her. I wouldn't be so easily fooled. Or swayed.

I dumped the salt on her, ensuring that the maggot was covered, along with most of the hole-ridden rug. I pushed the salt across the rug and into the cracks. I went to the doorway, ignoring the fluttering white curtains, to retrieve the second bag of salt. Perhaps I had bought too much, covering the rug so much that she appeared buried in snow. I couldn't even see her reaching hand that was knocking against the floorboards to be let out.

When the salt was placed, I glanced at the now-covered rug. Yes, that would do nicely. I slid the floorboards into their slots and bent my head in a silent prayer.

Seventeen

When Arthur came home that night, I had supper ready. Everything that was once covered in dirt, including our bedding, was now clean. I had burned coffee, aired out the house, and then spritzed my mother's perfume about.

Arthur paused in the doorway, cocking his head to the side. I knew that look was one of a man trying to find something amiss, but he couldn't. I had taken care of it like I said I would.

"Why the roast for tonight?" asked Arthur.

Crimson juices splattered the plate, oozing out in the growing pool. The slabs of meat were burned around the edges, but the inside was still warm, the white fat hanging off. I had seasoned the outside of the roast with salt, which offered the extra crunch.

I smiled at him. "I wanted to make something special for you."

Arthur linked his hand with mine. "How did I get to be so lucky?"

My heart fluttered. "It is I who am lucky."

I served him and then myself, sinking into the chair beside him. Our forks and knives scraped the plates. We sipped our wine, never gurgling and never slurping. It was a kind silence, one that was just us, and I felt safe in his presence. I also knew that it was partly an act: the more I smiled and focused on him, the less I had to think about how my body ached and my eyelids drooped. I kept my back straight before my head lolled to the side and the rest of my body followed, splatting against the floor.

"Would you like another piece?" asked Arthur, inclining his head toward the roast.

"I couldn't," I said, though I had finished my first piece in an unladylike quickness, barely remembering how to chew.

"You should."

"Are you trying to fatten me up?"

"I merely saw how hungry you are. More food could do wonders for you."

"You'll have to carry me upstairs."

"It would be my honor."

"It would be impossible."

"Then I would slumber down here with you."

I felt the words in my soul. It warmed me to think about it until I was warm for him, wishing to be freed from these clothes. I wanted him to mount me or hold me against the wall as he thrust into me.

Arthur was a gentleman and would never have such strange thoughts. I didn't think Arthur had much of a primal need, which made him better than me.

After supper, we retired to the back of the house, where Arthur pulled out whatever book he was reading and I sat with my embroidery. I leaned against his shoulder, though my body protested his sharp bones. It was like I was being stabbed, each prick of his collarbone worse than the last. If that wasn't terrible enough, the embroidery was hard on my trembling hands, my sight hazing.

"Are you tired?" asked Arthur, his voice husky like smoke.

"No," I lied, forcing my eyelids open. It felt like they would slip back over my eyeballs, falling into my head.

"You seem tense."

"I apologize."

I wasn't as good at hiding how I felt. What else had he noticed about me?

"It's your body," he said.

"My body?" I echoed, trying to parse through what he said and what he could mean.

My mind was like a speeding train with the worst possibilities aboard. They made me tense, my joints stinging and muscles like ice.

"I can feel it." Arthur laid his hands on my shoulders. "You rested today?"

"Yes," I lied, the word snappish.

If he noticed, he didn't say, rather pushing his fingers into my shoulders and muscles. His tender hands turned hard. He worked his fingers into me, gripping at my skin and muscle through my dress. It was like he was trying to reach for my bone and mold it the way he wanted. His massage felt so delightfully intimate that I leaned back into him, letting all my weight fall into him. I moaned softly.

"You like this, Virginia?" he asked in a coy voice.

"Yes." My voice wavered on the singular word.

"How much?"

"Very much."

He pressed his palms into me, working his way down my body. "I can tell you like it."

"Can you?" I asked breathlessly.

"Your body is relaxing."

"You're magic."

His hands stilled.

He was a man who didn't believe in magic. Perhaps he, as a man of science, didn't even wish for the comparison.

An apology built on my tongue, but then he resumed his massage, albeit hesitantly. It was the kindness that I recognized in him. I loved him all the same, but I wanted those hard hands again. He had been working toward my veins, but I didn't mind the pain. This softness was a disappointment.

Reaching up, I angled his face toward me. He again paused, allowing me to face him and press my lips to his. He let out a deep groan; it echoed from somewhere in his chest, shaking us both.

"Perhaps we shall retire upstairs," he said through the kisses.

He didn't pucker his lips as he once had, nor did he nip at my lips.

"We could." I shoved him on the sofa to be chest to chest.

The sofa groaned, obviously not liking how we sat, and I admitted to myself it wasn't comfortable. My dress was twisted like rope, cutting into my skin. I couldn't reach the buttons to undo my dress, nor could I hike up my skirts to press my lower lips against his bulging trousers.

Arthur looked away, cheeks red. Was that embarrassment or disgust that colored him?

"Virginia," he said in a husky tone, like a man arguing with himself.

"Have me," I said.

"I am tired."

"I shall be the one to work for it."

I reached for the waist of his trousers, and he caught my hands, his grip like iron. I raised my gaze to meet his, prepared for a discussion because we didn't argue. We were in love, so we wouldn't argue; that was the difference between my love for Ethel and my love for Arthur.

His gaze was like onyx, darker than night itself, the stars and moon blotted out. His chin jutted, his mouth dangling open. If only I could slip inside of him, piece by piece to make myself smaller…but no, he needed to come to me. He needed to be inside me.

I flexed my hands, and my fingertips grazed his tented trousers. He shivered. Yet he didn't release me. Even when I brushed my fingertips against the fabric again. He locked my hands together. His grip was like metal shackles, I the prisoner.

Look, Ginny, how he holds you away. Those rumors of your past are finally catching up to you. He finally realizes how true they are. He knows.

Terrified to see his mind working, I couldn't bring myself to look at him. He was a smart man, so perhaps he had put it all together, the pieces falling into place like they would for an investigator. Arthur said nothing about it, but wasn't that the kind of man that he was? Too kind.

"Why don't you want me?" I asked in a small voice.

"That's not true," he said on a brisk exhale. "I want you terribly. I want you more than any man wants a woman. You're my wife."

My belly did a flip because that was exactly what I needed to hear.

"Then why won't you allow me to touch you?" I asked.

"Oh, Virginia." He cupped my chin, bringing his forehead to mine. "It is not that I don't wish us to touch. Don't wish for us to be intimate. Rather, I wish for you to be safe and healthy, able to sleep at night. I don't want to work you into such a state that you cannot sleep."

I nearly laughed. Was that what he called it?

Was that what he thought would happen if we started to kiss one another, bringing our bodies closer and into ecstasy?

I wanted to scream *no*—the voice rubbing the back of my throat raw—but I couldn't disagree, not when I hoped he would understand. He only wanted the best for me, after all, so if he thought this was right...

Arthur kissed my forehead and then squirmed from under me, leaving me to flop onto the sofa like a dead fish. He offered his hand, and I slid my fingers into his and then stood. When we were face to face, he kissed my knuckles like when we first met.

I stepped into him, knocking my head against his firm shoulder, and locked my arms around him in a hug. He was stiff, planted to the floor, unmovable. I nestled my head into the crook of his neck and continued to hug him, and after a few long seconds, he relaxed.

Our bodies fit together, though not as they did during love making. I was at peace with him, having him take the weight off. Neither of us were poets, able to put into words what this meant, but it was painful to break apart.

We walked arm in arm up to bed like we were walking by the harbor again, courting and finding confidence in ourselves and one another. I had been so focused on this maddening house and Ethel that I forgot where I needed to be focused: Arthur.

To find our footing again, I needed his help. I was no expert when it came to men and no mystic, who could commune with his mind, so I needed him to tell me. Or I would have to go to the married ladies and have them whisper their secrets to me. I knew Arthur enough to know that neither of us wanted that.

Outside our bedroom, I stopped Arthur. "Shall we walk like this tomorrow?"

He drew his eyebrows together. "Inside the house?"

I giggled, knowing he was jesting. "Outside. If the weather is unseasonably warm again. I think the fresh air would do us both good."

He smiled. "I couldn't agree more."

Then his smile dimmed like someone blowing on a lit candle. "I'm not sure if tomorrow will work. I have a large project with John. It is very...inclusive. He argued with me not to go home today, hating how far away from work I am."

A mixture of anger and sadness built in me.

"No bother," I lied, walking into our bedroom.

We were polite in saying our good nights and laying down. He was quick to sleep, the weight of being a man pressing him into slumber. I stared at the ceiling, my fingers locked over my chest. As soon as I closed my eyes, slipping into slumber for a second, I heard the first *thump*.

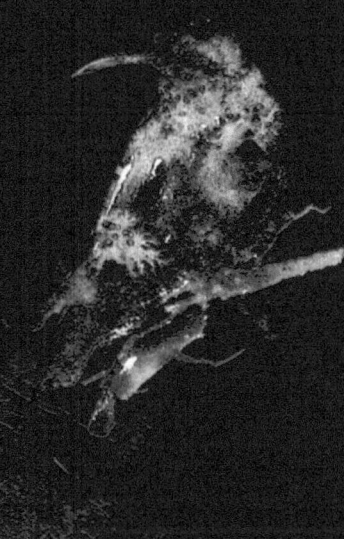

Eighteen

I stared at Arthur's form, wondering how he could sleep through the insistent knocking. If only I was a man who worked so hard that, when night came, it was easy to sleep. I had been awake for days and had been working tirelessly, but sleep escaped me.

Thump.

Thump.

Thump thump thump.

I sat up, the blankets toppling from me. The hearth was roaring like it had been when Arthur and I first settled in, gobbling up the wood and burping out embers, crackling with laughter. It should've been loud enough to keep out the knocking, but the sound was growing closer.

Ethel was coming for Arthur.

Jumping from the bed, I dashed out of the room, destined to meet her halfway.

Ethel was at the base of the steps, and I stood at the banister. Her clothing was pristine, recently cleaned.

"What is that look, Ginny?" she asked.

"Keep your voice down," I hissed, glancing over my shoulder at the closed bedroom door.

"You don't wish me to wake Arthur."

"Of course, I don't. He has no part in this."

She scoffed. "Doesn't he?"

"No."

"You've chosen to love him over me."

"You made it clear that you didn't love me when you tried to leave," I said.

Ethel sneered. "Look how well that turned out for me."

Thump.

Thump.

Thump thump thump.

"Stop that," I snapped.

Ethel raised her eyebrows. "Stop what?"

"You know what you're doing."

"Do I?"

"Don't be this way."

"What way is that?"

Balling my hands into fists, I wanted to scream in frustration because that was always how she made me feel: one step forward, two steps back. The concoction of love and hatred was overpowering.

I stomped down the steps and pressed my nose to hers. "You know. You want me to be upset. You say you want me to feel—"

"You often miss that ability," she interjected, "cut off from the rest of the world. You fit into the little dresses, and you play pretend, following whatever the latest trend is amid *your* society. You aren't you, Ginny. Just some creature that society has made."

Tears burned my eyes, and I couldn't stop how they overflowed. Ethel knew how to cut me to the bone, waving what I wanted to be the most in front of my face. How could a woman who was such a kind lover, such a smart person, be so devilish?

Ethel crossed her arms over her chest. "Yes, Ginny, cry. You obviously should be the one to do so."

"It's not like you're making this easy," I spat.

"I will not go quietly, Ginny. I will be with you forever."

"You will not." I stepped away from her, blinking the tears feverishly from my eyes. I needed to see her clearly, but it was hard to look at her, the pain bubbling to the surface.

She saw me too well to make me feel seen and loved and open, but our time... She had let it go. She said we were too different. We were born differently, raised differently, and lived differently, but it was our love that made us one, unique but similar. Until she ruined it when she tried to leave.

Ethel stepped close to me, thrusting her chest against mine.

Thump.

Thump.

Thump thump thump.

"We are bound. We will be together," she added.

"No," I hissed, throwing myself against the wall.

It breathed.

It pounded with the same beat that was inside my chest.

Then I sprinted up the stairs, yelling "No!" over my shoulder, as Ethel waited at the bottom step. Her one green and one blue eye traced me like a hawk following prey, and while she wasn't behind me—I checked—I felt her with me, her breath on the back of my neck and her hands wrapping around my center, lifting my nightgown for better access.

I slammed the bedroom door behind me, slumping against it to keep Ethel out. My heart pounded against my rib cage, threatening to burst free. So much that I barely heard Arthur.

"Virginia?"

Forcing a kind smile, I drew away from the door and climbed into bed. "Apologies, my love. I didn't mean to wake you."

In his tired haze, he drew his eyebrows together like he was confused, scrutinizing what it could mean. "Will you sleep now?"

"Yes," I lied, lying beside him and wrapping my legs with his.

Perhaps if we were tied together, I wouldn't leave the bed again.

Arthur covered us in blankets, tucking us in like we were children, and I imagined how he would be with our own children someday. What kind of stories would he tell them? How would he soothe their nightmares? He would be such a good father in our house filled with children. These thoughts almost allowed me to sleep.

Gray light filtered through the gauzy curtains that couldn't keep the day at bay, but Arthur was up at dawn, shuffling around the room and eating downstairs. I needed to hire servants or to get myself out of bed to make food for my husband; both were the last things I wished to do today. I wanted to sleep but the banging returned, louder than ever once Arthur left, so I pushed out of bed, changed, and practically ran from the house. The banging was swallowed by the noise of Boston coming alive.

The streets were like a wave. I was carried by them until I was deposited in the bowels of Boston close to where I had bought salt the previous day. Then I went deeper into the shadows, following the path I had taken to the apothecarist. I didn't venture there now.

What Ethel was, whether in my mind or of real body, was something of a mystic's inking, not one of a doctor who would prod me and make me bleed. A mystic, someone like in Mrs. Cox's employ, wouldn't save me from my ailment.

Buildings were built on top of one another, looming gloomy wood and broken glass, curtains drawn. The yells of the men at the port echoed down the dirt streets. The wind brought in the scent of fish from the harbor and oil from the ships. Plumes of dark smoke billowed from factories.

In a hefty gust, the smoke was on me like an attack. I coughed. When I managed to wiggle out of the hold, I grabbed a brick wall to keep myself upright and blink the coal dust from my eyes. It was also in my hair and on my clothes. I peeled it off my tongue with my teeth.

"You all 'ight, girly?" A woman stood outside a shop with a dirty sign hanging.

"Fine," I muttered.

My cloak had fallen off my shoulders when I stumbled out onto the street, and I righted it and then drew the hood to cover my features. Others didn't glance my direction, but I would rather not be recognized as the woman Ethel knew.

"No reason to hide here," said the old woman.

"I'm not hiding," I replied.

She lifted a white eyebrow, her wrinkled lips twisting in amusement. Her crystalline blue eyes, though seemingly hazy from age, were outlined in black charcoal. It enlarged her pupils so that they took up most of her eyeballs. They followed me too closely.

I didn't wish to speak to an old whore. The other women on the street were at least younger, wearing fewer clothes too, but this woman was covered in a shawl to her chin. Her liver-spotted hands only poked out so she could smoke.

I needed to find someone stronger than an apothecarist, but at this point, I would've taken a tavern and brandy. I peered down the street that I had come from and then turned in the opposite direction.

"Where do you think you're going so fast?" asked the woman, speaking quicker than I thought a woman of her age could. "I'm Mabel."

"I'm...I'm not interested." My cheeks burned.

"You don't know what I have to offer."

"I'm not—"

"Having trouble sleeping, are ya?" she asked, and I stilled. "You've lost weight, so I assume you can't eat. You have dark bags under your eyes, and you've stumbled for no reason. How ill are you?"

"I'm not ill."

"A woman like yourself would go to a doctor."

"How do you know what kind of a woman I am?"

"I know you don't belong here." She took a deep drag from her pipe, and when she spoke again, each word was punctuated by white smoke. "I knew you would come. I woke up this morning and could feel in my bones that there was a...*haunting*."

I shook my head, but desperation tightened its hold. The day was slipping away, and I needed to be home before Arthur. John McCarthy would try to keep him later, but I knew my husband: he would come home to be at my side, he loved me. And I loved him. I was making myself better for both of us.

I stalked toward her, and she raised her head to meet my gaze. An icy chill ran down my body.

No, Ginny.

There was no such thing as mystics communing with the dead. I wouldn't be tricked.

"What are you?" I asked.

Mabel shrugged. "The simplest term would be a witch."

The word struck me in the chest, making me fall back a step.

"You've heard the term before, no doubt," said Mabel, "but don't focus on what I am or what people call me."

She brushed her long yellow fingernail across my cheek, not hard enough to cause me pain but rather that she was looking at me intently.

"Follow me." She hobbled into the shadowy alleyway.

While no one was watching out for me on the street, I felt safer under the eyes of others. I didn't know Mabel, a supposed witch, or where she was taking me. I knew rumors sparked of private conversations—Ethel flooded my memories. Even away from the house, I was unable to escape her.

I chased Mabel and whatever supposed answer she could provide.

"In here," said Mabel.

I caught up to her. She had already stepped into a small apartment, leaving the door ajar and her back exposed.

"Close the door behind you," she added. "You're letting the warmth out."

I snapped the door shut, regretting the choice to follow as my eyes slowly adjusted. A few steps descended to a crowded room, a hearth leaking smoke. Glimmering rocks from a beach or...farther away—these weren't any rocks I had seen before—lined the windows covered in thin shawls, darkening her single-room apartment. The room smelled of mold, wet and cold, the walls expelling moisture. The ground was practically a sponge, most likely flooding with every hard rain in Boston.

I glanced around the apartment—though, there were no hiding places—for a watchman. Times were changing in Boston, bringing in the idea of police from abroad, but half the city was still crawling with soldiers. There was always another war, whether between us or someone else, on the horizon.

Mabel sipped from a teacup and then smacked her lips. "Tell me, can you pay?"

"Will you actually make me better?" I asked.

She frowned, the wrinkles sliding down her face. "That depends on you."

"That means no." I turned from her.

"Is she in your home?" asked Mabel to my back. "If so, you will need to cleanse the home. If she is in an item or on your clothes, then you need to destroy them, preferably by fire. If she is in your hair, cut it and throw it into the sea."

I snorted. She was no better than a mystic.

No matter what people called her, Ethel knew herbs, how to cut and grind them into tinctures that would soothe my aching muscles or calm my racing mind. She would make these oils, infused with lavender, to rub on my chapped skin. She put peppermint in my tea for a stomachache.

"Well?" prompted Mabel.

"She's in the house," I said, unsure why I was still talking to this madwoman. "You can't expect me to burn down the house."

"I said cleanse."

I faced her. "How?"

"There are herbs to burn."

"It will clear her away?"

"It will make it very uncomfortable for her to stay."

"She's desperate to."

"That is the life of a phantom," said Mabel. "There is nothing else for them to do. They are clinging to life. Did she die young and violently?"

"I..." My jaw dropped open. "I didn't..."

"I didn't say so," she said, giving me a knowing look. "I only want to know what kind of connection she has to this world, especially your house."

"Yes."

"To which one? Young? Violently?"

"Both."

"What was your connection to her?" asked Mabel.

I locked my jaw.

"If she was a servant that haunts you and you punished her, burn her hands. If she was a woman you hated, burn her mind. If she was a lover..." Mabel gulped down the remnants from her teacup and then set it off to the side. "Do you understand?"

I nodded.

"Then you must use salt," began Mabel.

"I've already used salt."

"Have you put it under the doors and windows?"

"What? No."

"It will keep the phantom out."

"But you said—"

"I haven't finished," snapped Mabel, landing her startling blue eyes on me. "You must get rid of every part of this woman. You must remove her things from her home. It will weaken her connection, and then you can be the one to break it. Do you understand?"

I didn't but nodded anyway because what Mabel spoke about... Ethel would've laughed, calling Mabel a crook.

"Is there anything else?" I asked.

"Anything else?" Mabel scoffed. "Have you not been listening to me? It will be a wonder if you manage to do it all. Especially in your state."

With my lips clamped shut, I reached into my coin purse and didn't count the money as I set it down on the table. We hadn't haggled in price, and I was too tired to do it now.

Nineteen

I had what I could buy tucked into the pockets of my dress, my heavy cloak sweat-laden from how I had traipsed all over Boston. All I wished for was to take off my clothes and lay in bed, letting my body relax and my skin cool, but I needed to set myself to work as soon as I returned home. The plan was written in my mind, and I would follow every step.

That changed when I entered the house, the door unlocked when I was sure that I had locked it behind me.

Arthur called out, "Virginia!"

I flinched. Was he home early, or was I late? I glanced toward the gray-hued light on the street, and while I was returning home later than I wished to, I was home before I thought he would be.

"Yes?" I called out to him, pushing my voice up an octave to sound chipper. Instead, I sounded like a young girl caught by her governess.

From where I was anchored by the door, I wrenched my head left and right and then toward the stairs, trying to figure out where Arthur was in the house and praying he hadn't gone into the sitting room.

Arthur came from the kitchen, his jacket off. "Where have you been?"

"Hello, dear," I said to interject a moment for my thoughts to relax, just as he looked with his ruffled hair and undone shirt.

I walked over to him and kissed him on the cheek. I didn't very much like the smell of him, something chemical and sterile that burned my nostrils. This was the first time the house hadn't smelled of my mother. I needed to spritz her perfume and then buy another ten bottles.

"Hello, Virginia," said Arthur after the kiss. "I hadn't expected you to be out."

"I hadn't expected you to be home so early," I said, removing my cloak. "I thought John McCarthy would be keeping you late."

"He was trying."

I hung up my cloak and turned to him, careful of how the contents in my pockets shifted. "I know how important work is to you."

He took my hand. "You are also important to me, Virginia."

Butterflies exploded in my stomach. I didn't know how many times he would have to say such romantic things before my body would finally calm. It was when he spoke, declaring things I didn't think possible for a man, that I fell in love with him again. When Arthur spoke so close to me, holding me on his body with his hot breath upon my exposed skin, I could barely think. I needed to keep my wits. I was protecting him.

"Where have you been?" he asked, wearing the smile that hadn't dimmed since I kissed him.

"I was out," I said, still trying to find my lie. "I was looking at new fabric. I was thinking about new rugs to spruce up the house. I hope that's all right."

"Of course, it is," he said, eyeing our surroundings.

I could tell that he was trying to understand, but his mind didn't work like that. Numbers, yes, but creativity?

He added, "I believe in your vision, but what of hiring renovators?"

My smile faltered.

"I'm inquiring," I said. "What would you like for supper?"

"I was thinking we could go out," he said to my back.

I halted before the ascending steps.

He continued, "You said you wished to go for a walk. I realize you already have, and I walked home, but I think it would be nice for the two of us."

I gripped the banister, fighting with what I needed to do—Mabel's words rattling in my skull—and how I needed to be a good wife. I *wanted* to be a good wife.

"Virginia?" he prompted. Hope leaked into his voice.

Once I cleansed the house and removed Ethel for good, I would have time to rest, and we would be back on a trajectory filled with love and a family. With so many things to worry about, he was leaving work early for me, so I needed to do this for him.

"Let me freshen up." I climbed the steps, ignoring how my body smarted.

I wouldn't have the time to work, not with him home, and as much as tiredness weighed on my bones, I knew it would be fruitless to lay down and try to sleep. I had survived the last three days without much sleep, so I could survive longer, even if my heart felt like it would explode from my chest like a cannon upon a ship.

Fishing the contents from my pockets, I threw them into the bottom drawer with my undergarments, knowing Arthur wouldn't look, and then stripped off the sweat-laden dress. The fabric was so tight it was like peeling off a second skin.

When I turned to the mirror and saw how disgusting I was, tears swelled. I barely recognized the reflected creature with stringy hair and sullen cheeks, dark bags hanging under her eyes. How could Arthur love a beastly thing like me? It was a wonder that he came home at all. Why would he want to go into public with me?

"Are you ready, Virginia?" called Arthur.

I pushed away from the vanity and grabbed the first nice dress I found in the wardrobe. Only as I was walking downstairs did I realize I'd picked a spring, not winter, dress. The colors were all wrong. If Arthur noticed, he didn't show it, standing at the door for me, his jacket already on and arm extended. I put on my cloak.

Arthur led me toward the harbor, the smell of damp and fish hanging in the air. Just when I thought he would take me into the slums near the factories and apartments brimming with people, he dragged me left. We followed along the river cutting through Boston alongside the others out strolling as the sun set. Shadows from the buildings crawled across the cobblestone roads, bringing a further chill.

While Arthur breathed warmth, goose bumps covered my skin. I pulled against him tighter but still the cold swept through my winter cloak and thin dress.

"Oh, Virginia," cooed Arthur. "You're shivering. Why didn't you tell me you were cold?"

I would've had to admit to many things I wasn't telling him if I unlatched my jaw and allowed my teeth to chatter.

"You're pale as snow," he said, removing my clutch on him.

I nearly growled like a dog not wanting to be moved from beside the fire. I wanted to grab him, sinking in my nails like they were claws. He peeled off his jacket.

"Take my coat," he said, already draping it around my shoulders.

"Then you'll be cold," I said.

"I am quite fine."

"You'll get cold."

"Don't worry about it."

"I will worry about it."

"Like I am worried about you." He tightened the jacket on my shoulders, but his were far broader than mine. "I dare say you are fashionable."

My cheeks warmed. "You really know how to make me feel wonderful."

"That is my hope." He slid my hand into the crook of his elbow. "Shall we continue, or are you too cold?"

"I'm fine," I said, propelling the words out of my mouth and keeping him on the path beside the river.

The cold cleared my mind, and I focused on survival—one step in front of the other. I took a deep whiff of Arthur's natural musk; it was much better than the fishy scent.

Tilting his head to the water, Arthur grinned, and I tried to look for whatever he saw. In the end, I smiled because he did. Boston lights fluttered in the waves. Foam bubbled on the surface, collecting near the stone built as a wall. When a heavy wave rushed through, the sea flashed up the sides and ran on the sidewalk. It doused on the hem of my dress.

We stood there, night descending, and I wondered how I could get Arthur home, undressed and in bed, my body pressed into his. But I felt the gaze on me and glanced over my shoulder to see the crowd huddled together, moving quickly against the night. Everyone wanted to get inside... except us.

Arthur pulled me along. White fog clouded his face.

"Let's go home," I said. "Let me warm you."

I knew exactly how I would rock my body against his, our skin turning slick with sweat. He could be on me, laying me flat on the bed...or tonight,

I could be on top of him, riding him. I would show him just how well I was.

"Perhaps we should eat," he said. "There are many restaurants."

Many of those restaurants served fish.

I locked my hands on his waist, holding him close, and he stilled. His eyes darted skittishly about, as though he were a cornered animal. I wondered what would happen if I kissed him openly right now. Would men chase after us with raised fists as they had when I kissed Ethel on the cheek?

"Take me home," I said to Arthur.

Red splotches bloomed on his exposed skin. "That's very forward of you."

I tried not to grimace, unsure where I had gone wrong. He liked it before when I had spoken openly about mystics, but when faced with the opportunity of love, he was stunted. I thought a man would've thrown me over his shoulder and taken me home momentarily, but he studied me like I was a specimen for a textbook.

Silver moonlight glinted in his eyes, bringing out a startling blue that reminded me of ice. Darkness overtook his eyelashes, rounding his eyelids. His pupils grew large enough to take up his face. The longer he stared at me, the more he scratched at my soul. It hurt.

I stumbled back, pushing out of his hands. Arthur rocked on his heels. He didn't reach for me.

The space between us was growing, and I wanted to take a step back...and then another. I would run all the way home, but then he would come too. Of course, he would; he was my husband; it was his home.

His home, Ginny.

His house.

"Virginia?" he asked. "Are you all right?"

"Yes," I said from gut reaction alone. "Shall we go home?"

"You're not hungry?"

"I can make you dinner when we get home."

"I can also make supper. Tell me what is wrong, Virginia."

"Nothing is wrong."

"Why are you acting as such?"

"I am not acting in such way."

He thinned his lips together. His eyes flashed, a transformation of an angry lightning strike and then the immediate downpour of rain, gray and heavy. It dragged down my emotional high, and I was shivering again. I wrapped my arms around my body like they were a shield.

Arthur was slow to fall asleep, lying with his body twisted toward me. He blinked his eyelids like they were bricks, forcing them open. His blue eyes pointed at me, glistening in the orange hearth light. He was a child, fighting tiredness, whereas I couldn't find it—wouldn't find it with Mabel's orders swirling through my mind. I waited for Arthur to sleep.

As hard as he fought it, he finally succumbed.

I waited a moment, each second punctuated by the bang of my heartbeat and the thud against the floor.

Thump.

Thump.

Thump thump thump.

Ethel was out again, creeping toward me.

Swinging my legs off the bed, I glanced over my shoulder at the slumbering Arthur. Someday, our children would also try to stay awake for the promise of a new year. Their little noses would scrunch, and they would fight their yawns. They would sleep just as peacefully as Arthur did. I would too after I rid myself of Ethel.

I tiptoed to the dresser, grabbed what I needed from the bottom drawer, and left the room silently.

Ethel's knocking grew louder as I entered the hallway. I followed the sound all the way into the sitting room. Ethel wasn't lingering openly, but she was in the corner of my eye. When I turned, reaching to catch her, she sprinted away. In the end, she wouldn't face me.

Because Ethel and I were connected through a loving guise, what I intended to do now was the hardest thing I'd done in my short life. Mabel had even given me herbs that Ethel herself had used to heal others.

As I ripped up the floorboards, the rancid stench slapped me in the face, and my hand dropped, the butcher knife clamoring to the floor. The rest of me slumped, sliding into the dirt and salt pit that surrounded the molding rug and husks of dead maggots. I didn't know how long the salt would last, but assuming the sea didn't overtake Boston or the sky didn't rain for months on end, I would be safe. For now.

"I am sorry, Ethel," I said, retrieving the fallen knife. "I'm sorry I did this, letting my love consume us—me. What I did was wrong, and I shall live with it for the rest of my life. You will not be forgotten."

I didn't know if I intended the words for her or myself. They flew from me freely, though I didn't know if she was listening.

"It is time," I continued, "for us both to be free."

Ethel said nothing, but I felt her presence behind me like a cold breeze, nipping at my exposed skin. The draft blew up my nightgown, which was already dirty from the floorboards and muck, and wrapped its cold claws around my legs, shifting my thighs apart. It blew higher. A shiver ran up my spine.

Ethel was here, even if she pretended not to be, but this was the end of her.

The end of us.

I peeled back the layer of rug and tried not to gasp at Ethel's grotesqueness. Death hadn't been kind to her, if it could be kind to anyone. Her body was now frozen in its half-bloated state. Bones that hadn't been eaten away like her flesh bulged from her skin. Her eyes lacked light, pupils narrowed, and color lost. She was not the woman I once knew.

"I'm sorry," I repeated and then launched the knife into her chest.

Her skin and bone opened with a sickening crack. Where there might've been the spurt of blood or the flow of organs, the only thing that came was more polluted stench. I tucked my nose into my hair and took a deep breath, hoping to calm my churning stomach.

When I could finally see through the haze and bile, I sliced the knife further into Ethel, wrenching her open piece by piece. Her body gave more than I thought it would or what it once had. The fight had left with her soul, but it was the shell that was the hardest. Her bones weren't malleable, and I had to use all my force—sweat dripping from my hair line and under my armpits—to dig a big enough hole for me to squeeze my hand inside.

Cold skin and bones flayed, I reached my fingers further back, kicking away veins and muscles to reach her heart. Something she once gave me so openly, and I had gifted her mine in return.

We had been in love, sharing each other's minds and bodies, tasting one another. We had offered everything of ourselves, intertwining until we were a singular person. Then we broke apart, severed by anger and pain. If there was a way to put to rest what once was us, it was this.

I pulled Ethel's heart from her chest. It released its hold with a wet squelch.

The thumping ceased.

Silver moonlight illuminated the brown glob. I was sure the muscle was supposed to have a discernable shape. I'd read newspapers and scientific textbooks about what the heart did and how it looked, but holding one in my hand... It was not what I expected.

In the silence, I scrambled from the sitting room. Her heart was heavier than I'd predicted, messier too. The brown goop splashed my nightgown. I ignored how the fabric caught on the heart like how Ethel's limbs used to entwine with mine. The heaviness made me drop my hand as I stomped into the kitchen, grappling for the oven and the fire inside, but I stopped at the last moment.

I couldn't have Ethel in the house—I needed to extinguish her. If I did it in the oven, she would stay in the kitchen, where she had been most comfortable in my home. I flung open the back door and stumbled into the night, meeting the small mossy area behind the house.

A dying tree hung in the corner, the branches brittle, and leaves covered the ground, damp and moldy. An old stone bench—the one my mother used when the weather had been nice—sat on the uneven ground. It caved in slowly, eroding into dust.

Leaves clawed at my foot, which sunk into the muck. I tried to kick away, but a tree root snaked out, tripping me. Consequently, my fingers ripped into Ethel's organ, macerating it. The deformed heart oozed.

Laying Ethel's heart on the stone bench, the moss fuzzy under my fingertips, I ran into the kitchen and grabbed a newspaper and matches. When I returned to the night, determination hardening my resolve, I was swept into the windy memories of Ethel and I in the small yard hidden behind the house, the stone walls acting as a barrier to keep out the world. It didn't quiet our laughter and shuddering screams. It didn't protect from others peeping. Now I saw the walls for what they were: a cage. I was setting Ethel free by doing this.

"I'm sorry," I whispered to the organ as if it were still connected to her body.

I wrapped her heart in the newspaper and then struck a match. The immediate flame burned orange, the heat grazing my fingers. I dropped the match onto the newspaper, which caught as if I had poured whiskey on the flames.

Orange clawed toward the sky, and I backed away before it singed my hair. Smokey tendrils escaped into the dark night. Clouds rolled across the sky, blotting out the moon and stars, though they felt impossible to see on the clearest Boston night.

The flames ate the wispy newspaper and the crusted heart, releasing the rancid scent of old meat and burned skin. I pressed my hand to my mouth. The fire burped embers that fluttered to the ground like discolored snowflakes. The ash collected on the leaves.

This was the least I could do, releasing Ethel, setting her and I free.

As the smoke flowed in the sky, swept up in the wind, I tilted my head back to watch it disappear, imagining Heaven finally taking Ethel home.

From this moment forth, I would be a good woman. I would be an obedient wife and a dutiful mother. I would go to church on Sunday without delay. I would give to the poor. I would not listen to the scurrilous gossip of society but rather bring them into the grace of God. I would make up for my past.

I glanced up at the house, Arthur sleeping inside, and while he wasn't with me now, I gave him my prayers too. I gave him everything, my vow when I became his wife. It was not just my earthly possessions or my body, but it was my love. With Ethel gone, it would truly be all his.

"Farewell, Ethel," I said.

When I returned inside, the house was silent, so I put it back together as though it were pieces of a smashed vase. Some were easier to fit than others, but they all slid into place eventually.

Leaving my nightgown to soak, I climbed into bed with Arthur, snaking my arms around him and pulling him close, silently announcing us as husband and wife.

 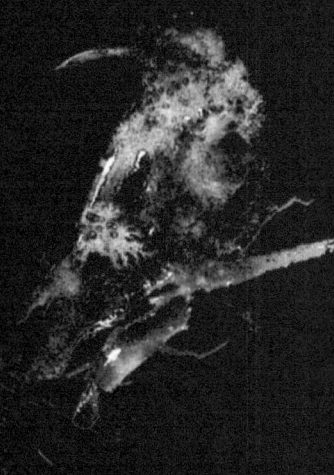

Twenty

When I awoke in the morning, pulling myself from the depths of a hard and dreamless sleep, I was refreshed. And being watched.

Arthur lingered on the far side of the bed, his head propped on his palm.

"Good morning," I said through an escaping yawn.

For a long few seconds, he said nothing.

The waiting lay heavily on my chest, so I forced myself into a seated position. My body ached, and the bed groaned.

"Good morning," whispered Arthur.

It was such a small voice, like he was scared to break the spell. I didn't blame him.

The last few days had been too much, but today was a new day. My past was officially behind us. From now on, we would build our future.

I leaned close to him, and we huddled under the blankets. His nightgown had risen in the night, and the scruffy hair on his legs tickled my skin. I tried not to wiggle away when I was desperate to be closer to him. I had wanted him last night, but that had been...

It wouldn't be that way any longer, Ginny.

Focusing on Arthur's gaze again, I said, "You're very peaceful when you sleep."

A smile crossed his face. "Is that your way of saying I'm not peaceful when I'm awake?"

"Not at all." I crept closer to him until his warm breath was on my skin.

"Did you sleep well?" he asked.

"Very much so. I was tired."

"I know." He brushed his thumb across my cheek. "You should spend the whole day in bed."

"I cannot."

"Virginia—"

"Nor do I need to," I interrupted. "I'm quite fine. Better than fine."

Before he could say another word, I pressed my lips to his to both say good morning and provide evidence that I'd rested well. Wrapping my arms around his neck, I brought myself closer, my perked nipples grazing him through his cotton nightgown. I wished to rip it from his body and press myself to him, tangling more than our limbs and tongues.

I parted his lips and drove my tongue into his mouth. He moaned, and I swallowed it. The sound radiated in my chest.

He broke the kiss, shattering my heart in the process. "Virginia, we don't need to—"

"You don't wish to?" I asked, trying not to shrink.

I never needed to beg for sex with Ethel.

Don't, Ginny.

I was only thinking about Arthur, giving him every speck of my love, injecting it into him and letting it grow between us. Come spring, we would have a garden.

"It is not that." Arthur traveled his hands up my arms, his gaze lingering on my breasts.

He nibbled on his bottom lip, and I waited for him to take one of my nipples in his mouth. I arched my chest, bringing my breasts closer, and his hot breath licked my skin. A shiver ran across me, and I tried not to quake. I had done too much of that recently; he needed to see how strong I was.

"It is not that," he repeated, his voice holding a dreamy tone. "I only want to ensure you are all right."

"Of course I am." I kissed him deeply. "Thank you for caring so much about me."

"It is what a husband should do," he said between the kisses, handing himself over to me.

"You are special in that way," I said. "Not many husbands would."

"They are fools. They are scum."

I tried not to laugh. "I like the passion in your voice."

A mysterious gleam took over his face, reminding me of a mischievous child about to steal a sweet. That gleam spread his lips into a grin, and then he was on me, his teeth leading the charge to nip at the soft part of my neck.

Hiking up his nightgown, I found his growing cock. I brushed my finger against it and felt it jerked. As I kissed Arthur, I dragged myself across him, and his body answered. Arthur was silent, not a moan or a gasp of my name, so I slipped him into me.

"Virginia," he hissed, his cheeks puffing out like he was already close to the edge.

He was so pent up, needing to be released, and I would release him. I clenched and unclenched around him, feeling how his body tightened under me. I milked him for my own pleasure too. It was building, albeit slower than his. I rocked on him as I so wished, moving at an increasing speed as I tried to reach the edge.

Arthur called out, jerking. His seed spurted inside me. My nether lips swallowed.

"I need to go to work," breathed Arthur, sliding me off him. "I'll need to wash before I leave."

He stumbled out of bed like a baby deer learning to walk. "You, Virginia…you should rest today."

I didn't need to, though I didn't say it. If it gave him the confidence to go about his business, I would keep my mouth shut because I, too, had work.

When Arthur arrived home early again, I had the house cleaned and everything settled. The house was in better shape than when Arthur had first moved in, though he hadn't much to bring. Arthur stopped in the front entryway, his mouth agape and eyes wide, and I smiled down at him from the top of the stairs, wearing a nice dress, one that was fit for winter.

"Virginia," he said on an exhale. "I don't know what to say."

"You don't need to say anything," I replied.

I walked down the steps. My shoulders pulled back, and I stood taller. I felt taller now that the weight of Ethel's haunting had ceased.

"I hope you don't mind," I continued, "but I also put out an ad for a housekeeper. I hope she'll bring recommendations for other staff."

Light twinkled in Arthur's eyes. "That is wonderful. I don't mind at all. I hope you didn't do all this today."

He motioned to the house; I knew how it glowed, the floor mopped, and the hand railings polished. The whole house smelled clean, fresh from flowers I had bought. I had opened the windows and aired out the stenches, and then I scrubbed the floors and walls that needed it the most. I'd wanted to spritz my mother's perfume like I had done many times before but then decided to leave that in the past, letting my mother's ghost be free of the house too.

I couldn't say how long I had left the windows open. The house had turned frigid, barely warmed by the hazy Boston sun coming in at a slant. But the sickness had been extinguished.

"It was nothing," I dismissed, answering Arthur's unspoken question. "Quite easy."

His brow creased, worry etching his face. I had rested, like he had told me to do, but I hadn't needed to, not that he would understand. He was a caring man, so concerned about my health. I was overjoyed to have a man such as him, but I was fine.

I kissed his cheek. "I was hoping you might be interested in a night out."

He dragged his gaze down my body like this was the first time noticing my dress. What a man. He hadn't noticed how I'd washed my hair and styled it, then added rouge on my cheeks and charcoal around my eyes. To top it off, I laid my mother's finest jewelry around my neck. It glittered in the candlelight.

"You look wonderful," he said.

I was sure I blushed redder than any rouge. "Thank you."

Then he startled, blinking rapidly like he was trying to clear away my beauty and see the root of the problem. There was none. I could've been a cloud flying through the sky. It was only my heavy dress that kept me weighed to the floor.

"You wish to go out?" asked Arthur.

"We were invited to a party," I said, grabbing the invitation from the front table. "It was sent with a note from Mrs. Cox that she expected us to be on our bridal tour, and since we are not, we should attend."

I hadn't written to Mrs. Cox to say we were coming, but my mind had been scattered and today seemed too late. She wouldn't mind—much—if we stopped by. Mrs. Cox always planned for unexpected guests, so she could flutter through the crowds with ease. She was a woman who ran Boston's society and had done so for years; nothing could surprise her.

Arthur stared at the note in his hand. "Are you sure you wish to attend?"

Stop questioning me.

I bit my tongue so hard that it started to bleed. "I'm already dressed."

The metallic tang slithered down my throat, and my smile wavered.

For another moment that felt like a lifetime, he studied the invitation as if it held an encoded message. He slid his thumb over the embossed cursive. With his eyebrows drawn together, he continued to form an indent in his forehead, cutting his face in half from the man I knew and the man I had yet to know.

My mind swirled, casting down into the shadows to say that this was all a mistake and perhaps I had married a man who didn't love me.

Stop it, Ginny.

It was because of how much he cared for me and how I had been acting that he didn't wish for us to go to the party. Or…was it because he didn't wish to see me in public after how I had acted?

I had disappointed him, embarrassed him, alienated him, and he now wished to only be known as husband and wife inside these house walls.

"Or we could not attend," I said, grabbing for the invitation.

He ripped it away from me. "I didn't say that."

I bit the inside of my cheek, blood flooding my mouth, and gulped it down. The pain was softer than I thought it would be, but perhaps I had bitten there enough times—by accident and on purpose—that it mattered little. I had nothing left to feel. It was a wonder with my past that I could feel anything at all. I was better left as a shell of a woman, wasting and waiting for the next illness to sweep through Boston.

Arthur raised his gaze from the invitation, studying me openly now, and I swallowed the last remnants of blood and brushed my tongue across my teeth. Even then, I ducked my head, keeping my mouth firmly pointed away from him before speaking.

"You do not wish to go," I said.

"I didn't say that," he repeated.

"You do not seem pleased."

"It is not that."

"Then tell me, Arthur. I'm not sure what I did wrong."

It was breaking my heart.

"You didn't do anything wrong. I only want to ensure you are up for this task," he said, waving the invitation in front of me. "You have said in the past that these things are…taxing."

I smiled sadly. "You've been listening to me."

"Of course I have, Virginia. How could you think otherwise?"

"It is because you are so special."

His cheeks pinked. "Don't flatter me."

"I don't say it to flatter you." I stepped closer to him. "Thank you for being concerned and caring for me, but I am fine. I want to go to this party. I have already set out a suit for you to wear; you'll have a tie that matches my dress. I bought it today when I went shopping."

He smiled, and ease rolled back his shoulders. "You think of everything."

"Now who is trying to flatter?" I jested, giggling.

Fluttering his eyes shut, he kissed my forehead and then lingered there for a few seconds. I leaned against his chest, allowing my heartbeat to match his own. We became tandem drums.

When he pulled away from me, he declared, "I'll change, and *we'll* go."

A genuine smile pulled across my face. "I shall call for a cab."

"Someone is very excited," he said.

"I am." I walked toward the door.

Twenty-One

Arthur held out his hand for me to step out of the cab, the cobblestone slick with a snow that had started on our ride to the Cox residence. I slid my hand into his palm and lifted my dress, meeting the cobblestone as softly as I could. Arthur paid the driver as I huddled under the awning. The Cox servants offered an umbrella to keep the snow off my face; unfortunately, my dress was caught in the moisture.

After he paid, Arthur ducked his head and offered me his arm, which I took, and we entered the residence together. We met another row of servants, who took Arthur's hat and jacket and my cloak. Then we were released into the throes of the party.

A lone celloist played something somber, and other partygoers wore their best winter dresses, sipping dark red wine that reminded me of blood. A mixture of holly green and brown moved throughout the space, and a flash of red irritated my eyes. Pale faces shot quick glances our way, but they slid past us. We were not noticed, and I could not say whether that was what I wished or if I hated the invisibility.

"Would you like a glass of wine, Virginia?" asked Arthur.

"Yes, please," I said.

He led me toward the table that had the glasses already poured and small bites of food. Dark meat peeked from thin slices of brown bread, slathered in butter and cranberry sauce. It was demure compared to the meals that Mrs. Cox was known to have, but this was only a small gathering of like-minded people.

A herd of women giggled and left a table at the far end of the room, and I recognized the mystic from the night Arthur and I had first met, not that I could recall his name. He was slipping money into his pocket after being handsomely paid for whatever fabricated service he just provided.

Arthur frowned, and I tightened my grip on his elbow. He was tense like a man about to go into battle, but the mystic was no match for Arthur and his superior mind.

"Let them have their fun," I murmured. "You don't need to partake in the foolishness."

He peeked at me from the corner of his eye, growing a smile. "You are so intelligent. So empathetic. So—"

"Stop it." I dipped my head. "Or we'll have to leave, so I may show you just how *empathetic* I am at home."

Red brushed Arthur's cheeks.

An excited thrill ran through me; I liked seeing him like this, having this power over him. It had been a while—in comparison to how long we had been married—since he looked at me with such...primal hunger. I hadn't wielded the power successfully, but now, I would use the pointed edge of the sword.

"Do not tempt me, Virginia." A small growl leveled his tone.

"Or what, my love?" I asked, edging closer.

Arthur dropped his smile. "Or—"

"Oh, good, Mr. Hunt, Mrs. Hunt, you could join us," declared Mrs. Cox loudly, forcing Arthur and I apart.

She used a cane to hobble toward us. A servant scurried after her while women crowded around Mrs. Cox like she was a priest giving sermon. She waved them all off and then extended her hand, which Arthur promptly took and pressed a kiss to her bulging knuckles.

"Mrs. Cox," said Arthur in a polite tone, "thank you for inviting us."

"I am happy you could come." She took her hand back.

Arthur straightened, allowing me to hold him again. He was my buoy.

Mrs. Cox was looking at me expectantly, and I hoped the heat didn't show on my face as much as I felt it.

"Apologies for the no reply. We have been…" My jaw dropped open as my mind struggled to fill the void.

"Oh, it's quite all right," Mrs. Cox dismissed. "I remember what it was like to be a young married couple. So many things to explore, so much to…conquer."

That was, of course, a simple way of stating it.

"Thank you for extending the invitation," I continued, "and allowing us into your lovely home."

Mrs. Cox broadened her smile, revealing her brown teeth. "You're too kind, Mrs. Hunt."

"I often tell her such," interrupted Arthur.

"Yes, Mr. Hunt"—she swung her attention to him—"how is your business coming along? My husband recently gave a summary, though I wish to have something more tangible. Would you have time tonight to speak to me about it in length?"

Arthur glanced toward me, and I tapped his elbow, so he answered, "Of course, Mrs. Cox. Whenever best works for you."

"Then now! I hate to drag you away from your doting wife, but the longer the party and more wine I have, the less my mind works." She chuckled. "This way. I have a private table."

Arthur had his arm on me like he meant to bring me along, but I slipped from his grasp, bidding him a fun time with Mrs. Cox and his adventures in his field. While I liked his passion, I couldn't say that I much cared for the business of it, and he would surely be giving a dull report to Mrs. Cox. He kissed me on the cheek and then followed Mrs. Cox to a table near the hearth, where the two of them seemingly set to business.

With a glass of wine in hand, I strolled through the room, gliding as if the cello's musical notes seized me. I wandered between the clumps of women and men, only some glancing over their shoulders and sneering. I tried not to return the vicious look because I was floating, held up by love, and all was right in the world. Their rumors tried to pop the bubble around me. Arthur, as my husband, offered the protection I needed against their foulness.

"Care for a fortune?" asked the mystic, reclining in his seat.

A propped-up sign leaning against a shawl-covered table said the Marvelous Auguste answered my earlier question. Candlelight danced over the gold thread on the purple silk, matching the mystic's jacket. He played with a deck of cards, though I didn't recognize the painted symbols or haunted faces.

Locking my jaw, I faced him. I had been too deep in my own head to realize how close I had gotten to the fraud.

"No," I answered him.

"Then to speak to a loved one who has passed?" he supplied.

"I don't speak to ghosts." The words fell from my mouth before I could think, and I looked over my shoulder like someone might've noticed.

"The spirits don't like to be called that." His tone was just as serious, offering a small warning like he was speaking to a child. "It upsets them."

"What do they have to be upset about?" I snapped, trying not to think of Ethel.

Blocking her from my mind had worked all day.

He uncrossed his legs and leaned forward, resting his elbows on the table. I dug my heels into the floor to not step back as he practically crawled toward me.

"They wish to have their voices heard," he hissed, "their final words said, to linger for the truth. They know more than you think. They stayed because they needed to be heard. All those things they didn't say and all the things they know."

"I have no need for that." I was a Godly woman and wouldn't peddle in ghosts.

He picked up his stack of cards. "Then you are not a believer?"

"I am healed."

"There is no such thing, Miss Jones."

I stumbled back a step. "How do you know who I am?"

"Who doesn't know who you are?" He shuffled the cards and then splayed them across the table.

Only then did he raise his gaze, cocking an eyebrow in challenge.

This mystic peddled in what could be read in gossip pamphlets and then read it back to society as fact, holding out his hand for exorbitant funds. I wouldn't play his game, so I stepped away from his table.

"I've missed my friend Ethel," he said in a small voice.

I cleared my throat. "You were friends?"

Ethel had never mentioned him, but she never mentioned many from her past life.

"People like us fall into the same circles. We've visited many times on trips up to Salem and back to Boston. I know the kind of work she was doing in the city. I know that she was *healing* you." He threw the word at me with malice.

My heartbeat thundered, roaring past my ears. I all but stumbled forward to catch myself on the table before I fell.

Steady, Ginny. He doesn't know.

He couldn't.

"No one has seen her," he continued. "Including her customers. She wouldn't leave them."

She had, though, for me. Many times. She had ignored her duties as an herbalist as I had ignored my duties to polite society. We chose each other and our bodily urges repeatedly. I had never been so happy.

Auguste asked, "Why was she coming to you, Miss Jones? Why not use a physician?"

"That's none of your business," I said.

"When was the last time you saw her?"

"What are you, a watchman?"

"Should I call for them?"

I forced a scoff, even as my body trembled, my organs liquefying and threatening to slide from me. "For what? Because a sham cutwitch sold me some herbs to rest."

I only gave what he probably already knew, the rumors slinking through Boston's bowels from beggars' mouths.

Suddenly, he stood, towering over his table. "I know she was with you."

"Because of rumors?" I pushed.

"Not just rumors," he said, though his gaze turned elsewhere.

For all the cards he could deal, he was no player of the game. I saw through his lie.

"Only rumors," I lied and walked away from him before his next taunting mumble could strike me.

I forced my strides to lengthen and rolled my shoulders back. I wouldn't bow to a man like him. Mabel's wonders had worked: Ethel was gone and I free. That was far more than the peddling crook mystic could do. Nothing he could say would bring the watchmen to my door, not for a delinquent like him. They would laugh him away, just as I should.

"Mrs. Hunt," said another voice.

I was a fly caught in a spider's web, the strings tightening around my throat until I couldn't breathe. I had to stop fighting if I wished to survive.

"Mrs. Clark, Miss Clark," I greeted, trying not to grimace at Agatha before facing Mrs. Clark, the woman like a wolf when she smelled blood.

How much had they heard? I tensed so I wouldn't glance back at the mystic, whose eyes peeled my skin away and dug toward my soul. He would find no answers there.

"I didn't realize you would be joining us tonight," said Mrs. Clark.

"Mrs. Cox extended the invitation," I said, hoping the matriarch of society would be a shield. "Now if you excuse me—"

"Don't go yet," said Mrs. Clark in a commanding motherly tone, leaving me stuck.

How could a woman so cruel have so much power over me?

Mrs. Clark stepped toward me, cutting the two feet of respectable distance in half, our wine glasses nearly clanking. Each breath of hers flowed into my lungs, and I turned my head away from the smoke, a mixture of tobacco and opium. My mind was hazy being so close.

"Yes, Mrs. Clark?" I prompted.

"I'm merely wondering how you are," said the older woman. "We have not had a chance to speak."

Agatha stood at her mother's shoulder, caught between glaring at me and sending a small, polite smile to any unwed man who walked past.

"I'm fine, thank you," I said to Mrs. Clark. "How are you, Miss Clark? Any closer to being married?"

She startled as if she were being coy, instead she seemed like a hungry mut. I knew the look—I had been her—but desperation didn't look well. Whereas Arthur had seen past my desperation, the stench that followed Agatha kept every man away from her. Well, that or her rabid mother. No man would wish to be close to her family, controlled into being the perfect puppet.

I worried for Agatha, truly, until I remembered how she had added to the gossip flames to burn me alive. That empathy could only go so far, and while I had promised God to be a better person, I was still only human.

"Mr. Martin is still unwed," I declared, reminding them and myself of the man I had chased only days ago—an old and plump man with burst veins on his nose and his eyes yellow. "If you are still in the market, Miss Clark. Mrs. Clark."

I turned away.

They were a storm brewing behind me, but I kept my sunny disposition. I inclined my head to Mr. Martin as I passed. I, too, could be a woman of elite. I could play the part and enact the barbs.

"Apologies for keeping him so long," said Mrs. Cox, depositing Arthur at my side.

"No need to apologize," I said, latching on to his extended arm. "I hope it was a productive discussion."

"Yes," said Mrs. Cox, "as well as very enlightening."

"I, too, find myself enlightened by Arthur," I gushed. "He has so much knowledge. We are lucky enough for him to share it with us."

"Perhaps he should give a talk to us sometime," said Mrs. Cox.

"It would be my honor," he said.

I squeezed his arm, already excited. "We should do it when everyone is back in Boston. We are missing society members from the holidays. I don't see Mrs. White."

"Which White do you speak of? There are many Whites in Boston." Mrs. Cox leaned toward us like she meant to share a joke. "It's the Catholics, you know. So many of them. However, you can't fault them for wanting such large families. It brings joy."

"I grew up with brothers," said Arthur. "I understand. Virginia had no siblings, so we look forward to a full house."

Mrs. Cox raised her eyebrows. My cheeks burned from speaking about this so openly.

Isn't this what you wanted, Ginny?

Yes, it was what I wanted. The marriage, the future children, my place amongst society. I blinked quickly to remove any lingering confusion.

"Then what are you doing at my party? You two should be... *familiarizing* yourselves further." Mrs. Cox waved her hands like she was shooing us away. "Enjoy the party, but enjoy each other more."

That gleam in her eye was like a beacon in the night, pointed toward us so everyone could see. It burned long after Mrs. Cox had found someone else to speak to. I had never thought to hear Mrs. Cox speak as such—nor did I want to hear it again—and wondered how many other women would speak of such.

Forcing a smile, I thrummed my fingers on the crook of Arthur's elbow. "Is there anything else you wish to do here?"

Arthur furrowed his eyebrows. "You want to leave already?"

"I'm only listening to Mrs. Cox."

He cleared his throat. "I was considering speaking to the mystic."

Please don't, I wanted to beg but resigned myself to asking, "Must you?"

He dragged his gaze down my body, eyeing me like a man not having drunk water in days. I brushed my hip against him, feeling the bulge in his trousers. His body gave a small jerk. He pointed his nose toward the exit.

I breathed a long sigh of relief, but he had to speak because we could not just leave without a round of goodbyes, where I must repeat the same lines: "Oh, yes, we're very busy at home" and "Yes, we're putting the house together" and "Yes, Arthur has had a long day; we must go."

Afterward, I towed Arthur out of the gathering, finding a cab waiting to take people away. We hopped in, gave our address, and waited for the carriage to take off before I kissed Arthur.

He grabbed my shoulders, pushing me back into the seat. "Wait until home."

The cab bumped under us, rolling over the ragged cobblestones. The winter chill slipped inside, wrapping a hand around my neck. It crept down my body, attempting to cool the yawning warmth. I inched closer to Arthur, but he kept to the other side of the cab, his face pointed toward the window, watching Boston pass.

The cab slowed, and the driver announced loudly, "We've arrived!"

Arthur lurched forward like he meant to scramble away from me. He went straight toward the house, and I trailed, stomping every step. He didn't look over his shoulder.

After I slammed the door behind us, I pounced upon him, and in turn, exposing his primality, he pushed me against the wall and hiked up my skirts. My knees were weak; my body grew weaker.

"Your cock," I begged.

I wanted a child.

"The bedroom." He put his hands on my shoulders and pushed me back. "We're not animals."

I growled, "Yes, husband."

In our bedroom, he laid me on the bed and brought up my skirts. I opened my thighs. He guided himself in, his mouth dangling open. Within a few thrusts, he flooded my womb. I took every last drop, bringing it deeper into my body and waiting for a child to grow.

"I love you." I held him close, listening to his heartbeat.

Twenty-Two

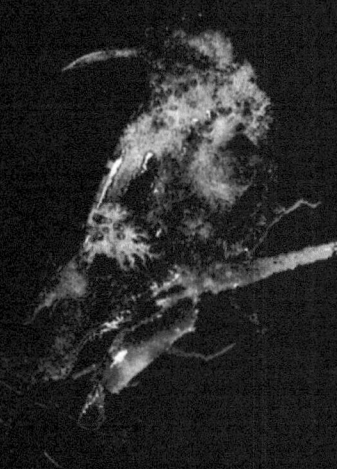

December 26, 1842

"Have you cooked before?" asked Ethel, peering over my shoulder as I chopped vegetables.

While I knew she didn't mean it with malice, the words still struck my breastbone.

"I make stew all the time," I replied, rolling back my shoulders.

"Stew is not the same," she said, shifting to my other side.

"Your question was if I've ever cooked, and I have."

"Then let me rephrase: have you cooked something other than stew?"

"I've made and baked bread."

"A meal?"

"No." I stopped my chopping to face her, placing my hands on my hips.

Eyebrows raised, Ethel wore an amused smile. I wanted to be angry at her but couldn't. Her smiles were rare.

"Can you prepare supper better?" I asked.

I had said that I would cook tonight instead of buying a meal, but I could see now that I had been unprepared.

"I have suggestions," said Ethel, widening her grin. She took my hands in her own, the carrot grime rubbing on her fingers. "Oh, Virginia, don't frown like that. You cannot help it. You are just not used to this."

"I wanted to do this for you," I said.

"I know."

"You already cook so much for us."

"I'm well practiced. It is a wonder you've managed to get this far."

I scoffed. "I'm not daft."

"I never said you were."

"You implied it."

"I implied that you are fortunate and didn't need to learn certain things that others would," said Ethel, "which is why I'm surprised—no, *impressed* you've made it this far."

"I thought you liked my stews," I accused.

"I do. But they remind me of my herb making."

"Don't you just usually pick them and bag them?" I asked.

She thinned her lips into a deep frown.

"Sometimes you also dry them," I added, fearful that I was about to be laughed at.

I was a sponge absorbing everything she said, but she didn't speak about her process of being an herbalist. Everything was locked in her mind.

"I will also bake them over the fire," said Ethel, turning to the kitchen counter to make supper for us. "Sometimes, I can only use parts of the herbs, depending on the remedy and type of plant, so I have to carve them, dice them, and muddle them if they should need to be a salve. Other times, I will need to brew what others might call potions—"

"Or stews," I interjected.

"In the winter months," she continued like she didn't hear me, "I'll have my head bent over pots, steam in my face and my eyes tearing up."

"From onions?"

"Other things, Virginia. How often do you put your face over a boiling pot of water?"

"I try not to if I can help it. I guess it would only be stew."

"I would also not do it," said Ethel, "but there are remedies that call for broth or the herbs to be boiled down. Depending on the patient or illness, it's necessary that it comes in something one can drink. Not that I recommend it because it seems to weaken the herb's impact."

She moved around my kitchen with grace, understanding where things were located whereas it had taken me weeks to find where the servants had put things.

"Are you watching or helping?" snapped Ethel.

Heat bloomed on my cheeks. "You do it so well. You work wonders."

She laughed. I ducked my head to the side because the bark of laugh vibrated the kitchen. Everything seemed too loud, and I tried not to grimace at my own foolishness.

"I am not calling you a witch if that's what you think," I said, forcing myself to jest.

She grinned at me, taking the weight off my chest for the moment, giving me the confidence to continue.

"You seem so knowledgeable," I said. "Please don't say you have been forced to learn to cook because of your upbringing. While that may be true, I think you have a natural affinity for this."

Suddenly, she drooped her chin, so focused on her work that she turned her back toward me. I peeked over her shoulder to watch how she cut the meat into long, fine strips like she was a surgeon. How she diced the potatoes made me wonder what else she could do with the knife.

"If only I wasn't a woman," said Ethel finally. "I could be a physician."

"Is being a woman what stops you?" I asked, knowing how naive I sounded.

"If one took gender out of it, there are the funds and the connections that would also cause challenges."

"I could provide those to you. You could have your shop."

"Are you offering me that?"

"If it will make you happy."

She kissed me, shedding the fear that I made her unhappy and how ridiculous I could be, so unknowledgeable compared to her. All I wanted to do was impress her because I loved her.

"Cut these up," she said when she broke our kiss. "I'll need to work more on the meat and bread."

While I didn't move as fast as her, I cut into the vegetables until they were chewable chunks and then slid them into the water, listening to the heavy thuds at the bottom. The vegetables would only boil for a little bit, but if we left them in longer, we could make a wonderful stew.

"Virginia, what is this?" she asked, holding up a stack of letters.

Most of the wax had been torn open, while the rest had collected dust. I should've used those as kindling long ago, but I kept them around like I would one day change my mind. At some point, they had become one with the kitchen, each new letter added to the heap.

"These are invitations to parties," continued Ethel when I didn't answer.

I grimaced. "I do not want to go."

"You must."

I put lard into the boiling pot, taking the moment to hide myself. "Please don't do this, Ethel."

"You haven't told me about these," she said.

"They are not important," I dismissed.

"Yes, they are." She shook the letters at me. "When I am not here, you are lonely. You stay in the house. You have told me so. What of this party? It is for tonight. It said you would still be going."

"I accepted that invitation months ago. Before my parents' deaths. I do not wish to go without you."

"I *wish* you to go without me."

The knife fell from my hand, and I took a deep breath, trying to corral the emotions filling me until I was boiling like water. Ethel waited at my side, saying nothing. Her cheeks flushed with either the heat from the kitchen or blooming anger.

"Please," I said in a small voice, "we are having a nice supper. Can we not bicker?"

"Not when you are purposefully keeping things from me." She threw the letters on the table.

"I did *not* do it purposefully."

The letters had kept coming, faster now, people pushing and prodding me to get back to society functions. I didn't understand why they wanted me. I wasn't interesting or intelligent, and I had no special skills. It had to be a duty to my parents that I was being invited at all.

"I asked you to tell me these things, so I could spend my time otherwise," she said. "I have patients to attend to. Brews to make. I have not been back to Salem in days. There are people who—"

"I do not wish for you to spend your time otherwise," I said, meaning the words.

My time spent without her was…cold, dark, lonely. I waited like a dog at the door for her to arrive, planting kisses on her and jumping into her arms.

"It's what we must do, Virginia," pleaded Ethel.

"Why?" I demanded, throwing down the knife. "Because the world dictates that we do so? It's mad!"

"We belong to this world, the church, the watchmen," she listed in a tender voice that cracked my hard shell.

She crossed the kitchen, taking my arms in her clammy hands. "Anything more than our played parts will lead others to grow suspicious, and then we will both be ruined."

"But—"

"Get ready for the party." She grabbed the knife. "You said you would go, and they obviously want you there. I'll finish supper here."

When she got this way, there was no arguing. Perhaps it was best to be out of the house, so I would let her win this one night. I would be back soon enough.

"Fine," I grumbled.

I desperately wanted to climb back into her arms until we could not be physically parted.

Twenty-Three

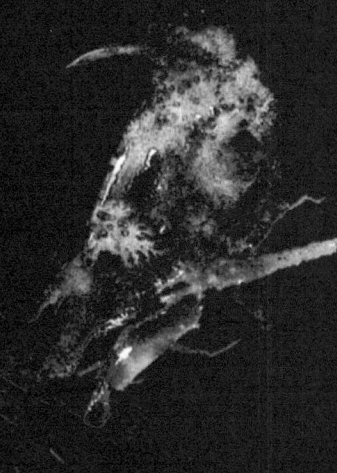

Thump.

Thump.

Thump thump thump.

I slammed my hand to my chest, accompanied by the immediate sting of pain. After lovemaking, I had been hot and gone to sleep nude. It was then that I felt how my stomach grew, skin taut, and I pressed my hands to my belly, imagining our child. His seed would take hold.

Thump.

Thump.

Thump thump thump.

Not my heart beating, no matter how long I laid my hand on the left side of my chest. I forced my breathing to calm because Ethel was gone. Mabel had helped me—I followed her instructions. Didn't I? What if I'd missed a step?

Ginny, you have done it. Yesterday, you were free. You're still free, Ginny.

What I was hearing now was just my own mind whirling, woken from a dream that could've been a nightmare. I tried to brush away the flare of panic.

Arthur radiated heat. His bones were like blades cutting through his skin. This was real, our limbs intertwined and minds in tandem.

Thump.

The heartbeat banged against the floor.

Thump.

How long would it continue?

Thump thump thump.

Peeling off the covers, I tiptoed from the bedroom and followed the pounding.

"Ethel?" I whispered and then cursed myself.

It wasn't her.

Though night was a blanket around me, I was still nude padding down the hallway. I should've returned to bed and snuggled into Arthur, but I knew sleep wouldn't come tonight. I wouldn't rest again until the banging was dealt with.

Reaching the bottom step, I paused. The banging had ceased in the house, but my own rattling heart took up the rhythm. It pounded against my rib cage, straining against my skin. I pressed my hand to my chest. My heart would rip out and thud on the floor.

Thump.

I jumped, placing both hands on the railing to keep myself upright. I was letting my mind get the best of me. There was a reasonable explanation for the banging. Who was calling on us at this time of night?

Thump.

I flew to the front door and whipped it open, practically ripping the wood from the hinges. The gas streetlamps illuminated soft orange that reached toward the sky, gracing the cobblestones just enough to allow people to see a few feet in front of them. This, of course, allowed me to see that no one was on the street.

Thump thump thump.

From across the way, Mrs. White sat in her front window, holding a steaming cup. The hearth was lit behind her, shedding more light onto the street. I took a step forward.

How dare she watch me? How dare she gossip about what happened in this house?

It was her fault that I had been cast from society!

A cold wind whipped down the street, grazing my exposed nipples. Shivering, I sunk into the house and closed the door.

What if someone had seen me? They most likely had. What a fool I was.

Tears sprung into my eyes.

Thump.

It wasn't the door behind me. No one was there.

Thump.

It wasn't this room, not the front entryway.

Thump thump thump.

Pushing off the door, I followed what I knew to be true—no matter if it were real—into the sitting room.

The floorboards rocked from their spots, someone clawing out from underneath.

"Stop," I hissed, wrapping my fingers into my hair.

Why hadn't Mabel's witchcraft worked? She had called it what it was, didn't deny that she was a witch. It was what Ethel had been too.

"You'll never be free of me, Ginny," hissed Ethel.

I spun toward her at the window, standing just behind the curtains, the white wrapping around the frame of her body. Why did she stand where anyone could see her so clearly? Mrs. White would tell everyone that there was a strange nude woman in my house.

"You'll never be free of me, Ginny," repeated Ethel, facing me now. "No matter what you do or where you go. I shall follow you—"

"Don't," I interrupted, balling my hands into fists.

"You think it's just that easy?"

"I have tried to cleanse you from the house."

"The house is not the problem."

"Then what is?" I asked, wondering what else I would have to destroy.

It hurt me more than it could hurt her. Her body wasn't her own any longer, instead latching onto me like a parasite, sinking claws into my flesh and ripping out chunks of me.

"You are," said Ethel.

I gasped. "Me?"

"Yes, Ginny. I follow you. I am you."

I shook my head. "I don't want you here."

Ethel laughed.

At one point in my life, her laughter would've been music to my ears, filling me with everything good in my life. She was my reason for survival, my long days in bed and quick nights filled with passion and love. Now when she laughed, it was like chasm opening beneath my house. I would fall into the depths and lie beside her body forever.

I turned back toward the door, and Ethel barked, "Where are you going?"

"To my husband," I said. "To my love."

"He's just your husband. You shall never love him as you loved me."

I hesitated, fighting back words that wanted to spew from me. It was what Ethel wanted: for us to speak all night as we had done before.

With her on my heels, I returned to my bedroom and climbed in beside Arthur, covering us in blankets like they were a shield. I did it for him more than myself, not allowing his body to be leered at by Ethel in the doorway.

Sun split the curtains, and I stared into the dusty light. Even after Ethel had disappeared into the night, I hadn't fallen asleep, waiting for her to return.

I followed what Mabel had said, but she had been a farce, as Ethel always said magic and witchcraft was. I had failed again, ensuring that neither Ethel nor I would be free. What I had done to rid myself of Ethel was not only for me but for Ethel, to allow her to move on!

A small cry worked out of my mouth unceremoniously, breaking the thin barrier I desperately tried to hold onto, and Arthur blinked awake. While tears wanted to swell in my eyes and everything that had been happening climbed its way up my throat, I only hid my face in the crook of his neck, taking in a deep whiff of his musk.

Arthur released a soft moan. "You're in a good mood this morning."

Lies escaped me. I didn't trust my voice, another cry lingering close to the surface. My limbs felt heavy like boulders. I kissed his soft skin, eliciting another soft moan. That was as much of an answer as I could give in my humble state.

"Oh no!" Arthur whipped his head back. "What time is it? I shall be late for work. I must go."

He rolled away from me, hitting the floor with a thump, and I braced myself. He was scrambling to find clothes, leaving a trail behind of what he didn't need. He found a white shirt and threw it over his head, looking for his deposited trousers.

Something slowed his movements, but I couldn't say it was my nude body stretched across the bed, beckoning his return.

"Did I hurt you last night?" he asked sheepishly.

I gasped. "No, of course not. How could you ask such a thing?"

"Your eyes are puffy, and you look tired. Like you haven't slept a wink—" He rocked back on his heels as if horrified.

This was what I received for marrying a scientist: how he would pick and prod until he saw the truth. He wasn't a normal husband, who overlooked his wife, deciding this was just how women were and leaving us to our woes.

"Virginia, are you…" He gulped. "Virginia, did you sleep well last night?"

"You have work," I reminded him.

"I am asking about you."

"I am fine."

He hesitated, but he and I both knew I would repeat the same lie after my voice had cracked. How many lies would I tell? How far would I drag him into the depths of my despair?

"I should stay home today," he decided.

"Please, Arthur," I begged, "don't on my account."

"I will." He raised his shoulders, lifting his head like he was preparing for a fight, but we were not two unruly drunkards behind a tavern.

I scrambled to find something to push him from the house and let me…

What would I do? Go see Mabel and waste more money and energy? Would I rip up the sitting room floorboards and burn the rest of Ethel's body? Would I screech at the top of my lungs until Ethel was gone, ensuring that someone would call the watchmen on me?

"Shouldn't you tell John you're not coming in?" I asked breathlessly.

"Let me worry about that," he said.

"There should be no worry. You should go to work."

"I will not." He sunk to the edge of the bed, resting his hand on my own. "I don't know what is happening, Virginia. You have not spoken about it with me—"

"You don't need to worry about it," I said. "I'm handling it."

"Damn that! I am your husband. You're not acting like the woman I know."

I pursed my lips, clenching my teeth to hold back that he didn't know me. Before we married, we spoke a few times and were watched by others who warned him away. He chose me over the gossip, and he was now living with the consequences of me latching myself to him like a leech. I would suck him dry.

"I have a right to be worried." His tone pitched up an octave. "I have seen this before—in my own mother—and I wasn't able to help her. I intend to help you."

My heart broke, proof that Ethel hadn't stolen it in the middle of the night. I doubted his mother had gone through what I did, haunted by a past lover, but to men, all women acted the same. Perhaps his mother *was* the same as me and the process would be repeated in the generations yet to come, haunted by the Hunt name, or perhaps the hysteria belonged to our gender.

"Arthur," I said, my body nearly falling forward. "I don't—"

"I have you." He tightened his grip on my hand.

"I don't know what to say."

"You don't need to say anything if you don't want to."

"I haven't the words."

"I agree they are also the worst." Clearing his throat, he stood. "You should rest. I'll send a message to my colleagues about my absence. Then I shall make you breakfast."

He didn't leave room for an argument as he walked from the bedroom, closing the door behind him like it would keep out the insistent heartbeat.

Thump.

Thump.

Thump thump thump.

I closed my eyes, as if that would keep out the sound.

But Ethel's voice echoed in the bedroom. "What a kind man he is. You're very lucky."

"I know," I croaked without opening my eyes.

"You should tell him about me."

"What would I say?"

"The truth."

I scoffed, and the sound jolted my head.

We settled into silence, neither of us breaking the tense comfort. I wanted to believe she had left me alone. However, a chill hung over me. Same with her scent. I had breathed her in so many times that I would forever remember it.

"I was lucky to have you too," I murmured.

Ethel barked a laugh, and I tried not to flinch.

"Don't lie to me, Ginny," she said.

"I'm not," I said.

"Then you are trying to wiggle into my emotions and push me aside."

"Or I could be paying you a compliment."

"You choose now to do so?"

I peeled back my eyelids, my lashes sticking together like cobwebs. How long had I been lying here, collecting dust?

Ethel lingered at the edge of the bed, her hands balled into fists. Fury burned in her eyes. The quivering hair wrapped around her neck. With her lips thinned together, she wore a grim frown, ducking her chin to glare at me more directly.

I had seen her expression many times; she wore the anger when she tried to leave. She wore it like it was her favorite dress as she haunted me. Ethel had always been quick to anger, and I was quick to argue.

There was a knock on the door, and Arthur opened it, holding a steaming mug. He smiled, though he openly studied me.

"Are you thirsty?" asked Arthur, stepping into the bedroom.

I reached to take the outstretched mug, but he stopped before letting our skin touch. I wasn't infectious.

The filled mug was like a stone, but I raised it anyway while Ethel glared at me, the acidic coffee stench curling in my nose. Bile burned the back of my throat. I wanted to throw it at her and scream for her to get out! Why did she need to do this to me?

With a smirk, Ethel strolled from the bedroom, stomping her foot against the floor.

Thump.

Thump.

Thump thump thump.

I gasped. She was doing it on purpose! What a horrible woman.

"Virginia, what are you looking at?" Arthur peeked over his shoulder to where Ethel had been.

I blinked away the memories of Ethel, trying to ignore how she banged on the house like she would bring it crumbling down and bury us alive. Only then would Ethel and I be bound again, our bodies and souls together forever in the muck of Boston.

"Nothing," I murmured.

He knitted his eyebrows together. "You were staring there intently."

"What would you like me to say?"

"I don't wish to hear you say anything."

"You keep pushing."

"Shouldn't I?"

"No!"

He ducked his head.

An apology bubbled on my tongue, and I should willingly give it to him. But I remained silent. I couldn't trust myself to speak. In my sadness and exhaustion, there was a flash of anger, embers burning in my lower belly. It was in my esophagus, and then it stretched into my intestines. It was under my skin. In my veins.

"You should rest," declared Arthur. "Perhaps I shouldn't have brought you coffee."

I ripped the mug toward myself as he reached. The liquid splashed over the side and onto my skin. There was no immediate pain but then my skin sizzled like melting wax.

A scream ripped from my lips at the same time Arthur lunged. More liquid spilled, hitting my hand. Arthur stood over me but then he yelped. It was only a few droplets, a sprinkle compared to the wash upon me.

He dried me off with the blanket. "Oh, Virginia, are you all right?"

"No," I whined.

"Is it your hand? Your chest? Should I call a physician?"

"No! No doctors."

"You're hurt."

"I'll be fine."

"You say that often, but it could be serious—"

"No."

Arthur rocked back. Anguished rimmed his eyes.

Hurting him was never my intent, but I couldn't bring anyone into the house.

"No doctors, please," I begged. "I have already been prodded enough by them, scolded and ordered, especially after my parents died. I cannot take it any longer."

"Take what?"

Tell him, Ginny.

I sprung from the bed, covered in grime and soggy skin, my stringy hair like snakes around my neck. Arthur reached for me, but I ducked away, rushing past him. He meant to lay me on the bed, strap me down, and let the doctors in. I fled our bedroom.

"Virginia!" he called, his footsteps thundering.

I sprinted, the hallway narrowing into a pinprick and the floor moving like thawing ice on the harbor.

"Virginia, tell me what it is," pleaded Arthur.

Ethel was at the end of the hallway, laughing like a madwoman.

"Virginia." He grabbed my hand, trying to spin me around, but I slipped away. "Where are you going?"

Ethel stood at the top of the stairs, blocking the exit. Short of dropping from a high window, I couldn't escape the house! She wouldn't let me.

I ran into the bedroom where Ethel and I had fucked our nights away and slammed the door behind me. I threw the lock into place.

"Virginia?" Arthur tried the doorknob but couldn't get in.

It rattled regardless. Hopefully, the lock would keep Ethel out too. Why couldn't she stay away?

"What is it?" asked Arthur, voice raised. "Virginia, what's happening?"

Unsure what would come out, I clamped my teeth shut.

"Virginia, just let me know you're all right," pleaded Arthur, his shadows inking under the door. "I know you don't want me to call a doctor, but I'm scared."

No doctors, Ginny!

"I'm fine," I called, trying to keep my wavering tone light. "I need to be alone."

Thump.

Thump.

Thump thump thump.

"Virginia?" asked Arthur hopelessly. "Please come out."

"Please go," I begged.

The floorboards squeaked outside my bedroom.

I froze, scared that he would stay, whispering through the door. He would join the others to create a chorus that would pound into me like fists during a beating.

"Fine," he said in a huff, "but I'm still home. I'm here in the house if you need me."

If I needed him...

I held my head in my hands. It quieted Ethel for the moment.

But then where was she?

What was she doing in the house? Was she around Arthur?

What would she do to him?

"Arthur, wait!" I ran to the door and tried to fling it open, but the damn lock wouldn't budge.

I jiggled it, but the door was jammed shut like someone was holding it from the other side. Was it Ethel keeping me hostage? Or was it Arthur, keeping me inside and away from him and others? Was this what I had become to him?

"Arthur, let me out!" I banged on the door but received no answer.

Ethel must've gotten to him if he wasn't responding. I wanted to scream, scrape through the wood, and release myself from this hold to get to Arthur, protecting him from Ethel. However, I was stuck like a pig in a pen for slaughter.

Slumping to the floor of my old bedroom, a place that I had once found refuge, I let the tears fall. I let them come because I was drowning, swallowed by Ethel's tide. This was my offering to God or the watchmen or Arthur to take me as their prisoner; Ethel had won.

What was her prize?

What was the price that I had to give? What did I have?

She had overtaken my house, my mind and body, and my life. What did she want?

What else did I have to give?

I couldn't eat. Sleep. Function.

Pulling my head from my hands, I stared at the bedroom we had once made ours. Ethel and I had lain in the bed, our hair braided.

In the wardrobe, now pushed to the back, were her dresses and other items she had left behind, collected to be mine. I still wore her nightgowns, those I had bought her when I found hers too scratchy. She didn't mind the rough material, but I didn't like the feeling when holding her. The nightgowns, if I were to bury my nose in the cotton, would still smell of her. The wardrobe, if I opened the doors, would let out her wicked sweetness.

On the vanity were items of mine she had used and more things I had bought for her, including a tin of cold cream, a small hand mirror, and a hairbrush. I would use the cream on her feet after her long days attending to patients. It had taken weeks for her to allow me to use the cream—she was prideful by being an herbalist—but as I massaged her feet, she couldn't argue any longer.

However, we found other things to argue about until the house shuddered with our voices. We bickered in this bedroom and in the kitchen and in the front entryway.

I curled in on myself until I fell to the floor, feeling like a splatter of water. If only I could leak through the cracks.

"Virginia?"

It was only a whisper, but I still raised my heavy head. The small movement exhausted me.

"Virginia? Are you all right?" The voice was clearer now under the constant thumping in the house. "I thought I heard a thud. Virginia?"

The door opened, and Arthur stood at the threshold, alarm written across his face. Then it slipped away like melting snow, slush collecting under his chin—no, that was just stubble growing into a beard. Shadows lingered on his face, murky under his eyes, and when he stepped into my old bedroom, everything about him was dark. The daylit Boston couldn't fight the gloom inside the house.

He rushed to my side, flinging his arms around me. "It's all right, Virginia. I have you."

When he entered, so had Ethel. Her lithe body flickered in the corner of my eye yet seemingly took up the whole doorway. She wore a smirk, one that I had seen her wear many times when she helped patients more than physicians, one that claimed she was smarter than anyone. I used to get a thrill from it and her, but now, I felt dread pool in my gut.

"Oh, Virginia," Arthur cooed, rocking me back and forth in his arms. "Virginia, tell me what it is. What can I do to make it better."

He could do nothing. If a witch could not and I could not, then he couldn't.

"Just hold me," I murmured, curling my fingers into his cotton shirt and bringing my face into his chest. I listened to his near erratic heart and wished to protect him but couldn't.

Twenty-Four

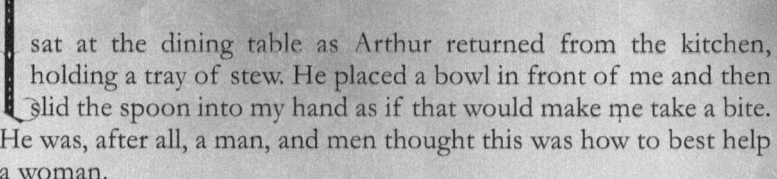

I sat at the dining table as Arthur returned from the kitchen, holding a tray of stew. He placed a bowl in front of me and then slid the spoon into my hand as if that would make me take a bite. He was, after all, a man, and men thought this was how to best help a woman.

On a normal day when my stomach was sour, I would've liked this kindness, helping me in the way that he thought best. In this moment, with my failure staring at me from across the table—Ethel wearing one of *my* dresses—I wanted to throw the steaming stew into Arthur's face and demand that he leave at once. This was my home!

Arthur placed the other bowl at the head of the table and then sunk into the seat, barely meeting my gaze, though he did look at me. His gaze prickled my skin, raising the small hairs on my arm. Of course, to meet his gaze, I would have to look at him but couldn't. Even if Arthur were able to ignore the chill in the room, it was in my bones.

"Eat, Virginia," said Arthur. "You haven't eaten all day."

There was much I hadn't done all day. He didn't need to throw my wifely failures in my face. What would he say next, supper or the cleaning? I tightened my grip on the spoon.

You're not being yourself, Ginny.

Ethel echoed, "You're not being yourself, Ginny."

"I know I'm not the best cook," continued Arthur after swallowing a bite of food. "Not that this is bad—I don't want to scare you off from it—but I have never been properly taught how to cook. I know enough to survive, as any person should. My mother taught me some."

His mother again, Ginny. He's always wagging her in front of you as if it's the same thing.

"I want to know more about his mother, Ginny," said Ethel.

"You should eat, Virginia," said Arthur. "I know it may seem difficult, perhaps one of the hardest things you'll do in your life, but these are the steps to take to make you better. I want you to get better, Virginia."

Would he say that to you if he knew this before marriage, Ginny? Or would he have run like every other man?

"I loved you once, Ginny," said Ethel, pouting.

"Did you?" I asked, the words scraping the back of my throat.

"Yes," breathed Arthur. "Of course, I do, Virginia. Have I given you reason to doubt it? Tell me what I did. Or you don't have to. Know that it is not what I meant. Tell me what I can do to make it better."

Ethel's unflinching gaze narrowed on my chest, where my erratic heartbeat was stifled under my nightgown and robe—placed on me by Arthur. My skin was rubber, gooey and hot. It kept my heart inside, or Ethel would've had her claws in my breast.

Arthur slurped stew off his spoon like a child wanting to be scolded. Perhaps he wanted to provoke me, but I wasn't his mother. Men often didn't seem to distinguish the difference between mothers and wives.

"Virginia?" prompted Arthur. "Please look at me."

I didn't know how many times he had said the same words today, each having less emotion. Would he next pull out paper and ink, play scientist by asking a thousand questions, and attempt to put me in a specimen jar? That was where my heart should go.

"Look at me," he repeated in a harder voice.

Was this not how a husband should speak to a wife? He would bend me to his will.

"You should look at him, Ginny," said Ethel from across the table. "His stew is getting cold. He'll blame you."

"Don't act like you know him better than me," I said.

"What?" Arthur craned his neck around the dining room. "Who are you talking to, Virginia?"

Ethel smirked. "You should tell him now. He knows."

Arthur took my hand, and I jolted. His hand was warm from the stew, his fingers tinged in vegetable juice and old meat, rancid. It was all over me now.

"I'm here, Virginia," said Arthur, squeezing until my bones protruded from my skin.

I blinked, focusing on how we touched—how he held me, wanting me to know that he had me, he loved me, and he would help me.

"Sure, help you, Ginny," mumbled Ethel. "Because men like him always do that, don't they? At least, they say that is their intent. You can't trust him."

"I can't trust you," I hissed.

Arthur stumbled back like he had been slapped. "What do you mean, Virginia? Of course, you can trust me. I never want to see you hurt. I don't wish to see you like this. I don't understand, Virginia. What have I done?"

"Thank Arthur for the lovely meal. I'm sure it tasted just fine." Ethel walked from the dining room.

I slumped in my seat, my bones near snapping under my weight. "What's happening to me, Arthur?"

Hot tears rolled down my cheeks, searing me from the outside in, as I shivered against the confines of mortality. Perhaps it was immortality that held me hostage. There wasn't kindness if there was no end.

"I don't know," he murmured. "Should we try more rest?"

"Do you really think that will help?" I sputtered through the tears.

"I'm hoping so, yes. I think you've had a shock, though I'm not sure what, and the best recovery is water, rest, and food. These are the basics to anyone's life. Once those are established, then we can work out other pieces of the puzzle, such as the nature of the ailment and the cause. Perhaps we should consider other actions too, who you've been around or how you are spending your day. We must look at the tiniest detail to find the truth."

I balled my hands into fists. "You're speaking like a scientist."

He frowned. "My apologies. I only mean to be the best husband I can be. What do you think will help?"

What hadn't I done? I had done everything and more, yet none of it helped!

What had I missed? I must be blindingly obvious if I'm staring it in the face.

I danced around the truth but couldn't bring myself to say the words. They were lost in the abyss of my mind, screaming as everything banged against my skull.

Thump.

Thump.

Thump thump thump.

"You," I whispered.

He rocked back. "There must be more I can do."

His blue eyes, outlined by his dark eyelashes, flashed, and his pupils narrowed on the thrumming vein in my neck. Ethel wasn't in the room, but I knew what she would say, how she would gasp at his evil eye. I knew this man: there was nothing evil about him.

"Come to bed with me," I said.

"I will tuck you in," he said. "I'll stay with you until you fall asleep. Even after that, if it makes you feel all right. No harm will come to you while I am there."

"I want you to make love to me."

He gulped. "Virginia, we should not."

"Because you think I need rest?"

"Yes. And to eat the stew. Please."

"Then will you make love to me?"

He furrowed his eyebrows. "I don't understand how it will help you."

"We sleep after we make love," I said. "Do you remember how we fell asleep in each other's arms?"

Or we would...if I fell asleep too. He would fall asleep draped across me. He was my blanket, and each time, I wished to be at peace like he was.

"Eat your stew, Virginia," said Arthur, pulling away from me.

He slurped another spoonful of brown vegetables and off-color meat chunks. He didn't know how to chop. Or he hoped I would choke. If I died, he would be free of me; he would have the house and everything that was ever mine.

Was that what he wanted?

I stood up, nearly throwing the bowl of stew into his face, hoping it would scald him. I marched from the room, but my movements were heavy, my mind swimming. I swayed, grabbing the wall to keep myself upright.

"Virginia!" Arthur wrapped his arms around me. "Let me help you to bed."

"No," I grunted.

"Please." His voice cracked on the singular word.

With his hand latched to my waist, he helped me up the stairs. The floorboards groaned under us, and the sound traveled down the empty hallway, echoing back a moan that I would've called orgasmic if it were mine. The house wanted us to make love as much as I wished to, so as Arthur helped me into our bedroom, I placed my lips to his, sucking him into me like I had done so many times.

He groaned, trying to wrench back, but I sunk my teeth into his bottom lip. Iron washed into my mouth. I swallowed.

Arthur pushed away from me, and I hit the wall. *Smack!* My head ached, and darkness blurred the corners of my vision. It receded too quickly.

"What the fuck?" He touched his bleeding lips.

I licked my lips, taking the last taste of him.

His cream hadn't made me pregnant. His breath hadn't done it nor his saliva. It would have to be his blood.

With his mouth dangling open, he asked, "Why, Virginia? Why did you bite me?"

"How does he taste?" asked Ethel, standing in the doorway, arms crossed over her chest.

I stumbled away from Arthur in front of the door and Ethel in the frame. They were a wall, blocking me inside the room. They were working together—how didn't I see that?

"Leave me," I said.

Arthur drew his eyebrows together. "I'm not sure that's a good idea. You—"

"You wish me to bite you again?" I asked.

"Will you bite me again?"

Salty tears swept into my mouth, taking away his blood. I spat both on the floor. The taste was making me ill.

"No. I don't want to do that. I don't know why I did that. I'm sorry. I'm—" My tears would drown the house. "I didn't mean to hurt you, I just…I want to be loved. Is that so wrong?"

"I love you," he pleaded.

I nodded because I needed to believe his words, even if Ethel smirked behind him, spreading her lips as she used to spread her legs, so easily. I would be in her mouth and her cunt, and I would fuck her mercilessly. I turned away from her—away from him too—and pinched my eyes shut.

"I need to rest," I whispered, "like you said."

"Do you wish me to stay?" he asked my back.

"No."

"Are you sure?"

"I don't wish to hurt you again." I pressed my fists to my eyes, blocking out the lingering speck of light.

"I don't believe you will," he said.

"Then you have more belief in me than I do."

The floorboards creaked, and I knew he stepped closer, so I stepped away. How many times had I walked over the soft spot in my parents' bedroom, inching toward my mother's perfume? A draft whistled through a small crack in the windowpane, the only sound for a pregnant moment.

"All right," said Arthur, adding a huff to his breath as though he were defeated. "If that is what you wish."

"It is," I said.

"Shall I leave the door open?"

"No, close it, please." And take the ghost with you.

The floorboards creaked again as he shuffled away from me. The groans softened.

"Good night, Virginia," he whispered, and then the door closed.

"I love you," I said, my voice echoing off the walls.

I hoped he heard it.

If Ethel wasn't with me, she was with Arthur, stalking his movements and learning him better than I knew him. Did she lead him to the sitting room, calling him from under the floorboards with her constant banging, and when would he finally know, giving into the truth that we both knew wholeheartedly?

"Ethel?" I asked, lying in bed.

The mattress was large and lonely without Arthur beside me. I ran my hand over the groove where he should've been.

Of course, she didn't come when called like a dog, claiming she was no bitch. Couldn't she find it in herself to come now?

"Ethel, please, come to me," I called into the void.

She wouldn't come. I was foolish to think she would.

"Don't hurt him, please," I whispered like she could hear me. "I deserve this for what I have done to you, but he is innocent."

Even that did not bring her to me.

I was admitting what I had done, handing myself over to her, but she didn't come the whole night.

Neither did Arthur.

I waited for them to enter the room silently to check if I was asleep, to lay beside me and whisper about my failures. Instead, I was alone until the sun broke through the Boston fog.

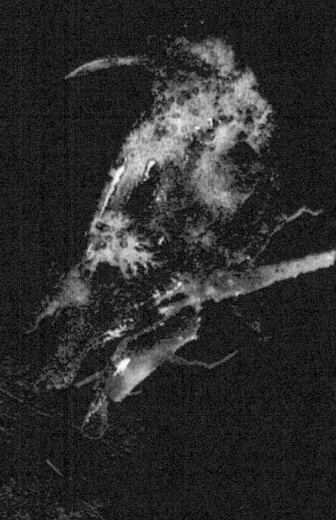

Twenty-Five

Morning light slunk through the windows. The bedroom door opened, and Arthur stuck his head in, his hair brushed and clothes fresh. He had shaved. Even the dark circles under his eyes had been removed. He'd returned to the man he once had been, so it was time for me to do the same.

I forced myself into a seated position, curling my fingers into the blanket. I tried to smile but feared I only winced.

"Good morning," he said, not whispering but not speaking too loudly. "How are you feeling?"

I didn't believe either of us wanted that answer, the truth or the lie, so I asked, "Are you going to work?"

"No."

"You should."

"I cannot leave you in such a state," he said. "I've called a doctor."

I gasped, the shock rushing through me like a wave. I was more awake than I had been in the last day. My heartbeat pounded, quieting the constant banging.

"I told you not to," I said.

"I know what you said, but I cannot allow this to continue, Virginia." His voice was hard as if I had pushed him too far.

I murmured, "I'll get better."

"When?" he demanded. His gaze was filled with something dark.

I clamped my teeth shut, struggling to find what I should tell him. As I peeled back the blankets and placed my feet on the floor, the room twisted. I tumbled back into bed, landing with a splat. My bones and skin had betrayed me like snow melting to slush.

"You are not eating," he spat. "You did not sleep. I heard you talking last night. Not the exact words, no, but how you talked to yourself until dawn. Every time you moved in bed or in this room. This cannot continue—for you or for me—so I have called a doctor, and he should be here—"

There was a distant knock, and I tried to lurch into a seated position. I didn't dare try my feet again. Acidic bile burned the back of my throat.

"That must be him now." Arthur left our bedroom.

"No," I groaned, reaching toward him.

The space was empty.

Polite manly tones floated from the front entryway, and I cringed, burying my head into the pillows as if the act would keep the men out. Perhaps I could slice open the mattress and crawl inside, hiding amongst the feathers, flinging the blanket across the mattress so they wouldn't know where to look. Or perhaps I should go further, leaving this room. I wouldn't be able to via the bedroom door, because Arthur would undoubtedly be close by, so I would go out the window, meet the backyard, and crawl over the fence, running all the way to the harbor. If Arthur couldn't get to me, neither could Ethel.

"She's in here," said Arthur from outside the ajar door. "Resting."

"Does she do that often?" asked a second male voice.

I didn't need to see the man—let alone be introduced to him—to know that he was a physician. The air of condensation and drawl of superiority were enough.

"No," said Arthur. "I think she suffers from exhaustion."

"I shall inspect her myself," said the man.

The door opened the rest of the way, Arthur strolling into the room first with the older man on his heels. I didn't recognize him. He wasn't one of the many doctors I had asked to save my parents, nor had he attended to me after my parents' deaths.

The doctor had no facial hair, though it didn't make him look younger. His hair was gray, and wrinkles crossed his face like newly laid railroad tracks. I doubted he was from Boston. I waited for him to speak so I could listen to his accent and dissect every vowel to decide.

"My wife," introduced Arthur, "Mrs. Virginia Hunt. Dear, this is Doctor Anderson."

"How bland of a name for a man as bland," said Ethel from the doorway, standing behind both Arthur and the doctor.

I grimaced as the physician walked over, placing his leather bag at the end of the bed and then extending his hand to me in greeting.

"Hello, Mrs. Hunt," said the doctor. "I wish we met under different circumstances."

"Do you know me?" I asked.

"No," he said.

"Do you know of me?"

"Only by name."

"Because of gossip."

"Because I know your husband." The doctor inclined his head toward Arthur. "From the university. He wrote to me, asking me to come."

My husband stepped forward, giving a small nod. "Doctor Anderson is a good physician. He's previously helped me."

"You?" I asked, dragging my gaze across Arthur, wondering if I had missed his ailment.

Perhaps he hid his from me as I hid mine, proving that we were made for each other because we both lied. He infected me!

"Don't trust him," muttered Ethel.

I glared at her, and the physician tracked my gaze all the way back to the door, sweeping past Arthur. My husband, too, looked. Then the men shared a glance—one that openly stated I was to be shipped to McLean Hospital—before they returned their attention to me. Arthur dragged himself in front of the door, blocking Ethel from the room.

"Mrs. Hunt," began Doctor Anderson, "do you know why your husband has asked me to come?"

"Exhaustion," I said, repeating what Arthur said in the hallway. "Lack of nourishment. Lackluster cleaning abilities. Excuse the upkeep of the house. Dehydration, I'm sure, and whatever scientific words come along with that."

Arthur looked down at his feet as the doctor asked, "Do you think that, or is that what your husband has said?"

"My husband cares for me," I replied.

Arthur lifted his head slightly.

He was like a dog listening for a command, and I was the master. After kicking him one too many times, he would bite.

"Your husband cares for you very deeply," confirmed Doctor Anderson. "I would like to hear from your own words what you believe is happening."

Tell him, Ginny.

Ethel echoed from the back of the pack, "Tell him, Ginny!"

I flinched. The words rattled in my skull, loud against my ears. What could I say that wouldn't get my house searched? I clenched my teeth until I felt like they would break. I would spit tooth shards and blood onto my lap, letting the physician attend to that instead of my mind.

"My parents died," I said, choosing my words wisely, "and since then, I have been...not myself. With Arthur, I feel better, almost normal. I love him—I love you," I added to Arthur. "There are good days and bad days. I thought I was getting better before I met Arthur."

Doctor Anderson pinched his eyebrows together. "Do you think you're getting worse because of Mr. Hunt?"

"No!" I rushed to say. "I didn't say that. I said that I was getting better before I met Arthur, so much so that I took him as my husband and brought him into my home, married him. I never wanted him to deal with a decrepit wife. It is not fair to him."

Arthur stepped forward. "Virginia, in sickness and in health. I take my marriage vows seriously—"

Doctor Anderson waved for my husband to stop.

Why must he? I wanted those kind words to be my balm, but Arthur snapped his mouth shut.

"Please, Mrs. Hunt, continue," said the doctor.

Glancing between Arthur and the doctor, I worked my jaw to find the correct words. Things that weren't right—or made me sound crazy—popped into my mind, fizzling behind my eyes and draining toward my ears.

"Mrs. Hunt?" Doctor Anderson hung over me like a willow tree.

His spindly arms were at his sides, but the slightest wind could've snapped him toward me, his fingers slapping my face. I braced myself for a blow.

"I love Arthur," I said, "but I cannot deny that something is happening to me."

"What do you think it could be?" asked the doctor.

Before I could stop myself, my eyes fell toward the door Arthur now blocked. He flinched like he had been punched in the gut, nearly doubling over. My hand inched forward. I wanted to reach out to him but kept myself huddled in bed, my fingers woven in the blankets.

"Mrs. Hunt?" prompted the doctor.

"Well, Ginny," said Ethel, raising to her tiptoes to peek over Arthur's shoulder. "What are you going to say?"

"Does she do this often?" the doctor asked Arthur.

"More often over the last few days," answered my husband.

"Before?" asked the doctor.

Arthur shook his head, and Ethel rolled her eyes. A smile crept across her face like this was all some jest.

"Not before or not that you know of?" asked the doctor.

Arthur jutted out his jaw, his eyes narrowed to pinpricks. The makeshift wheels turned in his head as he considered what he knew about me.

"He doesn't know you, Ginny," said Ethel.

"Stop," I murmured.

"What did you say, Mrs. Hunt?" The doctor peered at me again, scrutinizing me as Arthur did, dragging his gray eyebrows together until they were one furry caterpillar.

"Not how I know you, Ginny," added Ethel.

Arthur and Doctor Anderson were waiting, and I wondered how long they would wait. How long could I lay in bed, silent? It would be Ethel who would break my spell long before the doctor did.

Arthur moved to the edge of the bed, still blocking my view of the door, and placed his hands on the blanket covering my feet. The pressure was like a swaddle. I could've been a baby, wrapped in blankets and held, and only then would I sleep.

"I'm exhausted," I said finally.

The coarse words rubbed my throat raw.

So many doctors had failed me before; Doctor Anderson wouldn't be different.

"What does this exhaustion cause?" asked the doctor.

"What does it matter?" I snapped.

"Virginia," said Arthur, anger flashing in his eyes.

I had disappointed him. What was new?

"Apologies, Doctor Anderson," I said because that was what I was meant to say, and I followed up with ducking my head, acting like I was a good girl.

Be a good wife, Ginny.

Be a good daughter, Ginny.

Be a good woman, Ginny.

"I shouldn't have spoken like that," I added when the doctor didn't immediately respond.

He forced me to wait, dangling his acceptance of my apology, but he wouldn't take it until I gave in. I would be clay for him.

"Sir?" I prompted.

"It's all right." He chuckled, and it was…gentle. Somewhat endearing. "Though back to my original question, Mrs. Hunt. What does the exhaustion cause?"

"I cannot eat. I feel sick. I'm sluggish," I listed. "I upset easily. I cannot focus. I cannot do the tasks about the house. I cannot be a good wife."

Each aftermath rolled off my tongue with ease like I was undressing after a long day, wanting to free myself from the layers of clothing I wore. I didn't think about what I said, only that it needed to come out. I bit my tongue before I mentioned Ethel.

With her arms crossed over her chest, she wore boredom. What about a doctor being called to attend to me was boring? Was it because he didn't already decide to lock me away in McLean Hospital? No doubt, she would be stuck with me there too.

"Ah yes," agreed Doctor Anderson. "That all will happen because of exhaustion. Lack of sleep is no laughing matter. It has made men go mad, jump off roofs, thinking they can fly. It has made women kill their own babies, drowning them in bath water. It has made priests take their own lives, sure that God was whispering in their ear to do so."

The last one struck me, and I slumped against the pillows because of the blow. "You don't believe it?"

"No," said the doctor. "The mind is a complicated thing. It controls our bodies as well as our lives. Without our minds, we are nothing. Humans have such strong minds—it is how we have become what we are today with industry and science and the world at our fingertips. We are so much smarter than even our ancestral counterparts.

"Mr. Hunt told me how smart you are, Mrs. Hunt," continued the doctor, "and I assure you that is why you are having such troubles. Your mind does not know how to numb itself. You can't snuff out the thoughts like a candle. I know how to help you."

"You do?" I echoed, leaning forward like a child about to see their present.

Doctor Anderson reached into his leather bag and pulled out a small brown bottle. "This is laudanum."

"No, Ginny!" gasped Ethel, shifting behind Arthur.

By the way she screamed, I knew in my gut that it was exactly what I must do. I didn't exactly know what the medicine was, but it wasn't the hashish Ethel had once prescribed or the leeches the previous practitioner had used.

"This will help me?" I nodded to the brown bottle in his hand. "This medicine? Nothing else has helped."

"Has the other medicine included opium?" asked the doctor.

I recognized that word. "No."

"What will happen?" asked Arthur.

"With a few drops in a glass of wine, Mrs. Hunt will be able to fall asleep," explained Doctor Anderson. "Depending on how tired she is—and how much sleep her body needs—she shall be asleep for some time. Do not be concerned about this, Mr. Hunt. Mrs. Hunt's body will take what it needs."

I would open my mouth and drink the whole bottle now if it meant sleep. I would tip back my head and drop my jaw, and I would suck on the bottle. I would swirl my tongue around the lip and the neck.

"Don't take it, Ginny!" Ethel had taken a step back.

Arthur's gaze never left the brown bottle, as if he feared it. How could a man of science fear a bottle? Perhaps I should point at Ethel standing behind the two of them, revealing the ghost in the room with us. That was what Arthur should fear.

"Here. You can administer that to Mrs. Hunt." Doctor Anderson offered the bottle to Arthur, who carefully took it between his forefinger and thumb.

Arthur frowned. "Shouldn't you do it?"

"You're an intelligent man, Mr. Hunt. I have full faith in you." The doctor turned to me. "I shall return to check on you, Mrs. Hunt, in a few days to see how you're progressing, but I am sure you'll be quite fine."

He gave a polite smile, grabbed his bag, and started his walk out.

"Mr. Hunt," he said before leaving, "will you join me? We can discuss payment not in front of the woman of the house. It's nothing for your wife to worry over."

While now might be a time to tell the doctor it was my money, I was focused on the bottle as it left the bedroom with Arthur. He closed the door behind himself and the doctor, the low voices sailing away.

"Ginny, I beg you not to take the opium," said Ethel, flinging herself toward the bed.

"You're not here, Ethel," I said. "You need to not be here. I've tried everything to—"

"Not this," she interrupted. "Don't do this."

I rolled my eyes, refusing to hear whatever excuse she had this time. "I let you stay because of our past, but my future is with Arthur. You haven't accepted or respected this choice. I cannot let this go on any longer. It is affecting my health. Arthur and I want a child."

Ethel rocked back on her heels as if I had slapped her, but I had made my intentions very clear. I was sorry about what happened, but we couldn't continue to live in this pattern. The laudanum would free us from the stalemate. I was doing this for all three of us.

"Please," I said, my shoulders slumping forward. "Just go."

"Go where?" asked Arthur, walking into the bedroom. "Virginia, who were you speaking to?"

He swept his gaze around like he would catch sight of Ethel. He hadn't before.

"No one," I murmured, focusing on him. "Do you have it?"

"The doctor's orders." He held up the bottle of laudanum and a glass of dark wine. "I'll just put in a few drops."

"Should there be more?" I asked.

"On the first time, no. We want to start out slow."

He put the glass on the vanity and then dripped in the laudanum. My mouth watered. The scent curled in the room, a mixture of alcohol and poppies. I took a deep whiff like it would go straight into my lungs. My eyelids would grow heavy, and I would fall into bed, finding immediate sleep.

"Here you are, Virginia," said Arthur, offering the glass to me. "Drink it slowly."

I licked my upper lip. "Is that what the doctor suggested?"

"Yes."

"Not that I don't believe you," I added hastily.

"I didn't think that at all." He sat on the edge of the bed, and the mattress tilted down.

"Do you not trust that I shall drink it?" I asked and then sipped the wine.

It was disgusting. The few drops of laudanum had twisted the tart apple wine into acidic bile that tasted more like vomit. I wanted to spit the wine back into the glass but forced myself to have another long sip.

"I believe you'll drink it," said Arthur. "I never doubted. I only wish to see you well."

After another gulp, I asked, "You don't think the medicine will work?"

"I didn't say that. I would drink it slower."

"The taste is bad. You have to drink it quickly."

"I was scared of that."

"Is that the only thing you're scared of?"

He peeked at me from under his dark eyelashes. "That is a queer question."

I leaned forward. "Will you give me the truth?"

Hesitation made him pull back. "Is that what you want?"

"Of course," I answered because that was what a good wife would say.

I strove to be a good wife—the best wife that Arthur could ever have.

After the words left my mouth, only a second before Arthur spoke, I regretted my request for honesty and his assurance that he would give it because, no, I didn't want it.

I wanted to go to sleep and wake up and be all better, to ignore what happened between us or, better yet, to forget. If only I could wake from the nightmare the last few days of my life had been and find myself with Arthur on our bridal tour. While I could've wished more—for Ethel and my parents' deaths to not have happened—I didn't want to lose Arthur.

Swallowing another gulp of wine, I licked my teeth and then sucked any opium-laced wine off. When would sleep settle over me like I was a corpse?

"The truth, then…" He knotted his fingers together until his knuckles were white. "I don't know you. You're not the woman I met or grew to know. You are a stranger now. You confuse me, perhaps disgust me. You scare me."

Everything he said was another blow to my chest.

"But I married you," continued Arthur. "I made those vows in front of God and others. I will stand by your side, Virginia. I will help you get better. Someday, then, we can return to who we were once. We could start to build the life we have spoken about."

"Do you love me?" I asked.

"I have loved you."

"Do you love me now?"

"No."

I grabbed at my aching chest, strumming my collar bone, and then drank the rest of the opium-laced wine in two gulps. I did it so carefully that there wasn't a lost drop.

"Virginia, please slow down," begged Arthur. "You may make yourself sick if you drink like that."

"You don't think I'm already sick?" I asked, dropping the empty glass to my side.

"I think you are ill, but you can get better." He set the glass on the nightstand.

"Then you will love me again?" I questioned.

Pinching his lips together, he stood and wandered across the room, taking the brown laudanum bottle from where he had left it on the vanity. He pocketed it.

"Arthur, answer me," I pleaded, leaning forward in the bed.

The smallest movement tightened my stomach, and I slammed my teeth shut.

"Arthur, please," I begged, curling my fingers into blankets.

"It will take time," he said in a small voice, "but yes, I will love you again. Someday. I first need you to get better. Can you do that, Virginia?"

"I shall rest now, Arthur," I said with determination.

He turned to the door, about to leave without another word.

"I love you!" I called to his back.

He paused, hand on the doorknob.

"I love you still, and I will love you forever. I will get better, for you, for me, for our child, may it grow." I pressed my hands to my lower stomach and hoped that his seed had taken root. "We'll be a family. We'll leave this terrible past behind, and we'll be happy. You'll see, Arthur."

He nodded. "Sleep well."

When he left the room, he closed the door behind him. Gray light shrouded me, Boston still living in day outside the curtains, but darkness pushed at the corners of my eyes like waves of fog.

Laying on the bed, I looked up at the ceiling and blinked the crawling shadows away. I couldn't break free from how they crowded me. I couldn't swat them away when I couldn't lift my own hands. They had become boulders at my sides. I was as heavy as one too, sinking into the bed like it was the harbor.

"Arthur," I tried to call out, but my jaw had locked together. All that came out was a soft groan, too quiet under the pounding.

Thump.

Thump.

Thump thump thump.

"Go away," I groaned, but of course it wouldn't leave me.

It never did.

"I'll never leave you, Ginny," said Ethel in bed with me. She placed her chin against my shoulder. Her hair tickled my nose, but I couldn't wipe it away.

I couldn't move but couldn't sleep.

Darkness dug its claws into my body and lurched up, overtaking me slowly. It was in my hair, dancing its talons across my cheeks, and dragging down my chin. It caught in my throat. I coughed, trying to expel it.

"Just breathe, Ginny," said Ethel, petting my hair.

Sweat collected on my temples, but I shivered. The darkness had brought a chill, turning my bones to ice. Then it was in my veins. My body wasn't my own.

What was happening to me?

What was inside of me?

It wiggled under my skin like maggots that would come for my eyes and my tongue.

Was I dying?

"It's all right, Ginny," cooed Ethel. "Let it happen. You wanted to get better."

Yes, I wanted to get better, but I didn't know what this was.

"It's the opium, Ginny," said Ethel.

You told me not to take it. I just want to be free from you. I was supposed to be free from you.

"We both know it's not that easy, Ginny." Ethel snuggled her nose against my cheek. "I didn't want you to take the opium. It's not good for you."

I want to be free from you.

"I know, Ginny, but this isn't the way."

Tell me how.

What more could I do? What hadn't I done already?

"You already know, Ginny." She kissed my cheek. "Tell the truth."

What?

"Tell Arthur what you did to me, Ginny. Tell him where to find my body. Tell him to get the watchmen. Tell him to send you to jail, hang for what you have done to me."

You want me dead?

"I want us both to be free, Ginny."

Or us tied together for eternity.

"Are we not already, Ginny?"

No!

I tried to roll away, tried to get away—*run away for God's sake, Ginny!*—but my body was too heavy.

"Our souls, our bodies, our minds," listed Ethel between kisses.

She dragged her lips across my cheek, pecked my lips, and then down my neck, nibbling on the rise of my vein.

"Ginny, look how well we fit together," said Ethel. "How well we are together. We shall never be parted in life or in death. It is as you always wanted."

No.

I tried to shift away from her, but she was on me, leeching away my soul.

My body.

My love.

She overtook my body, grinding herself against me, and I hated how my body rose to meet her like a marionette on strings, how close I wanted to be to her. The want was overpowering, not only by body but every other part of me. I moaned.

"Yes, Ginny," whispered Ethel, dragging herself across me. "Tell me how much you want me. Let me hear it."

Too much. Not at all.

"Virginia?" asked Arthur, poking his head into the bedroom. "Are you all right? I heard you moaning."

No, Arthur. Don't come in! Don't see this.

Ethel trailed her kisses down my chest, nipping at the skin exposed from my nightgown. She slurped her way to my breasts, taking my already pointed nipple. It felt so good.

"Virginia?" Arthur stood at the edge of the bed. "The doctor said you should be sleeping by now."

I let out a soft moan, not that I had any control over my body or what sounds it made. Pleasure—how Ethel worked me just as I liked—was sculpting me.

"Can you not sleep?" asked Arthur.

"She can never sleep," hissed Ethel, pausing her kissing. "Can you, Ginny?"

She twisted her tongue around my nipple, and another moan rolled across my body. I shifted in the bed, moving as if I were at sea, when I was sure that I was nothing more than a dead fish. My body was just as slick.

"Do you want more, Ginny?" asked Ethel.

Yes, I answered and then eyed Arthur moving across the room, standing by my head.

He shouldn't see this.

Shouldn't have to see this.

Please go, Arthur.

"I was thinking about what I said, Virginia," continued Arthur. "It was unkind, even if true. I hate myself for it. I know better. There is more truth than just the base, and that's all it was: the base. I needed to delve deeper, which is what my ask is as a scientist. I am only a man, never good with my feelings. I am no poet or even well-read unless you count scientific books, so I am no good with words. I am sorry, Virginia. I hope you can forgive me."

He kissed my temple as Ethel sunk her teeth into my nipple. I let out a deep moan. At the same time, she slid her hand lower, collecting my nightgown and slid her palm against my pearl. I released a hiss of a breath as she fucked me.

Damn her.

Damn her movements.

"You could tell him now, Ginny," said Ethel, quickening her pace. "Tell him how you killed me."

"No," I groaned, trying to unlatch my jaw.

Arthur fluttered his eyelashes. "No? I don't know what you mean, Virginia."

"Tell him how you hid my body, Ginny," continued Ethel, shoving her fingers deep into me and tearing back my folds.

It burned with how she held me, digging her fist into me like I was giving birth in reverse. I bared down, feeling a contraction build in me. My walls clenched around her, ecstasy looming.

I screamed, "No!"

Arthur stumbled back, pink tinging his cheeks. "My apologies, I should let you rest. Like Doctor Anderson said."

No! My jaw had locked again, holding back my scream of pleasure and pain.

How could it feel so good and hurt so much? I wished for Arthur to take over how Ethel touched me, bringing his cock into me and planting his seed a hundred times. One of them would have to take root. If I had his child in me, I wouldn't have Ethel too. One would have to be expelled; I would ensure it was Ethel.

"Yes, like Doctor Anderson said, Ginny," whispered Ethel, jamming her fist into me. "Before he gave you opium. I told you not to take it. Now see what is happening, Ginny."

Arthur ducked his head, leaning toward the door.

Come back, Arthur!

Continuing to move against my body, Ethel worked me into a frenzy. I was like a rabid dog, wanting more and humping everything in sight, including my ex-lover in front of my husband. I was a whore.

Yes, Ginny.

He spun around. "What did you say, Virginia?"

Stay.

"Don't do that, Ginny." Ethel thumped against me, riding me for her own pleasure. "Don't ask him to stay. He'll never understand."

"It must be the laudanum," he said. "Rest well, Virginia. We shall speak tomorrow."

Then he left, leaving the door ajar like he meant to listen.

Arthur!

"Yes, Ginny, scream for your husband as I fuck you," hissed Ethel through her powerful thrusts, bringing me closer to immense pleasure. "I know you have thought about me while he fucked you. It is the only time that you imagine him with me. Come for me, Ginny. Let him hear you."

I swallowed my moans. My arousal. My pleasure. Even my grunts, hoping he would come back, see Ethel on top of me and expel her from me.

"You don't want that, Ginny," said Ethel, flicking my pearl. "You want me here. It's why nothing has worked to get rid of me. Your life is nothing without me, Ginny."

No, get out. I don't want you here.

Then ecstasy turned me to mush on her hand, black dots overtaking my vision. I moaned, a scream ripping from my throat but barred behind my teeth. The sound rattled in my empty skull.

Empty.

I was so empty without Ethel, her having disappeared with my undoing.

I lay in the empty bed.

I lay alone.

Twenty-Six

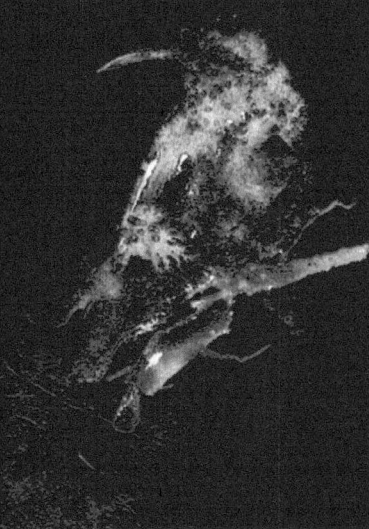

Night—true night and darkness—descended over the house. No, over Boston.

The darkness covered my vision and me like a blanket, and while I had tried to fight through the haze, I only accomplished to do so now.

I lifted myself from the bed, my legs working—perhaps too well— and sprung forward a step, catching myself before I fell on the vanity. My hairbrush fell to the floor with a *whack!* I twisted toward the bed, about to apologize for waking Arthur, but he wasn't there.

I knew that, or so I reminded myself. He left me to rest, though I couldn't say I had. Even after Ethel had disappeared, along with Arthur, I stared at the ceiling, unable to move, and counted my banging heartbeats. The thumping against the floor continued. It was Ethel, telling me to come play.

This was no game. I wouldn't let this continue longer.

How long have you been saying that, Ginny?

I didn't know, but I had meant it each time.

It spurred me down the hallway. I passed the open door to my old bedroom, Arthur on the bed. His back was turned to me, and he let out soft snores as he always did, sleeping with ease. That would be me one day.

No more Ethel.

No more ghosts.

"I will make this all right, Arthur," I whispered to his sleeping form. "We will be happy."

I shut my old bedroom door softly and then listened a moment longer to his snores. I imagined that it only worsened with each breath filled with dust and old lust, the culmination of Ethel and myself. I wondered if we now lived in his dreams and if he would wake, thinking it a nightmare about his wife with another woman as all the rumors had said. He must now believe they had merit, in the same way he must think he had made a mistake. After all—even for a scientist—he was still a man.

"Soon," I whispered, stealing down the hallway and the steps and into the sitting room, closing the door loud enough that it stopped Ethel's incessant knocking.

"I'm here," I declared, but she already knew. "Ethel, come out. Let me see you."

"Why don't you open the floorboards to see me clearly, Ginny?" asked Ethel, but when I whipped toward the voice, she wasn't there.

Thump.

Thump.

Thump thump thump.

"Let me out, Ginny," she said.

"Do not act like you cannot get out. You've done it before," I snapped. "You were in my bed earlier."

"Was I, Ginny?"

"Yes. You kissed me. You..." I swallowed the saliva building my mouth.

"What did I do, Ginny?"

"You made love to me."

"No, I fucked you."

"Is there a difference?"

"I didn't do it because I loved you. I did not make love to you, Ginny."

My chest ached, same with my core. It was bruised and battered, yet I wanted more of her. Of the love we'd made a hundred times when we had been happy and living together in this house, creating a home.

"What would you call it before?" I asked.

"When before, Ginny?" asked Ethel. "Before you killed me?"

A lump formed in my throat, and I tried to speak over it. "Yes."

My voice cracked.

"Say it aloud."

"Before I killed you, Ethel. What was it before? Was it love?"

Silence answered, echoed by a cold wind that bristled the curtains by the windows.

Thump.

Thump.

Thump thump thump.

I flinched away, grabbing my heavy head and placing my palms over my ears like it would block out the sound.

The thumping increased tenfold. It was inside my skull; it banged against my chest; it rattled my bones.

"Tell me, Ethel!" I pleaded.

Each thump was a jolt to my body, nearly sprawling me sideways.

"Yes," she hissed between the cracks in the floorboards.

I ventured a step forward. "You used to make love to me, Ethel?"

"Yes, Ginny."

"Because you used to love me?"

"Yes, Ginny."

"Do you love me now?"

"Do you love me?" asked Ethel.

I fell to my knees over the weakened floorboards. "Yes, I still love you, Ethel. I have never stopped loving you. Sometimes, it hurts so much. I ache for you. I yearn for you. However, these things I now feel for Arthur too. I love him."

"More than me?" asked Ethel.

"No, Ethel. Not more than you."

"Less than me?"

"No." I placed my hands against the cool floorboards. "I love you both. Why can you not understand that?"

"Because it's impossible," said Ethel.

"It isn't," I insisted. "If you were still alive—"

"You would choose him over me."

"No, I wouldn't."

"You would because you wanted to be a member of the elite, a pretty wife on a man's arm. You wanted children, which I would never be able to give you."

"You gave me so much more!"

"Yet you killed me."

"You tried to leave me!" I banged my fists against the floorboards like I could reach her underneath. "You were going to leave me. What about that love, Ethel?"

"I wanted you to be happy."

Her voice seeped through the cracks in the floorboards like smoke. It curled around my neck, bringing my head down further, and then flew into my nostrils. I was intoxicated. I was falling into her again.

I jerked back. "You were leaving me."

"Do you hate me for it?" she asked.

"Yes."

"You hated me enough to kill me?"

"It wasn't hate that made me kill you." I pressed my eye between the wood like I would be able to see her hiding in the darkness. "I loved you so fiercely that I couldn't let you leave."

"Would you do the same thing to Arthur?"

"No." My thoughts echoed for him the distance of the house. "If you were alive now—this being a different time and place, of course—you would love him too. He would love you. He would've joined our family, and we would've been happy."

Ethel barked a laugh, and the floorboards shook. The knocking skipped a beat.

"Don't be daft, Ginny," said Ethel.

"Don't say that," I begged, tears welling in my eyes. "Please. He would've loved you as I did. He would've accepted you as part of me. We are together—"

"Then why won't you tell him now?"

I pushed to my quaking knees until I thought I would topple forward, sliding between the cracks and into her. "I will."

"Tell him that you killed me, Ginny."

"How many times must I give you the same answer, Ethel?"

"How many times will I ask you to speak the truth? It will set you free."

"You shall leave me?"

Silence answered.

Pushing up from the floor, I stomped loudly and then jumped, thudding against the wood. I kicked faster and harder, quieting her knocking for the moment and hoping she would stay silent, locked away and dead because that was what she was: dead.

Turning on my heel, I grabbed the matches from above the hearth. The floorboards could catch, and the flames would eat the wood and the body beneath, tearing into what was left of her. I would burn her, turning her into ash and dust.

Before I struck the matches, I paused. Arthur was sleeping upstairs. I could get him and myself out; I could let the house burn.

For a moment, when I thought of him, it was like gray clouds parted, revealing clarity I didn't realize was missing. It was soft and lingering in the corner of my eye, and I turned in that direction. It cleared my mind as much as it blew the cobwebs from my lungs.

Arthur was upstairs sleeping. I needed to protect him and build our lives, because if I burned down this house, I would destroy our future together.

Returning the matches to the mantle, I exited the sitting room. Each of my steps punctuated by the thump under the floorboards. Still, I returned upstairs and looked in on the sleeping Arthur.

Near the door, like he expected me to come or for him to need it, was the bottle of laudanum. It was easy to grab it, twist the lid, sip the rancid-tasting liquid, and place the bottle back on the desk. The hardest part was the horrid taste, a mixture of vinegar and rank sweat, but I sucked it down.

Returning to the hallway, I snapped the door shut and then faltered. I barely caught myself on the wall, digging my fingernails into the wallpaper as if to hold myself upright. Still, I was teetering. The floor leaped up to meet me.

How did the opium get to me so quickly, faster than alcohol? This had to be it, right? The walls twisted, the end of the hallway narrowed into a pinprick, and the floor ebbed like waves in the harbor. I was a ship knocked out to sea, my masts no longer leading me straight and my sails twisted.

They tripped me, and I sprawled out on the floor, my chin hitting with a sickening crack. Then there was a searing pain, hot against my skin. The pain ate up the sides of my jaw. With darkness pushing in, my heavy head splatted against the hallway floor.

Twenty-Seven

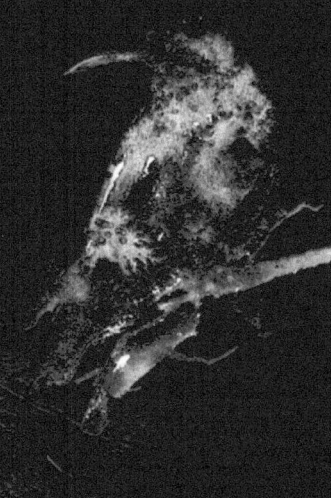

"Virginia," hissed a voice somewhere in the distance.

The snake wrapped around me, attempting to swallow me whole. I was pressed close to someone hard but breathing.

Each hot breath seared my skin.

Each hot breath was ragged.

Each hot breath brought the mouth closer to me, unhinging its jaw.

"Virginia," it repeated, only knowing one word.

How did it know my name?

I tried to roll away but was ensnared in the coil of the monster's body and then the weight of my own. I was a boulder sinking in Boston Harbor. I would stay with the destroyed ships beneath the surface.

"Virginia, wake up," the disembodied voice said from somewhere above me. "Open your eyes."

Didn't I already have them open?

"Virginia, you're injured. How did that happen?" The monster took my chin between his fingers, and I groaned in pain. "You're bleeding. I should call for Doctor Anderson again."

"No," I said, peeling back my clinging lips.

"Virginia, you're injured," repeated the male voice—yes, it was male.

Think, Ginny. You know this voice. It's the opium in your system.

Yes, the opium. And if this was darkness, it meant I had finally slept!

Was this what sleep was like? I couldn't remember. There had been no dreams. I didn't feel well rested as much as weighted.

Sinking.

I landed on a hard cloud—*Think, Ginny*—and then realized I was on a bed. My bed, it had to be. The tension released me.

"Here," said the man, pressing a cool, damp cloth to my forehead.

He dragged the towel across my eyelashes and down my face, careful of my chin. He patted that tenderly.

"Virginia, can you open your eyes now?" he asked. "I've gotten most of the blood off your lashes. It should be easier now."

Wrenching my eyes open like I was a baby entering the world, I took in my blurry surroundings before finding one head ducked toward me, a mixture of concern and awe written on his face. Arthur would look at our children like that one day, covered in blood after they were expelled from my body, hopefully not on the hallway floor.

"Virginia," said Arthur in a heavy tone, "are you all right?"

"Yes, husband," I said, still trying to find my voice.

"What were you doing in the hallway? What happened? Why did you—" He thinned his lips together. "I should call for Doctor Anderson. He should look at the cut on your chin, and he should explain further about the laudanum. I don't trust—"

"More," I said.

His eyebrows were drawn, creasing his forehead as if his skull could be cut in half, right down the center. One half drooped more than the other. His eyes weren't the same shape, though both were blue and rimmed with his dark eyelashes, and purple bags hung underneath. How terrible for him to grow so old already. His lips, thankfully, were the same shape, and I arched my neck as if to close the distance.

"What do you mean 'more,' Virginia?" he asked.

"More laudanum," I said.

He shook his head. "I don't think it's a smart choice."

"Doctor Anderson prescribed it to me." My voice was returning to normal. I was recognizing my own words. "You know Doctor Anderson from the university. You trust him. Why do you not trust him now?"

"I don't trust opium."

"It's laudanum."

"Opium is in it."

"The English are using it."

"I'm not sure we can count on the English for anything. Look what they have made of the world," he said in disgust, scrunching his nose.

He was adorable when he was angry. I tried not to giggle because I knew that would make his anger worse. Men didn't like to be laughed at, after all. He was being angry for me, though I didn't see why we needed to bring the English into it. But he was such a smart man—much smarter than me. His mind worked differently than mine, like a clock!

Tick tock tick.

Thump.

Thump.

Thump thump thump.

I froze in the bed, stuck and bewildered, because the knocking had returned after I hadn't heard it for hours. Now, it was haunting me again.

Ethel was stalking the halls. She was coming for me!

"I need it," I begged Arthur, grabbing his hand. "I need the laudanum."

He stared at where we were connected. "Why?"

"I was finally able to sleep."

"Do you feel better?"

"On my way to it."

"Do *you* feel better?" he repeated, voice harsher this time.

"Almost."

"Why do you say so?"

I flipped my gaze toward the open bedroom door, and Arthur craned his neck like he would be able to see Ethel stroll inside.

The laudanum had kept Ethel away with the higher dose, so I needed to take it to expel her.

"Virginia?" asked Arthur, facing me again.

"I'm tired, Arthur," I pleaded, tears welling. "Please give me the laudanum. I wish to sleep."

He grimaced. I wondered if his mother had said something like this before. Had she been prescribed laudanum? And was that why he was so hesitant? His mother and I were not the same.

"Please," I whispered, my voice cracking.

I was exhausted and only felt at peace when I was asleep. I needed the opium to silence the thumping under the floorboards. If he heard the knocking, he would understand.

"All right," he said on an exhale, as though it physically pained him. "Only a little, though."

I dropped my mouth open, ready for what he called "a little." I would be a good girl.

"Don't you want it in something?" he asked, the brown bottle in his hand. "Wine?"

"No, by itself is fine," I said.

"The taste doesn't bother you?" he asked.

"No."

"The smell is horrid."

"It's not the worst taste or smell ever."

"You have a stronger stomach than I."

More than he knew.

Arthur crept forward like a man scared of a dog, extending his hand with laudanum. I opened my mouth, stretching my lips wide until they pulled tight, dropping my jaw like I was taking his cock in my mouth.

One.

Two.

Three drops were all he gave.

I closed my mouth and gulped, scraping my teeth over my tongue to get every last speck. I swallowed again.

Raising his eyebrows, he said, "You're very strong, Virginia."

My cheeks warmed at the compliment. "I need the medicine. I understand that."

He pushed the stopper back into the bottle and then tucked it into his pocket for safekeeping. I memorized the brown of his jacket, readying to climb out of bed the moment he took it off to have a few more drops.

Already, darkness was pushing in on the corners of my vision. I should be scared like I had been before when the opium took me, but those were fading memories, slipping behind me as I flew into the darkness, welcoming it with open arms.

"I should leave you to rest unless…" He grimaced.

"Unless?" I prompted, arching to see him clearly.

I was sliding into the mattress, the blankets like ropes across my body.

Arthur stepped toward the door. "You need to rest. Apologies for disturbing you."

"You haven't disturbed me," I murmured over a yawn.

He nodded, so sad and soft.

"Would you like to stay with me?" I asked, my tongue turning to molasses, my words slurring. I worked my jaw, forcing my eyes open. "Unless you have work. I don't mean to keep you."

"I wrote John for the time away. He understood," said Arthur.

"Did he?" I asked.

Based on the way Arthur wouldn't look at me, he couldn't hide his lie. We knew John too well: a man who didn't like me, played with Boston's finest women, used Arthur for his own bidding, but couldn't lose Arthur or his popularity amongst those funding the university projects.

"No, but I didn't give him a choice. You are my wife." Arthur sat beside me on the bed, interweaving his fingers with mine. "I'm so sorry—"

"Please don't." I shook the darkness away, freeing my tongue in the process.

"What I said was—"

"The truth."

"It was terrible."

"I know about terrible things."

He drew his eyebrows together, a face that I believed he made too often in my company. I was a puzzle he meant to figure out, stripping me to the bones, sucking my blood into vials, and laying my skin flat. I, too, wanted to see inside him, wanted to better understand his mind.

"What have you seen?" asked Arthur in a small voice.

Thump.

Thump.

Thump thump thump.

I thinned my lips together, unwilling to squeal like a swine for slaughter. That was what Ethel wanted, why she picked up her pace now to knock against the walls of the house, my heartbeat quickening against my rib cage. I wouldn't let it out!

Thump.

Thump.

Thump thump thump.

It was all around me, inside my body, shoving my blood through my veins. It knocked against my skull.

Ethel walked past the door. Where was she going? Did she think she could just leave and return whenever she liked, injecting herself into my life?

"Do you believe in ghosts?" I asked.

Arthur cleared his throat, squeezing my hand until I thought my bones would break. "Doctor Anderson mentioned that McLean Hospital might be able to—"

"The asylum, you mean?" I jerked awake now, throwing off the opium-induced shadows. "You want to send me to an asylum."

"No," he gasped. "I, of course, do not want to send you to an asylum. I want to help you. Unfortunately, I'm not finding much of a solution because you won't talk to me or tell me the truth."

"The truth?" I spat. "Like you have given me?"

His cheeks pinked. "Yes."

"Then," I began, building up my breath, "the truth is that all the rumors are true. You chose to ignore them, and I lied to you."

Blinking like I was speaking another tongue, he sat back but didn't release my hand. It kept us anchored to one another. Yes, this was how much he believed in his vows of marriage that he would still hold my hand after I spread the truth, the embers turning to wildfire, threatening to consume the house with us inside.

"Virginia?" he prompted, glancing to his left and right as if others could hear. "I don't know of what you speak."

"Don't start lying now, Arthur. Please."

His eyes flashed dark. "If I am innocent?"

"Would that be complacent in a lie?" I challenged. "Arthur, you can play innocent and choose to ignore what Agatha, Mrs. Clark, and surely what others have said."

"I didn't believe it. I don't listen to such gossip. It is known to be false. Tell me it is false, Virginia."

"Some of it is," I said.

Specifically, how they called Ethel a witch, how she bathed in virgin blood, and prayed to Satan. I had checked her body many times, but she didn't have extra nipples to nurse a familiar. Absolutely no witch's mark.

Arthur released a low breath. "Then, yes, it isn't true."

"The base of it is," I said. "True, I mean."

His finger stilled on my vein, right over the pulse on my wrist like he meant to press down and feel my hard heartbeat. It was the quick successions: *thump, thump, thump-thump-thump*, repeating in my mind for my life, no matter how long or short, for sickness or in health. Our wedding vows wove an invisible string tying us together.

"What is it?" he asked.

"What is what?" I asked.

"The truth. Tell me the truth, Virginia."

The words were sticky on my tongue, clinging to me like they had for so long. However, they had worked their way up my throat from the deepest parts of my body. I scraped my teeth over my tongue, slicing the truth off, so I could finally spit it.

"Ethel and I were together," I said.

"Ethel?" he repeated like he was tasting the name for the first time.

"Yes, Ethel and me. Together."

He knitted his eyebrows, aging him twenty years. I was sorry for that, age wearing on his already delicate features, teetering between young and old.

"What does that mean?" he asked.

Was it a mask, or was he a man who truly didn't see past his science? It was how he so plainly turned from the rumors because he found no evidence behind them.

"You're women—they go out all the time," he continued. "Hold arms and such. I see society women promenade by the harbor or the shops. They giggle and talk. It all seems rather...mundane."

"We did not go out," I said. "Ethel and I, I mean, though people saw us on the street. We tried to be...discrete, but people saw us. They drew their own conclusions."

"Some of them not true."

"Some of them true. Like I am trying to tell you, Arthur." I scratched at the memories that I had tried to hide, placing them into the furthest reaches of my mind, but I couldn't deny that Ethel wasn't so far away in spirit, body, or time. "Ethel and I were close, like you and I are. Not in marriage—for two women cannot make vows in church or in the government—but we were together in every way that you and I have been, Arthur."

"She touched you?" he asked.

"Yes," I said.

"We should tell the watchmen."

"No!"

"She assaulted you."

"She did not. I liked it. I wanted it."

He rocked back, his mouth agape. His eyes were just as wide, glimmering like moons on a clear crisp winter night.

I released his hand, ready for him to storm away as I expected any man would. Perhaps this would be the time for him to call the watchmen or bring Doctor Anderson back to our home with the intent of throwing me into McLean Hospital. How many women were locked in those walls for kissing those of their own gender?

I looked away, not wanting to see the moment he chose my fate. It hovered above his hands. He only needed to grasp it.

"You liked it?" he repeated, glancing toward the bed.

"Yes," I whispered.

"Why did it end?"

"What?" I dragged my gaze to him, trying to parse out what he was asking me. Surely, it couldn't be the obvious.

"Why did the...relationship end?" he asked. "How you two were, I mean. Did the rumors become too much? Did you fall out of...the relationship? Why stop?"

"She died." The words escaped me before I thought them; I wished to take them back.

Ethel appeared in the doorway behind Arthur. "Tell him the truth, Ginny. I'm not just dead. You killed me."

"I'm sorry, Virginia," said Arthur. "For your loss."

I shifted away from his awkward kindness that rubbed me roughly. I couldn't move far in the bed, the laudanum weighing me down. I needed another few drops to still be able to speak, and perhaps I should stop talking altogether.

"That will get you into McLean, Ginny," said Ethel, "but it will not stop this conversation."

"How did she die?" asked Arthur.

Ethel laughed, clapping her hands. "Tell him, Ginny."

"It is very morbid, I know," continued Arthur, ducking his head like an embarrassed young boy. "One to die so young, even with the flu and a harsh life does seem odd. How did it happen?"

Creeping forward, Ethel peeked over Arthur's shoulder, drawing her face nearer, teeth elongating like she would take a bite of him. She would take her chunk like one did a piece of cake, deciding if he was spongy and his blood would come out like cream.

Did he feel how she breathed on him? Did he feel the chill creeping across his cheek?

Why didn't he swat it away? Why didn't he hit her?

She dragged her face toward him, growing closer to almost touch. She would cling to him, digging in her claws. He would never be free.

"I did it," I said.

Ethel halted just an inch from his face. "Tell him, Ginny."

She was too close to him.

"I killed her." The words ripped from my lips.

I wanted to slap my hands over my mouth and hold back the words, but they slipped from my body like weight during the flu. I felt ill, but then my stomach unclenched. The pressure lifted from my shoulders, sweated off my body. I took a breath.

Arthur's jaw dangled open. "What?"

Ethel lingered. Her fingers reached out like she meant to brush his hair back, freeing it from the collar of his shirt.

I couldn't let her touch him!

"I killed Ethel," I said. "Murdered her."

My voice cracked on the words, and tears swelled in my eyes, burning like fire. I blinked them away quickly because I wouldn't cry in front of her, though I had done so many times before and she wanted me to grovel.

"I didn't mean to—"

"Stop, Virginia," muttered Arthur.

At the same time, Ethel said, "Continue, Ginny. Tell him how you slaughtered me. Tell him what you did with my body. Tell him that I live in this house too."

"I—" The truth was right there, and I had to harness it. "Will you leave?"

"Yes," said Ethel.

Arthur stared at me, giving no answer, but no, he wouldn't leave me.

We were married. Soon, we could return to how we had been—better actually. All that we could be without Ethel in our lives.

"I killed her," I repeated as Arthur rocked back on the bed like he meant to put physical distance between us, so I tightened my grip on his hand, ensuring that he hear me. "She was in the house, and we had been arguing, and she tried to le—"

"Stop, Virginia." He ripped away from my grasp.

My fingernails shredded his skin. He drew his hand toward his face, one look to see how it bled, before dropping to his side.

"Please listen, Arthur." I tried to reach for him, but my hands were like boulders.

So much for the freedom. It was thin to begin with.

"No, Virginia, I won't." He took another step back.

"But I—"

"Don't say another word."

"Arthur, it is the truth."

"It is not."

"You don't—"

"No, *you* do not, Virginia." He released a shaky breath, schooling his features.

He gave me a hard stare, one that put distance between us. One that proclaimed we were no longer man and wife but scientist and subject.

"You don't know what you're saying, Virginia," he continued. "It is the laudanum in your system."

I protested, "It is not—"

"It is," he cut in with venom. "Doctor Anderson didn't want to tell you this—something about the fairer sex's minds and if someone is already ill—but laudanum could make it worse. It can make you see things."

My gaze flickered to Ethel involuntarily; she still waited as if I had not just admitted the truth like she wished. I did as she asked! It wasn't my fault if Arthur chose not to believe me. She should be gone.

"Do you see something now?" asked Arthur, glancing over his shoulder.

He faced Ethel directly! But he didn't see her, nor had he ever seen her or felt her or knew that she was there, thumping against the floor and humming down the hallway.

"Virginia, there is no one there," he added.

"No one?" I echoed, wanting to believe him because Arthur told me the truth even if it was painful.

The truth was his bible more than any Godly word. He had tried to hide his snickering when we wed with the priest like a little boy. He was a man of science, and he had no proof—with his eyes, ears, or nose—to show that Ethel was standing before him. Thus, she wasn't there.

"You know I am here," said Ethel, nearing him like a monster about to strike. "How I have followed you."

"Virginia, you are ill," said Arthur. "I want to make you better, but you also need to make yourself better. That means turning your back on hallucinations. We are the only two people—beings or whatever—in this room. In the house. You and me."

"Don't listen to him, Ginny," hissed Ethel, stomping around him. "He doesn't want you to get better. He wants you away. He'll take your home."

"Focus on me, Virginia," said Arthur loudly. "Everything will be all right. I will ensure you are safe."

"Safe?" Ethel snorted. "You shall never be safe with him, Ginny. He is a man. You let a dog into the house, and he now thinks that he is master. You should've left him out in the cold, but you have always been so desperate for the love of man. You wanted someone like your father, and when an old man looked away from you, you found someone young but smart—or so he thinks—and fell into bed with him. Does he remind you of your father, Ginny?"

"No," I groaned, clenching my teeth.

"Don't look there, Virginia," said Arthur. "Focus on me."

"Does he remind you of me, Ginny?" asked Ethel.

"No," I said.

"Please, Virginia." He hung over me like a gray cloud, blotting out the Boston daylight.

"Please, Ginny," repeated Ethel.

"Fight this, Virginia."

"Fight him, Ginny."

"Listen to me, Virginia."

"Listen to me, Ginny."

I tried to grab my head, meaning to hold back the voices that pelted me like icicles, driving into my skin, but of course, with the opium finally taking a hold of my body, I could not reach. I was in the grasp of Arthur's and Ethel's bickering. I wouldn't let them have the last word; I would take their tongues from their mouths until they could say nothing at all. They would groan like I did on the bed, withering into a husk.

Arthur stepped back. "I understand, you're tired. It's the laudanum."

"More," I grunted, but the word didn't sound right in my head.

He wouldn't be able to understand, so I dropped my jaw open, hoping he would understand—I wanted more.

Needed more.

From over Arthur's shoulder, Ethel shook her head. She had no right!

She said she would leave when I told the truth. Why was she still here?

Did she understand what she had done?

"I don't think more laudanum is a good idea," said Arthur, worrying his bottom lip. "What you've just said, and your side effects paired with your mental state... What you said about" —he lowered his voice— "*murder*, that is the laudanum. It does things to your mind."

I dropped my jaw further, letting it clank against my chest from how I lay in bed. I would let my jaw fall off, creating an abyss if it meant that he would give me a few more drops. I moaned, sounding like the ghosts wandering the halls before Ethel had shoved them into the cold and crowned herself queen.

"All right," said Arthur, pinching the bridge of his nose like he, too, couldn't take the thumping any longer. "I'll give you more, but we cannot... after this. The laudanum will not help you. I shall ask Doctor Anderson to come by. We must try another course of action."

"McLean Hospital," murmured Ethel as Arthur withdrew the brown bottle from his pocket. "That is what he means, Ginny. Close your mouth. Don't allow this to happen."

Even if I wanted to close my mouth, I couldn't.

The opium was in my body, in my veins, and with a few more drops—one...two...three four five—the laudanum rolled down the back of my throat. It was so easy to become the puppet dancing for the drug that allowed me to sleep.

"Ginny, please," begged Ethel as Arthur tucked the bottle into his pocket. "Stop this, Ginny!"

"Virginia, think of us. You and myself, I mean. Our future." He kissed my knuckles and then backed toward the door. "Sleep well."

"Stop him, Ginny!" Ethel pointed at the door. "You are the only one who can."

Was I?

Am I, Ginny?

The laudanum brought darkness around my vision, across my body like a fast wave, brought in by a heavy tide in a strengthening storm. I was twisting around, preparing to be spat out. I clung to the bed as I closed my eyes, letting it take me.

"Ginny, wake up," said Ethel from somewhere above me. "Don't do this."

Why are you here? I asked. You said you would leave.

"You want me to leave?"

That's what I've always wanted.

"You kept me here."

I couldn't move your body.

"You didn't allow me to leave, Ginny."

I'm allowing it now. Leave, Ethel! I yelled into the darkness, and then…she was gone.

Twenty-Eight

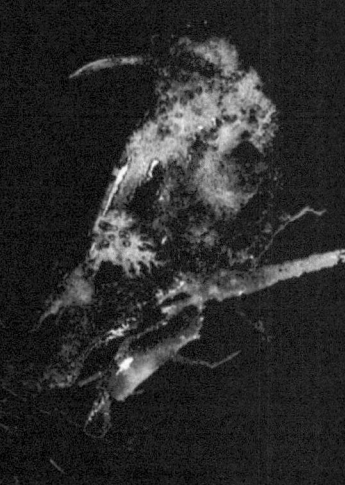

As if I was already at McLean Hospital, I was chained to the bed, listening to *thump, thump, thump thump thump*. Why couldn't Ethel leave?

When I tore my eyes open, I didn't find her hanging over me but the blue of the evil eye.

For a time, I thought her one green eye and one blue eye were beautiful, stealing both my breath and my thoughts, but it was at night that her blue snuck out. I would find her watching me, the blue almost like the white glow of the moon, illuminating us. It tracked me when I moved.

The blue of her single eye blasted through the darkness, swirling around me. This was her witchcraft. It climbed on me like she had been before. The eye crept over me. I was powerless to stop it, caught under the thick blankets with my temperature rising and my limbs like raw bread dough, waiting to rise but unable to stiffen.

Ethel, I wanted to scream, trying to call her back to take her beast from me, but she wouldn't return.

They—the doctors, society, the watchmen—would know I killed Ethel, and I would be put in prison. Perhaps hanged. No, for my crimes and mind, Arthur would ensure I would be in McLean Hospital, surrounded by those screaming profanities and throwing feces.

Not me. I wasn't mad.

When was the last time they had hung a woman in Boston? I couldn't remember. Surely not in this century.

No, Arthur wouldn't let me die.

As the caring man that he was, he would think the hospital as mercy, allowing me to live with whatever comfort there was to be had for a person like me. Confining me there would give me the help he believed I needed. Because I had told him I killed Ethel.

My own stupidity stared at me.

How dare I speak the truth? It would be my undoing.

Where was Ethel? I couldn't believe I was truly free.

Unless she knew my fate. Whether because she was dead, or because she was a witch. She had come from Salem, joined Boston in the craze of mystics and seances, and claimed she was a healer. She had only ever caused me harm, leading up to the moment I told Arthur the truth.

Was it too late?

Had he called for the doctor or the watchmen, telling them his wife had admitted to murder? They would have to come at once. Anyone would believe him, myself included. If he called me crazy, I would say I was. I would have to bite my tongue if he pointed at me and called me *killer*. No matter how true, I wouldn't recite the heinous murder of Ethel.

Our future—that of Arthur's and mine, of course—was built in this house, made in this home, and I glanced down at my stomach as if I would see it grow with our child. If so, he would retract whatever he said. He would protect us.

I took a deep breath, pushing it down into my belly and feeling my skin grow taut. My stomach swelled. I held my breath and reached my hands to the apex of my belly, grunting in the process to move…just a little further. A little bit bigger. Finally, I let my hands rest on my bloated stomach, imagining how a child would kick, and I would laugh and tell them to calm themself; Arthur would lay his hand on me so gently as if I would burst.

It would be that, or I would waste away in prison until I died, my body rotting and collapsing in on itself, leaking into the cracks of the walls.

Arthur wouldn't tell the watchmen what I had said I did, not because he had no proof of Ethel's death, but because he was a good man.

A kind soul.

A clever mind.

A righteous superiority.

I released the breath I had been holding, letting myself deflate on the bed until I was returning to the child I once was, shrunken. During the day, I'd had my parents and the servants as company, but at night, shut up in my room and in the darkness, I had been alone. Empty. Waiting for someone else to arrive. But I had the ghosts. They kept me company until Ethel sent them away, and then I had her. Now, she was gone too.

Your own fault, Ginny.

I rolled my face away. I knew.

I rolled further, hooking my fingers around the edge of the mattress. With all the strength I could muster—the laudanum lingering on my tongue—I pulled myself to the ledge.

Thump.

Thump.

Thump thump thump.

It was coming faster now.

Of course, Ethel wouldn't leave me. Those were idle threats.

I didn't call out to her now, scared of what might be said or the animalistic grunt rushing up my throat. I swung my legs off the bed, hips groaning in protest. My feet because they didn't feel like mine.

As they dangled off the bed, I told them to strengthen, so I could carry myself through the house. My legs were braided hair, released at the end to create toes, and I tried to curl them in. Strand by strand, I was grabbing control of my body again.

I tilted my head to the side, feeling how heavy it was.

Just my mind? My brain?

Or my soul?

What was mine and my body's? What was the third party, a leech on my physicality?

What would Arthur say the answer was?

The name brought me into focus.

I blinked night away, allowing my gaze to travel around our bedroom still smelling of his musk, a mix of sweat and grime. A man tracked in so much mud, not caring where they stepped or how they carried themselves, not caring how my back ached and my hands cramped from cleaning.

Arthur was better than other men—how many times did I have to remind myself of that?—and he cared.

Cared so much to put you in the hospital, Ginny. To spill your secrets.

I craned my head.

Yes, Arthur was better than other men. He was a good man.

But he was still a man.

Sliding to the edge of the bed, I pressed my feet to the cold wood, my toes elongating like flimsy roots. They wouldn't carry me forward—I would need to do that myself.

Stand.

Walk.

One step in front of the other, I fought the opium in my system, in front of my eyes and glided my hand through spring's icy slush. I fought through the hold and tumbled forward, catching myself on the wall.

Another step.

Another.

Out of the bedroom that smelled of Arthur and into the house, which also smelled of him. He clung to the walls; he dragged himself across the floor; he was deep inside the cracks and me.

Down the hallway, his snores.

In.

Out.

In out in.

It rubbed against the walls, a wind blowing down the hallway. I grabbed the wallpaper, digging my fingers in as if to anchor myself. I would flutter like dust in the house, scattering into the far reaches and waiting for someone to clean me up. It would be Arthur's next wife.

While I was locked away, he would get another, bring her inside, lay her down in my bed, dress her in my clothes, run my house. For a good man like him, women would line up around the block, waiting through day and night to have a moment.

What a poor man. Distasteful what happened to him. That horrid wife.

The murderess.

The name hissed in his snores, blowing back my hair.

Arthur rested his head on a pillow, his eyelids shut. His long eyelashes fluttered. How peaceful he could be when he slept, so trusting of the world. So vulnerable. Nothing could ever happen to a man like him. I thought nothing could happen to me either. Both of us were wrong.

I couldn't go to prison for Ethel's murder. Only Arthur knew my crime.

My mind held me next to the bed, my words haunting me.

As I loomed over him, I didn't know exactly what I would do or how I would do it, but Arthur had to be interrupted before he spoke a word.

Reaching into my old nightstand, I withdrew a pair of shears. The metal was rusted, the tips dull. Yet they cut so easily into Arthur's neck.

He gasped awake.

He reached for the wound, wrapping his fingers around the now-red metal.

Don't pull it out, I wanted to say, but he gripped the shears and ripped.

Blood rained.

It got everywhere, in my hair and in my mouth, across my nightgown and around my feet. What a mess. How could a body have so much blood? Was this what it was like when a pig was slaughtered? Ethel hadn't bled so much.

"I'm sorry," I whispered.

His eyes found me in the thick darkness and rush of crimson. The light that once had been in his eyes was dimming, peeling back around the edges of skin. His eyes were so large. His life was so fast. He too must've seen how fast it was, fleeting and deafening.

His eyelids drooped for a second too long. He forced them open with a groan.

His jaw dropped, and he gurgled. Whatever he wanted to say was lost in the bubble of blood.

He reached for me, the shears on the floor, and I took his hand. He turned it into a fist, holding onto me, so I held onto him in return. It was a kindness.

"I didn't want to do this," I whispered through his wheezes. "I'm sorry, Arthur. You didn't deserve this."

He opened his mouth, grunting like he meant to say, *You didn't deserve it either, Ginny.*

"It was the damn opium. I never should've told you," I continued, fighting my tears. They blinded me, mingling with his blood dripping down my face, running into my mouth.

Tendrils of blood ran from the corners of his mouth, splattering the pillows and sheets. I wouldn't be able to remove the stains. I would need to burn the blankets, the pillows, our clothes.

I brushed his matted hair off his forehead, accidentally dragging blood across his paling skin. I hadn't meant to paint him so. It would stain his skin pink.

"Oh, Arthur," I murmured. "It's all right. I am here."

I wrapped my other hand around his, keeping him close as though we could fit as we once did.

"I love you. Please don't think otherwise. I have done this for you—for us," I corrected because it probably sounded selfish that only one of us lived. "I fell in love with you in front of the mystic because of your intelligence and kindness. You have shown me such kindness. I meant to do the same for you. My love just isn't enough."

It had never been enough. Not for Ethel either.

His eyes, darkened by anger and lingering death, narrowed on me.

He grunted like a swine, a sniffle that acted like an oink.

"It's all right," I cooed.

He peeled back his lips, letting out a deep groan that was meant to be a scream. A scream the neighbors would hear.

I threw down his hand and reached for a pillow, intent on muffling the sound, but his neck had been cut. He couldn't scream without his precious throat, couldn't even breathe, so he was dying.

Slowly.

I didn't mean for him to die slowly. Not quickly, per se either. What I wished was to have him die, not have these last moments where I stared him in the eye. I wanted him to be at peace, to die without pain, but everything was hurtful.

Grabbing the shears from the floor, I tried to point them at him only for them to fall, clattering. I stooped as Arthur grabbed for me, sliding his fingers through my hair. He twisted sharply.

"Don't, Arthur," I hissed.

He ripped me toward him, and I fell to my knees. Pain jolted through my bones.

"Let me go, Arthur," I groaned, jerking my head back.

He wrapped his fingers in my hair, palming my scalp. Pain seared my skin.

"Let go!" I found the shears on the floor and ripped them across Arthur's arm.

He let out a gasping yelp, dropping his grasp.

I stumbled back, using the shears as my protection. Slipping on the blood-slicked floor, I backed against the wall and pointed the tip at him.

Arthur rasped, slammed against the bed.

His blood rolled off the edge, splattering across the floor and leaking into the cracks.

Drip. Drop. Drip.

It was a wave across the shore, brought in by the return of the thumping.

"What?" I gasped.

I had done what Ethel wanted. Why couldn't she leave me alone?

The thudding was faster now. It rattled the house, seeming to knock down the walls. It rattled the floorboards like they were rickety ships in Boston Harbor.

Then it was silent, the air stolen from the room.

I waited for Arthur to breathe or the blood to stop dripping from the bed.

Arthur didn't move.

Didn't breathe.

I was now sure that he was dead but couldn't bring myself to check, terrified of what I would find on my childhood bed.

Thump.

Thump.

Thump thump thump.

Too fast now.

It was in my head, down my bones, like Arthur was breathing on my neck.

Releasing the shears, I buried my head in my hands, placing my palms over my ears to stop the thumping for God's sake!

Ethel said she would go, but she never left me. Not even her ghost had abandoned me.

Perhaps this was Arthur, increasing the tempo and the sound, driving me mad.

Where was the opium? He kept it on his person.

As I scrambled to my feet, a wave of nausea hit me. I fell, landing in a pool of blood that worked its way into every crack of my skin and into the roots of my hair.

Leaning against the wall, I sucked in a deep breath tinged with iron. It made my stomach twist...or perhaps it was the sight of Arthur's bloody hand hanging off the bed.

Drip.

Drop.

Drip drop drip.

I had cut him along the vein, nearly hitting the bone. That must've hurt, but how much pain did he feel when dying?

The iron scent was in my nose. It slid into my stomach as if I drank it, taking gulp after gulp of Arthur. It filled me like he never had.

Twenty-Nine

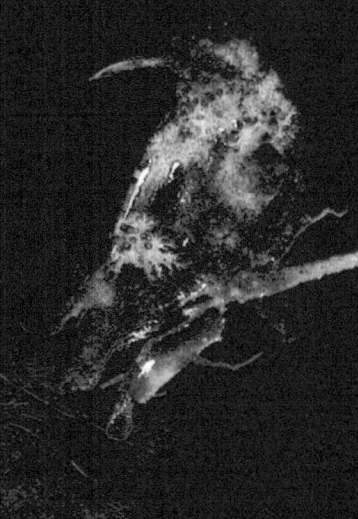

January 05, 1843

Ethel stormed toward the front door as I yelled, "You cannot leave!"

She whipped around. "I shouldn't stay."

"What do you mean?" I asked, my heart shattering.

She hesitated, gnawing on her bottom lip. Tears washed down her face, and down mine.

Rushing to her side, I took Ethel's hands. "Please, don't go. I don't know what I'll do without you."

She shook her head. "I have to go, Virginia. I never should've come here."

"I want you here."

"We're too different."

I dropped my jaw to speak but couldn't find the words. They slipped out with my tears and created a pool around my bare feet. We had been in bed together, making love, when she suddenly pulled away from me, muttering that she must go. I didn't know what I had done wrong. I had given her my body and my mind—my soul belonged to her—let alone my house and all my belongings.

"We're happy," I whispered, breaking through the differences she claimed we had.

"No, Virginia." She ripped her hands from my grasp. "We're not."

Balling my trembling hands, I tucked them behind my back. "When did that happen? You never said you weren't happy."

"I didn't think I would have to."

"I'm not a mind reader," I spat. "I'm no witch."

She rocked back on her heels like I had slapped her.

At one point, that raw hurt upon her face would've left me in pieces, because I would never hurt her—I never wanted to hurt her, only love her and make love to her. I was addicted to her, praying to her at night. I had devoted myself to her on more than one occasion, turning my back on what I had always known from society, the church, and my parents.

"It is that right there," she said, jabbing her finger at my chest, her nail attempting to slash through my cotton nightgown. "You call me a witch."

I began, "You make potions—"

"Those potions have helped you," she spat. "You sound just like the women in the ruling class, how they whisper in your ear, and you echo whatever they say. You mirror them, forgetting your own reflection. Who spoke to you this time? Mrs. Cox? Agatha Clark?"

I locked my jaw before I gave her answers she would only throw back in my face like boiling water.

Ethel waited, hands on her hips and eyebrows raised like she knew she was right.

I finally unhinged my jaw to say, "I have stayed with you. I have loved you. I have chosen you—"

"Enough, Virginia!" She backed toward the door. "I will not stay here or with you. This will be the end of us."

"You cannot! We are bound together."

"This is not a marriage. We are women who make our own choices. Something you fail to realize."

I knew about making my own choices. I made one now as I grabbed the vase off the front entry table—something my mother had imported from the far east—and I swung it at Ethel's head. It was met with a sickening crack, both the vase opening as well as Ethel's scalp. She screamed, falling to the floor, landing in the blue and gold vase shards.

She didn't move.

Blood streamed down her face, brighter red than I thought possible, but it darkened by the second, mixing with the shadows or the ghosts coming for their taste. Blood began to soak through her dress, the fabric cinching to her breasts. It pooled around her head, which was twisted at an unnatural angle.

When Ethel stood and walked out the front door, what would the neighbors think when they saw her in this state? What new rumors would pop up around me like weeds, except this time Ethel would be the one to spread them instead of fight them with me?

She chose to leave me after all I had given up for her, losing my place in life to be in love with her, and she would now leave me to rot, forgotten and shriveled. I could do the same to her, sending her back to Salem.

"Get up," I snapped because lying on the floor was her punishment.

She always wanted me to learn, so neither of us would sleep.

Still, she said nothing.

Didn't move. Not even to breathe.

"Ethel?" I whispered, looming over her mangled form. Her chest pointed toward me, but her head had fallen back.

How could a vase do so much damage?

Look what you have done, Ginny.

"Ethel!" I dropped beside her, gripping her shoulders and shaking her.

The vibrations moved across her body, her head flopping like a fish on a dock. She was just as heavy as something dredged up from the sea; her blood acted as water, washing down her and across my floor.

"I'm sorry, Ethel," I said as if that would coax her into movement, but she only slumped against me when I wasn't strong enough to hold her up any longer.

We both crumbled on the floor, our bodies intertwined as they always had been in bed and should be forever. My thick robe and sturdy nightgown were my cushions against the broken vase under us. I laid her on top of me to soften the blow, letting her head loll to the side. Her glossy gaze found me through her curls.

Unblinking.

Stagnant.

Distant. Nothing. Oblivion.

"Ethel," I whispered, dragging the hair from her face and tucking it behind her ear.

Something slimy inched across my fingers, falling sloppily from the back of her head and landing in thumps on the floor. I pulled my hand back to meet gray clumps and shards of bone that looked oddly like the vase. Rubbing my fingers together, I knew how to repair her like one did a vase.

I would shove the blood, brains, and bones inside and then stitch her back up. She would be fine.

She's dead, Ginny.

"No," I muttered, concentrating on picking through her hair to reach the back of her scalp.

Like your parents, Ginny.

The thought struck my chest like a knife straight through my heart, and I hunched over Ethel, holding her neck to keep her eyes trained solely on me. She looked past me regardless, tracking something on a wall like it was a ghost. She finally saw them too.

"Ethel," I said, tilting her face to mine again and staring deep into her eyes.

My vision went blurry, burning with the oncoming tears. I tried to blink them away but only splattered her in the process. It felt as though we were drowning in the harbor together, each breath ragged and forced and clinging to fading life.

"Ethel, no—I didn't mean to...I only wanted you to stay with me. Why did you want to leave?" I pressed my forehead to hers, so we could be one mind. "Why did you decide to go? It never had to be this way. Think of all the people you could've helped. Think of all the love I was giving you—so much I could give you."

Detaching from her, I let her body fall to the floor with a bang, and I flinched at such a racket. The neighbors would hear if they hadn't done so already, so I couldn't leave Ethel out in the open. She needed to rest, like my parents did in a cemetery, but she was a cutwitch and never would've been accepted.

Your neighbors, Ginny.

Anyone would see Ethel. I wouldn't be able to move her myself, so who would I call upon? Who could I tell?

No one, Ginny.

"You cannot do this, Ginny," hissed Ethel, and the hair on the back of my neck stood. "You say that you love me, but you really will just leave me."

Her cold breath cut through my robe. I brushed past her into the sitting room and closed the front curtains; Mrs. White couldn't see inside.

As the old flooring creaked under my steps, covered in a rug, I knew what must be done. Like she could read my mind, Ethel glared at me. I pulled up the rug and ripped up the molding floorboards, the wood weakened and discolored.

"I'm sorry, Mother," I said, laying the rug flat and then rolling Ethel on top.

She seemed heavier now, like a pile of rocks. I flipped her over.

Front.

Back.

Front back front.

Lowering her between the floorboards, I whispered good night as the sun rose. Gray-tinged light spilled through the white curtains. I reached for them, wanting to open the window to breathe in the cold winter air, but only pulled my hand across my slick forehead.

"I had to do it. I didn't want to, but I had to. It's like how you left your other lovers for your future. This is my future." I gripped a floorboard, my knuckles turning white. "I love you, Ethel. I always will."

Then I slipped the floorboards back into place and stood, the room twisting. I grabbed the nearby table to keep myself upright, though sleep called my name, darkness clouding the corners of my vision. It fought the day and the neigh of horses on the street, their hooves clacking on the cobblestones.

I stumbled out of the sitting room and into the front entryway, the vase shards and blood taunting me from the floor. I needed to clean in case someone arrived.

Who is going to come to the house, Ginny?

"The watchman," responded Ethel behind me.

No one came because I hadn't been out in society, but if they did arrive, then I needed to be prepared. I strolled into the kitchen for a bucket of water. An invitation on the stack of letters caught my eye: Mrs. Cox was inviting me to a party tonight with the mystic Marvelous Auguste to entertain us.

Thirty

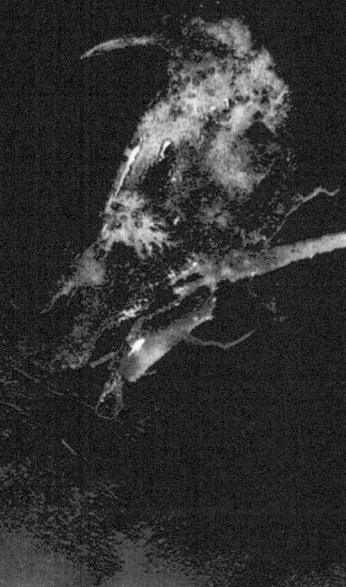

When gray light cascaded into the bedroom, I blinked my heavy eyelids. The movement was difficult, blood crusted to my face and hair, chapping my lips.

Thump.

Thump.

Thump thump thump.

Groaning, I reached for my head, feeling the weight of it and the banging. My brain leaked from my ears. I drew back my hand covered in blood.

The gray light sliced Arthur's body, revealing the horror in daylight. The crimson had transformed to maroon, darkened to a color I would wear as a shawl. The blood upon me offered no protection as if my lower belly should've been split open, letting my organs fall out with a splat. Perhaps I would see a small baby, curled tight and sucking its small thumb, looking for life that I couldn't give.

"What have I done?" I asked. "Arthur, will you speak to me? Ethel, I know you're still here. I can hear you."

The banging continued, so loud I pressed my hand to my chest to calm the heartbeat.

Me.

Ethel.

Arthur now too.

When would it be the watchmen banging at the door? Arthur hadn't made a sound, but Mrs. White must've seen because she saw everything.

"Arthur?" I stepped to his side.

His eyes stared passed me. He no longer tracked me in a scientific way, as if I were a woman who should be trapped in a jar, my heart removed from my chest. I hoped he would keep the small baby that had to be inside me and watch it grow and suckle on my dead breast.

Perhaps I should reach inside of my cunt, pull out the small thing, and stick it deep inside Arthur's mouth, forcing him to chew and swallow. It would breathe life into him. We could always make another baby, but I couldn't make another him.

"Arthur." Tears sprung into my eyes. "I'm so sorry. I didn't mean to kill you, not really. I just couldn't have you tell the watchmen. I couldn't go to prison."

I fell onto the creaking bed beside him.

Blood flaked off like discolored snowflakes. Snow, brought on the factories blowing plumes into the air, would dust the ground red.

Perhaps the opium in my system still clouded my mind.

"Arthur, I'm sorry," I whispered, brushing his hair back. "I know it is hard to believe, but I didn't wish for it to come to this. I love you—I've always loved you. I had to do it. The same way with Ethel. Do you understand?"

His mouth hung open, a dark abyss waiting inside as if something would crawl out. A spider, a snake, a rat…I didn't know.

I buried my face against his hard chest.

Thump.

Thump.

Thump thump thump.

That beating wasn't his.

I pushed into a seated position. "Ethel?"

Of course, she wasn't gone.

"Ethel, how dare you?" I asked the house. "How dare you make me do this? How dare you make me kill him? I wouldn't do this to him—you drove me to this, Ethel! I killed him because of you! How dare you? Face me!"

She won't come, Ginny.

"Shut up," I hissed.

Was the banging coming closer?

I rolled off the bed, ready to meet Ethel halfway.

She's not coming, Ginny. She's gone!

"Then why can I still hear it?" I asked. "Why can I still hear her?"

Thump.

Thump.

Thump thump thump.

The sound doubled, rattling the windows and shaking the doors that slammed shut and squeaked open. Ethel and Arthur were like unruly children running down the hallway, stomping their feet on the old wood. They threw their fists against the walls, meaning to rip them down and get to me.

I stared at Arthur lying in my bed as Ethel once had, wrapped in my blankets and snuggled with his head on my pillow. He indented the bed with his weight as Ethel had. He claimed this as his own like Ethel had. He created a home with me. His house was mine.

"Enough you two!" I snapped.

I pushed out of bed and from the room, slipping on the crusty blood and falling to the floor with a thud. I landed on my chest, air rushed from my lungs with a *whoosh!* Pain rocked from my thighs to my breasts. I would be bruised and would ache.

"Leave now," I begged, pushing to my knees.

Wood from the floorboards had sliced into my body, drawing blood, as if the house hadn't already taken enough. It had licked the blood that came through the cracks in the floorboards, gnawing at the body I fed it. I didn't wish to see what was left of her, perhaps hair and shredded clothing, her bones sucked dry of marrow.

I expected she would be much like my parents in their final days: sunken cheeks, skin tight to their bones and hair laden with sweat. They had been husks of the people I knew, the ones that had given me love. They were barely able to speak, groaning out each word, each breath a wheeze that sucked the air from the house and exhaled mold. The doctors were surprised that spores hadn't been in my lungs, creating a withering creature. They needed mercy. I gave it to them.

Where were the watchmen? Surely, they would come after John McCarthy realized his coworker was missing.

The rumors would surround me eventually, consuming me, and the house wouldn't be able to keep them out. It was only wood and stone, so flimsy and old.

Thump.

Thump.

Thump thump thump.

I balled my hand into a fist and lowered it to my belly, pressing it deep into my navel like it was a hole that would swallow my fist and then my arm. I would reach into me. I punched my lower belly, no longer a house for the thumping that was inside of me.

No one wanted me either way, Arthur's seed never took root. There would be no future for Arthur and me—no future at all if I allowed his body to rot in bed, to stink up the house as Ethel's body once had. It would seep into the wood, and no matter how I aired it out, they would linger.

I twisted my face toward the window, the daylight gracing my skin and showcasing how red it was. How bloody it was. On me, inside of me.

I scraped my skin, tearing off the crust, drawing more out. The house groaned like a hungry stomach. What did it want to be fed next?

What could I feed it?

Stop, Ginny.

I jerked my head away like I could get it out. I didn't want to hear it anymore!

"Ethel," I gasped, glaring at the shadows. That was where she liked to lurk.

I pushed to my feet, running into the hallway to catch Ethel before she escaped. The thumping was behind me, and I twisted back into the bedroom.

"Husband?" I asked. "Is that you?"

No, Ginny.

"Ethel!" I sprinted into the hallway and then down the stairs. "Ethel!"

Thump.

Thump.

Thump thump thump.

Where was she?

"Arthur, are you here?" I asked. "Ethel, you were meant to stay away from him! I told you so."

Think about what Arthur said, Ginny.

"I'm trying to listen," I hissed. "Arthur, are you here? I never meant for this to happen. It was Ethel! Ethel, where are you? I know you're here."

I flew into the sitting room, nearly tearing the door from its hinges, and stalked across the floor, bouncing on the boards above Ethel like I was dancing on her grave. I brought my fist down, banging like she did against the walls, and I wondered how she liked me waking her up, reminding her that I was still here.

When she didn't respond, I marched to the hearth and grabbed the matches, striking one and letting it fall to the floorboards. The flames spread like the wings of a bird. They sprang from the floor toward the ceiling. Heat brushed my face, and I jerked back.

The fire was growing, closing in on me with a mouth full of teeth. As the flames ate the elderly floorboards, it cackled.

"No," I mumbled, gasping a smoky breath.

It seared my lungs, and I raised my hand again to shield my eyes from the light and heat.

"No," I repeated, stomping my foot like the flames would listen to me. "No!"

I grabbed a blanket and swatted at the grasping hands. I beat back the fire like they were beggars in the street wanting money I wouldn't give. They could claw at me, ripping my dress and reaching my skin, but I would fight, damn it! I wouldn't let myself die so easily.

Everything I had done was to survive.

The fire crawled toward me, engulfing the wood. I jumped back. The fire kept coming, gnawing its teeth and arching toward the walls.

"No!" I screamed. "My house!"

It was mine no more.

Nor was it Ethel's or Arthur's or any other ghost trolling these halls.

Run, Ginny!

I sprinted from the sitting room, swinging the door shut. Pain blistered my hand, and I let out a squeal only to intake more smoke. It rolled into the house.

Knock.

Knock.

Knock knock knock.

"No!" I kicked away from the door and ran toward the kitchen.

I needed water, lots of it, and I would put out the flames before they ate the rest of the house—before they reached my father's study and grabbed at my mother's clothes. Her old dresses would surely be kindling.

The house itself was kindling, embers to stoke the fire. Like seeds that needed water. For so long, I had waited for something to bloom. In a time like this, it grew like vines toward the ceiling, tendrils of smoke collecting when they couldn't reach any further.

I flew to the kitchen for water but hesitated in the doorway, holding the frame. My knees quaked under my singed nightgown. Pain thrummed on my skin, across my feet, and I couldn't tell what was red with blood or with blisters. I stayed like that for a moment, stuck in safety and in fear, somewhere between accepting life and death.

It was nearing my back, dragging itself across the floorboards like Ethel had once tried to drag herself away from me. This time, it was growing nearer. It smelled my blood. It wanted a taste.

I faced the flames, wanting to scream like I had done before, but it wouldn't listen—no beast did—so I was speechless. The flames wanted the house, the bodies—myself included—and everything else. It would take all of Boston.

"Fire!"

Yes, Ginny, fire.

It was beautiful and dangerous.

The heat leaked under my feet before the flames touched me, holding out their long arms to embrace me.

"Fire! Someone get the brigade. Call for help!"

"Get water! Need water!"

I wanted to tell the ghosts that water wouldn't help them because we would burn together.

Wasn't that what Ethel wished? I would meet my doom. We would never be parted.

Thump.

Thump.

Thump thump thump.

I sucked in the dark plume, letting it fill my body. It was in my lungs. It molded to my bones, blackening them from the inside out.

"This is what you wanted, Ethel," I said, holding out my arms. "Shall you take me now?"

"Mr. Hunt! Mrs. Hunt! Are you home?" Someone banged on the front door.

No, Arthur was dead, long gone, though his soul might've answered the door. It was the only polite thing to do, and as the woman of the house, it was what I needed to do, allow the guests inside and offer them refreshments, ignoring how my husband was still asleep in bed.

Yes, I would say, *he is ever so tired. I will pass along the message to him, and could you—perhaps—tell Mr. McCarthy that Mr. Hunt is ill? No, I don't know when Mr. Hunt will return to work. Yes, thank you.*

I recited my speech, pulling open the door to a man on the other side, Mrs. White's son. The old woman must've sent him over. How kind. She must've been watching from her perch as she always did.

"Mrs. Hunt!" Mrs. White's son gasped. "What happened? Are you all right?"

"Yes." I coughed so hard that my bones clattered. I didn't have time to cover my mouth. How rude of me. "Apologies, sir. I must be coming down with an illness. If you'll excuse me."

I tried to close the door, but the man slammed his hand on the wood, pushing it open.

"Excuse me," I yelped. "This is my home."

"Fire!" he yelled into my face. "Your house is on fire."

I glanced over my shoulder at the orange working across the floor, burping out ashes. The flames ate up the stairs and toward the back of the house, taking succulent bites from curtains and savoring their sweetness. They must've been like candy compared to the hard floor.

"Oh," I said, searching for words but missing many of them. "Is your mother home?"

The man rocked back on his heels. "My mother?"

"I see her. Mrs. White!" I walked out of the house, hit by the immediate stench of Boston and tried not to recoil at the mixture of fish and grease and smoke.

"Mrs. Hunt, your house!" he called.

I paid him no heed, spying Mrs. White in the front window.

"Fire!" the younger Mr. White called to my back. "Fire! Get water! Fire!"

I stomped up to the front window of Mrs. White's house and tapped on the glass, leaving smudge marks. I dragged my fingers across the window, digging in my nail to make an awful high-pitched ring, scratching like a feral cat to be let in on a cold night.

Mrs. White swirled her gaze toward me, pupils blown and taking up her whole eyes, covering the white and the blue that used to be there. For a woman who watched so much, she had terrible cataracts, but they had disappeared. The blackness of the pupil had opened like the night sky to consume her vision.

I gasped. It was no wonder Mrs. White had been kept away from polite society. I should've shown the woman mercy—it was what any good person would do—but I had walked through fire and was covered in blood.

Thump.

Thump.

Thump thump thump.

It banged against my back like a leather belt, lashing me until I fell face-first against the glass. I breathed hard, my cheek cracked, but the window was left unmarred by such a blow.

The fire was supposed to consume the heartbeat—why hadn't it stopped?

Peeling my face off the window, I turned back to my house. Flames rose from the windows like tinted hands, smoke gobbling up the air. People lollygagged; half turned toward the house and half toward me. I would never hear the end of these rumors.

Through the black smoke, the blue eye shone. It was Ethel's evil eye, piercing my soul and dragging me into the depths. I wouldn't go!

Spinning to face Mrs. White's house, I slammed my hand against the window. "You did it! You told everyone about Ethel and me. You spread the rumors. Do you see what you have done?"

My family's home was in flames, and the bodies inside were turning to ash. I would escape. I would survive.

"Is that what you think you will do, Ginny?" asked Mrs. White, standing at the window.

Her words slipped through the panes like they weren't there at all, so clear against my ears that it would have only been us on a quiet street.

"You shall be like the rest of us, Ginny," she hissed, leaning out the window, dark eyes now flashing the evil eye, one so blue that it was like the sea rising to drown me.

"No." I jumped back. "Ethel, it is you!"

She was out of the house. She was following me.

"Make way!" yelled men in the distance. "The fire brigade is coming through. Move! Help us before the fire spreads."

I could've laughed. The fire would spread and consume the whole of Boston, and Ethel would be trapped. She would be caught in the smoke. Same with Arthur.

"No, not you, Arthur. I didn't mean—" I cut off, the smoke sinking into my lungs.

"Mrs. Hunt!" called out a man.

I spun toward the crowd a second too late, forgetting that yes, I was Mrs. Hunt.

Not Miss Jones, an unmarried woman.

Not Ginny, a young girl.

"Where is your husband?" asked Mrs. White's son. "Is he inside?"

"He is dead," I said, clawing at my blood-stained nightgown. It was maroon, covered in soot, darkened so that it almost looked like it was meant to be this color. No wonder they didn't understand that he was dead because this blood could've been mine or something fashionable for the season.

"Mrs. Hunt?" questioned another man, but the younger Mr. White grabbed the man by the arm.

"We need to call the watchmen," he hissed.

"Or the hospital," he offered.

I bared my teeth. How dare the men speak to me that way? I had a right to be how I was—my house was on fire, my husband was dead, and the damn thumping wouldn't fucking cease!

Someone was banging against the floorboards so regularly that it rattled like the heartbeat in my chest, marching me to their drum.

Always there. I never had the chance to live my own life.

"What happened, Mrs. Hunt?" demanded the younger Mr. White.

I wished that Mrs. White would keep him on a leash in the backyard like some yippy dog. My head already hurt. He was making it worse.

Thump.

Thump.

Thump thump thump.

"Do you hear that?" I asked, rubbing my temples.

"Hear what, Mrs. Hunt?" asked Mr. White.

Rising from the smoke beat back by the fire brigade and people dousing the flames was the evil eye, the blue of the sky so bright that it could've been a star. It threw itself from one of the top windows—the one that Arthur lay in. The eye brought down its weight and shook the street with the incessant banging, throwing me to my knees.

As if I was in a pew at church, I clasped my hands. The saints' judgmental gazes hooked into my skin to move me like a puppet. I had tried to cut the strings but failed. The blood linked us together like shackles. Arthur wouldn't ever be free—neither would I.

"I did it!" I yelled to the house.

Others twisted their necks at unnatural angles, their pupils like pinpoints and sticking into my skin with a thousand tiny cuts, letting my blood bubble to the surface.

Thump.

Thump.

Thump thump thump.

The evil eye drew closer with the ticking of the clock—the rush of heartbeats that jumped to the base of my throat, sucking out my breath.

This would be how I died, crumpled on the street like some common whore overcome by disease. The infection had seeped into my blood—brought by whatever had sickened my parents—and it had infested my mind, eating away my thoughts after it consumed my soul. It was terribly hungry.

"I killed Arthur!" I screamed.

It rang across the street as if the fire had also quieted.

The thumping didn't stop. The evil eye drew closer, the pupils enlarging to swallow me.

"I killed Ethel too!"

The air whooshed from my lungs. I landed on the ground, hands between the cobblestones.

I was not in pain, rather it was different, like I would not be pained again.

The shackles that had bound my wrists and held my mind captive had fallen off. I shook, unsure what it was like to have this freedom, yet I knew there would be no pain, for it had slipped away like the tide rushing out to sea, leaving memories but nothing real, just discoloration.

I rose, meeting the fire and people, mirroring one another with wide eyes and mouths agape. I imagined my face was the same, the truth like a beacon. I couldn't escape it as it shone from me now, following me into the recesses of my mind and where my body could physically be.

I curled my toes into the squishy muck. The mud grabbed like I had roots, holding me to the ground.

The thumping had ceased, and the evil eye had disappeared into the blue sky. Faces crowded together.

I snapped my jaw shut, hearing it click in my skull, but at least I heard it—not the thumping!

"Mrs. Hunt?" asked the younger Mr. White, blinking at me. "What did you say?"

My heartbeat quickened, the sound in my skull. It quaked the ground.

"I killed them," I said, forcing the words out, but they flowed so naturally.

It felt like the spring melt, and the words burst the dam, rushing from me like a violent flood.

"I killed Athur, my husband," I said, "and I killed Ethel, my…lover."

I whispered the last, not to hide what we were to one another but the love that we shared, tucking it close to my chest.

"I killed them," I said again. "I have done it—I am a murderess!"

People gasped as the words broke me, leaving me in shambles like shards of glass hanging from the windowpanes, fluttering in the breeze.

Surely, the truth had set me free, but it also brought something terrible. It tore down the wall to let in the truth that I had kept at bay: it was I who killed them, only I to blame.

What had I done?

I balled my hands into fists, pressing them against my chest. My heart was calm, my body at ease. Although, tears welled in my eyes, burning my cheeks as they slid down and plopped onto the street. The Boston rains were weak compared to my brewing storm, bringing in wind and anguish, swelling the harbor over its banks, throwing the ships onto land and destroying the masks with my howling wind.

What had I done?

Their deaths—their murders at my hands—hit me like a train that I should step in front of, killing myself so immediately and sparing anyone the trouble.

What had I done?

I had killed them, stolen away their lives as well as their breaths. I had left them in beds or buried them in the house. They would never be free.

I should offer my wrists to the watchmen, bound them for them, so they could take me to prison, where I would wither and die.

No, they—Ethel, Arthur—wouldn't even be free then. Their souls were tied to mine, so they would stay with me in prison. I needed to free them!

I fled.

Shocked eyes were upon me, watching my every movement, but no one dared to catch me. To touch a murderess would have their souls stained or else they may become my next victim.

While the evil eye had left me, evil was inside of me. I sprinted like I could leave it behind.

The evil eye chomped at my heels, nipping at the back of my nightgown; it would drag me back with its immense force, so I propelled myself.

Crowds on the sidewalk jumped out of the way, yelling at me, but their words flew away with the wind. I wanted to scream for the people to stay away or else be infected because—like the sickness had overtaken Boston—my evil would spread and infect them, sinking in its teeth and inhaling marrow with each breath, gnawing for their souls.

In the faces that blurred together, I saw Arthur and Ethel standing among them. Somewhere in the mass of bodies, my mother and father looked down on me, their faces drawn from the sickness that consumed them.

Boston Harbor rose in the distance, the waves gray and washing the stones in winter lashes. I hurled myself forward, skating and then flying. I shoved out my arms to take flight, letting every heartbeat stop.

I splashed into the icy water that rushed up to gobble me; the white-tinged waves met the cloudy sky, covering an escape. I sank.

Down.

Deep.

Into the depths.

Don't do this, Ginny.

Where did the voice come from? I twisted into the inky darkness.

Swim, Ginny.

My father taught me how. He taught me many things, like any father should. Same with my loving mother. And Ethel and Arthur. I thought I had taught myself survival, but it was all a farce, much like the corsets that kept me skinnier.

My lungs burned, yearning for breath, and when I opened my mouth, bubbles fluttered before my eyes. I bobbed in the undertow, toward land and away.

With my nightgown spiraling around me, I raised my hands toward the surface, but I was sinking like an anchor. Tendrils of cold wound around my feet, and I was yanked down, only for someone haloed in gray to grab my hands.

Their dark hair covered their face, and their blood-covered nightgown molded with mine, interweaving us together. We floated in neither death nor life, tempted by what was before and after, seduced by love and possible life.

I interlocked our fingers, taking them with me, close to my breast and deep in my searing lungs and water-logged brain.

Ethel.

Arthur.

Ethel Arthur me.

Together at last and forever.

If you loved the fatal devotion in *Temptation of a Haunted Heart*, don't miss the dangerous seduction and immortal revenge in *Masquerade of Vengeful Hearts*.

Continue the series:

Serpent of the Bells by Susan Stradiotto

Echoes of the Oval Portrait by Meadoe Hora

Temptation of a Haunted Heart by Sophia-Rose Johnson

Masque of Red Love by Ashley Steffenson

Masquerade of Vengeful Hearts by Sara Sines

Serenade of the Spectral Heart by Stephanie B. Whitfield

The House of Hollow Graves by Mackenzie Kate

Beneath the House of Usher by Airicka Phoenix

Whispers from the Abyss by M.S. Weaver

Shadows of the Ravens Wing by K. Rose

Silence of the Damned by Elise Knight

Ballad of the Broken Mirror by Hayley Whiteley

https://books2read.com/rl/OnceUponAMidnightDreary

Also by Sophia-Rose Johnson

Wives of the Vampire Queen Series

The Blood She Claimed

The Woman She Craved

The Thread She Unraveled

The Wrath She Awakened

The Day She Lamented

The Carnage She Devoured

The Death She Sired

The Immortals They Became

The Castle of Skull Series

Castle of Skulls

Counts Her Souls

By She Who Is Death-Touched

Mermaids of Lake Superior Series

Beneath the Surface

Thaw the Heart

The Coven Thirteen Series

The Favorite Kind of Wild Magic

The Least Kind of Controlled Magic

The MacLeod Trilogy with Susan Stradiotto

Fight for Darkness

Hunger for Darkness

Conquer the Darkness

Poisoned Darkness with Susan Stradiotto

Stand-alone Novels
Temptation of a Haunted Heart

Short Stories
"Bloody Mary's Day Off" in *Twice Upon a Name*
"The Haunting of Neve Ravensblood" in *Third Name's a Charm*
"The Prophecy of a Powerful Witch" in *Four Names of Fortune*

Acknowledgements

Firstly, I would like to thank you, the reader, for taking the time to read this (and hopefully review).

Whether you are reading part of the Edgar Allan Poe-inspired Once Upon a Midnight Dreary set or picked up *Temptation of a Haunted Heart* individually, I thank you for making my dreams come true!

Secondly, I would like to thank every person who helped me write and edit this book from the first draft to the final edits.

Thank you, Susan Stradiotto, for being my copy editor, mentor, and friend. You pulled me into this set (even though I don't think I had ever read Edgar Allan Poe before) and said to do "The Tell-Tale Heart." Without reading the short story, I accepted it as my piece of to retell that because you said so, and you were right, Susan; this is right up my alley.

Thank you to my beta readers, including E.A Spellman, Meadoe Hora, K.E. Hartley, and Sara Sines. Sorry if I missed anyone!

Thank you to J.A. Armitage at Enchanted Quill Press and Sara Sines for the amazing book inside and out.

Thank you to all the other authors part of the Once Upon a Midnight Dreary for the support!

Thirdly, I would like to thank my parents and my friends. I tend to forget about them all in these acknowledgements (and when writing), so sorry!

To my parents who love and support me but never read my books, thank you for allowing me to explore my passion with my feet on the ground. You didn't stifle my strange growing up, but I could blame my strange on you for allowing me to watch *Criminal Minds*, *CSI*, and *X-Files* as a young kid. I tend to know how the insides of bodies work really well for someone who has a humanities degree.

To my parents who love and support me but never read my books, thank you for Tuesday trivia and random events. While we rarely ever swap books to read, I know that you are the first to purchase it for your TBR and say you'll get to it someday. This book will not be the day you start reading my horror stories.

Temptation of a Haunted Heart—in my mind—is a story about love. Susan—my editor—would say it's horror, so we'll agree to disagree. But we agree to leave in the fiction realm. To write and edit this novel, I did a lot of research and stretched myself as an author. I learned some hard lessons about the craft and myself, including that I will never be a historical fiction author.

Once again, thank you to all who have *Temptation of a Haunted Heart* and support me as an author.

- Sophie

About the Author

Sophia-Rose Johnson, who has also written under S. Johnson, is from Minnesota, USA, and is a northerner by heart and accent. She graduated from the University of Wisconsin-Superior in 2018 with a writing degree. While she first published in 2022, she's been writing since 2011. She is a queer woman.

Stay connected with her via social media or website:

https://www.sjohnsonbooks.com/

www.ingramcontent.com/pod-product-compliance
Lightning Source LLC
Chambersburg PA
CBHW030641020726
47493CB00006B/1821